I0716153

THE DIGITAL CORONER

THE DIGITAL CORONER

THE FENWAY STEVENSON MYSTERIES
BOOK 10

PAUL AUSTIN ARDOIN

THE DIGITAL CORONER

Copyright © 2024 by Paul Austin Ardoin

Published by Pax Ardsen Books

All rights reserved. No part of this book may be used or reproduced in any manner whatsoever without written permission from the publisher, except in the case of brief quotations embodied in critical articles or reviews.

This book is a work of fiction. Names, characters, businesses, organizations, places, events and incidents either are the product of the author's imagination or are used fictitiously. Any resemblance to actual persons, living or dead, events, or locales is entirely coincidental.

ISBN 978-1-949082-58-6

For information please visit:

www.paulaustinardoin.com

Cover design by Ziad Ezzat of Feral Creative Colony: feralcreativecolony.com

PRAISE FOR THE FENWAY STEVENSON MYSTERIES

"Be warned: to read one Fenway mystery is to want to read them all. If you love page-turning, unputdownable mysteries, then Ardoin is the real deal."

—Mark Stay, host of the *Creative Differences* podcast

"This is as good a mystery series as you will find in print. You do not want to miss a single one of these books."

—David Marvin, Scintilla Book Reviews

"I adore Fenway from her amateur sleuth abilities to her wit and from her relationship struggles to her insatiable appetite for Mexican food. I highly recommend the Fenway series for mystery lovers."

—C.B. Samet, EVVY Award Winner

"Keeps you guessing the entire time. This series has been getting better with every book—be prepared to stay up all night!"

—Tess Baytree, author of *The Penelope Standing Mysteries*

"Fenway Stevenson is my new favorite heroine! She has the analytical mind of Kay Scarpetta, the street smarts of Maura Isles, and the sardonic wit of Temperance Brennan. Crime fiction doesn't get any better than this."

—John Ling, USA Today Bestselling Author

"There's nothing better than a well-plotted mystery investigated by a witty, wonderfully clever (and flawed) heroine... well-paced and suspenseful crime fiction not to be missed!"

—Gabriella Messina, author of *The Kate Gardener Mysteries*

"Fenway Stevenson's latest mystery had me really turning those pages! The smooth prose kept me interested not only in the outcome, but the characters themselves. Ardoin is a fantastic writer."

—Carlie Lemont, author of *Murder at a Discount*

"Deftly woven storylines, quirky but relatable characters, and 'wow, didn't see *that* coming" twists and turns. Highly recommended!"

—D.F. Hart, author of the *Vital Secrets* series

"The perfect balance of tension and rich detail that makes it impossible to put down. I simply loved it!"

—L.J. Regan, author of *Before the Devil Knows You're Dead*

"An intelligent and immersive thrill ride reminiscent of Patricia Cornwell and John Sandford...You don't want to miss this!"

—Meghan O'Flynn, author of the *Ash Park* series

In memory of my mother,
Carolyn M. Ardoin,
who was the last proofreader of
every mystery book
I've written

The people who make art their business are mostly impostors.

PABLO PICASSO

PART 1

THURSDAY

CHAPTER ONE

"HURRY UP," PIPER PATTEN SAID, BOUNCING UP AND DOWN ON the balls of her feet, setting down her cherry-red duffel bag on the cheap dresser.

Fenway Stevenson rolled her basic black suitcase next to the second queen bed as the hotel room door shut behind her. How had she let Piper convince her to stop in the middle of the Nevada desert? A bead of sweat started at the nape of her neck and skittered down her back, between her shoulder blades, and she involuntarily shuddered despite the heat.

"You okay?" Piper's green eyes focused on Fenway.

"Glad to be out of the truck," Fenway muttered. "It's roasting in here." She stepped over to the thermostat on the wall. 83°F—yuck.

Piper stopped bouncing for a moment. "The museum is air-conditioned, you know."

Fenway turned the thermostat down to seventy-four. "*Everything* here is air-conditioned."

Piper pulled her phone out of the pocket of her denim shorts. "I know you think the museum is ridiculous, but you'll see."

"If you tell me that NNoV8 is a 'unique immersive experience' one more time..." Fenway rolled her eyes.

"I've only said it *twice* in the last eight hours."

The museum's name was pronounced "innovate," but Fenway was sure the founders of the museum had purposely made the overly hip spelling to attract investors who were too busy staring at the bright, shiny NFTs the museum was supposedly based on to care about things like financial viability. Seriously—who puts a high-tech Vegas-style "immersive experience" an hour northeast of Sin City?

She sat down heavily on the bed. The room might have had cheap furniture, but the bed seemed comfortable enough, and the room was rapidly cooling in the blazing June afternoon. "Give me a minute."

"The museum closes at seven."

"That's two hours from now."

"And it's a ten-minute walk from here. And I want to make sure we have enough time to see all the exhibits." Piper narrowed her eyes. "Unless you want to park the moving truck in their lot. That'll save us a good six minutes."

Fenway shook her head. "All right, all right. I'm almost ready."

"Awesome." Piper tapped her phone, a grin spreading across her face. "They've got this room you go into, and these beams of light turn on as you walk through, and then it activates these visualizations of the art the founders commissioned using these e-ink projections. It's a different art experience every time."

"It still sounds like they're trying to ride this whole crypto wave. And they're a little late."

"Well—they could have incorporated technology in other ways or with other types of artwork, I guess, but my understanding is that the NFTs allow those commissioned works to be seen, felt—fully *experienced*."

"Where did you hear that?"

"That's from the website."

Fenway sniffed. "Do you need some water before we go?"

"No. Sunblock?"

Fenway considered for a moment, then nodded.

Piper dug in her purse. "Ten minutes out in this and I'll get burned to a crisp with my complexion." She pulled out her wallet, a large ring of keys, and—

Fenway blinked. "Is that a tactical knife?" The folding knife was almost six inches long, the blade tucked into the handle.

Piper pulled the tube of sunblock out. "What, that? My dad insisted on getting it for me when I went to college. Said it was for self-defense." She laughed. "But I use it for cutting zip ties when I'm untangling cables in the office. Plus, it's got a can opener on the end." She uncapped the tube and squirted a pool of sunblock directly on each shoulder next to the spaghetti strap of her floral top.

Fenway leaned over the stainless-steel folding knife, examining it. An etched message just under the release button: *You'll always make us proud.*

Like a punch to the gut. Yes, Fenway and her father had smoothed things over—but he'd said nothing like that when Fenway was growing up. She knew why, now—her mother had pretty much cut off all contact and redirected his financial assistance—but the pain was still there. Maybe not fresh, but envy pinged around the inside of her skull.

Piper held out the sunblock. "Your turn."

Fenway nodded, taking the tube.

After a few minutes of glorious silence—except for sunblock application—Fenway sighed and pulled herself to her feet. "Mission accomplished. We can go now." Her stomach rumbled. "But dinner right afterward."

Piper nodded, opening the door and letting a blast of heat into the room. "You got it. Now let's go."

———

Halfway across the parking lot, Piper elbowed Fenway gently in the ribs. "You didn't call McVie when we got in."

Fenway tilted her head at Piper. "You looked like you were going to shoot off into space if we didn't immediately leave for the museum."

"You didn't even *try* to call him, though."

Fenway shrugged. "He's probably still at work. I don't want to bother him his first week."

Before inviting Piper along, she'd planned on taking Interstate 15 all the way to the Interstate 70 turnoff in central Utah, finding a hotel there for the night. The junction was more than halfway to McVie's apartment in Colorado, just south of Denver, and with the brutal drive through the Rockies ahead of her, she'd wanted to speed through the desert and the salt flats on day one.

But Fenway didn't want to make the trip alone, and Piper had some of McVie's work files he'd left in the office. She figured with the two of them driving, they could cover more ground per day. At least they could give each other a break every few hours, especially when the highway started winding through the mountains in eastern Utah.

And McVie was effusive in his thanks. He tried to insist on giving Fenway his credit card for gas. He'd paid for the room at the Cartwheel, even though money was a little tight for him. He promised he'd treat Fenway to a fancy dinner when she arrived. And a big raise for Piper, now that she was taking care of McVie Investigations for the next year or so. The drive so far had been long and exhausting, and Fenway wanted to rest.

But she hadn't counted on Piper's exuberance about the technology museum. She'd had Dez explain NFTs to her before—though the acronym's full name of "non-fungible tokens" shed no light in her mind about what they actually were. She read an article comparing NFTs to the tulip market of Amsterdam in 1614. According to the author, the NFT market was built on sand and inflated expectations, just like the tulip bulb market, and many investors would lose everything.

Fenway stopped and dug a rock out of her sneaker.

"Come on," Piper said.

"It's ninety-five degrees," Fenway said.

Piper nodded. "I was just thinking that you and Craig haven't been talking much since he proposed—"

"We've talked plenty."

"Is he mad that you said no?"

"I—look, I think he's fine. He's okay with me being in charge of all his stuff while driving across three states, right?"

Piper scoffed. "I guess so."

Fenway paused. "It just came out of left field, you know?"

Piper shook her head. "Left field? The two of you have been dating almost a year. More, if you count the months you were hiding it while you were running for office."

"Wait—you and Migs have been dating for as long as Craig and me. Don't tell me *you* talk about marriage?"

"I mean, maybe in vague, general terms, but we're both too young. Like, 'if we ever got more serious.' If we wind up working in the same city. Stuff like that. But I mean, come on. Migs just passed the bar. He's applying to law firms all around the state. He doesn't even know where he'll be in three months."

Fenway nodded vehemently. "Exactly. If you don't know what's going to happen in three months, why would you even talk about it?"

They arrived at the parking lot beneath a black sign with white lettering: NNoV8. Piper had been right: the lot was narrow and the spaces tiny, and the lot was about half-full. No way they'd have fit the moving truck in any of these spaces. The building itself was low-slung and squared off, a near-cube in the middle of the vista of sand dunes, with no windows except for a set of glass doors to the right of the parking lot, inset and within the confines of the shadows. Keeping the windows at a minimum probably made the place cool, but the futuristic black building looked out of place among the dunes and scrub brush.

Piper picked up the pace as they got closer to the double doors.

"You're bouncing again, Piper."

"And you're *not* bouncing, Fenway. Come on—this is the coolest thing to happen to the art industry in a long time."

"Do you actually own any NFTs?"

Piper paused. "Well—no. I think the market for them is in a hyperinflated realm of expectations right now. When it bottoms out, that's when I'll buy some."

That was exactly what the article about the tulip market had said. "When do you think it will bottom out?"

"Maybe in six or eight months. And a little later—maybe six weeks, maybe a year—you'll see an explosion of practical applications for NFTs that we can't even conceive of right now. Remember how everyone thought touch-screen phones wouldn't be popular? Or handheld tablets? I even read an article from the nineties saying the internet was just a fad."

Fenway screwed her mouth up as they crossed the NNoV8 parking lot. Right near the door, a red Alfa Romeo convertible, its canvas roof up, in a sea of silver sedans and white SUVs. "So you think this museum's going to make it?"

Piper shrugged and stepped up on the sidewalk next to the museum. "I wouldn't have put my money in otherwise."

"You *invested* in this place?"

Piper pulled open the right-hand door, ignoring the question; they entered a hallway, the floor cool gray tiles and the walls painted black. Three sets of double doors on the right bore the numbers "01," "02," and "03." To their left, a low counter and a tablet-based point of sale system stood, next to a young man—probably no more than twenty—standing with a smile plastered on his face, a name tag reading *Roberto* pinned to his chest.

"Are you ready to innovate?" he asked.

"Uh," Fenway said, "we want two tickets, if that's what you mean."

"Sure."

Piper held her credit card out before Fenway even opened her purse.

"My treat," Piper said. "I know it was a pain for you to stop here. I appreciate you humoring me."

"One hundred eight dollars," the man said.

"For two tickets?" Fenway asked.

Piper's smile faltered as the man took her credit card.

"I'll get dinner tonight," Fenway said.

They walked through the double doors marked "01," and immediately darkness enveloped them. Lights on the far wall lit up as they took a few more steps, growing closer as they walked through the corridor, passing by them, then going behind them. Fenway took a few steps back; the lights came closer again. The lights were turning on in the opposite direction of Fenway's location in the room, like a funhouse mirror.

Piper stared at the bulbs on the corridor wall and blinked a few times.

They both made their way down the dark hallway. The lightbulbs activated farther and farther behind them as they approached a thick black velvet curtain.

Pulling it aside, Fenway revealed a thirty-inch monitor mounted to the wall that read:

Galápagos
By Benjamin Bartok
Mixed Media, NFTs
Bartok captures the mystique of the magical Ecuadorian islands in this immersive installation. Non-fungible tokens of artwork depicting the native flora and fauna interact in real-time with the viewer, instantly programming the hundreds of light bulbs with a

unique "fingerprint" of electricity. The NFTs are owned by the orig-
inal investors of NNoV8, imbuing the viewer with the curated
choices, the unique artwork, and the light of literally dozens of
creators.

"Oh no," Piper whispered.

Fenway tilted her head. "Why do they need NFTs to—"

"I thought the NFTs were going to—actually be part of the experience."

Fenway motioned to the sign. "It looks like they are."

"But not like this. You can't even see the art that the NFTs represent. It's all under the hood."

"Kind of like those paintings that are just blocks of color. Uh— Maximilian Renfro, right? Those sell for millions. Some people don't think that's art, either."

"Not really," Piper said. "You can see what Renfro painted. It's not a sign saying 'red rectangle.'"

"Yeah."

"Let's go to the next room." Piper sounded slightly nauseated. "Maybe the other installations will be better."

Next to the mounted monitor hung a second dark velvet curtain. Piper pulled it aside to reveal a door. She pushed it open.

Another dark room. What did Fenway and Piper have to do here? Piper took a step forward. Then a spotlight from above shown down upon her.

"A motion sensor?" Fenway murmured. "Is this the room from that article you were talking about?"

"There must be more to it than that," Piper said.

Then, as if the room were listening to her, the far wall lightened to a medium gray. And darker gray dots appeared. Then more dots. They had numbers and characters. Fenway blinked; a large black-and-white screen, like an etch-a-sketch or an e-reader, covered the wall. No color, just shapes, and only the faintest light by which to see. The e-ink screen Piper had talked about.

The dots continued to propagate. Oh, maybe *they* were NFTs. Or represented NFTs. Or whatever. They began to swirl, taking shape. A star? A dreamcatcher? Or just random shapes? Fenway couldn't determine anything, but then she saw it.

"That's you and me," Fenway said. Representations of their bodies, shapes made by the flying NFTs.

Piper folded her arms.

"What's wrong? I thought this was right up your alley."

"This is a travesty of how NFTs should be used in art. Don't you see what they're doing?"

Fenway grunted. "I don't really get NFTs."

"They're files," Piper said. "And they're stored in blockchains."

Fenway nodded. "Another word I've heard. Cryptocurrency, distributed systems of trust, right?"

"There's a little more to it than that."

"You can't just enjoy the art for its own sake?"

"This isn't art," Piper seethed.

Fenway looked through the glaring waterfall of light over at Piper and took a few steps forward. "I didn't think you—" Then her foot caught, and she almost fell. Piper grabbed her elbow and steadied her.

"What was that?" Fenway asked.

"Can't even pick up after themselves," Piper muttered. "One of those black velvet curtains that separate the rooms—it's on the floor. Right where everyone's walking." She pushed it with her foot against the wall. "At least there it'll be out of the way."

"A lot of artists leave their stuff lying around." Fenway grinned, trying to add levity, but Piper was having none of it.

"I won't deny there are problems with NFTs," Piper said, standing in her ray of light. "Everyone knows that. I know the validation of NFTs doesn't necessarily prove anything. Can't be trusted as a signature. Easy to create an NFT of an artwork you don't own. I think sometimes the people who come back to this technology *want* us to go back to the Dark Ages." She bit her lip. "But I thought NNoV8 was different. I thought this museum would show the value that NFTs could bring to the art world. Not just the art world—to humanity."

Fenway nodded and opened her mouth to change the subject, but Piper was on a roll.

"Art connects us with who we are as humans," Piper continued, her words gathering steam as if she were giving a seminar. "Just because I can't draw or paint doesn't mean I can't be an artist. I can reconfigure technology in ways that make people think differently. Put things into perspective. Make a political statement. But this?"

Piper was one of Fenway's closest friends, but she was still young. Only a few years younger than Fenway, but obviously had a more sheltered upbringing. Piper was more idealistic in a lot of ways. Piper took a step away, fuming.

After a moment, Piper turned to Fenway. "I read a profile of Vaughn Trask in *Emerging*."

"Sorry—who? In what?"

"*Emerging*. It's an online news site about new technology and new ways to use existing technology. Some fascinating stuff."

"Okay—and who's Von Trapp?"

Piper rolled her eyes. "Vaughn Trask, not Von Trapp." She spelled the name. "Anyway, he was talking about how art was under attack since the advent of artificial intelligence and pirating. 'The loudest voices for advocacy have prioritized democratization over privacy.' That was one quote in the article. He talked about how art will go away if artists can no longer support themselves."

"Sounds reasonable."

Piper looked around, the spotlights from the ceiling flicking on and turning off with every step she took. "Sounds like he was giving lip service to people like me who actually believe that technology and art go hand-in-hand." Piper extended her hand, another light coming on. "Canvases, paint, the discovery of bronze—all technological advances." She scowled. "You think Michelangelo could have painted the Sistine Chapel ceiling if he *hadn't* studied corpses? If he hadn't been a driving force to advance Western society's medical technology—" Piper stopped herself. "Sorry. It's just—I expected so much more. I expected something new."

"Something 'innovative,'" Fenway offered.

Piper smiled, though her eyes still looked sad.

They walked into the next exhibit—and this was a small room, barely large enough for two people. And a surprise: hanging on the wall was a painting, about three feet square. An image of a man sitting at a table, back to the viewer, staring at a purple-and-blue desertscape through the window. Interesting—a southwest theme without the strict red-and-dusky-gold color palette that often came with the subject matter. Powerful use of line, too, a little reminiscent of early twentieth-century artists from France and Spain. A large placard, almost as big as the painting itself, was on the wall next to it.

Desolation
O. Lockberry
Oil on canvas
What is an NFT? NFT stands for "non-fungible token," a one-of-a-kind digital asset that asserts ownership of a piece of digital, or increasingly, in-real-life artwork. Blockchain technology is at the heart of the NFT process; a digital ledger stores each NFT's information and ID code. The NNoV8 museum takes artwork like Desolation, converts it to an NFT, and uses those assets to create the experience you see in these exhibits.

"How about that?" Fenway said. "Real art."

Piper studied the painting. "Yes. I like the use of color. Unexpected." She shot a glance at Fenway. "Not exactly using technology in a new way, though."

They trudged through six more exhibits, Piper's tutting and

grumbling becoming more pronounced as they walked, especially as they encountered a stray cardboard box or a piece of packing foam.

"We sure paid a lot of money for a museum that looks so unfinished," Piper muttered.

"Probably need it for all the slip-and-fall lawsuits," Fenway said, moving another box out of the way with her foot.

The last room was huge, like a warehouse. A long bench stood on one side of the warehouse room. Beanbags and floor pillows filled the vast room. Must be a nightmare for a germaphobe.

An enormous screen took up the wall opposite the bench, at least fifty feet high, filled with swirling, whirling shapes. Fenway stared, blinked, and stared again. What were those shapes? Floating books, open with the spines cracked? Thousands of them, appearing to flap wings and float in and out from the sky. At first, the flapping units looked like a flock of birds, but quickly turned into two distinct groups that lengthened vertically.

But the shapes moved too quickly, and the resolution of the film wasn't good enough for Fenway to figure out what the shapes were. Piper, her scowl now deeply etched on her face, stood next to Fenway, her arms crossed.

"More NFTs." Disdain dripped from Piper's whisper.

"The birds?" Fenway whispered back.

Piper nodded. "They're all NFTs. All loaded onto a cloud-based server and displayed on this large screen."

"Who's the artist?"

Piper pursed her lips. "It's listed as *Vaughn Trask*, if you can believe it. Not only is he the founder of this museum, he sells most of the NFTs here *and* he's the artist behind this steaming pile of—"

The door behind them opened. A white couple, the man in his late fifties and the woman in her early forties—entered the space. They dressed like tourists: the man in an aloha shirt, khaki shorts, and sandals; the woman in faded jeans and a tank top with the famous neon Las Vegas welcome sign at the top and "If You Win It, I'll Spend It" in a bold font underneath. The man's sunburned face wore a scowl that almost rivaled Piper's. The woman's eyes were wide, staring at the large screen.

"I've never seen anything like this," the woman said, her voice full of wonder.

The man grunted. "Me neither."

The woman frowned and hooked her arm around the man's elbow. "Now, Stan, don't be like that. You can see the work Vaughn put into this."

"Can you?" Stan said. "There's a lot of darkness and some big screens and a lot of words on the wall I don't understand. You might see art in those weird lights. I see my money going up in smoke."

"Keep your voice down."

"Sorry." Stan continued speaking, but Fenway could no longer make out his words, although his tone was rushed, urgent, angry.

Piper leaned to the side and whispered in Fenway's ear. "I think that's Dr. Stanley Schup."

Fenway grunted. "You're making me feel old. I don't know who that is, either."

"President of Brush & Charcoal Venture Partners. A private equity firm specializing in art-related startups." A smile touched the corner of Piper's mouth. "He won an auction at La Vincenza for one of those Renfros you were talking about."

"So he knows art."

"He knows what makes money." Piper stifled a giggle. "Schup posted to Photoxio—he'd donated the Renfro to his rich friend's foundation. His rich friend hung it upside down. Lots of people made fun of it online."

Fenway glanced over at the couple, the man becoming more animated. "Come on," she said, "let's get out of here."

"I wanted to be inspired," Piper mumbled, walking toward the exit and ducking behind the blackout curtain.

Fenway followed a few feet behind Piper, then paused. "I don't care if he..." Schup said, then lowered his voice.

Fenway listened closely, standing a few feet behind the curtain. She looked out of the corner of her eye at Schup, whose voice had increased in volume again.

"...thinks he's going to get any more money out of me, he's sorely mistaken."

Oof. Fenway turned away before the couple caught her eavesdropping, ducked under the blackout curtain, and pushed the door open into the bright light of the foyer.

"...don't know how you think you can get away with it!" Piper shouted to Fenway's left.

Fenway blinked, disoriented, her eyes not used to the bright light. She was blinded for a moment as Piper continued to yell.

"You've taken work by *real* artists and you've reduced their work to a label flying around on a screen!"

"Miss," another voice said, "please lower your voice."

"Nonsense, Roberto," a third voice said, this one deep and rumbling. "This is exactly what the NNoV8 museum is here for. Discussion. Transformation."

Fenway's eyes started adjusting to the brightness. To her left, Piper stood in front of two men, one the person who took their ticket money, and the other a tall white man in a tailored suit with a pink-and-blue dress shirt with an oversized collar, open at the neck, no tie. The ticket-taker looked horrified; the man in the suit looked amused.

"Transformation? You've transformed art into *nothing*!" Piper's left hand was at her side, clenched in a fist, and her right hand gripped the purse strap around her shoulder so tightly, her knuckles were white.

"And perhaps that's what makes NNoV8 such a unique experience," the man in the suit responded coolly.

"I'm not just a visitor," Piper said. "I'm an investor. And you're not just transforming art into nothing—you're transforming *my* investment into nothing." She stamped her foot like a toddler who wasn't getting her way. "This is theft, Mr. Trask. It might be legal, but make no mistake. This is *theft.*"

Fenway's eyes focused on a group of five people gathered inside the front entrance, gaping at Piper's outburst. A woman in front of the group had her phone out.

Pointed straight at Piper.

CHAPTER TWO

Oh no.

Whatever Piper thought she was doing, she was losing this battle. Fenway stepped forward and took Piper by the elbow.

"Fenway," Piper snapped, "what are you—"

"You'll end up getting doxxed if you don't shut your mouth and leave," Fenway murmured into Piper's ear. "You're being recorded, and you'll end up as one of those crazy-lady-yells-at-employees videos on Photoxio."

"But that's Vaughn Trask, and he can't get away with—"

"I don't care," Fenway hissed, pulling Piper into the gift shop, out of range of the phone camera. "You might be right, and you might have an excellent point, but if that woman posts that video without context, you'll look like an entitled white woman yelling at employees. It won't end well for you."

"I—"

Fenway kept maneuvering Piper through the gift shop, toward the exit, and finally out the door. The heat of the desert smacked Fenway in the face, but she pushed forward with Piper at her side, past the red Alfa Romeo and into the parking lot.

"I had something to *say,* Fenway."

Fenway continued walking, almost pushing Piper forward. "And you have every right to say it, but it doesn't mean it's a good idea. I dealt with Barry Klein and the stupid politics of small towns and the internet way too much over the last year. Viewers won't give you the benefit of the doubt in that video. You scared the bejeezus out of the guy who took our tickets."

Piper shook Fenway's arm off, though she kept walking forward. "I'm sick and tired of shutting my mouth to make *other* people comfortable." She turned to glare at Fenway. "And you should be too. Vaughn Trask is ripping people off, and someone needs to say something about it."

"I don't care about anybody's comfort level," Fenway said, more firmly now that they were almost halfway through the NNoV8 parking lot. "I care about *optics.* It looked like you were lecturing an employee on your opinion of what the museum would be."

Piper stopped. "Well, so what?"

"Because I don't want a video to go viral." Fenway kept eye contact with Piper. "And I don't want you to be the poster child for yelling at employees."

"I didn't—"

"That's what it looks like, Piper."

Piper frowned. "Agree to disagree, I guess."

"You spent a hundred bucks on something that disappointed you. I get it." A bead of sweat, this time at Fenway's temple, dripped down the side of her face. "But the recording won't show what you spent. The guy in the suit—"

"That was Vaughn Trask."

"The guy in the suit wasn't facing the camera," Fenway continued. "No one will see the smug look on his face. They'll see you shouting at two employees telling you to lower your voice."

Piper exhaled in exasperation.

"I've been there," Fenway said. "I've been right, but I sometimes need to shut the hell up to help my cause." She gave Piper a small smile. "Even when I was in the right. It's not about making others comfortable, it's about survival."

Piper kicked the ground with her sneaker.

"Come on, Piper. When you were working at the sheriff's office, you were right, but HR forced you to resign anyway."

Piper was quiet. "I guess I see your point."

They both turned toward the parking lot exit and began walking, threading their way between the cars and SUVs.

"I still think I'm right, though—" Then the strap on Piper's purse slipped off her shoulder and she squeaked as she tried but failed to catch it on the way down. A few items spilled out of the top of her purse—the key ring, a small tube of lip balm, and more, glinting in the harsh sunlight.

Piper cursed loudly.

"It's fine." Fenway bent down and retrieved the lip balm before it could roll underneath a white SUV.

Piper grabbed her keys and a few other items and dumped them back in her purse, then stuck her lower lip out and exhaled loudly, the red hair above her forehead ruffling.

"Got everything?" Fenway asked.

"Let's just go," Piper said.

Fenway nodded.

They walked in silence for a few minutes before Fenway spoke again. "Did you really invest—"

"I believed in their approach," Piper said. "McVie gave me a bonus, and I wanted to do something good with it."

"So you invested in an art museum? *This* art museum?"

"Better than a hedge fund." Piper thrust her chin out. "Or so I thought."

"Okay, I get it." Fenway cleared her throat. "Can I ask—what were you expecting to see?"

"Something immersive. Something new. Maybe to experience myself inside some of the art pieces using technology. Maybe something interactive."

"Well, those lights were activated—"

Piper scoffed. "Please. A five-year-old with a My First Science Project kit could set up a sensor to make lights turn on." Piper kicked at the ground. "I don't know what I was expecting, but it wasn't this."

Fenway paused. "So—dinner? We can complain about the museum over a good meal."

Piper groaned, pulling her purse strap back up onto her shoulder. "After all that, I'm not sure I'm hungry."

"Huh. I thought with you getting so angry, you would've worked up quite an appetite."

Piper shrugged.

"Maybe you'll feel differently when we get to the restaurant," Fenway said. "After that terrible museum, I need *something* satisfying. I'm thinking the enchilada plate at the Mexican place just past the museum. Can't replace a bowl of chips and salsa with an NFT."

"I guess I could use a cold drink," Piper muttered.

"Yes. A margarita. On the rocks."

"I meant like an ice water. Because it's so hot."

"Sure," Fenway said, "you can have one of those too."

———

Six empty margarita glasses between the two of them. Fenway signed the credit card receipt and pushed the payment tray to the center of the table.

"See?" Fenway said. "You *were* hungry."

Piper pushed herself to her feet and tottered slightly. "Oh," she said. "That was—those drinks were a little stronger than I thought."

Fenway stood up. They'd been there almost two hours, and the burrito in her stomach was working overtime to soak up the tequila in the margaritas. She was steady on her feet—plus, she'd had three glasses of water, too, so she knew she wouldn't have a hangover tomorrow. Driving was out of the question—or she wouldn't have felt comfortable getting behind the wheel, anyway—but an early alarm and ten hours of driving tomorrow shouldn't be a problem. She checked her watch—eight fifteen—then grinned at Piper. "I'm just glad you're feeling better."

"Yeah, it's just the hopes and dreams of my whole life, completely *shattered*." Piper's words were a little slurred, but not bad; she might be tipsy, but not drunk. "The marriage of technology and art, destroyed in an hour of walking through a shitty museum."

"Three cheers to late-stage capitalism," Fenway said, offering Piper her elbow. She might only be tipsy, but Fenway wasn't taking any chances, especially with the purse-spilling incident in the parking lot. "I say we go back to the hotel room and go to sleep. We have a long drive tomorrow."

"I can take the first shift," Piper mumbled.

"Sure," Fenway said. They'd cross that bridge when they got to it.

Holding onto Fenway but trying desperately to *look* like she wasn't, Piper took a few uncertain steps, then steadied herself. They left the Mexican restaurant and turned right on the sidewalk toward the Cartwheel Hotel & Casino.

"Maybe an hour of blackjack instead of going right to bed?" Piper said.

"Absolutely not," Fenway said. "Nevada makes me smell like cigarettes as it is. I set foot in that casino and I'll have to set myself on fire to get the stink out of my hair."

"I'm a *superb* blackjack player," Piper said. "Betcha I'll win us a few hundred bucks. Get our money back from that idiotic museum."

"We're here to move McVie's stuff," Fenway said.

"You're no fun." Piper pouted, her lower lip protruding.

"Oh, well, with that convincing argument, I will for sure go to the blackjack tables now."

Piper stuck her tongue out.

They walked down the side of the road in silence for a few minutes. The sign for the Cartwheel Hotel & Casino, bright neon, loomed larger and larger in front of them.

"Thank you," Piper said.

"For what?"

"After I got fired," Piper said. "Forced to resign. Whatever. You got me on my feet working for your father. You never doubted me. Not for a second."

"Neither did Craig," Fenway said. "He wanted to hire you. I mean, I would have recommended you, but I didn't need to. This was all you, Piper. You're the one who proved how valuable you were. You don't need to thank me."

"But I do. You're a good friend, Fenway. You stick your neck out for people you believe in. Not many people do that, and I appreciate it."

"I didn't do anything special."

Piper giggled and shook her head. "You're terrible at taking compliments."

"Sorry." Fenway paused and took a deep breath. "You're welcome, Piper."

They entered the parking lot to the Cartwheel and walked around the right side of the casino building to get to their room. Piper was steadier on her feet and walked up the single flight of outdoor stairs with no problem. Fenway held her key card and opened the door.

Piper walked in and collapsed on one of the queen beds. "It's not even nine o'clock and I feel like it's midnight. Maybe you're right. Blackjack would be a bad idea."

"Welcome to adulthood." Fenway stretched her arms above her head and caught a whiff of her underarms—and after drinking three margaritas and three glasses of water, her bladder was screaming. "I think I might take a shower tonight so we can get an earlier start. You need to use the bathroom?"

"Nope," Piper said, staring at the ceiling.

"You okay? Room spinning?"

"I'm good. A little bit of a buzz, but that walk back took the edge off it." Piper sat up on the bed. "Maybe I'll watch something mindless on TV."

"Sure," Fenway said.

Fenway gathered her pajamas and a hair wrap from her suitcase, then went into the bathroom and closed the door. She took her time, going to the bathroom, wrapping her hair carefully—not too much of a cigarette smell, she hoped. She would have liked to take a long shower to get the feel of the long trip off her, but Piper was waiting for her—and that they had a long drive the next day.

After showering, she reluctantly turned off the water, used one of the two white, scratchy towels to dry off, then donned her pajamas, brushed her teeth, and opened the door. She could finish the rest of her bedtime routine later.

The room was empty.

"Piper?"

No answer.

Fenway frowned. Maybe she'd gone to get dessert? Something from the vending machine? Or did she go to the blackjack tables?

She stood, tapping her finger on the doorframe of the bathroom, then went back in and finished moisturizing her face.

Fifteen minutes later, Fenway came out of the bathroom, but still saw no sign of Piper. She frowned. Maybe the lure of blackjack had been too much. Fenway shook her head. Just what they needed —Piper gambling while tipsy.

She reached for the remote on the dresser and tried to come up with a reasonable explanation for Piper's absence. They each had a room key. But—what if something had happened? Did Piper go out for ice and get assaulted or kidnapped?

Fenway folded her arms. There wasn't another option: Fenway would have to go look for her. She took her pajamas off, put on the clothes she'd been wearing that day, and checked her phone. They'd gotten back to the hotel room about eight thirty, and it was almost nine fifteen. Forty-five minutes where Piper was unaccounted for. Fenway felt her blood pressure rise. She slipped on her sandals, then opened the hotel room door—

—and almost ran into Piper.

"Where were you?" Fenway said, then noticed Piper's stricken face.

"I—I'm sorry," Piper said. Her lower lip trembled.

"I was just worried when you weren't in the room."

"I lost my knife."

Fenway stepped to the side and Piper walked into the room, shoulders slumped, and sat down on her bed.

"I don't know what happened to it," Piper said, looking distraught. Ah, yes, the knife her father had gotten her.

Fenway thought back. Had Piper put it back in her purse after they put on sunblock? She thought Piper had. Then it hit her.

"In the parking lot, when your purse—"

"That's where I've been," Piper said. "And I found the exact spot where I dropped my purse, too, because I found something *else* I didn't pick up—a little packet of mints I bought when we stopped for gas in Banning. But I couldn't find the knife."

Fenway was quiet. She wanted to tell Piper not to go out by herself—a woman walking through dark parking lots at night by herself was a terrible idea, especially in a remote desert town like Ruby Dunes, but Piper was clearly upset, and Fenway's admonishments would have been counterproductive.

Piper shook her head and her voice wavered. "My dad bought me that knife when I went to college. I know it didn't cost a whole lot, but it was just the idea of it, you know? I was going to school hundreds of miles away—and it's just like there was always a part of him with me."

"Yeah." Fenway felt her mouth go dry.

"And someone probably saw it under that SUV or just lying on the ground and took it. I mean, it's a cool-looking knife."

"We can go out and look for it. Two sets of eyes—"

She shook her head. "It's not there, Fenway. Someone took it. I went to the restaurant and asked, and I even looked in the booth where we were. I had it when we walked out of the museum, I'm sure of it, and now it's gone."

"I'll go," Fenway said.

"It's not there," Piper said. The sides of her mouth turned down at the corners, and her makeup was slightly smeared around her eyes. She looked like she'd shed some tears.

Fenway couldn't blame her. "I'm not getting any sleep until I look for it." She turned to the dresser and grabbed her purse.

Piper following behind her, Fenway walked out of the hotel room and back to the parking lot of the NNoV8 museum. She was determined to look under every sedan, SUV, and sports car in the parking lot. She and Piper almost ran, and what had taken them ten minutes in the ninety-five degree heat of the day took less than five.

But when they arrived at the parking lot of the NNoV8 museum, the cars were all gone—all except the red Alfa Romeo parked by the entrance.

"Oh," Fenway said. "There aren't any—"

"I tried to tell you," Piper said. "The knife isn't here. It'd be sitting on the asphalt—I wouldn't have missed it."

"Maybe..." Fenway began, but she couldn't figure out how to end that sentence. Maybe nothing. Her mind was blank—the knife obviously wasn't here.

Even though it was pointless, Fenway shined her phone's flashlight all over the parking lot.

Nothing but pebbles and dirt.

Fenway walked to the red convertible and got down on her hands and knees.

"I already looked there," Piper said.

"Can't hurt to double check." Fenway shined her flashlight under the Alfa Romeo. Nothing. She stood back up.

Beside Fenway, Piper wrapped her arms around herself.

Dejected, Fenway trudged back to the hotel room, Piper

following close behind. It was a little past nine o'clock—plenty of time to get a good night's sleep. She didn't know what to say to Piper—she could buy another knife, but it wouldn't have the etched words of Piper's father into the handle. Piper went into the bathroom to get ready for bed, and Fenway put her pajamas back on. She thought she could hear Piper softly crying over the loud whir of the modesty fan.

Fenway's mind raced. How could she make this okay for Piper? What could she say that would help? Would they be up all night worrying about it?

But, exhausted from the drive, from the three margaritas, and from the adrenaline leaving her system after the rush of the parking lot search, Fenway fell asleep as soon as her head hit the pillow.

PART 2

FRIDAY

CHAPTER THREE

FENWAY OPENED HER EYES. LIGHT FILTERED IN THROUGH A crack in the curtains and Fenway sat bolt upright in bed. Oh no— she hadn't set her alarm the night before, and they had to get on the road.

She grabbed the phone off her nightstand.

Okay, phew. 6:07 A.M. She wanted to wake up at 6:15 or 6:30 anyway, so this was all right. She pushed herself upright. "Hey, Piper, we should—"

Piper's bed was empty. The rumpled sheets and squashed pillow showed Piper had been in bed at some point. Fenway lifted her head to see into the bathroom, but the door was open and the lights were off.

Maybe Piper couldn't sleep, or woke up early, and went to look for the knife again. She remembered the admonishment she hadn't given Piper the night before about looking for the knife on her own in a dark parking lot—but it was early summer now, and it had been light for an hour. They could look for Piper's knife for another hour or two before leaving. And they needed breakfast, even if they just grabbed something quick before they hit the road.

She got up. The room was chilly. Piper must have blasted the air conditioning last night. Good thing; a cool room meant Fenway was relatively fresh from her shower the night before. Enough that she didn't need another shower before the drive, anyway. She went to the bathroom, quickly brushed her teeth and put on deodorant, then threw on a fresh change of clothes, pulled her hair back into a low ponytail—her hair was finally long enough for that again, after she'd shaved her head in Los Angeles—and was out the door.

She walked down the concrete stairs and scanned the parking lot, halfway expecting Piper to be peering under cars. Fenway's stomach rumbled. Maybe Piper had been hungry—and the twenty-four-hour diner in the Cartwheel Casino would have drawn her in. They'd both need breakfast, anyway.

She found Piper sitting at a booth in the Cartwheel Diner. Fenway expected Piper to look terrible, but she didn't. Her hair was tidy, a fresh T-shirt and shorts. Ready to take on the day, not a hungover mess like Fenway might have been in the same situation. A coffee cup sat in front of Piper, whose head was bent over her phone.

"Hey."

Piper looked up. "Oh—hi. I meant to give you another fifteen or twenty minutes. I didn't wake you when I got up, did I?"

Fenway shrugged. "I don't think so."

"I was just about to order some breakfast. You want something?"

"Absolutely." Fenway scooted into the booth across from Piper, narrowing her eyes. "Are you okay?"

Piper shrugged. "I'll get over it. My dad wouldn't want me to freak out about it." She reached out and grabbed her coffee. "Besides, we need to get on the road."

"Did you look in the parking lots again, now that the sun is out?"

Piper shook her head. "Maybe we can give the area another

once-over before we go, but I don't think we'll see anything this morning that we didn't see last night."

"We should see if someone handed it into the museum."

Piper nodded, her eyes brightening. "They don't open until eleven, and we'll leave long before then, but I can call from the road. Maybe have them ship it to me."

"And another once-over of the parking lot before we head out."

The server came over, and they both ordered breakfast as the server turned over the mug in front of Fenway and poured her a cup.

Piper took a deep breath, closing her eyes, then sitting back in her seat. When she opened her eyes, she looked straight at Fenway and a smile appeared on her face. "So, you get to see Craig today."

"Yes."

"Excited?"

Fenway paused. "I mean, it's barely been a week."

"But you haven't been apart for a week since you started officially dating, right?"

"Uh..." Fenway thought back. "There was my little adventure in Los Angeles."

Piper tilted her head. "Two or three days tops, though. Didn't McVie drive you all around Southern California to prove your innocence?"

Fenway laughed. "I guess he did. I can't believe it seems like those were simpler times."

Piper leaned forward, her elbows on the table. "Are you two okay?"

Fenway rubbed her chin. "I think so. I guess I don't really know —he left right after..." Her voice petered out.

"Right after he proposed, and you told him no," Piper said.

Fenway rolled her eyes. "Okay, but that makes it sound so much worse than it was. Craig was already supposed to be on the road. He was super stressed. And he knew I was worried about our relationship surviving long distance. He—"

"Did he?" Piper asked.

Fenway paused. "Did he what?"

"Did he know you were worried about your relationship surviving long distance?"

"Of course."

Piper raised her eyebrows. "You sure about that?"

"He knows I haven't had a relationship last longer than a few months," Fenway said. "He knows I have commitment issues."

"Does he?"

"Stop it," Fenway said. "You worked with him for eight hours a day since he and I started dating. What do you know that I don't?"

"Maybe," Piper said, "he thinks that you've been waiting for the right guy. That you haven't had a long relationship before because you've never had someone care for you the way he does."

Fenway scoffed.

"Don't be like that," Piper said.

"You know about my father. About how he and I barely talked for twenty years. You think I have modeling for what a healthy romantic relationship should look like?"

"I don't know," Piper said. "You don't really talk about it. Do you talk about it with McVie?"

"Of course I—" Then Fenway stopped. Maybe she didn't talk about it. Maybe she mentioned it once or twice. Maybe she didn't want to scare McVie off. The dreaded "daddy issues"—always perceived as the daughter's fault even though the issues manifested due to circumstances far beyond the daughter's control. But she didn't want McVie to think she was broken, did she? Fenway didn't want McVie to think that she was jealous of him moving to be near his daughter. And she wasn't, was she?

She and McVie *had* talked in the week since he'd left. He'd said he understood, and they talked about the move. Fenway offered to drive the moving truck, and McVie didn't want to impose, but Fenway insisted. And he accepted.

Oh. They'd really only talked about logistics.

Ugh.

"Look," Fenway said, "Craig moved a thousand miles away. He'll be in Colorado at least until Megan graduates high school. I know his daughter is his priority. I wouldn't want it to be any other way."

"Wouldn't you?"

"No," Fenway said sharply. "I wouldn't. I would hate him if he abandoned his daughter to date a younger woman."

"But—"

Fenway raised her hand to stop Piper. "But nothing. It's not lost on me that after my mother left my father, he married a woman who was much closer in age to me than to himself. And I'm closer in age to Megan than I am to Craig."

Piper blinked. "I don't think that's true."

"Thirteen years and nine months between me and Megan," Fenway said. "Fourteen years and three months between me and Craig."

"You did the math? Besides, it's not the same. You're not your stepmother." Piper narrowed her eyes. "And isn't there only seven years between you and Charlotte, and there's, like, twenty-five years between Charlotte and your dad?"

Fenway sighed. "You're right, you're right. But there is no good reason for me to marry Craig right now. I have my career in Estancia. I don't think he knows what he's going to do after Megan graduates high school." She paused. "Or if he *does* know, he hasn't told me."

"I hope he plans to come back and keep McVie Investigations going," Piper said. "I mean, I'm pretty sure I can keep it viable for the next year without him being around, but it'll be tough."

"And he's got a full-time private security job in Colorado," Fenway said. "What if he gets promoted? What if he thinks his career is there? If his life is there with Megan? I wouldn't begrudge him that."

"You wouldn't?"

Fenway closed her eyes. "I *shouldn't* begrudge him that."

The server set two plates in front of them. Fenway grabbed her fork and started eating—mostly to stop the conversation with Piper.

Piper took a bite of her omelet—and stopped talking about McVie. Fenway was grateful for the silence. Every time she looked up at the willowy redhead, though, she saw a question on Piper's face. And Piper wasn't asking anything.

Fenway took another drink of coffee, then bit off a piece of rye toast. They'd left Estancia at eight in the morning the day before, and Piper had blasted some new music when they'd gotten on the road, bleary-eyed and sipping a large coffee. When they'd stopped for gas in Barstow, Piper had asked if Fenway had heard from former Dominguez County Deputy Celeste Salvador. Fenway had bitten her lip and shaken her head. Hopefully, wherever Celeste was, whatever detective position she'd taken, she'd be successful. But Fenway didn't know where Celeste had taken her job, and she wasn't sure how much longer it would be before she felt comfortable reaching out.

She was glad Piper didn't have follow-up questions. Though with another ten hours of driving in front of them, Fenway wasn't sure she could avoid any more uncomfortable questions.

Fenway stopped herself after two cups of coffee, then asked for the bill and went to the bathroom as Piper was finishing her omelet. After washing her hands, Fenway checked the time on her phone. 7:08 AM. They could give a once-over to the parking lot here at Cartwheel, then get ready and get packed—that would probably take only a few minutes if Piper didn't have to shower.

Fenway walked back to the table, where Piper was signing the credit card slip.

"I was going to get that," Fenway protested.

"You can get lunch."

"We won't do much more than stop at an All Access Burger."

"Fine, then you can get dinner, too."

They walked out of the hotel restaurant, toward the exit to the room, then Fenway stopped. "Did you check the hotel's lost-and-found?"

"For my knife?"

"Right."

Piper shook her head. "I guess it's worth a shot."

Unlike the larger casino hotels on the Las Vegas strip with the automated check-in kiosks, the Cartwheel still had real people to interact with. Fenway stepped up to the front desk. A man with deeply tanned skin and long curly blond tresses stood behind the counter, his green eyes heavily lidded, and his posture straight. His blue dress shirt, with the Cartwheel logo on the left chest, was rumpled, like he hadn't ironed it, and it was too large for him across the shoulders. *Orlando* was etched on his metal name tag. He looked up as Fenway and Piper approached.

Fenway pointed to his nametag and grinned. "Is that your name, or where you're from?"

"What?"

"Your name tag. Orlando. You know—all the name tags I've seen in Vegas have both the person's name and where they're from originally."

Piper elbowed Fenway in the side. Yes, right, she should stop talking.

"It's my name." Orlando smiled back, but his levity was forced. "I'm afraid my location is too boring to put on my name tag. I'm from here." He cleared his throat. "Checking out?"

"In a bit," Fenway replied. "Do you have a lost-and-found?"

"Of course. Are you missing something?"

Fenway put a hand on Piper's shoulder. "My friend lost her, uh, pocketknife. We think it was in the parking lot. I wondered if anyone had turned it in."

"I can check."

"Can I see? It's a stainless-steel folding knife, about six inches long, and it's got a message etched into the side of it."

Orlando shook his head. "We've had too many problems with

weapons in the lost-and-found disappearing. We've got them in a safe now. I'll see if the knife is there. Stainless steel, you said?"

"Right."

Piper leaned forward, watching Orlando walk away. Now it was Fenway's turn to elbow Piper in the ribs.

"What?" Piper said.

Fenway tipped her head toward the back room where Orlando had gone.

"I can *look*," Piper replied, color rising to her cheeks. "Migs and I are exclusive, but we're not dead."

"He is a handsome young man," Fenway said, in her best schoolmarm voice.

"Shut up." A slight smile touched the corner of Piper's mouth.

Fenway and Piper stood waiting, only the sound of country music on the sound system, tinny and quiet, keeping them company. Fenway looked at the clock on the back wall of the check-in area. Three minutes passed, then four.

Orlando came back. "I'm sorry. No knives in there. I'll keep my eyes peeled, though."

"We're checking out today," Piper said.

He shrugged, making eye contact with Piper. "Give me your address, and if someone finds it and turns it in, I'll mail it to you."

Fenway stepped forward. "You can send it to the coroner's office in Dominguez County," Fenway said, producing a business card from her purse and sliding it over the counter.

"Coroner?" Orlando's eyes went wide. "You're a coroner?"

"Someone had to get the job. Might as well be me." Fenway took a backward step. "Thanks, Orlando. I'll see you when we check out."

Piper followed Fenway out. "What was that about?"

"He was clearly hitting on you," Fenway said.

"You're not my mom," Piper said playfully, though a note of admonishment hung in her voice.

"I'm not Migs's mom, either, but a hotel clerk in Ruby Dunes doesn't need your address." She cleared her throat. "What do you think—should we head to the parking lot now, then pack up and get on the road?"

Piper was quiet, and soon, there was just the sound of their footsteps on the gravel walkway through the parking lot.

The U-Move-It truck was parked behind a low concrete separator between the regular parking lot and the one for oversize vehicles.

"Did you go back to the truck yesterday? After we put on sunblock?"

"Why does it matter after we put on sunblock?"

"Because I saw you put your knife into your purse just before we left for NNoV8."

Piper nodded.

The low concrete separator grew closer. Piper walked ahead, her eyes on the ground—and then she jumped back and let out a shriek.

Fenway rushed forward.

Between the U-Move-It truck and the concrete separator lay a body, supine, arms above the head. A man's body, in a black tailored suit with a familiar pink-and-blue dress shirt, large collar.

Fenway took a cautious step forward and looked at the corpse's face.

The guy in the suit from the museum: Vaughn Trask. And a knife stuck out of his chest, his pink-and-blue dress shirt stained with a bloom of dark red, almost brown from the oxidation.

Another cautious step forward. The body and the knife were in the long morning-sun shadow of the moving truck, but Fenway could tell the knife was stainless steel. She craned her neck. Something was on the side of the knife's handle.

You'll always make us proud.

———————

CHAPTER FOUR

"That's my knife," Piper whispered.

"I know," Fenway said. "I'm trying to make sense of this."

"How did my knife get—" Piper said, her voice rising in pitch. Then she squinted. "That's Vaughn Trask."

Fenway nodded.

"Oh, no," Piper said, rubbing both temples. "I—I told him off yesterday. People *saw* me talk to him at the museum." She looked at Fenway, her eyes wide. "That woman *recorded* me talking to him. You said I looked like I was yelling at him."

Fenway nodded again. What was the best thing to do here? They'd have to call 9-1-1. Part of Fenway wanted to just drive off, pretend like this had never happened. Pull Piper's knife out of the dead museum founder's chest and drive to Colorado. Without Piper's knife, there'd be no connection to her—

Fenway closed her eyes. How, exactly, did she think she'd get away with doing that? The truck hadn't moved from the parking space for the last fourteen hours. She pictured a prosecutor in front of her; the courtroom stifling. "Ms. Stevenson, you mean to tell us you drove the truck away, and you didn't notice the dead body lying next to the driver's door?"

She shook her head to clear the cobwebs. Surely Cartwheel Hotel & Casino had cameras set up in their parking lot. Even if this was Piper's knife—and there seemed to be no doubt about that— Piper had lost it the day before. The parking lot cameras would show that Piper had done nothing.

Right?

She took her phone out of her purse.

"What are you doing, Fenway?" Piper's voice sounded panicked. "Are you calling the police?"

"You didn't do this, right, Piper?"

Her eyes widened even more. "How could you think I killed someone?"

"I don't," Fenway said. "But I want to hear it from you. If this guy attacked you in the parking lot, if he chased you, if he made you feel unsafe—"

"I didn't see Vaughn Trask after we left the museum," Piper said evenly. Her voice had lowered to its regular range. "And I didn't kill him."

"Okay," Fenway said. "Because if it was self-defense—"

"I didn't kill him," Piper repeated.

Fenway crouched next to the body, phone still in her hand. Vaughn Trask's face was much paler than it had been at the museum. The blood had likely pooled in his back, which meant he'd been dead at least a few hours. Maybe she could check for rigor mortis. She reached in her purse for a pair of blue nitrile gloves— and then realized she wasn't in Estancia. She had no gloves with her.

A dead body in front of her, and she wouldn't be investigating this death.

Fenway turned her phone over in her hand, thinking. She tapped the phone app.

No question about it: she should call 9-1-1 first.

She tapped the screen.

It rang once, twice, three times. Then a sleepy male voice. "Fenway?"

"Hi, Dad."

"It's—it's early," Nathaniel Ferris mumbled. "Is everything all right? Did you get a flat tire on the freeway?"

"First, I'm safe. We're still at the hotel east of Las Vegas."

"What's wrong?"

"I hate to ask you for this favor—"

"Fenway, *what's wrong?*"

"Do you know a good criminal lawyer in Nevada?"

"What?"

"Not for me. At least, probably not for me. For Piper."

"For Piper? What happened?"

"I'll explain everything later. I need to call 9-1-1 next. You're a part-owner of the women's soccer team here. Your corporate lawyer *must* know of someone. Please—if you know a good criminal lawyer, get a name and contact information over to me immediately."

"Of course." A brief pause. "Piper is the reason I stayed out of jail last year," he said. "This is on my dime."

"Thanks, Dad. Okay—I'm sorry I have to hang up, but my next call is to 9-1-1."

"You sure you're okay?"

"Nothing a few months of therapy won't fix." Fenway attempted to keep her tone light and jovial, though she probably missed the mark.

"Okay. Let me know if you need anything. And I mean anything."

"Okay, Dad."

Another brief pause. "I love you, Fenway."

"Oh—uh, me too." Fenway hesitated. "Thank you."

They ended the call.

"What was that about?"

Fenway shook her head. "I'm getting you a lawyer. Or rather, my dad is getting you a lawyer."

"But—why? I didn't do anything."

Fenway tilted her head. "Piper, come on. Take a step back. Pretend you don't know where you went last night. Look at the things that a prosecutor will see. You argued with this guy in a public place. You own the knife that's sticking out of his chest."

Piper pointed to the supine body of Vaughn Trask. "Whoever did this will have blood all over them," she said, raising her voice. "I didn't have any blood on me."

"And hopefully the cameras in this parking lot will catch whoever really did this," Fenway said. "But I work for law enforcement, Piper. Hell, you did too, not even a year ago. You know a district attorney will take one look at this and you'll be their prime suspect. So until we have video evidence that clearly exonerates you —or a confession by the real killer—you're getting a lawyer."

Piper's shoulders slumped. "But I can't afford—"

"My father is paying for it," Fenway said.

"No way. I can't have your father—"

"Piper," Fenway said, "you don't get a vote. You didn't do this, but I think chances are decent you'll be arrested for Vaughn Trask's murder. And I can't let you take the fall for something you didn't do. And neither can my father."

Piper was silent.

"Now," Fenway said, "the first domino is about to fall."

She tapped 9-1-1, then tapped *Connect*.

———

Fenway ended the call. The dispatcher had asked a lot of questions, as she was supposed to. The nature of the emergency. Their location. Fenway had given the dispatcher the dead man's description and had described his dark suit, his pink-and-blue dress shirt with the big collar. She'd stayed on the line for what seemed like an hour, but was only a few minutes.

And now, how long did she have? Five minutes, maybe, before the police showed up? A small desert community like Ruby Dunes would surely have deputies show up as close to immediately as possible. But in a small town like this, Fenway didn't imagine the deputies were out in force. Maybe someone would need to be woken up. Maybe they'd need to review protocol before coming. And she'd bet the paramedics were at least ten minutes away.

Okay. She took a step toward Vaughn Trask's body—hold on. She reminded herself she didn't have jurisdiction here. Not to mention no coroner's kit. Not even a pair of blue nitrile gloves.

But she could still look, right?

She crouched next to the body, then looked over her shoulder. The cement divider hid her from view of the entrances of the hotel, most of the parking lot, and probably whatever cameras were set up. A few other oversize vehicles were in this part of the lot, but the truck hid her from them, too. All right, she was reasonably sure no one would see her leaning over a dead body.

A lot of blood, especially on the left side of Trask's dress shirt. His eyes were closed, and his arms were above his head and his legs were straight. Not like he'd fallen here—like his killer had moved his body. She looked at his hands and wrists.

"Hey, Piper? You see this?"

"What?"

"His suit jacket sleeves are pulled about a third of the way up his forearms."

"So—what does that mean? Does he have needle marks or something?"

"No—I think someone dragged the body to hide it here, between the concrete barrier and the moving truck. Keep it out of sight for as long as possible."

Fenway studied the body more closely, but without turning him over or touching his arms and legs, she couldn't tell much. His face was pallid, so the blood had likely drained closer to the ground with gravity. No way to tell when the body had been dragged here, but probably at least a few hours ago. Fenway had no liver thermometer, and she couldn't legally move the body to check for rigor mortis.

"If he was dragged," Piper said, "wouldn't there be scuff marks on the heels of his shoes?"

Fenway nodded. "Probably. But no way to tell without touching him." Maybe the back of his jacket or the rear of his trousers were torn. But that would only confirm Fenway's suspicions that his body had been moved—not necessarily new information. Besides, the clock was ticking. She pulled her phone out.

"Now who are you calling?" Piper asked.

"My last call was to get you a lawyer. Now I'm taking pictures." Fenway tapped her phone's camera app and took pictures of the knife, the wound, his hands and wrists, his legs—especially his shoes. Maybe she'd miss something now that she'd figure out later.

She pushed herself to her feet and examined the asphalt. Although it was early, Fenway could tell the day would be a scorcher. It got cold at night out here in the desert, and it was only seventy-five degrees. Downright pleasant. But Fenway could feel the air itching to bump up another twenty or thirty degrees in the next few hours. The asphalt could get hot, maybe as soon as the paramedics arrived. She squinted and knelt near Trask's feet. Maybe there were a couple of faint lines on the black asphalt. Slowly, she made her way from Trask's feet to the end of the concrete barrier. A concrete walkway about thirty feet away. Fenway turned her head first one way, then the other: the walkway ran from the edge of the lot toward the NNoV8 museum, stopping and starting where cars would drive, almost to the entrance of the hotel. Fenway and Piper hadn't taken this walkway; the hotel rooms with the external facing doors were farther down, with a different, more efficient route to the museum.

The parking lot was flat and open. No trees in this part of the desert, so nothing to stop the sun from beating down on the walkway and the vehicles parked in the lot.

But two large black SUVs—man, the interiors must get awfully hot in this climate—had parked perpendicular to the walkway about a hundred feet back from the casino. And on the other side, parked parallel to the walkway, taking up six or eight spaces and pointedly not in the oversized vehicle lot, was a big white pickup truck towing a boat. The trailer of the boat was perhaps twenty feet long.

But the concrete walkway between the boat in the trailer and the SUVs would have been a perfect place for an ambush. Fenway walked toward the boat, determination in her step.

And if Trask had been walking from the museum to the hotel, someone could have been hiding right there. Or maybe not even hiding—if Trask had known that person or expected them, it would have been easy enough to kill him as soon as they passed between the SUVs and the boat. Late at night, there'd be no reason for anyone else to be on that walkway: the museum was closed, the restaurants down the road would be closed, too. The perfect crime.

Fenway walked around the boat. Didn't seem suspicious. But on the concrete walkway, a smear of rust-colored brown, the size of her fist. She crouched, peered around. A couple of drops on the edge of the walkway, too.

This was the murder scene, she was sure of it.

She snapped several pictures of the bloodstains, then stood and took a few steps away, getting a wide-angle shot of the SUVs parked in the spaces on the left and the big pickup truck and boat parked on the right.

Next, Fenway walked between the two SUVs, then examined the asphalt. Nothing. No cigarette butts, no discarded matchbooks... no neatly folded notes saying *I Did It* with a signature. Fenway frowned. What did she expect? She took a few pictures of the empty ground, expecting little.

A siren in the distance. No need, in this case: the victim was already dead. But maybe the novelty of a murder victim in Ruby Dunes spiked everyone's adrenaline.

And it was a convenient warning to Fenway that she had to get back to stand near—but not too near—the corpse of Vaughn Trask.

———

Fenway stood about six feet away from the paramedics as one of them examined the body. The medic attempted to gently move Trask's arms, but they were stiff. Legs too, and—yep, neck as well. Full rigor. He'd been dead for at least eight hours.

Fenway glanced at her phone. 8:03. So he'd been killed sometime between six-thirty—when Fenway and Piper had left the NNoV8 museum and seen him alive—and midnight.

Next, the medic cut off Trask's pink-and-blue dress shirt. Fenway couldn't be a hundred percent sure from her angle—and with all the blood—but it looked like a single stab wound on his left side, just above the sternum. She saw no additional stab wounds on Trask's torso.

She glanced over her shoulder. Piper sat on a concrete bench twenty or thirty feet behind the U-Move-It truck, her shoulders hunched, her face tilted toward the phone screen in between her knees. Probably texting with Migs.

Oh—Fenway's phone. Not just for crime scene photos and checking the time.

Fenway tapped on the phone app, then pulled up her Favorites and tapped McVie's name. Two rings.

"Fenway?"

"Hey, Craig."

"Oh, hey! Great to hear your voice!"

"You too."

"I'm really sorry, but I can't talk long. I just pulled into work. Everything okay?"

"I just wanted to tell you we've been, uh, delayed."

"Delayed?"

Fenway hesitated, trying to figure out how to tell him.

"Look," Craig said hurriedly, "it's fine. I know it's a long drive, and it's a long time to be on the road. Just text me your ETA."

"I'm not sure when that will be."

It was McVie's turn to pause. "Oh no. Did something happen?"

"A dead body next to the moving truck."

"A dead body?"

"A murder victim."

"And you found the body?"

"Piper and I, yes."

McVie paused. "Are you okay?"

"Yes."

"Is Piper?"

"Both of us are okay."

A sigh of relief. "That's good. Thanks for telling me. So you probably have to give your statements. If the sheriff's office is anything like the one in Estancia, it should only be a couple of hours."

Fenway was silent.

"Even if it's longer," McVie said, "the important thing is that you're okay."

"It's complicated."

A slight pause. "How is it complicated?"

"You have to get to work. I'll tell you later."

He was silent for a moment. Then: "I read this funny science fiction book when I was a teenager."

"A—a funny science fiction book?" Where was McVie going with this?

"A hilarious science fiction book, as a matter of fact. It had this guy in it. Wherever he went, rain ruined everything for him. Every vacation he took, every sporting event he ever went to, even his wedding day. Turns out he was a rain god."

"Did you say 'a rain god'?"

"Yep. And you're like that. Only for dead bodies, not for rain."

Fenway chuckled.

"I hate to ask," McVie said, "but do I need to get on the next flight to Vegas?"

"Uh—I don't know. Can I call you later?"

McVie exhaled. Was it with suppressed exasperation? "Text me if you know whether you can leave. If it's before one o'clock, I can probably still make a reservation to get on the next plane out there."

"One o'clock your time?"

"Yeah. Sorry—I'll be late if I don't head in right now. Love you."

"Okay." Fenway paused. "I'm sorry about this, Craig. I'll get your stuff..."

Fenway looked at the screen. McVie had hung up.

She pursed her lips. He was usually such a Boy Scout about politeness. He'd never—well, rarely—hung up without saying goodbye.

She closed her eyes and remembered him, just over a week ago, on one knee in Dos Milagros. Given how much Fenway loved the taquería's lengua tacos, there were definitely worse places he could have proposed.

But she had gently taken his hands in hers before he'd even gotten all the words out.

"Craig," she'd said quietly, "what are you doing? You're about to leave for a year. I know you love me. And I love you. And I don't want to lose you. But this long-distance thing has me freaked out."

"I know," he'd said. "Me too. That's why—"

"I won't be any less scared with an engagement ring on my finger," Fenway had said. "In fact, I might be more scared. Because if the distance is too hard—if we get to where we feel like this isn't right—it's going to be that much harder to do the right thing."

He'd blinked at her. "The right thing? Breaking up is the right thing?"

"Well, not *now*," Fenway had said, taking her hands away and crossing her arms. "And maybe—*maybe*—not ever. But getting engaged won't fix the next year. I hope it won't be rough, but I'm scared it will be."

"And you want options."

"I—" Fenway had stopped. The tone in McVie's voice—an edge to it. "I don't want to stay with you just because I feel trapped. And I don't want *you* thinking I only stayed with you because I feel trapped. That would suck, right?"

Fenway opened her eyes. The two paramedics were taking the wheeled stretcher out of the ambulance.

The first paramedic out of the ambulance had asked her where the victim was, but had asked nothing else. She looked at her phone again. 8:04—had it really only been a minute? She tapped her phone app and scrolled. She'd found the body at, what—seven twenty? No later than seven thirty. There couldn't be so much crime in Ruby Dunes that it would take the county sheriff's office forty-five minutes to show up for a murder.

Then her mind spun again. Yes, she'd done the right thing and called the police. But now that the paramedics were tending to Trask's body, could she and Piper just... drive away? She thought for a moment. The knife belonged to Piper. Fenway expected Piper to at least be a person of interest, and probably the prime suspect.

If they found out Piper owned the knife.

They'd alerted the authorities. Technically, everything they were supposed to do was complete. Legally—well, Fenway didn't know Nevada law that well, but she was pretty sure they didn't have any obligation to stick around.

The paramedics were blocking the driver's door of the moving truck, but Fenway could get in the passenger side, climb over the seats, start the engine, and drive off.

Could they pretend they didn't recognize the victim? That they didn't know it was Piper's knife?

Fenway squeezed her eyes shut.

They'd told the front desk agent Piper had lost the knife. They even said the knife had an etching on the side. No, if the sheriff's office spoke to—Orlando, that was his name—if they spoke to Orlando, and they most certainly would, they'd get Piper's name. Fenway had paid for the room, but Piper had signed for breakfast using her credit card. And the sheriff would hear about the lost knife.

And they'd talk to the workers at the museum. The ticket-taker —Roberto, right?—would almost certainly tell the sheriff that a tall redhead had shouted at the dead man. Fenway pictured the sheriff —in a tan cowboy hat with a badge affixed to the front, like out of a noir movie—holding Piper's picture in front of him. "This her?" he'd say in a Southern drawl.

"One of our guests recorded the entire argument on her phone," Roberto would say. "I can get her name from our ticket system if you like."

Fenway shook her head. Only terrible options for Piper. Either leave before the sheriff could show up and get chased down later— maybe on a lonely stretch of Interstate 15 in the middle of the Utah desert—or wait here for the sheriff, almost certainly facing questions that could easily turn into an interrogation. For that matter, Fenway was on the video, too—no telling how the sheriff's office would treat her. She knew how annoyed she was when persons of interest kept secrets during her investigations, and this sheriff would probably be no different. Her law enforcement identification might get her out of a traffic ticket, but it probably wouldn't get her out of a murder investigation.

The thought wasn't even out of her head before a white sheriff's cruiser appeared in her peripheral vision. The car drove down the street in front of the casino—a bit lazily, Fenway thought.

Didn't really have a choice now—there was no way they could get the moving truck out of there without the police noticing. And they wouldn't be able to pack and go before getting stopped for questioning. The only thing for sure: Piper wasn't getting her knife back any time soon.

Fenway walked over to Piper. She glanced at Piper's phone screen: a text conversation with Migs. That was good—Migs had passed the bar, and he'd give her useful information. And Piper would listen to him, whereas she might not listen to Fenway.

"Migs giving you advice?"

Piper nodded. "Keep my mouth shut. I told him your dad was getting me a lawyer. He said to expect to be taken into the sheriff's office, maybe get interrogated, maybe even get—uh." She cleared her throat, but when she spoke again, her voice cracked. "Maybe even get arrested."

Fenway frowned. She should have gone into the hotel while she was waiting and asked Orlando to cue up any parking lot video footage from the night before. That would show that Piper wasn't in the parking lot at the time of the murder. She hoped.

She shook her head—no, that was the wrong thing to think. She had no power here. Fenway needed the police to do their jobs.

The sheriff's cruiser pulled into the driveway of the casino, only traveling about five miles per hour. The car came to a stop next to the concrete barrier on the other side of the body, and the engine turned off.

Fenway blinked at the sheriff's cruiser, but the sun glinted off the windshield and she couldn't see inside. She looked away, having no idea if the driver was watching her watching the car.

A moment later, the driver's side door of the cruiser opened, and a tall man got out in a beige short-sleeved sheriff's uniform. No hat, and a badge centered on his shirt pocket. His blond hair was disheveled and perched above a high forehead. He wore aviator sunglasses and stretched languidly as he got out of the car.

"Mornin', Jake," he said to the paramedic. He reached in the car and came out with a paper coffee cup with the telltale yellow lid from Sassy Sunrise Coffee.

"Sheriff," the paramedic said. Oh, he was the sheriff, not just a deputy.

"Another overdose?" the sheriff said, then took a long drink from his coffee. Hadn't he heard the news from the dispatcher?

"Stabbed," Jake said, turning away to arrange a piece of equipment in the ambulance.

The sheriff lowered his coffee. "What was that?"

"Stabbed," Jake repeated, then stood and hooked his thumb toward the NNoV8 museum. "I recognize him. He was one of the owners at The Box."

Huh. *The Box.* That didn't sound complimentary—must be how the locals referred to the museum.

"Ah." The sheriff took off his sunglasses. "Not Brock?"

"No, not Brock." Jake was terrible at hiding his annoyance. "You didn't get the message from dispatch?"

"Got a call from Izzy. I'd just won a big jackpot on the five-dollar slots at Breakwater. Ten million dollars. And she had to wake me up from the nicest dream I had since Alyssa left."

"Why didn't Deputy Bardot come?"

"Izzy? She's up in Mordecai Gulch. Domestic dispute. I don't expect her for another half-hour. Didn't get a lot of info—just a dead body in the Cartwheel parking lot." He jerked his thumb toward the body. "My money would have been on Brock."

Fenway made a mental note. Brock. She didn't think that was the name of the investor who'd been in the museum at the same time as Piper and her. Who'd that been? Stan. And something monosyllabic for the last name. Brock was obviously one of the other owners.

"Vaughn Trask," Jake said.

The sheriff let out a low whistle, and he straightened his posture. He motioned his head toward Fenway and Piper, but Jake didn't take notice. Or didn't respond, anyway.

Raising his chin, the sheriff turned toward Fenway. "Ma'am? You the one who found the body?"

Fenway nodded, and he walked toward her, more urgency in his step—now that someone *important* was dead, she thought.

This might be trouble for Piper.

CHAPTER FIVE

"WHEN DID YOU FIND HIM?" THE SHERIFF ASKED.

"About seven thirty," Fenway replied. "We were about to get on the road."

He pointed to the hotel. "You stay at the Cartwheel last night?"

"That's right."

"You've checked out?"

"Not yet."

"What are you doing here in Ruby Dunes?"

She pointed to the truck. "I'm moving my boyfriend's stuff to Colorado."

He smiled, just a hint of cruelty. "That's quite a task. Wish my ex had done stuff like that for me." He cleared his throat. "Mind if I see your identification?"

Fenway pulled the Dominguez County badge out of her purse. "I'm a county coroner in California. Fenway Stevenson."

The sheriff stepped closer and stuck his hand out. "Sheriff Bartholomew Jeffcoat, Correos County."

Fenway shook his hand, trying to express as much friendliness into it as possible.

He clicked his tongue. "You deal with corpses all year, come out here for a little vacation, and you can't get away from the dead bodies."

She gave the sheriff a little smile. "My boyfriend says I'm like a rain god, but for murder victims."

He frowned. "You think this is funny?"

She widened her eyes and took a step back. "Sorry. Sometimes you need a little levity to get through the week."

He harrumphed. "So you're just passing through?"

"Yes."

"You ever meet the victim?"

Fenway paused, and Jeffcoat tilted his head.

"What is it?"

"I don't know if you'd call it *meeting* him. I saw him yesterday afternoon at the museum."

Jeffcoat nodded. "You visited the museum? Or just one of those gift-shop looky-loos?"

"A visit. Bought tickets, went through the exhibits. We—" Fenway paused. She'd had forty-five minutes to think about how she wanted to characterize their meeting but still couldn't figure out the best way to do so. And should she mention Piper in her answers? She didn't want to get her involved, but with Piper's knife sticking out of the dead man's chest, there was little chance of that. She'd already said 'we,' so she was committed now. "We spoke to him briefly just before we left. That was about six fifteen yesterday —I suppose that's more evening than afternoon."

The sheriff turned to Piper. "And you, miss?"

Huh. Fenway had been called "ma'am" and Piper was a "miss."

"Yes," Piper said.

Ah. Monosyllabic answers. Possibly an effective course of action. And likely something Migs had coached her on.

Jeffcoat arched an eyebrow. "Yes? To which part?"

To her credit, Piper didn't flinch. "What Fenway said." Good— no use of any formal language; no use of *Ms. Stevenson*. That might have tipped Sheriff Jeffcoat off that Piper was evading specific answers. Probably wouldn't get her off the hook—not once they discovered the knife was hers, anyway—but it would keep her out of the sheriff's sights for a while.

From this distance—well, from *any* distance, really, that wasn't leaning over the body as Fenway had done earlier—she couldn't read the etched inscription on the knife. And stainless steel folding knives were common. Already, Fenway could imagine the sheriff barking at Piper, "Why didn't you tell me the knife was yours?" Fenway couldn't picture Piper's response.

The sheriff scratched his scalp, looked past Fenway toward the casino hotel, and sighed. Oh—maybe he saw through Piper. "Ordinarily," he said slowly, "I'd let you folks get about your business."

Fenway followed the sheriff's gaze over her shoulder. Several people filtered out of the hotel exit, and three of them jerked their heads up, then began walking toward them. Looky-loos. One of them was Orlando, still in his rumpled, ill-fitting dress shirt with the Cartwheel logo on it.

"But I'll bet a hundred bucks," the sheriff continued, "that those Cartwheel folks haven't fixed the camera situation in the parking lot yet."

Fenway's ears perked up. "What camera situation?"

"Maybe two or three weeks ago. Coupla teenagers smashed all the cameras in the parking lot with a baseball bat." Jeffcoat sighed again, this time more dramatically. "We caught the kids, of course—they uploaded the whole thing to Photoxio—but I don't think the company has fixed the cameras yet. Told 'em it was a condition of their operating license here in Correos County, but I think they've got sixty days to make the fix. I've worked with the Cartwheel folks before. They won't let go of their money without a fight."

Oh no. That meant there'd be no footage to exonerate Piper.

"So that means we'll be relying on your statements, rather than camera footage," Jeffcoat said. "I'm afraid I'll have to ask you to come to the station to make your statements."

The wheels in Fenway's mind spun. "Who knew about the broken cameras?"

Jeffcoat blinked. "I'm sorry?"

Fenway looked Jeffcoat in the face, then pressed her lips together. "I'm sorry. My office investigates all the suspicious deaths back home. Just where my mind went."

Jeffcoat smiled, though the smile didn't reach his eyes. "Sure, sure. Comes with the job, right?"

"That's it. Sometimes, I wish I could stop my brain from going a million miles an hour."

The looky-loos stopped about ten yards from them. Orlando craned his neck.

"Can we cordon off the scene?" Jeffcoat barked.

Jake, who'd been attending to the body, stood. "With what, Sheriff? You're the only law enforcement official here. We don't carry police tape in the ambulance."

"Uh huh." Jeffcoat shifted his weight, turning back to Fenway. "Being a fellow law enforcement official and all, I'm sure you wouldn't mind helping us out."

"Of course I don't mind," Fenway said. "I can put up the police tape while you—"

"That's not what I mean," Jeffcoat interrupted. "I mean, you and your friend come down to the station, give your statements."

"Ah." Fenway pressed her lips together. How did she want to play this? "If I weren't pressed for time, I would. My boyfriend's waiting for this truck." She opened her mouth again and almost blathered about McVie.

Hmm—maybe that wouldn't be a bad thing. Might give the sheriff pause.

"He just moved to Colorado, and his company wanted him to start a week early—and he couldn't get keys to his apartment until today. So I got stuck driving this truck a thousand miles, and luckily my friend came along to keep me company." She raised her head and looked Jeffcoat in the eye. "Have you moved across the country before?"

Jeffcoat gave Fenway a wan smile. "Not for a long time. Now, if you'll—"

"This is the second long-distance move I've done in two years, and I hope I'll never have to do one again." Fenway pointed at the sheriff. "Ever been in a long-distance relationship, Sheriff? I don't mind telling you, I'm not looking forward to it. He says it'll be fine, it's only supposed to be for a year, but can you believe he asked me to *marry* him before he left?"

The sheriff put up his hands in front of him, palms out. "Listen, I'm sure this has been rough on you. And I'm sure you have lots of reasons for getting back on the road. But I'll tell *you* something you might find interesting." He cocked his head. "I just saw an American Institute of Crime report, and it estimates that—uh, let's see, what was it—thirty-two percent of people who report a body that's been a victim of a homicide are the ones who committed the murder."

Fenway ran her tongue over her teeth. The sheriff was tenacious; she couldn't scare him off with her irrelevant babble. Then it hit her—interrogators *loved* people who wouldn't shut up. They often gave information they shouldn't. Hell, *she* loved interviewees who wouldn't shut up. She could have kicked herself.

"So," the sheriff continued, "you see my conundrum. If I *don't* bring the two of you in and interview you, there's a one in three chance I'll be letting the killer go." He pointed to the highway. "And you're on your way out of town."

"It's not like I'm leaving the country."

He tilted his head. "So you say. But why would I give myself an advanced degree of difficulty when you're standing right in front of me now?"

Jake turned to the sheriff. "Hey, Bartholomew, you want to—" He stopped midsentence, giving a quick, furtive glance to the five people standing with their mouths open at the scene.

Two more police cruisers appeared on the road and turned into the parking lot.

"Hold your horses, Jake," Jeffcoat called back. Then to Fenway: "Don't go anywhere."

Orlando was still craning his neck. "Hey," he said, in a voice just a little too loud, "isn't that your missing knife?"

Fenway closed her eyes.

The sheriff's head snapped up. "Someone's missing a knife?"

Orlando pointed to the body of Vaughn Trask. "That knife. Stainless steel folding knife, right? Does it have an etching on it like you said?" He stared at Fenway. "No wonder I couldn't find it in the lost-and-found."

A shadow of fury fell across Bartholomew Jeffcoat's face as he raised his face to look Fenway in the eyes. "This is *your* knife?"

She hesitated, just for a half-second. "No."

Jeffcoat inclined his head. "Why did you hesitate?"

Piper stood, her face strangely impassive. "Because it's *my* knife." She pointed at Orlando. "Fenway reported it missing this morning to the front desk, and Orlando..."

Orlando raised his hand as if a teacher were going to call on him.

Piper nodded. "Orlando helped us by looking through the lost-and-found."

"What's your name, miss?"

"Piper Patten."

"And do you know the victim?"

Piper paused. "No." A careful *no*, for sure. Truthful—but not the whole truth.

"And what's the etching?" Jeffcoat asked.

Piper frowned; Fenway could see the gears turning in her head, but she couldn't figure out a way to get out of answering the question. Besides, she'd already admitted it was her knife—probably not the smartest course of action, but the bell couldn't be un-rung. "'You'll always make us proud.'"

The sheriff turned toward the body, took three purposeful strides over, then squatted and peered at the side of the knife. He exhaled loudly, then stood and turned.

"Now," he said, as the cruisers parked thirty feet behind the ambulance, "I *insist* that the two of you come to the station with me."

———

The back of the police car smelled like barbecue: a not altogether unpleasant smell, but the sweetness was cloying. The cruiser had been moved to a spot in the shade of the casino building, so the heat inside the car wasn't unbearable. At least the front windows were rolled down. She looked through the rear window toward the other cruiser, the one Piper was in. They must not have wanted Fenway and Piper to have the chance to coordinate their stories. That meant Fenway would likely spend some time in an interview room.

The woman in the front seat wore the same uniform as the sheriff, but with fewer stripes on the sleeve. A deputy. Her skin was several shades darker than Fenway's, but her brown eyes were bright. She sat for a moment, typing on her phone. Fenway couldn't be sure if she was entering notes from the case or if she was texting with a friend or relative, but she didn't want to interrupt.

The minutes ticked by, and Fenway closed her eyes and breathed deeply despite the too-sweet smell of barbecue. She wouldn't be driving anywhere in the next hour, for sure. She'd told the sheriff check-out time was at eleven; the sheriff said they'd finish in plenty of time. But the longer Fenway sat in the back seat, unmoving, the more she doubted it.

Especially since she and Piper were going in different cars. If the plan was to interview the two of them separately, making them both wait for hours—worrying about the stuff left in the hotel room, late check-out charges, getting on the road—would lead one or both of them to say something that would get them arrested. Fenway set her jaw. She couldn't worry about any of that. Her freedom—and Piper's freedom—was worth far more than late check-out charges. Even extra days renting the moving truck.

McVie wouldn't like the delay, but he wasn't one of those guys who'd be mad at her. Because he used to be sheriff back in Estancia, maybe he knew law enforcement officials in the Vegas area. Perhaps one of them owed a favor and could pull some strings.

Fenway's phone rang in her purse. She lifted her head and met the deputy's eyes in the rear-view mirror. "Mind if I get that?"

The deputy grunted noncommittally.

Fenway pulled the phone out. Dez. Fenway tapped *Answer*.

"Good morning, Sergeant Roubideaux."

Silence for a second at the other end. "So formal, Fenway. You on the road yet?"

"I'm in the back of a police car in Ruby Dunes."

"What are you doing in—" Dez sighed. "I swear, Fenway, trouble follows you everywhere."

Fenway cleared her throat. "Would you contact Craig and make sure he knows we're delayed?"

"We? So—Piper too?"

"That's correct."

"I'm up to my eyeballs in paperwork, but I'll see if I can call him on my lunch break." She paused. "Is this some bullshit charge like going 35 in a 30 zone, or is it—"

"A dead body was found next to our moving truck. Vaughn Trask is the victim. Appears to be foul play."

"Hey—" the deputy began.

"I'm speaking to my detective sergeant," Fenway said. "No information is being revealed to the public."

"You still can't talk about the case."

Fenway arched her eyebrow. "Deputy—are you a deputy?"

Another grunt.

Fenway searched her mind for clues from what she'd heard from the sheriff. Then it clicked. "Izzy Bardot, is that right?"

"Yeah."

"Deputy Bardot, I'm a county coroner. You got to the scene after I introduced myself to the sheriff, but I'm a law enforcement officer as well."

"Coroners aren't law enforcement—"

"In California, they are."

"You're not in California. And no talking about the case."

Fenway frowned. "You called me, Sergeant. Did you need to give me some information about *your* case?" She glanced at Bardot as she said the last few words; Bardot didn't respond.

"It can wait till you get back," Dez said.

"We haven't moved in ten minutes." Fenway pushed herself more upright in the rear seat. "I think I have time."

The deputy started the engine and blasted the air conditioning, rolling up the windows.

"It's official," Dez said. "George Pope pled 'not guilty' to the murder of Mathis Jericho."

Fenway's brain had to shift gears—this was from last week's murder investigation. "What?"

The deputy put the cruiser into Drive and they rolled through the parking lot.

"Don't pretend you didn't see this coming," Dez said. "We went over your statement. George Pope didn't mention Mathis Jericho in his confession."

"But he's not withdrawing his guilty plea for Seth Cahill?"

"No, just for the murder of Mathis Jericho."

Fenway blinked; she flashed for a moment on the image of Mathis Jericho in the driver's seat of the stolen Corvette, bricks of drugs all around his dead body, the flies swarming.

The cruiser turned left onto the main road of the casino. Fenway hoped the sheriff's office wouldn't be a long drive. "I'm only surprised that he's defending himself," Fenway said. "I figured he'd want his secrets going to the grave with him; that he'd want to protect his wife from the emotional fallout."

"The truth will set you free," Dez said.

"In this case, it makes our job harder."

"You say that like it's a bad thing."

"Sorry—you're right."

"And what about you?" Dez said. "This Vaughn Trask—you want me to look into him?"

Fenway glanced up. The deputy focused on the road, and as they drove onto the on-ramp to Interstate 15, the noise of the road and the engine increased. But Fenway still wanted to be careful of her side of the conversation. "I'd appreciate it."

"Are you under arrest?"

"No."

Dez paused. "Do you think they'll accuse you of murder?"

"No."

"How about Piper?"

"Less clear, but I think that's the direction it's headed."

"Why do you say that?"

Fenway was silent.

"Oh—you can't talk. Just yes or no answers."

"Correct."

"Is there some evidence that implicates Piper?"

"Yes."

"Beyond just the location of the body? Next to your truck?"

"Yes."

"Are you worried about a motive?"

"Yes."

"A weapon?"

"Yes."

"The time of death? Opportunity?"

"Yes."

Dez let out a loud exhale. "Are you sure she didn't do it?"

"Yes."

"What makes you so sure?" Dez clicked her tongue. "Right, right, you can't say. Listen—if they're looking at her but not at you, there's a good chance they'll stash you somewhere like a break room or something. Keep your eyes and ears open. Or say you have to stretch your legs, walk around or something, and get somewhere you can call me as soon as you can."

"What about—" Fenway clamped her mouth shut. Yesses and noes only.

"What about the Jericho investigation?" Dez said, as if reading Fenway's mind. "I know I've got my hands full with you being gone and Callahan not starting until next Monday, but it's already been a week and a half since we found Mathis Jericho dead. The trail isn't exactly blazing hot anymore."

"You could talk to Celeste," Fenway said quietly, turning her head away from the deputy. Celeste Salvador was intelligent and insightful. She'd been a great asset to the sheriff's office and was Fenway's choice to promote to one of her detectives. "She was with me when we found Jericho's body, after all. Celeste took good notes, but you know how these things are. Could be details she can provide that aren't in the report."

Dez grunted. "That'd be a great idea—if I knew where Celeste was."

"I knew she was mad at me for screwing up her promotion, so I'm not surprised Celeste didn't tell me where she'd taken another job. But she didn't tell you, either?"

"I can track her down, probably. Must be *someone* in Estancia she confided in." Dez paused. "But it feels like we need to start from square one. We assumed—like anyone would—that the same person committed both murders. Now that we know they're not—"

"Assuming George Pope is telling the truth."

"—we'll have to reboot the investigation," Dez finished.

Fenway was silent. She glanced up; Deputy Bardot watched Fenway out of the corner of her eye. Ugh. Back to yesses and noes.

"You have a lawyer?" Dez said.

"No."

Dez cackled. "You've been in law enforcement long enough to know you *always* need a lawyer when you're talking to the cops. Or are you in denial about what happened to you in L.A.?"

"No," Fenway said.

"Ah. Piper. Does she have a lawyer?"

"Yes."

"Your daddy paying for it?"

"Uh, yes."

"I'm glad," Dez said. "Piper got him out of his scrape. Now he has the chance to help her out. Makes me think billionaires aren't all soulless ghouls."

"Just most of them," Fenway said.

The deputy clicked on the turn signal, and they got off the freeway at the Tenth Avenue exit, only a few car lengths behind the cruiser in front of them. A sign on the shoulder with an arrow pointing to the right: *Sheriff's Office.* They were almost there.

CHAPTER SIX

THE SHERIFF'S OFFICE BUILDING WAS A LOW-SLUNG TWO-STORY concrete box—beige instead of the NNoV8's black, but otherwise not too dissimilar, except in size. The building took up an entire block of Tenth Avenue from A Street to B Street. Ah, the beauty of cartographers' creative naming conventions.

Fenway expected the deputy to immediately park next to the cruiser in front, but she waited.

Oh: they wanted to get Piper inside first.

Yep. They didn't want Fenway and Piper talking. And obviously Fenway's status as a law enforcement representative held little to no sway here. But this wasn't a speeding ticket: there was a corpse with a knife in the chest. And Fenway supposed she should be glad that the county didn't give special treatment to other law enforcement representatives.

"I apologize for my manners, Deputy Bardot."

"Happens to the best of us."

"Bardot," Fenway said, turning the name over in her mind. "Like Brigitte, the movie star from the fifties?"

The deputy grunted. "I'm sure you can see the family resemblance."

"Fenway Stevenson," Fenway responded. "And yes, I realize I'm the spitting image of the baseball stadium."

Bardot cracked a smile. Good.

The driver of the parked cruiser, an olive-skinned deputy of medium height with a bushy mustache, got out. He closed the driver-side door, then opened the rear door, and ushered Piper out of the backseat and into the building.

Bardot steered her cruiser into the parking space next to the first cruiser. It had the air of a well-rehearsed process to it. Methodical. Fenway was impressed despite her situation: Jeffcoat looked like he ran a tight ship.

Bardot opened the back door of the cruiser and Fenway slid out. She wasn't in handcuffs, but Bardot kept uncomfortably close as they walked to the building.

They didn't go through the main entrance: this was a side door where Bardot used a keycard to gain access. The same door the other deputy had taken Piper through.

Beige walls and bad lighting. Gray vinyl flooring. Not the most attractive of spaces, but Fenway had yet to see a police station or a sheriff's office that would win any design awards. Bardot turned left down a hallway, then a right, then the hallway opened up into a bullpen area with six or seven cubicles. She turned right again and came to a closed gray metal door. A plastic slider sign mounted next to the door read *In Use*.

Bardot nodded slightly, barely slowing down. That must be the interview room, and Piper must be in there. Fenway continued following Bardot down the corridor. They passed a set of restrooms on the right, then an open door on the left with six round tables, four plastic chairs at each. Two vending machines, a coffee maker on the counter, a microwave, a plain white refrigerator.

"Can I get you anything?" Bardot asked.

Breakfast was still sitting in Fenway's stomach, and she didn't want any coffee. "Just the restroom." She got up before Bardot could object. If she'd be next in the interview room, she didn't want her bladder screaming at her. Sheriff Jeffcoat might run a tight ship, but Fenway had over a year of experience interviewing suspects and knew some tricks of the trade.

She walked out of the break room and into the women's restroom. Two sinks on the left, three stalls on the right, all with open doors. Fenway went into the last stall and closed the door, sliding the lock shut, then hanging her purse on the hook on the back of the stall door.

She emptied her bladder and was about to flush when she heard the door slam open and a woman crying.

"I don't know what happened, Mom," she sobbed. "Vaughn's dead. Someone killed him. I heard they have a suspect, but they won't tell me anything else."

That suspect was probably Piper. Fenway clamped her mouth shut and didn't move a muscle.

The woman's voice caught, then she stopped crying. "That's not why Vaughn is dead. You mean to tell me—"

Quiet for a moment. Fenway was about to clear her throat and announce her presence, but Dez's voice rang in her head: *Keep your eyes and ears open. People say the damnedest things when they don't think other people are listening.*

So she listened.

"I don't know where he was last night," the woman said. "I just told you, the police aren't telling me anything."

Another moment of silence.

"I don't know, Mom. People can change—"

More silence.

"Totally unfounded, Mom." Anger in her voice. "And for your information, I moved in with him. I don't care if you don't approve, he and I were married."

She paused again, listening.

"Oh, don't tell me it was a blessing, Mom. That's horrible.

Maybe you never liked Vaughn—"

Another moment of silence.

"That was over a year ago, and the two of them are through." A sigh, then she cleared her throat. "Look, I'm in the bathroom at the police station." The woman's voice had a caustic bite. "They want me to give them a statement of where I was last night. I'll call you again in about an hour and you can insult my dead husband all you want."

A beep of the call ending.

The woman sighed loudly—it sounded like she was in front of one of the sinks.

"Okay, Aurora," she said, so softly that Fenway could barely hear. "Yeah, it sucks that the last thing you said to him was that he was an entitled asshole, but he knew you loved him. And he knew he *was* an entitled asshole, and he just didn't care." A deep breath. "You're going back out there, and you will *not* tell them that the last thing you did was fight with him. You were in love, you just got married, and you'll go home and wear nothing but black for the next two weeks. If they find out, they find out."

The faucet turned on, then a few seconds later, off. A paper towel dispenser rumbled once, twice. The sound of crumpling. Then the door opened and closed.

Fenway exhaled.

Aurora.

She grabbed her phone from her purse. Two bars—that should be enough. She opened a browser and searched for *Vaughn Trask Aurora*.

A Photoxio URL was the first search result. *Aurora Horn's Photoxio Feed*. A candid picture of a brown-haired white woman, athletic build, in a black tank top, standing next to Vaughn Trask in a *Neon Lights Brewing* T-shirt, a rocky vista out of focus behind them. "I said yes!" was the caption. In the next photo: two hands, a smaller feminine hand with a big diamond ring, resting inside a larger masculine hand.

Aurora and Vaughn, getting engaged while out on a hike—at least, that's what it looked like to her. She scrolled until she found the date: January of the previous year. That made sense—one of the few decent months to be outside in Vegas. But wow—eighteen months since the engagement pictures, and no pictures of the wedding. Had they eloped? Maybe that's why Aurora's mother was so upset.

Fenway felt a pang of—well, *something*. Was it regret? She'd said no to McVie. Not "no" exactly. Just a not-yet. Not until we figure some stuff out. And he'd understood.

But Fenway knew her clock was counting down, too—McVie wouldn't want to wait eighteen months for Fenway to figure out what she wanted.

She put the phone back in her purse, then flushed, exited the stall, and washed her hands.

When and where had this fight between Aurora and Vaughn taken place? Maybe it had been later in the evening, which might give Piper more of an alibi.

She opened the door and nearly ran into Deputy Bardot.

"Coroner," Bardot said. "Let's go have a chat."

Fenway followed Bardot into the break room. Bardot motioned Fenway to sit at one of the round tables and Bardot went to the vending machine, tapping her credit card and pushing buttons until a granola bar on the top row pushed itself out and into the retrieval tray.

"Sure you don't want anything?" Bardot asked, grabbing the granola bar.

"I'm good."

Bardot pulled the plastic chair out opposite Fenway and sat, tearing open her granola bar. "These aren't too bad once you get used to them," she said. "Not as good as a Chocolate Chunk bar, but probably better for me, you know?"

Fenway nodded.

"Okay, then." Bardot bit a chunk of granola bar off, then chewed as she talked. "The decedent was found next to the driver's side of your truck."

"The rental truck," Fenway said.

"You talked to Mr. Trask at approximately six-thirty."

Fenway paused.

"It's a simple question, Coroner."

"I don't believe I ever addressed Mr. Trask," Fenway said carefully. "So technically speaking, I didn't talk to him. I left the exhibits, I saw Piper in a conversation with Mr. Trask, and she and I left. I don't even think it was a full minute between the time I exited the exhibits area and that time we went into the gift shop. Mr. Trask did not come into the gift shop while we were in there."

"What was the subject of Ms. Patten's discussion with Mr. Trask?"

Fenway pressed her lips together. She was positive that Piper would have more information about this—because Fenway only caught the last snippet of their conversation after it had turned confrontational. "I came into the conversation late, Deputy."

"But what were they discussing when you entered the conversation?"

Fenway drummed her fingers on the table. "Piper was discussing the artistic merits on the use of NFTs, to the best of my recollection."

"And what was Mr. Trask doing?"

Fenway shook her head. "He may have responded to Piper, but I can't remember clearly."

Bardot nodded. "Where did you go after you went into the gift shop?"

"We left the museum and walked back to the Cartwheel Hotel."

"You didn't drive?" An accusatory note in Bardot's voice.

Fenway opened her mouth to say *It's not that far* or *We didn't want to drive the rental truck into the museum lot.* But simpler was better. "No."

"Then what did you do?"

"We went to dinner." Ugh—Fenway closed her eyes. Had they gone straight to dinner before going back to the hotel? She thought back—and yes, the Mexican restaurant had been on the other side of the museum from the hotel. "Hang on, Deputy. I don't have the order of this right."

Bardot narrowed her eyes.

"We didn't go back to the hotel. We went to dinner."

"Where?"

"The Mexican restaurant."

"La Comida Verdad?"

"I don't remember the name."

Bardot crossed her arms. "First you say you went back to the hotel, then the restaurant. Which is it?"

"We went to the restaurant first," Fenway said, feeling the heat rise to her face. "We had a few margaritas, and we ate dinner. I think it was probably about eight thirty when we left to walk back to the hotel."

Bardot leaned forward. "What route did you take to get back?"

"Route? What do you mean?"

"I mean, how did you get back? Did you walk along the road, or did you take the back trail behind the parking lots?"

"Oh. The sidewalk next to the road. I didn't know about the trail."

"You both went back to the hotel?"

"Right."

"And what did you do when you returned to the hotel?"

Fenway blinked. "I got ready for bed, and then I went to bed. We wanted to get an early start." None of that was technically lying. But it omitted that Piper went out to look for her knife while Fenway was in the shower. Time Fenway couldn't account for Piper's whereabouts. She wasn't sure if it was smart to leave that part out. But something didn't sit right with Fenway, and the fewer details they had about Fenway not being able to provide an alibi for Piper, the better.

And a seed of doubt popped into Fenway's mind.

Maybe Piper *had* gone back to the museum to fight with Vaughn Trask.

No—that was ridiculous. Piper wouldn't stab someone over a hundred dollars—or over a philosophical disagreement about the true nature of artistic expression. Besides, she would have had blood all over her clothes if she'd stabbed Trask.

But the police didn't know Piper like Fenway knew Piper. And the police hadn't seen Piper's unstained clothes when she got back to the hotel room after searching for her knife. So the less the police knew, the better.

At least, that's what Fenway hoped.

Then a thought hit her.

"What was Vaughn Trask doing in the Cartwheel parking lot, anyway?" Fenway asked. "He worked at the museum, not at the hotel or the casino."

Bardot shrugged. "This is the only casino in a twenty-mile radius," she said. "A rich guy like that probably gets his drinks comped at the high rollers table. We're looking into it, but an employee who works half a block away from the casino in their parking lot? It's not unusual."

Fenway nodded; only in Nevada casino country did "half a block" take ten minutes to walk. It made sense for museum employees to play craps for a couple of hours or sit at a blackjack table after their shift. Trask would have been no different.

Bardot flicked her eyes up to meet Fenway's. "Did you and Ms. Patten have different rooms?"

"No, we were sharing a room. Saving money."

"So was Ms. Patten with you all night?"

Fenway leaned forward, resting her elbows on the table. "I took a shower last night. And this morning, Piper was already in the restaurant when I woke up."

"So the answer is no."

"I mean," Fenway stammered, "for all intents and purposes, yes, she was." Except for when she was looking for her knife. Which ended up being the murder weapon.

"But you wouldn't swear to it in a court of law."

Fenway broke with Bardot's gaze. "No, I guess not."

"And you were in the hotel room the whole time?"

Fenway inwardly grimaced. Nope. She'd gone out looking for the knife *with* Piper. Yes, maybe the cameras were broken for the parking lot, but she'd bet a camera somewhere had captured her and Piper either leaving their hotel room or heading to the parking lot. And that would have been later than they got back from dinner—it had been about ten o'clock, hadn't it?

Ugh. Any way you sliced it, Fenway and Piper looked like suspects. Maybe the medical examiner could determine time of death. Maybe it was when they were at dinner, when they had witnesses at the restaurant and credit card receipts to prove when they were there.

Fenway shook her head. "No."

"Where did you go?"

"After my shower, Piper and I went out to the parking lot."

Bardot leaned forward another inch. "And did you see Mr. Trask next to your rental truck?"

"No." There was more to that—they'd been looking for Piper's knife, of course. But as that was now the murder weapon, Fenway went monosyllabic.

"Why were you in the parking lot?"

"We'd—" Ugh. She couldn't say they'd left something in the truck, because what if Trask had been killed before nine forty-five? They'd have surely seen the body then. But they didn't go by the truck—not on that side of the concrete barrier. Trask might have already been dead by then.

The truth, then. If the police were to ask both Piper and Fenway why they were in the parking lot, only the truth would guarantee they'd both answer the same way.

"Piper had lost her knife. It was a gift from her father, and she'd had it with her earlier in the day."

"Her knife. This is the same knife we found sticking out of Mr. Trask's chest an hour ago?"

"I haven't examined the knife," Fenway said carefully, "but if the etching is the same, then I have no reason to think otherwise."

Bardot barked a laugh. "A very measured answer, Coroner."

"A very *accurate* answer, Deputy."

"Had you ever met Vaughn Trask before yesterday?"

Fenway shook her head. "I wouldn't even say he met me yesterday. He and I weren't introduced. I doubt he'd know my name." Of course, now that Trask was dead, it was a moot point.

Bardot leaned back in the plastic chair. She hadn't taken a bite of the granola bar since that first one when she'd sat down. Fenway watched Bardot closely, hearing only the ticking of the clock on the wall above the vending machines.

Finally, Bardot sighed and pulled herself to her feet. "Wait here a moment."

As Bardot left the break room, a palpable sense of relief washed over Fenway. She stood, stretching her arms over her head, and paced around the break room.

Though it was the mid-morning, no other employees walked in or out of the break room. Fenway scratched her scalp. Perhaps the police used the break room for a second interview room when the main one was taken. Happened often enough in Estancia.

She sat back down and pulled out her phone. McVie should know what was going on.

We're still in Ruby Dunes

Piper and I are being questioned

Not sure when we'll be able to head out

I will let you know when I have an update

As she tapped away, she heard voices outside the break room. Two men came into view on the other side of the glass wall separating the break room from the hallway: a tall man perhaps in his late fifties with a sunburned face, and a younger, shorter man with slicked-back light brown hair and bushy eyebrows. The older man had a paunch visible despite his tailored black business suit; the younger man in a dark gray pinstripe suit that didn't fit his shoulders just right. Both men spoke in hushed tones.

Fenway's stomach rumbled. Maybe she should have taken Bardot up on her offer to buy her a snack. She grabbed her purse, got up, and squeezed her way past the tables to the vending machine. The granola bar was only seventy-five cents. The county must subsidize the cost. She opened her purse, took three quarters out, and immediately dropped one on the ground.

She shook her head and knelt. The quarter had rolled to the other side of the vending machine from the door. She crawled over —then the voices got closer. The two men had come into the break room.

She turned and was about to stand up and make herself known.

"I know *I* have nothing to worry about," the older man said.

Fenway froze. Wow—the men didn't see her crouched beside the vending machine. First the victim's wife in the bathroom, now this. Was she invisible to these people? She should listen to Dez far more often.

Fenway blinked; the older man with the sunburned face looked familiar. *Nothing to worry about*: did that refer to Trask's death?

Fenway looked down at herself. Did she look like a member of the janitorial staff? Well—shorts and a T-shirt weren't very professional. The two men in suits might not think Fenway mattered—or maybe Fenway didn't even register on their radar.

"Kim was with me all night," the older man continued. "Craps, slots, blackjack—we're probably on about twenty different camera feeds. We had dinner at what passes for a steakhouse there. What about you?"

The voice made everything click in place for Fenway. He was the other visitor in the museum—his wife had called him *Stan.* Short last name. Was it Shay? No. Schup? Fenway thought that sounded right.

"It doesn't matter if you have an alibi," the shorter man said. "With our policies, they'll be looking at whether we've hired someone to do this."

"I didn't hire anyone, Brock," Stan said. "Did you?"

Ah—Brock, the other investor. Must have a poor reputation if Sheriff Jeffcoat expected him to be the murder victim instead of Trask.

"That's not my point," Brock said. "The point is, if they think we might have done it, they'll look at the museum's finances, won't they? And I don't know about you, but I'm not sure our financial statements will pass muster."

"Vaughn was in charge of the books, not us," Stan said, but a note of panic rang in his voice.

"Our names are all on the partnership agreement," Brock said. "Our fiduciary responsibility—"

"Well," Stan said, straightening to his full height, "seems like we ought to worry about this murder charge before we worry about whether our revenue recognition will pass an audit."

"We should worry about both. If we've violated the Guran-Beissner Act, the fines alone could bankrupt us."

"The museum will need lawyers."

"With what money, Stan? Vaughn poured everything into those stupid NFTs." Brock glared at Stan. "And I don't think I have to tell you about the backlash against NFTs right now."

Stan grunted. "I don't know how I let the two of you talk me into this."

"Because you wanted to triple your investment in six months."

"Hasn't exactly worked out like that, though, has it?"

Brock gave Stan a mirthless grin. "Buy low, sell high, Stan. You just have to ride it out."

"And now you're sounding like Vaughn. He might have been scamming us with the whole idea of a museum out here in the desert. NNoV8 isn't exactly in the middle of the Strip."

"If we can avoid getting arrested," Brock said, "we should have an extra two million each to either make the museum work or cut our losses."

"I can see the speech now," Stan said. "'Without Vaughn Trask's vision and leadership, we feel it would be best—'"

"To sell you a pile of horseshit," Brock said, chuckling. He clapped Stan on the shoulder. "Come on. Let's see if we can get the cops to finish up with us, and then let's get out of here. I've got to call my financial advisor and see when he thinks the policy might clear."

CHAPTER SEVEN

Fenway sat for a moment until Brock and Stan were out of her peripheral vision, then she brought up a browser on her phone and loaded the NNoV8 website. Tapping the *About Us* tab, she scrolled down until she saw *Leadership Team*, then tapped that link.

Soon, the smiling faces and suit-and-tie shoulders of Stanley Schup, Vaughn Trask, and Brock Shellwater—ah, that was Brock's last name—appeared on the screen. Decades of experience, previous positions as CEO and vice president and chairpersons of companies Fenway hadn't heard of. Possibly startups with weird valuations that got bought by other conglomerates for millions. Yep—there it was in Shellwater's bio: *exits obtained with more than 200% return.*

If she'd interpreted their conversation in the sheriff's office break room correctly, both Brock and Stan had taken a policy out on their partner Vaughn. To the tune of two million each. Considering what their track record was, that might have been chump change, but if NNoV8 had been close to bankruptcy, those two-million-dollar payouts might be enough to let the two of them fight another day. Wonder if they could use a life insurance payout in their exit valuations. Even if it *was* chump change, comparatively speaking, two million wasn't nothing—even to rich people.

A minute later, Bardot came back into the break room, lines on her forehead and arms at her sides. "You're free to go, Ms. Stevenson, with the caveat that you don't leave the county."

Fenway blinked. "But—I've got to get this moving truck to Colorado *today*."

Bardot shook her head. "That's not the deal."

Fenway stood and crossed her arms. "Am I under arrest? House arrest? Anything like that?"

"Well, no…"

"Look," Fenway said, "I've been on that side of the table, and it sucks sometimes, but you can't force me to stay in the county. Piper and I have to go. We'll cooperate, but we can easily be on a phone call or a videoconference."

"Oh, Ms. Patten isn't leaving," Bardot said. "We're keeping her here for questioning."

Fenway's jaw snapped open. But she shouldn't have been surprised—Piper's knife was the murder weapon. Depending on the time of death, Piper might not have an alibi. And if anyone saw Piper shouting at Vaughn Trask—well, it ticked off all the boxes for *prime suspect*.

"I understand," Fenway said wearily. "You know Vaughn's wife, Aurora, fought with him the day he died?"

Bardot blinked. "How do you know what Aurora Horn did or didn't do?"

"I also know Vaughn was unfaithful to Aurora. You might want to check out his romantic relationships."

Bardot narrowed her eyes.

"And have you checked out who took out seven-figure life insurance policies on Vaughn Trask?" Fenway asked, taking a step forward. "Piper's missing knife might have been the murder weapon, but she didn't get a seven-figure payday when Vaughn died. If it were me, I'd want to look at who did."

"Coroner Stevenson," Bardot said, "I appreciate that you don't think your friend committed murder, but these accusations—"

"I'm not accusing anyone of anything. I'm just saying a lot more people had more motive—and just as much opportunity—as Piper."

"Enough," Bardot said firmly. "I had hoped you'd go back to the hotel and extend your stay before checkout time. That way, you won't get a penalty tacked onto your stay." She narrowed her eyes. "But, hey, maybe you can drive that moving van to Colorado and back before your friend gets arraigned."

"You're arresting her?"

"Not yet," Bardot said, "but she's asked for her lawyer." She scoffed. "One of the best in Vegas, too. A counselor named O.K. Ubosi."

Fenway's eyes widened. Even she'd heard of Okpara Ubosi, known as "O.K." by the media. He'd successfully defended the famous poker player Erik Zoltan from a murder charge that the media called a slam dunk for the prosecution. He was a talking head on many of the political shows when they did a segment on legal analysis.

Bardot raised her eyebrows. "Your friend must have a rich daddy."

"*Somebody* must have a rich daddy," Fenway muttered under her breath.

———

A different deputy drove Fenway back to the Cartwheel Hotel & Casino. The sun in the cloudless sky baked Fenway in the back seat of the cruiser. The deputy pulled in front of the hotel, got out, and opened the back door, letting in a blast of heat. Sweat dripping down her temple, Fenway scampered out of the car, murmuring her thanks, with her purse over her shoulder.

She pushed through the revolving door and made a beeline for the reception desk. A woman of about fifty, her hair pulled back into a ponytail, stood behind the desk and smiled brightly at Fenway.

"I wonder if I could extend my stay," Fenway said.

"That shouldn't be a problem," the woman replied.

Fenway gave the woman her room number. The nightly charge was less than she'd thought. One additional night for now—the hotel wasn't full, as few tourists were visiting in the heat of summer.

"Sorry," the woman said, groaning. "The computer is taking forever today."

"No worries, I've got time." Fenway looked up and down the reception area. "No Orlando today?"

"He clocked out early this morning." She pulled a small flier out from behind the counter. "He's in an art show at the museum next door. You should go, if you have time. Big opportunity for him."

"Orlando—he's an artist?"

"Yes, ma'am. Pretty good, too. He just started here a few months ago. I think he wanted a steady paycheck to supplement his art. He invited a few of us to an independent showing he had in Henderson last week. I don't pretend to understand it, but it's a lot better than those modern art people who paint red squares in the middle of a canvas and charge a million dollars for it."

Fenway pointed over her shoulder. "At NNoV8?"

"I know, I know," the woman said. "Maybe that museum isn't really for me. But you should see Orlando's stuff. It's good. Thought-provoking." She smacked the counter. "What am I talking about? I've got a few pictures on my phone." She leaned forward conspiratorially. "I wasn't supposed to take pictures when he had his gallery showing, but there's no way I can afford those paintings on my salary." She grabbed her phone, tapped the screen a few times, then thrust it in front of Fenway's face. A woman's face, in olive green and muted lavender. A bit like Picasso's expressionist period, but different use of line. He had something to say, for sure. A duck on a pond, again somewhat abstract, the shimmering surface tension of the water in oranges and blues. Then another woman—face turned away, a bit more realism in this one, especially in the colors. The woman had a gray and orange blanket with squared-off pyramid shapes. This wasn't a nude, but the scene felt sensual, like Fenway was invading an intimate moment.

"I don't know if this is art or smut," the clerk said, "but it takes your breath away, doesn't it?" Then she scrolled again: a man sitting at a table, back to the viewer, staring at a desertscape through the window.

Fenway squinted. "I've seen this one before."

"Oh—was it on display at the museum?" the clerk asked. "Orlando told me it might be there. Said he had to talk to one of the owners."

A ping in Fenway's head. "Wait—'O. Lockberry.' Is that Orlando?"

"Sure is." Another scroll on the clerk's phone: a black cube in the middle of the desert.

"That's the museum," Fenway said.

"Paint what you know, I guess," the clerk said. "Pretty good, aren't they? Maybe this will be his big break."

"Let's hope so," Fenway said, looking down at her nametag. *Theodora.* "I went there yesterday, and I wasn't impressed. But maybe today will be different." Would NNoV8 even be open today, given the death of the founder and one of the three major partners?

Theodora blinked. "Oh—that's disappointing. I thought Orlando had a lot of artwork on display at the exhibit. You didn't see it?"

Fenway shook her head. "I just saw the one piece of artwork— the man at the table. But I think all the other art had been converted to flying NFT birds."

"Flying what?"

Fenway grinned. "Birds. I don't really get it, but I guess I need to read up on NFTs, blockchain, cryptocurrency, all that stuff."

"The casino's more my speed," the woman said with a shy smile. "It's why I work here."

Fenway nodded, then smiled warmly. "So—do you go by Theodora?"

"Teddi."

"Well, Teddi," Fenway said, "you heard that one of the owners of the NNoV8 museum was killed, right?"

"Of course—right in our parking lot." Teddi tutted. "Such a horrible thing."

"What was he doing over here? He like to gamble?"

Teddi turned her face down, and the color rose to her cheeks. "Well, let's just say he had an arrangement."

"An arrangement?"

"He would often call and request a room."

Fenway raised her eyebrows. "I assume this wasn't for him and his wife—well, probably fiancée, back then."

Teddi leaned forward. "Housekeeping found a pair of those fur-lined handcuffs. We had them in the lost-and-found for a few weeks."

"Sounds like you get interesting things in the lost-and-found."

"Mostly boring stuff. That's why the handcuffs were the talk of the staff." Teddi tapped her chin. "We found a gun once—I think it must have been a collector's item. Real pretty, one of those Colver .38 pistols, a stone blue handle and eight-pronged gold stars. That was too dangerous to have in the lost-and-found, though. Someone put it in the hotel safe."

"*That* wasn't in Vaughn Trask's room, was it?"

"Oh, no. At least, I don't think so. I wasn't here." Teddi clicked her tongue. "But it wouldn't surprise me. Mr. Trask wasn't a rule-follower. He'd usually reserve his hotel room under the company name. Paid for it using the NNoV8 corporate card." Her eyes twinkled. "And I don't think those fur handcuffs qualify as an artistic expense."

Oh. That might not be legal. Embezzlement, fraud, financial malfeasance.

"But it might have been above-board most of the time," Fenway said. "He could have been keeping the room for investors, maybe artists who were exhibiting their work."

Teddi chuckled. "Oh, honey, that little thing he had in the room was exhibiting *something*, but it sure wasn't painting." She leaned forward. "Some people might call it art, but you'd know it when you see it."

Fenway nodded. "Right."

"I never got a name—not that I asked." She clicked her tongue. "None of my business. But once, I gave them the room above the dumpsters over in the plaza area." Teddi leaned forward conspiratorially. "Management are cheapskates. Those dumpsters are always overflowing, and it can stink to high heaven. Especially in the summer."

Fenway grinned. "Nice way to silently voice your disapproval."

Teddi shrugged. "A lot of good it did. Trask was down here in a flash, and Orlando upgraded them to a suite on the casino level at no charge." She sniffed. "I hated it back then, but it gave Orlando the opportunity to show Trask his work." She gave a sly grin. "He had to be polite, didn't he? Since he was cheating on his wife. Had to give Orlando a little leeway so he wouldn't say anything to anyone."

"How often would Mr. Trask make this, uh... arrangement?"

"Once or twice a month." She leaned forward again. "I got the feeling she wasn't from Ruby Dunes."

Fenway blinked. "You'd have to get a license plate number, though, wouldn't you? I mean, I had to go back out to the rental truck to get my license plate."

"That's a good point. Well, now, we'll have to go through the computer, so let me see if it's done with its update." Teddi turned toward the monitor. "Yes—we're back. Finally." She put her hands on the keyboard. "All right—now, let's search for

NNoV8." Her head tilted to the side. "Well. Last night. That's interesting."

"Vaughn Trask had a room reserved for last night? No wonder he was here." Fenway tapped her fingers on the counter. "Was there a vehicle associated with the room?"

Teddi tapped the keyboard. "Yes. A Volkswagen Jetta. California plates."

"Hold on." Fenway pulled her phone out. "What's the license plate number?"

Teddi paused. "I don't think I should give that information out. Are you a reporter or something?"

Fenway looked at Teddi wide-eyed for a moment. "Uh—no. I'm actually a coroner."

"A coroner?" Teddi narrowed her eyes.

Fenway dug in her purse and pulled out her badge.

A quick glance at the badge. "Oh—well, shouldn't you be with the dead body?"

Ah. Teddi thought Fenway was the *local* coroner, not some random coroner from a California beach town. The badge didn't loudly proclaim the county or state, and Teddi hadn't studied it. Would Fenway be able to use this to her advantage?

Of course, it didn't make much sense that Fenway was the local coroner while staying in a casino hotel rather than in, presumably, a home within the Correos County limits, but if Teddi was going to give up information that might exonerate Piper, Fenway wasn't going to argue. "Coroners investigate all suspicious deaths in the county," she said. "And that license plate will save me a lot of time getting to the truth." She raised her eyebrows.

"Protocol," Teddi said. "I'm sorry."

Fenway nodded. "You know Sheriff Jeffcoat."

Teddi rolled her eyes.

"Look, I haven't known the sheriff very long, but he likes to be a big fish in a small pond, right?"

Teddi scoffed. "You don't know the half of it."

"Well, look, Teddi, if the sheriff is forced to get a warrant, do you think he'll keep things quiet, make sure no one knows the cops are visiting the casino? Or would he be as loud and disruptive as possible?"

Teddi was quiet.

"Look, I get it. People at craps tables get nervous when they see the police all over the place, don't they? They might decide to go somewhere else—and if they go into Vegas, they might not come back."

Teddi frowned. "Bartholomew's a good guy, but he doesn't seem to understand that gambling pays for his salary."

"And he doesn't exactly listen to reason," Fenway said. "It's not like you can put him in the room over the dumpster."

Teddi laughed, then tore the top page off a notepad next to the keyboard and scribbled seven characters. "There. You take that. If someone from Cartwheel Hotels calls you and asks where you got that information, it wasn't me. And it wasn't anyone in the hotel. Say you wandered around the parking lot looking at license plates or something."

"My lips are sealed."

Teddi took a deep breath. "Now, let's get your room extended for tonight."

———

Fenway stepped outside the casino and tapped the screen of her phone, calling Dez at her desk. It rang five times, then went to voicemail. She called Sarah Summerhill next.

Sarah answered on the second ring. "Hi, Fenway."

"How's it going holding down the fort?"

"The coroner's office is pretty dead today. No pun intended."

"Ha ha."

"Is everything okay?" A note of genuine concern in Sarah's voice.

Fenway's assistant was perceptive, as usual. "Not really," Fenway said. "I'm still stuck in Ruby Dunes with Craig's truck."

"He needs to have everything unpacked this weekend, doesn't he?"

"Kind of tough when one of the drivers is being held for questioning in the murder of Vaughn Trask."

"I figured that's who the victim was," Sarah said.

"You—what? Did you know Vaughn Trask?"

"It made the news—at least of the tech blogs I follow," Sarah said. "Besides, McVie called the coroner's office this morning. Based on the information you'd given him, I had enough to put two and two together."

"I've got some more information now." Fenway told Sarah about the life insurance policies taken out by Trask's business partners, as well as the hotel room reserved by the museum's credit card. She read the make, model, and license plate number of the car in the lot reserved by the room.

"You're thinking this is somebody that Trask is cheating on his fiancée with?"

"Wife, now," Fenway said. "And yes. Aurora Horn. She and Vaughn were married recently. I don't know if you can find anything out about what she might know—but she was on the phone with her mother earlier, and I know she caught him cheating a while ago. Maybe a year or two. And if he did it then, it's more than likely he's still cheating."

"Don't I know it."

Fenway coughed lightly. "So, I'm not asking you to do anything illegal. But you can find stuff out."

"I'm sure I don't know what you're talking about," Sarah said breezily.

"And Dez isn't in the office?"

"She's following up on a lead."

"A lead? We have open cases?"

"Hmmm," Sarah said.

"Oh. After George Pope entered the not-guilty plea."

"That's correct. And Dez is the only detective in the office right now."

"Maybe Sheriff Donnelly can help us out. She could maybe get someone from vice."

"Callahan starts next Monday."

"I know. I'll be back in plenty of time."

The sound of Sarah's keyboard clicking. "Donnelly's lost two of her top deputies in the last couple of weeks. She's just as short-handed as we are."

"I'll have to do something soon. McVie might be able to wait another day, but if I stay to make sure Piper's okay, it'll mean he has to unload the whole truck by himself."

"Oh, poor baby," Sarah said. "At least he's not currently being interrogated for a murder he didn't commit."

Fenway hesitated. "Have you met Piper?"

"I've heard nothing but good things, but I've only met her in passing." The sound of more typing. "I imagine I should be jealous of her computer skills."

"Yours are pretty formidable, too."

"I do what I can." She clicked her tongue. "Nadine Ryeo."

"What?"

"R-Y-E-O. First name Nadine. The license plate you gave me. The car's registered to a Nadine Ryeo of Palmdale."

"Palmdale, California? Out in the high desert?"

"California plates, California address."

"Wow, that was fast. It's a Volkswagen Jetta?"

"Red, according to the registration. Not sure if the Palmdale address is current."

Fenway paced in a circle. "She's probably still here in Ruby Dunes at the Cartwheel. Unless she's the one who killed Vaughn Trask, and if she is, she probably took off last night. She could be anywhere by now." She looked out across the parking lot—and the sun glinted off a red sedan about a hundred yards away.

"Hang on, I think I see it."

"The Jetta?"

"Yes." She hurried across the lot.

"You know you don't have jurisdiction."

"I don't need jurisdiction to look at a red Volkswagen Jetta in the hotel parking lot."

"No—but what are you going to do if you find this Nadine person? You can't exactly interrogate her."

"I can ask her some questions in an unofficial capacity. Or I can let the sheriff's office know they should talk to her."

A brief sigh, barely noticeable. "You should think this through, Fenway. If Vaughn Trask has Piper's knife sticking out of his chest, don't you think someone *wants* the police to think it's Piper?"

"That's why I have to—"

"I mean it'll be dangerous to ask questions," Sarah said. "The murderer has already killed once. You don't think they'll kill again if they think you're onto something?"

"But—"

"You no longer have the full force of the Dominguez County sheriff's department behind you," Sarah said.

Fenway didn't respond, but stopped at the red Jetta and looked down at the license plate.

"California plates, all right," Fenway said. "And the number matches. Looks like Nadine is here."

"So that means she didn't kill him, by your logic. You said she'd be long gone."

"Unless she thought she could get away with it," Fenway replied. "Can you dig into Vaughn Trask's financials? I have a feeling he was doing some shady stuff with investors' money. Maybe Nadine isn't a mistress, but rather an investor."

"An investor? Driving an eight-year-old Jetta?"

"Who knows?" Fenway asked. "Maybe she's an artist he screwed over. Or maybe he didn't tell her he had a fiancée—wife, now."

Sarah chuckled. "At least there's no lack of motive with this guy. Everyone who met him seems to have a motive to kill him."

"Yeah, it's an embarrassment of riches."

"Let me get on this financial research. I want to get Piper Patten out from under the thumb of the Ruby Dunes sheriff as soon as possible."

"Right. Thanks, Sarah." Fenway ended the call, staring at the license plate number. Sarah was right—what *would* Fenway say to Nadine Ryeo? Her badge might do for a quick flash, but if she wanted Nadine Ryeo to answer some questions? That might require getting Nadine to study the badge, and that would cause a "you don't have jurisdiction here" conversation.

Her phone rang. Sarah hadn't uncovered financial information already, had she? Fenway looked at her phone screen. McVie. She tapped *Answer*.

"Hey, you."

"Hey—sorry I had to cut the call short with you this morning. I'm on my break now. They're real sticklers here for the schedule."

"Not like the flexibility you have when you're running your own business."

"No. I didn't think I'd miss the demanding clients, but going back to punching a time clock is taking some getting used to."

"So we're still in Ruby Dunes. Piper is at the sheriff's office. She's giving her statement, but she's asked for her lawyer."

"Her lawyer? Who's that—Migs? He just passed the bar in California—he's not licensed to practice in Nevada."

"Not Migs. O.K. Ubosi."

McVie let out a long, low whistle. "Ubosi, huh? I take it your dad is paying for that?"

"Piper can't afford a lawyer that expensive on the pittance you pay her, that's for sure."

"Hey, now, I've given her two raises over the last six months. She's worth every penny and then some."

"I know, I know, just giving you shit." Fenway sighed. "I don't know what to do, Craig. I don't want to leave Piper, but you've got all your stuff here in this moving truck, and it's just sitting in the parking lot."

McVie was quiet. "This is my fault."

"Why is it your fault?"

"Because I gave in to Payback Systems when they asked me to start earlier. If I'd stuck to my guns, *I* would have been the one driving the moving truck. And you and Piper wouldn't be stuck in a little town in Nevada giving statements about a murder."

Fenway sighed. "I told you, I was happy to drive. I wanted to make your life a little easier."

"Yeah. I really appreciate it. I just feel terrible that you and Piper are stuck there."

"If everything goes smoothly, we'll be on the road this afternoon."

"Okay. I'll call U-Move-It and extend the truck another day. That way, you don't have to worry about getting all the way to my apartment tonight." He paused. "I can look at hotels for tonight—"

"I don't know when we're going to leave, Craig. We might have to stay the night here. But it's okay, really. You had no way of knowing a dead body would be next to the truck this morning."

A loud exhale. "Okay—let me see if I can get a flight tonight from Denver to Vegas. Maybe I can take a seven or eight o'clock flight. I can drive up to Ruby Falls and see if I can use my former-sheriff status to smooth things over."

"Ruby *Dunes*."

"Right, Ruby Dunes." He chuckled. "Definitely wouldn't help smooth things over if I get the name of their town wrong."

"No."

"And if it helps get Piper out, then maybe I'll drive the truck home tomorrow, and the two of you can fly back to Estancia. I know this has screwed up your plans, too."

Fenway felt a pang of guilt. "I'm sorry, Craig."

"This isn't your fault, Fenway. Unless *you're* the one who stabbed the guy because you didn't like the way he was talking to Piper."

"Aw, Craig, you know I prefer strangulation. So much less messy."

McVie chuckled.

Fenway looked up and down the parking lot. No one was around. The morning was hot and dry, with the heat shimmering off the asphalt. It would get hotter today—much hotter.

"Also," she said carefully, "I was kind of hoping to talk with you. You know, you had to leave right away after, you know, after—"

"After I proposed, and you said no."

"It wasn't a *no*," Fenway protested. "It was a *not yet*. And I want to—I want to explain myself a little more. Give you an idea of where my head is at."

"It's not that complicated, Fenway. It was a little crazy, anyway. I mean, look, you and I have only been dating for what, six or seven months, officially? It was too quick." Fenway could feel his embarrassment coming through the phone. Fenway couldn't blame him; she supposed her "no" had felt like rejection.

"I only said 'no' because you'd never have asked me to marry you if you were staying in Estancia."

McVie paused. "I don't know about that."

"Sure, maybe down the road. But, come on, the ink on your divorce papers is barely dry."

"That didn't stop Amy from getting married," McVie said.

"We're not talking about—" Then Fenway paused and closed her eyes. No, they weren't talking about his ex-wife, but that was exactly who had taken McVie's daughter out of the state. Amy's new husband was dead—and for the first time the thought struck Fenway that moving to Colorado, dragging Megan with her, knowing that McVie would follow Meghan because—well, because he was a supportive father...

Was this all part of Amy's plan to get McVie back together with her?

Fenway's mouth went as dry as the asphalt beneath her feet.

"No, you're right," McVie said. "Amy's terrible relationships are no barometer for ours."

"And you *know* I've got issues," Fenway said.

"No more than anyone," McVie said.

"It wasn't the right time. You could be the right person—and I've *never* thought that about anyone else. But I know it wasn't the right time."

"I mean," McVie said, "when you know, you know."

Fenway was quiet.

"Although," McVie continued, a little more gently, "I suppose that sometimes when you know, you freak the hell out instead."

"But in a good way," Fenway said.

CHAPTER EIGHT

McVie had to get back to work, so Fenway ended the call with him. She tapped the phone on her hip, then turned. Not knowing what else to do, she went back into the hotel.

She hadn't planned to be gone from Estancia for more than a few days, and spending all that time on the road—and planning to have a long, serious conversation with McVie about their relationship, Fenway hadn't even bothered to bring her laptop.

But Piper had, and it was back in their room.

Fenway could never get into Piper's laptop, but if she could get back to the sheriff's office, she could get to Piper, find out her password, and get into her computer.

And then what? Do her own research? Besides typing faster, what could she possibly get from Piper's laptop that she couldn't get from her phone?

Fenway walked around the front of the casino and went up the concrete staircase to her hotel room door. In a few years, Cartwheel would probably make improvements to this property so that everyone would have to walk through the casino to get to the rooms. But until Cartwheel made those upgrades, Fenway had to endure the heat of the Nevada desert instead of the cigarette-smoke-filled casino.

Fenway unlocked her hotel room and went inside. House-keeping hadn't been in yet to make the beds, and she still had to pack her small suitcase. She had two more days' worth of clothes. She sat down on the unmade bed and stared at the floor.

In all her previous murder investigations, she'd had a plan—except for the time she was stuck in Los Angeles. That was another situation where she was without a computer or the resources of the Dominguez County coroner's office.

And this was different. She was not only in another city, but in another state. And she wasn't trying to save herself, she was trying to save her friend.

She rested her chin in her palm. She had to get evidence that someone besides Piper had committed the murder.

Fenway pulled her phone out and connected to the hotel wi-fi.

Now—where to start?

She typed in *Nadine Ryeo*.

Huh. Quite a few options. Some in Delaware, some in Nova Scotia. Ah—a LinkProfs photo. She clicked on the picture and Ryeo's profile came up: Las Vegas, Nevada. Must be a recent trans-plant if her car still had California plates. Her occupation: "Dealer, Casino Table Games" at the Monaco Resort Casino on the Strip. Fancy.

She pressed her lips together. The Cartwheel was an hour northeast of Las Vegas—not really far enough to spend the night if she lived in the greater Vegas area. She searched for Ryeo on Photoxio and found a profile with forty or fifty pictures of a young black-haired woman with a perpetually bored look on her face.

And a comment from *ryeosookie78:* "glad 2 see ur having fun hope u can come home this wkend"—ah. Maybe a parent, if the "78" in the username was a clue as to the birth year. Did that mean the first name was "Sookie"? Fenway tilted her head: she'd heard the name before in TV shows, but never met someone with that name. Of course, Fenway wasn't one to judge. She tapped *ryeosookie78*, but most of the photos were of nature: flowers, a desert landscape, a close-up of a cactus, another flower, a Joshua Tree—then one picture of Nadine, a forced smile on her face, with an older Asian woman, grinning ear-to-ear; both women wore Santa hats. A comment: *Good to see you, Sookie! Such a great picture with your daughter! Glad she came home for Christmas!* Okay, so that meant that Sookie was Nadine's mom—and perhaps Sookie lived in Palmdale.

Fenway texted Sarah.

> Nadine's mom is Sookie Ryeo. Probably lives in Palmdale. Can you get me a phone number?

A moment later, a thumbs-up appeared on her text.

Fenway kept scrolling. More nature pictures; maybe Sookie was a professional photographer. Or maybe she just enjoyed going on hikes. The photos were good. One of Half Dome in Yosemite. A selfie of Sookie on a rocky trail. A couple of days before: two steaming bowls of noodle soup.

Her stomach rumbled.

Really? Fenway shook her head and admonished her stomach. She'd eaten a good-sized breakfast since she thought they might not be stopping until one or two o'clock. And now, here it was, not even eleven thirty, and her stomach was imitating a freight train.

She stood, glancing around the room—for what, she wasn't sure—and then grabbed her purse and headed to the door. Fenway wasn't sure how she was going to help Piper. She had to come up with a plan. But she needed to concentrate, and that meant some food. She'd gotten so distracted by the two NNoV8 owners that she'd forgotten to get food from the police station's vending machine.

No. She had more work to do.

A knock at the door. "Housekeeping," a woman's thin voice with a thick Eastern European accent called from the other side.

Well, that settled that. Fenway opened the door to see a woman with a cart full of towels and cleaning supplies. Her nametag read *Nadezhda.*

"I come back later."

Fenway shook her head, holding the door wide open. "I was just about to leave."

"Okay, thank you," the woman said, reaching out a hand to hold the door open. Fenway walked out of her hotel room, a little frustrated at herself. She'd only spent fifteen minutes trying to get information on the other suspects—people she considered other suspects, anyway.

She walked down the concrete stairway and surveyed her surroundings. The diner attached to the hotel, where Piper and Fenway had eaten breakfast, was still open. The Mexican place past the NNoV8 museum was probably open for lunch. A visit to the museum was on the list too, but it might not be open because of Trask's death—and she needed food in her stomach.

Even in the fifteen minutes that Fenway had been in her room, the air had gotten thicker with heat, though the dry desert meant low humidity. No frizzing of Fenway's hair. But a walk in this heat to the Mexican restaurant would be unpleasant. And probably sweaty.

She walked to the edge of the casino and stood in the shade of the building for a moment. There, across the side street from the museum, a small brick building with an orange hexagonal roof that betrayed its previous life as a Captain Pizza: Albie K's Bar & Grill.

Something pinged in Fenway's memory banks. Her father, when not following the Red Sox, had an affinity for watching Texas Hold 'Em poker on TV. Was there a poker player named Albie that used to be a featured player? Kitsopoulos, or something like that. Fenway didn't think Albie Kitsopoulos was famous for good food, but his namesake restaurant looked better than the diner and closer than the Mexican place.

She walked slowly, the sun pounding on her shoulders, and a

bead of sweat starting at her temple and racing down the side of her face. Not a pleasant feeling, so even though she'd have preferred tacos to a famous poker player's burgers-and-fries, she kept her eyes focused on Albie K's.

Only two cars in the parking lot. Were they even open? But as she got closer, the red-and-white *Open* sign was visible in the front window.

As Fenway opened the door to Albie K's, a blast of air conditioning smacked her in the face, blowing her hair back slightly. The tables and booths were empty, and only a single person sat at the bar, a tall schooner glass of light-colored beer in front of him. The bartender was cutting limes at the side of the bar.

She needed to do some more research on her phone while she ate, but sitting at the bar seemed like the best idea. Bartenders were usually attentive servers, and she could get in and out quickly. But hopefully still give housekeeping enough time to finish up.

"Oh—hi there."

Fenway's head snapped up. The man sitting at the bar had turned his head and was grinning at her. Oh, it was Orlando Lockberry, the desk clerk from the night before. He was dressed in khakis and a blue short-sleeve button-down shirt; he'd changed from his rumpled blue shirt with the Cartwheel logo.

"Hi," Fenway said. "Orlando, right?"

"That's right. For a minute, I thought—" He scrunched up his face, then took a sip of his beer. His hand shook slightly. "Never mind."

Fenway tilted her head.

Orlando sighed. "I had a date. Or—I thought I had a date." Ah, that would explain his hand shaking; he might be a little nervous.

"In the middle of the day?"

He paused and drummed his fingers on the table. "Lunch is a perfect first date. A set amount of time since most people work day jobs. Public place, daytime, so the girls aren't as on guard. Plus, no one gets angry if you leave after half an hour."

"Are you on a first date?"

"Well—no. But it's something to keep in mind."

Fenway nodded. He seemed like a pleasant guy—and was definitely attractive enough that he could get the opposite sex to pay attention to him. Didn't seem like he'd need to resort to internet dating or blind dates. But Fenway reminded herself that everyone did that—she was either a throwback to a different era or an anomaly for someone who wasn't even thirty yet.

She pulled up a stool three seats away from Orlando. "If your date shows up, I'll get out of your hair."

The bartender walked over. "Get you something to drink?"

"A margarita." Her stomach gurgled. "Oh—on second thought, maybe not. I overdid it a little last night. You have sparkling water?"

"Club soda. Or a bottle of the fancy French stuff."

"The fancy French stuff sounds good. And a menu."

Orlando sighed. "I might as well get some lunch so it's not a complete waste of a day."

"You want a menu too?" asked the bartender.

Orlando nodded, and the bartender reached under the bar and handed two menus to Orlando and Fenway.

Fenway perused her menu. "You're not at the Cartwheel today?"

"I had the overnight shift. Ended this morning."

She nodded. He must have been in the parking lot this morning at the end of his shift. "I was talking to the desk clerk—uh, Theodora, I think."

"Oh, yeah, Teddi. She's cool."

"She said you're quite the artist. Likes your stuff."

Orlando sat up straight on his stool, then nodded. "Nice to know she meant it and wasn't just blowing smoke up my ass at the exhibit last week."

"I think I saw your work on display at NNoV8."

Orlando's jaw clenched. "Ah, well, I suppose you did."

"Part of that NFT exhibit."

Orlando shrugged. "One of a thousand artists in there."

Fenway wanted to bite her tongue—all the questions she had were too invasive. But she couldn't help herself, and besides, her loyalty lay with Piper. "You know, I went to the museum yesterday, and I can't imagine most of the artists were happy with the way the exhibit turned out."

Orlando took his hands off the table and clapped them on his knees. "Yeah, I had—" Then he stopped, staring at his beer, then picked it up and took a long drink. He set it back down carefully. "It's a good learning experience for me. Especially in this new paradigm where art is getting devalued. I mean, there are more places to get my name out there, but there's less and less money to be made."

"At least you've got an actual piece on display."

"Not the five pieces the museum promised." Orlando shook his head. "But NNoV8 didn't screw me over as bad as all the other artists in the show."

"How many of the NNoV8 artists live in the same town as the museum? I can't think it's easy for any of the artists to come see that NNoV8 buried their art as an NFT inside a, uh—what do they call it? An immersive experience?"

Orlando stared at the menu, not responding. Finally, he said, "My mom would tell me to look at it as a net positive. Sure, maybe no one will see more than that one piece of mine, but I got a little money out of it, and it's something to put on my résumé. Could be worse."

"That's right. You could be Vaughn Trask, dead in a parking lot."

The bartender set a green glass bottle in front of Fenway and twisted off the top with a flourish. "You know what you want?"

"The BLT," Fenway said. "And what's your soup today?"

"Clam chowder." Oh right, it was Friday.

"Yeah, I'll take a cup of the chowder as my side."

The bartender turned to Orlando. "And you?"

Orlando ran a hand over his face. "The Albie K Burger," he said after a moment.

"Good choice." The bartender took back both menus and disappeared into the back.

Fenway glanced over at Orlando, whose mouth turned down at the corners. She grabbed the glass bottle; it was cold, but not as cold as she was hoping for. She took a long drink, then set the bottle down. "I guess I should be mad at you," she said, "for telling the sheriff that was my friend's knife."

Orlando nodded. "Yeah. I realized as it was coming out of my mouth that it wasn't a cool thing to say."

"Don't worry about it." Fenway scooted back on her stool. "I probably would have done the same thing."

Orlando glanced over at Fenway. "Why?"

"Comes with the job, I guess."

"You a cop or something?"

"Or something. A coroner. Back in California."

Orlando looked straight ahead and gave a slow nod to the bottles of liquor against the back wall of the bar. "What about your friend?"

"Used to be my go-to person for all my computer forensic needs."

Orlando narrowed his eyes. "The tall redhead? Looks like she could, uh—"

"Yes," Fenway said, before he could say anything she didn't want to hear. "She's brilliant. If she weren't working for the good guys, I have no doubt she'd be able to siphon money out of a hedge fund somewhere and be living on the beach in the South Pacific sipping cocktails."

Orlando nodded solemnly and took another sip of his beer. He stared vacantly at the back wall, then put his hands flat on the bar. "So your friend was the one who owned the knife?"

"Right."

"And she's at the sheriff's office right now?"

"The cops are probably asking her why her knife is sticking out of the victim's chest, yeah."

"And you're a coroner from California." He tapped the bar with the tips of his fingers. "I didn't think coroners acted like detectives."

"I'm in charge of investigating all suspicious deaths in the county. I've got two detectives who report to me."

He nodded. "So you'll help with the investigation?"

"I'm out of my jurisdiction," Fenway said, "but I won't let my friend get charged with a murder she didn't commit."

Orlando was quiet for a moment, then said, "I guess I better come clean, then."

Fenway turned toward Orlando. "Come clean?"

"I'm not here on a blind date."

Fenway arched her eyebrow. "And... why would you lie to me?"

"I'm here meeting a job recruiter. I figured since you're a guest of the hotel, you could say something and get me in trouble."

Fenway smiled. "Desk clerk not your dream job?"

"I thought I'd be meeting a recruiter for the Vegas galleries." He cleared his throat. "Sure, it's still a retail position, but given my background, I thought I'd give it a shot."

"So why did you feel the need to come clean to me?"

"Well—if your friend gets out on bail, and if she's as good at computers and hacking and stuff as you say, then all she'd have to do is look at my online dating profiles to find out I didn't have a date today. And that would make me look suspicious, right? Lying?"

Fenway chuckled. "You're overthinking it, Orlando. But I appreciate the honesty." She glanced over at his beer; only a quarter of the liquid remained. "So instead of being stood up by a woman, you got stood up by a recruiter."

"Right. I mean, he texted me a couple of minutes before you came in and said he didn't realize how far away this was from Vegas, and asked if we could we reschedule."

Fenway nodded. "Did he think Ruby Dunes was an off-strip casino or something?"

"Cartwheel is, technically, off-strip."

Fenway chuckled.

"So after he cancelled, I ordered a beer, since I'm not interviewing today."

The bartender came out of the back with their food, setting each plate in front of them. "Can I get you anything else? Ketchup? Hot sauce?"

"A job that doesn't suck," Orlando mumbled.

"Another beer?" Fenway said, and Orlando looked up. "If you want."

"Sure. Uh—thanks."

"And put it on my tab," Fenway said.

"Same?" the bartender asked Orlando, who nodded, popping a french fry into his mouth.

The bartender stepped away toward the beer taps.

Fenway turned forward and examined her BLT. Looked decent enough. The sourdough was toasted perfectly—it looked crisp, but not like it would tear up the roof of her mouth. The lettuce and tomato looked fresh and vibrant, not wilted and old like she might have gotten on an All Access Burger. She picked a half up and took a bite. Mmm—not bad at all. The tomato wasn't ripe, but the sandwich was better than she expected.

"So," Orlando said through a mouthful of Albie K Burger. He swallowed with difficulty. "Besides telling you the truth about why I'm in this bar and grill, what can I do to help you out?"

"Help me out?"

"I mean, I have access to records at the hotel. Guest check-in and check-out times, credit cards, who paid for what. I've only been there a few months, but I already know some of the regulars—and that their credit cards don't match the name on the reservation."

"I didn't think hotels were supposed to do that."

"First thing Teddi taught me were the workarounds," Orlando said.

"I don't want you to get fired."

Orlando shrugged. "Not like I don't have one foot out of the door."

Fenway took another bite of the BLT and chewed thoughtfully. True, she wouldn't be able to use the hotel records she found through Orlando to *prosecute* anyone. But to establish reasonable doubt, or show the sheriff that pursuing Piper was the wrong way to go? It could free her. Now the only question was: how quickly could Orlando get the information?

"You have any thoughts of, uh, hotel records I might want to see?" Fenway asked, picking up a fry. She bit into it; it was delicious. Crispy on the outside, well-seasoned, still with the softness of the potato on the inside. This might even be better than the Mexican place down the road.

Orlando paused for a moment. "You know prostitution isn't legal in Clark County, but it is in Correos County. When a rich client gets a suite for the weekend, we don't ask a lot of questions." He took another bite of his burger.

"You think that's why Vaughn Trask was murdered? He cheat a prostitute out of money?"

Orlando chewed, then swallowed. "I know the museum did some sketchy things. I mean, I wasn't too happy with the situation. A lot of other artists were more pissed off than I was, especially since no one else got their artwork visibly displayed."

"But—sketchy things? Having a contractual dispute with an artist is a far cry from paying for prostitutes on the company credit card."

"Yeah," Orlando said, "you're right. But maybe it wasn't Trask. Maybe it was one of those other two."

"Right." Fenway searched for their names in her head. "Stanley Schup and Brock Watershell."

"Shellwater," Orlando corrected. "They're just as bad as Trask.

Well, maybe not, because Trask is the one who actually cheated the artists, but the other two just sat back and let it all happen."

"So what do you think their involvement is?" Fenway wouldn't tell Orlando that they had each taken out a large life insurance policy on Trask, but anything that could establish an alternate view of the case was a good thing.

"Where do you think those two multi-millionaires stay when they're visiting their precious museum?" Orlando said. "They're not driving all the way to Vegas. And the outside rooms—the ones you and your friend are in—those might not be upper-crust, but we've got casino-side rooms that are pretty nice."

"Schup is here—"

"*Doctor* Schup." Orlando grinned. "Used to be a thoracic surgeon before he got into the private equity game."

"Sorry. Dr. Schup is here with his wife, right?"

"Right. But she doesn't know about his penchant for—uh, *desert contemplation.*"

"What?"

"He brings his wife here. Far enough from Vegas where she gets bored and wants to go home. He says he stays for museum business, but then he calls this local guy, goes out into the desert, and two days later he comes back with his eyes glazed for a few days and a bad sunburn. Sleeps it off for a week and then goes back home. Like his own personal Burning Man Festival."

"You said he goes with a local guy?"

"I only know him as Entropy. I expect that's not his real name."

"And Stan's wife has no idea?"

Orlando shrugged. "I don't know. He and Kim have been married twenty years. Maybe she figures an acid trip and a sunburn every six months is the price of admission. Better than an affair, I guess." He picked up the burger again. "And I don't judge." He took another bite.

"But it's not public knowledge," Fenway said, "and if Trask threatened to expose his drug use..."

"And Shellwater's no saint, either," Orlando said. "He had a hooker in his room last night, I'm sure of it." A smile turned up the corner of his mouth. "Or maybe he was role playing with his much younger mistress. Either way, I can't imagine he'd want it coming out either."

"So you think Trask blackmailed him? Or both of them?"

Orlando shrugged. "Honestly, I've never thought about it before."

Fenway nodded. "That's certainly given me a lot to research."

"Yeah," Orlando said. "If anyone can find out who was black-mailing who, I bet it's your friend." He drained the rest of his beer.

"If you know about Trask's little dalliances—" Fenway began.

Orlando grunted. "I never said anything specific. Said I thought it was really shitty that he told all the artists he'd display their work, and then everything is just an icon representing the NFT." He arched his back, still sitting on the stool. "I might have said that when he was making a reservation for his little getaway. Because the next week, I found out that the museum had installed one of my physical art pieces in front of the second exhibit."

"But you didn't blackmail him."

Orlando shook his head. "I didn't say anything about anything. Not about how I was keeping quiet about his hotel guests."

"But you implied it."

Orlando looked at Fenway and studied her face for a moment, then broke into a wide smile. The dimples in his cheeks grew. Yeah, he was a handsome guy. Fenway would bet he got away with a *lot*. "I hated studying English," he said. "But one thing always stayed with me. Ms. Kerrigan, my junior year of high school, taught me the difference between *infer* and *imply*. Trask might have *inferred* that I would open my mouth if I didn't feel like the museum treated me fairly. But that absolutely doesn't mean that I *implied* it."

Fenway chuckled. "Touché."

Orlando turned back to his burger. "Sorry, I got a D in French." He took another bite with a twinkle in his eye.

Despite Orlando's insistence that he hadn't blackmailed Trask, Sarah could research if there were signs of blackmail. She had plenty of connections and plenty of know-how—maybe not as much as Piper, and maybe not the resources that Patrick Appleby in IT had, but all Fenway needed was an alternate theory to get Piper out of this mess.

The bartender came back and set a full beer down in front of Orlando.

Fenway shifted on the stool. "I heard a bunch of kids smashed up the cameras at the Cartwheel last week."

Orlando took another bite of his burger, chewing without looking at Fenway. He swallowed, then nodded. "They don't tell me a lot of stuff about hotel security, but yeah. Cartwheel was supposed to get additional security patrols, but they don't start until next week. I hope the company replaces the cameras soon, but knowing them, they'll wait until the last possible minute."

"You'd think there'd be a little more urgency. Someone could get murdered in the parking lot."

Orlando snorted. "Sorry—I shouldn't laugh at that. But yeah. We've been telling management about the liability issues."

"We? I thought you didn't know about it."

Orlando paused. "Well—I'm not *supposed* to know about it."

Fenway furrowed her brow. "What about employee safety? People walking to their cars at night?"

Orlando laughed. "You think Cartwheel cares about their employees? The regulations say they have sixty days to fix the cameras or add security personnel. And I'll be shocked if they don't wait until day fifty-nine."

"Now that someone got murdered in their parking lot and it's getting press—"

"Yeah, maybe." Orlando gave Fenway a sardonic grin. "If the murder affects the CEO's bonus, *then* he'll move the dates up."

"'No one wants to work anymore,'" Fenway quoted. "'If you can't tolerate getting murdered in the parking lot, what kind of loyal employee are you?"

"Sure thing, Ayn Rand," Orlando said. "Now you know why I'm looking for a new job."

They ate in silence for a few minutes.

"How'd you end up here?" Fenway said. "Was it the museum?"

"I grew up here. My dad worked at the Air Force base twenty miles down I-15. My mom worked at the truck stop at the U.S. 93 interchange."

"You grew up here? Never left?"

He smiled sadly. "A couple of years at North Vegas Community College. But it really wasn't for me. The art classes were okay, but it wasn't exactly Parsons. Plus, my dad wouldn't pay for me to go to art school. He wanted me to become a doctor."

"It sucks when parents want to live vicariously through their kids."

Orlando smirked. "Took an upper-division anatomy class. Dad wanted to pay for that. Then he was pissed off that I only took it to get better at painting the human body."

Fenway remembered a conversation with Piper when they were in the museum the day before. "Didn't Michelangelo do that too? Except instead of anatomy classes, it was with corpses he dug up?"

He laughed. "That story is the stuff of legend. Probably apocryphal. But hey, I learned a lot. Got an A."

Fenway nodded. "You still live here?"

"Not with my folks. They moved to Florida. And if I get that job in Vegas, I hope I can get a cheap place near the Strip."

"You wouldn't be near NNoV8 anymore," Fenway said.

He shrugged.

"Can you get out of your artist contract with them?"

Orlando frowned. "Uh—I don't think so. It's with the museum, not with Trask."

"You read it, though, right?"

Orlando hesitated, then nodded. "Of course I did. It's not like agreeing to the terms of service for a phone app. It's my art."

Fenway took the last bite of her BLT. She didn't believe him; he wouldn't have ever agreed to the terms that NNoV8 put forth had he read them. Unless NNoV8 had worded it in a way that meant they were technically following the letter of the contract, but the execution of the contract wasn't what the artists expected.

Fenway wiped her mouth with her napkin. The phrase "prominent display," for example: the contract between the artist and NNoV8 might state that the electronic art would be "prominently displayed" to all visitors. But if the museum turned each electronic artwork into an NFT, then presenting that NFT rather than the artwork itself, like in that lightbulb display or in the sweeping bird-like movie, might technically meet the contractual requirement and yet be completely useless for all the artists. It would be especially maddening if the artist took a significantly lower fee from the museum in exchange for the "prominent display."

A thought struck Fenway.

Her mother had been an artist; a couple of her canvases were on Fenway's walls back in Estancia. Joanne Stevenson and Nathaniel Ferris had met because of her gallery showing. Fenway hadn't paid a ton of attention to the ins and outs of her mother's art "side hustle," but she knew that her mother would always shun galleries that asked for money to represent her, to rent wall space in their facilities, or for participation in art fairs. She didn't even like paying membership fees to the Dominguez Art Collective—Fenway still remembered overhearing the phone conversations when the Collective's sales team accosted her mother with fundraising requests after they'd moved to Seattle; the calls had gone on for years. Joanne Stevenson always abided by the rule that money needed to flow from the gallery or the museum to the artist—not the other way around. Fenway tapped her temple; what term had her mother used for those companies? It would come to her.

Fenway pushed the empty plate toward the back of the bar

counter. "Did you and the other artists pay for, uh, renting virtual wall space?"

Orlando set his half-eaten burger down and put his napkin over it. "I got duped once, a few years ago, by this fly-by-night gallery in Sedona who wanted three thousand dollars to exhibit my work there. They wound up not promoting the show—they weren't making money off sales of the art, they were making money off the artists who were desperate to get their work shown. I wound up selling a few of my paintings anyway—my parents had some friends who had vacation homes in Sedona. But most of the artists I met through that gallery weren't so lucky. Not so funny when people can't make rent because a gallery lied like that."

"But?"

Orlando pushed his stool back from the bar by a few inches, then leaned forward, grabbed his beer, and finished a third of it in one pull. He set it down. "Fool me twice, shame on me, right? It wasn't three thousand dollars—it was only five hundred. I mean, when I had a show for my canvases, I'd pay about four hundred—sometimes more—to frame and ship my paintings to each gallery. So I didn't really have a problem with a couple hundred bucks. I figured, since it was electronic-based art, they'd have to run everything from servers in-house, or they'd have cloud computing costs, or they'd have additional electricity costs."

"And you felt ripped off."

"Like I said," Orlando said evenly, "I'm lucky. I was preparing to eat those costs. Some of my friends, not so lucky."

"I'd be pissed off if I were those other artists. All the blood, sweat, and tears you poured into your art, and all they get is the representation of the NFT flying around a screen."

"At least I got one of my paintings as part of the exhibit," Orlando said.

"Because of what Vaughn Trask inferred?"

Orlando's eyes danced. "Yeah, you get it. I knew you were a cool chick."

Ugh. Fenway tried not to physically recoil at the term. Instead, she pulled her phone out, launched her browser, and brought up the NNoV8 website. She searched for a moment, but there weren't any numbers of how many NFTs were being used in the artwork. Fenway closed her eyes and tried to see the bird-like NFTs swirling on the gigantic screen in her mind. There had to be hundreds, maybe even thousands, of NFTs represented in that one piece of art. Or maybe "art" should be in finger-quotes.

And that didn't include the light-bulb installation, or the piece with the floodlights in the ceiling, or any of the other pieces.

She went to a web search screen.

```
NNOV8 number of NFTs artists
```

And there it was: the second listing on the second page of results. From a private equity firm's website from two years before:

> The firm has chosen a site in the Las Vegas area, and 6,243 artists have currently signed up to have their art presented using the latest blockchain-based technology, although the museum has extended invitations to thousands more. The firm will realize an immediate 140% return on investment when the museum opens.

Ha. "The Las Vegas area." That was stretching the truth. And as far as the financial discussion in the press release, the museum had been almost empty on a Thursday afternoon. She remembered wondering how it could stay in business, and after overhearing the conversation between Schup and Shellwater, she figured they were looking for a way out of museum bankruptcy.

But if what Orlando said was true, NNoV8 staying in business wasn't an issue. The artists themselves—over six thousand of them, paying five hundred dollars each—dumped over three million dollars into the museum before it even opened its doors, and were owed nothing in return.

And this big black box off Interstate 15 in the Nevada desert wouldn't cost more than a few hundred thousand to prep like this. Even the real estate here—they could buy it outright and still make a huge profit. And with the casino and the restaurants popping up around it? That real estate investment probably already tripled.

Follow the money.

Vanity gallery. That's the phrase her mother had used. Galleries taking advantage of artists who had always dreamed of seeing their paintings on the wall for sale.

Orlando might be able to afford a vanity payment of five hundred dollars, but not all artists could. And besides, it was the principle of the thing: turning the blood, sweat, and tears of art into not just a commodity, but essentially a Ponzi scheme, where the museum left the artists with nothing. Fenway was livid just thinking about it, and she hadn't poured any of her time, effort, or money into it.

Piper? Well, she invested additional money into the NNoV8 museum, too, and her idealistic streak ran a lot wider than Fenway's.

If the police thought Piper had a motive, thin as it was, there were thousands of artists who had more reason to want revenge on Vaughn Trask.

Her eyes came back into focus, and Orlando Lockberry took another sip of his beer.

"You said that some of your friends weren't so lucky," Fenway said.

Orlando nodded.

"Mind telling me who some of these friends are?"

A smile touched the corner of his mouth. "Nice try, Coroner. No, I won't give you an excuse to bother my fellow artists. And I'll tell you right now, they didn't do this. Most of them live hours away, anyway. But I appreciate that you want your friend to stop being a person of interest."

"Thanks, Orlando," Fenway said. "You've been really helpful, even if you won't give me the names of your artist friends."

He leaned toward Fenway slightly. "Maybe I should get your number."

"I have a fiancé," Fenway blurted. The words were out of her mouth before she could stop them.

"Oh." Orlando's ears reddened, then faded. "Well, I mean, if I come across any other information from the hotel that might prove your friend didn't do it. I'll need to get in touch with you."

"Right," Fenway said. Now it was her turn to feel embarrassed. "I didn't mean—"

Orlando shrugged. "That's okay." He took another drink of his beer. "Your friend is being held by the sheriff, and your fiancé isn't here, though, right? Unless your *friend* is the one who you're—"

"No," Fenway said quickly. "My friend and I are driving the truck to my boyfr—to my fiancé's place."

"Okay," Orlando replied. "Just—well, look, you're in town for another night, anyway, especially if your friend doesn't get released. So if you want company—"

"If I need anything from the hotel records," Fenway said, "you'll be the first to know."

"How are you going to get in touch with me if you don't have my number?"

"I'm sure I can get Teddi to get in touch with you," Fenway said, thinking quickly. "But you've been more than helpful. I've got to make a phone call." She pulled her wallet out—thankfully she'd gone to the ATM before leaving Thursday morning and had enough cash to cover lunch. She tossed the bills on the bar, put her wallet back in her purse, and held her phone out like a sword as she exited the restaurant.

CHAPTER NINE

"Yes, I understand that Mr. Ubosi might be at lunch," Fenway said on the phone, pacing outside the bar and grill. "But I have some crucial information for him regarding the Piper Patten case."

"He can call you back on Monday." The man on the other end of the line had a clipped, no-nonsense tone, which Fenway would have loved if he'd been on her side. But his ruthlessly efficient blocking of her talking to Piper's lawyer was getting under Fenway's skin.

"I don't really need to talk to him," Fenway said, "but I need him to talk to the Correos County sheriff's department regarding Piper Patten. With this information, his client could be released this afternoon."

"Mr. Ubosi is at lunch," the man repeated, "and is due in court after that."

Fenway closed her eyes and took a deep breath. "Can I leave a message?"

"Name and number?"

"I don't need him to call me back," Fenway repeated. "I need him to follow up on the information I'm trying to give him."

"As I said, he can call you back on Monday."

Ugh. They were going in circles. Fenway was glad her father was footing the bill for Ubosi, because she wouldn't have wanted to waste money on a celebrity lawyer who was fine letting a client stay in jail over the weekend.

"Thanks, I'll call back later." Fenway ended the call, then took a deep breath as her words rang in her head.

I have a fiancé. What the hell was that? No, she didn't have a fiancé. She had a boyfriend: a boyfriend who she loved, true; a boyfriend who she loved spending time with, true; and a boyfriend who she was scared to admit she could see building a life together, also grudgingly true.

But a fiancé? No.

Plus, there were complications. Look at the situation she and Piper were in right now. If McVie hadn't been the Boy Scout he was, if he hadn't been the white knight trying to protect Megan from herself, if he hadn't been the kind of dad who—

Oh, this was getting her nowhere. True, Piper wouldn't be at the sheriff's office in the Nevada desert right now, but that wasn't because McVie was in Colorado. It was because Piper had lost her knife. She was the one who insisted on stopping at the NNoV8 museum anyway, instead of stopping at the Supreme Value Super Inn at the I-70 junction in Utah. Would have been two additional hours of driving yesterday, but would have saved two hours of driving today. In fact, they would have been stopping for lunch on the west side of the Rockies right about now. Instead, Fenway was trying to get Piper out of jail.

Ugh. She hated that she was jumping to conclusions: the sheriff's office hadn't arrested Piper yet, and might not hold her over the weekend. Yes, the police had circumstantial evidence, and they had the murder weapon. But if the sheriff canvassed the area, someone might have seen the real killer. The medical examiner hadn't even established the time of death—and if it was when Fenway had been with Piper, she could provide an alibi.

Surely they'd take the word of a fellow law enforcement representative.

Unfortunately, the cameras didn't work. And unfortunately, Cartwheel hadn't hired security staff to walk the parking lot.

But the NNoV8 financial scheme might be enough to get the sheriff to realize that hundreds—even thousands—of other people could have done it. And if Fenway could convince the sheriff that Piper had lost her knife hours before Trask's death, maybe that would be enough to get Piper released and get them on their way.

She looked at the clock on her phone. 12:18 PM. A deep sigh. She raised her eyes to look across the street to the parking lot of the Cartwheel Hotel & Casino. Fenway could see the top of the U-Move-It truck in the parking lot.

Probably time to go back to the sheriff's office.

She traipsed across the bar and grill's parking lot, crossed the side street, and walked alongside the concrete barrier—on the same side as they'd found Trask's body.

This side of the parking lot was empty now; no sheriff's vehicles, no ambulance. The asphalt next to the driver's side door of the truck showed an asymmetrical dark stain. If she hadn't known it was blood, she might have thought it was another vehicle's oil leak. A big oil leak.

She unlocked the door and climbed in, putting her purse on the floor and wedging it under her seat. The beast got ten miles to the gallon—probably less off the highway. The gas tank was just under a quarter tank; she should fill up before getting on the road. Whenever that would be. Fenway started the engine, cranked the air conditioning to high, took a deep breath, then put the truck into gear and drove out of the parking lot. The moving truck shuddered and groaned as she turned left from the side street onto Ruby Dunes Road. A sign for Interstate 15, with an arrow pointing straight ahead, went by on the right shoulder.

Fenway remembered the route from her earlier ride in the cruiser. She congratulated herself for taking the correct exit from

Interstate 15, and she remembered to turn right at the stop sign. The sheriff's station loomed ahead on the left.

She slowed down, the truck complaining with its squeal of brakes, and navigated into the parking lot. The parking lot was half full, but there was nowhere for a large truck to park. Maybe on the street?

Nope. A series of *No Parking Any Time* signs lined the curbs on both blocks. She exited the parking lot and turned down the next side street she came to. An industrial park, with warehouses and dirt lots surrounded by chain-link fences. And of course, the fences had more signs on them prohibiting parking.

After another hundred yards, a different lot appeared with another rectangular red-and-white sign. Fenway frowned, but then her heart leapt: it was a *For Lease* sign, not *No Parking*. Interesting that such a relatively minor thing could bring her joy. Maybe this was a sign that she'd have to work at it, but that she *could* get Piper out of this mess without getting her arrested. Maybe they *would* be able to make it to his apartment in Colorado before midnight.

Her phone rang.

Fenway pulled to the side, hoping her wheels were close enough to the curb, and put the truck in Park. She picked up her phone: it was McVie. Ah. His lunch break. She tapped *Answer*.

"Hi, Craig."

"Hi, Fenway. How are you doing? Holding up okay?"

"Piper's still being held for questioning. I just got back to the sheriff's office. I found that thousands of artists paid a fee to Vaughn Trask for exhibiting, but he cheated them out of exposure. And maybe money. So that's another six or seven thousand suspects."

McVie was quiet.

"Craig?"

"I'm still here," he said. "So—sorry, but it's the investigator in me. You're in the middle of nowhere in the Nevada desert, right?"

"It's only an hour and a half from Vegas. If someone wanted

Vaughn Trask dead, they could get a cheap last-minute flight, drive out here, and kill him."

"With Piper's knife?"

"She dropped her purse in the museum parking lot yesterday afternoon. So yes, with Piper's knife."

"Anyone see her lose the knife?"

"I saw her drop her purse, and the stuff inside went everywhere. I bet her knife skidded under a car and we just didn't see it."

McVie was quiet again.

"You don't think she did it, do you, Craig?"

"Of course not. But I'm looking at it through the sheriff's eyes. I'm thinking what *I* would do if a coroner from Nevada showed up with her friend and found a prominent businessman murdered in the parking lot with her friend's knife sticking out of his chest."

Fenway blinked. "I know what it looks like, but I'm officially a law enforcement officer. I can give her an alibi—and why wouldn't they trust my testimony?" Although Sheriff Jeffcoat had strongly suggested that, since Fenway had been asleep, she wasn't able to provide Piper a proper alibi.

"You're officially a law enforcement officer in *California*," McVie said. "Not true in every state. And in Nevada, not only is a coroner *not* a law enforcement officer, but coroners must have a medical doctorate—and be licensed to practice medicine in the state, too."

Fenway chuckled mirthlessly. "So they won't afford me the same courtesy they would if I were a beat cop or a sheriff's deputy from another state."

"If they don't, now you know why," McVie said. "And, look, I believe you. I know Piper. I know she wouldn't kill anyone. But if I were in the sheriff's shoes, I'd be preparing for an arrest. And it's Friday, so her arraignment probably won't happen until Monday."

"But O.K. Ubosi—"

"*Especially* with a high-priced lawyer," McVie continued. "The sheriff has the murder weapon. He knows it's Piper's. And he only has the word of her traveling companion that Piper lost the knife *before* the murder, and only your word that she was in the hotel room with you when the murder occurred."

"We reported the knife missing to the front desk," Fenway said. "So it's not just my word that Piper lost the knife. The sheriff already heard it from the desk clerk."

McVie gave a soft grunt. "You and Piper *said* the knife was lost. Do you know how many times I arrested someone for assault with a deadly weapon or a hit-and-run and they reported their handgun or their car or their baseball bat as stolen, conveniently right around the time of the crime?"

Fenway was quiet for a moment. "The time of the crime."

McVie paused. "What about it?"

"We don't know when the murder occurred. Or, at least, I don't. The sheriff's office isn't telling me anything. From what I saw, he could have been killed any time between six thirty and midnight."

"Even more reason to hold Piper," McVie said. "But if you have the names of some of those artists who got fleeced, you could give that list to Piper's lawyer and he could work on cross-referencing that list with travel records. You said thousands of people, right? Chances are at least a few of them were in Vegas and don't have alibis."

Fenway paused. "I don't have any names. Would—would you have any ideas on how I could get those?"

McVie snorted. "Honestly, that's a job I would give Piper." Then he exhaled loudly.

"What is it?"

"It's nothing."

"No, it's not. Something's bothering you."

McVie was silent for a moment. "I don't really want to burden you with my problems when you and Piper are stuck in the desert being questioned about a murder."

"It's fine," Fenway said. "Maybe it'll distract me."

"Okay, well, I'm in a weird spot," McVie said. "It's my first week on the job, and it's—well, much more strict with my time than I'm used to. They already said I took too long in the bathroom this morning. Apparently, if you pee for more than a minute and a half, you get written up."

"That—that's not legal."

"I'm thrown off my game, that's all," McVie said, and there was a note of worry in his voice. "One of the other guys on my shift said he was written up for taking a day off to attend his father's funeral."

"You don't want to work for a place like that," Fenway said.

"No. But it'll have to do for now. I'll lose my apartment if I quit in the first thirty days."

"Really?"

"It sucks, but yeah. So I'll have to grin and bear it. I'm not sure I can take the afternoon off and catch the early flight—I probably won't be able to leave until five o'clock."

"Not that big of a deal. It looks like I'm going to be stuck here for at least the night. Maybe the entire weekend."

The worry left McVie's voice. "Oh, Fenway, that sucks. I'm sorry."

"And you're counting on getting all your stuff today."

McVie sighed, a note of sympathy in it. "I know I am, but it's just stuff. You and Piper—you're more important than my stuff."

Fenway was silent.

"Plus," McVie said, "I already called U-Move-It and extended the truck a day." He hesitated. "Okay, let me see what I can do. I can still catch a flight tonight. And I haven't had time to call my Vegas connections, but I could do that."

"You did say you might be able to cut through the red tape. Thank you."

"Are you kidding? Thank *you* for driving the truck—and I know this is a pain in the ass. Besides, after tonight, I have the whole weekend to figure things out," McVie said.

"Right." She cleared her throat.

"Oh." McVie's voice was startled. "I didn't realize what time it was. I have to get back to work right now. Let's text each other with updates. Bye."

"Wait," Fenway said hurriedly. "Look, I won't deny that things have been weird between us since I—I said no when you proposed. Well, I didn't say no, exactly, but I sure didn't say yes." She took a breath, and when he said nothing, she pressed on. "Anyway, things have been so crazy with your move, I didn't get a chance to explain myself very well. I still—" She paused, then swallowed hard. "I still love you, Craig. I know I haven't had a relationship like this before, and I know you're the most serious boyfriend I've had in..." She closed her eyes. "Ever. And you know it scares the shit out of me, and I *might* be ready to take another step forward with you, but marriage right now is too much. I'm still, uh, I'm still broken, Craig. I have trust issues and commitment issues, and you're a thousand miles away. And it's the right decision—for you to go and support Megan through her senior year even though Amy doesn't want it. You're the kind of dad my father never was. He never fought for me, and I see you fighting for Megan, and I—"

Fenway stopped and took a gulp of air. "Part of me loves that you fight for Megan so hard, and part of me loves *you* for it, and part of me is jealous as hell because I never had that, and I—I'm on the short end of that again. And that's how it should be. But that's why my answer was *not yet*. Because I need time to process it, and I need to be sure I'm the kind of person who can choose someone who makes the right choice even when it's not advantageous to me."

She paused. "Look, I know this is a lot for you to process on your lunch break, and especially when Piper could get arrested at any minute. But if I've learned anything since coming to Estancia, it's that there's never a good time for interpersonal messiness like this to come out. But if it doesn't, it'll just fester and fester and we'll both make bad assumptions and misunderstandings and then we'll never move forward. And what we have is the best I've ever had." She took a deep breath. "And I wanted you to know that."

Silence.

"Craig, are you there?"

She looked at her phone. No active phone call.

McVie had hung up after saying goodbye.

———

"Didn't expect to see you back here so soon," Deputy Bardot said. Fenway looked up from her phone. Nothing yet from Sarah. After Fenway had poured her heart out to an unconnected cellphone, she had needed to calm down before going into the sheriff's office. From the cab of the moving truck, Fenway had texted the sheriff about the "exhibition fee" that all the artists had to pay. She'd done a little more research on the artists, and not surprisingly, there was no public information on who the artists were. That struck Fenway as a little strange, since museums usually pushed the artists' names like crazy—they were, after all, the biggest draw. But was it the technology itself that was the draw for the NNoV8 museum? If so, maybe it didn't matter who the artists were. Particularly if the artists were hungry or desperate for exposure and were willing to kick in the equivalent of framing and shipping costs directly to the museum. She'd been hoping she could get the name of one or two of them—maybe there'd been an artist complaining to their local news station or something. But no, nothing she could find.

Still, the information was something that the sheriff needed to know. And if Deputy Bardot was out in the waiting room to meet Fenway, chances are Bartholomew Jeffcoat was still in the interview room with Piper. And, especially after McVie had given his opinion on how he'd act in the sheriff's shoes, it had the distinct feeling that this was an interrogation, not just an interview, which meant at any point, it could become an arrest.

"I've got some information on this case," Fenway said, standing from her seat.

Bardot pressed her lips together. "You're outside your jurisdiction."

"I had lunch with one of the artists from the museum," Fenway said, "and he told me about a scheme Trask had." She pulled her phone out, tapped the screen to the equity partner statement where Trask promised the high rate of return. "Thousands of artists paid over five hundred dollars each to exhibit their work, but the installations used representations of the NFTs instead of the actual work. Trask defrauded all the artists."

"And his investors too," Bardot said.

Fenway blinked.

"We know your friend invested a thousand dollars into the museum."

"She's not a starving artist. Some of those artists spent money they didn't have—"

"And we've got footage of her shouting at the murder victim."

Ah. So the sheriff's office *had* obtained the phone footage from the woman pointing her cellphone at Piper and Vaughn Trask in the museum's lobby the afternoon before.

But also important is what Bardot *didn't* say.

"Fingerprints haven't come back yet?"

Bardot said nothing.

"Oh," Fenway said. "The knife was wiped clean."

"I'm not at liberty to give out that information."

But the look on Bardot's face made it clear: there were no fingerprints on the knife. She tried a different tack.

"I've found out a *lot* of information, Deputy. And more people than just the artists have strong motives. Like—did you know both of Trask's business partners had life insurance policies out on him? Two million dollars each, that's what I heard, anyway."

"His business partners? Schup and Shellwater?"

"Right."

Bardot shook her head. "Bigger fish to fry. They might not be billionaires, but they're awfully close. Two million might sound like a lot to you and me, but it's not enough to kill for. Not for them, anyway."

"Look at Shellwater's extramarital affairs. Schup goes on drug holidays. Trask could have been blackmailing them."

The deputy cocked her head. "Any proof of that?"

"The Cartwheel," Fenway said. "You could get the records for the rooms that the museum paid for and then see who actually stayed in those rooms. I heard Schup goes out to the desert and gets high with a guy named, uh..." Fenway's mind raced, then finally clicked. "Entropy. A guy named Entropy. You could ask Entropy where Schup was the night of the murder."

Bardot chuckled. "Man, I wish I had a friend like you. You've been busy. You'd probably help Ms. Patten bury a body in Mexico if she asked."

"Piper Patten didn't commit this murder."

"I hope you don't hold it against us if we don't take your word for it."

Fenway took a small step back. "Can I—uh, can I see her?"

"Ms. Patten?"

"Right." Fenway paused, then turned the words over in her mind. Was this the right thing to do? Had she even talked to the high-priced lawyer yet?

Fenway thought back—and remembered when McVie was still sheriff. He had caught a suspect in a burglary who had requested a lawyer. While they were waiting for the lawyer to show up, and after reading the suspect his Miranda rights, McVie just started chatting. The suspect didn't have to respond to anything McVie said—and McVie was careful not to frame anything as a question. He'd talked about how the burglary suspect had cheated on his wife and how he'd stolen the victim's electronics to sell it and buy a necklace for his mistress. After McVie outlined the case against the suspect as a cheat, a philanderer, and a liar, the suspect cracked, angrily saying he'd never cheat on his wife, and he'd used the money from the electronics to buy his wife an anniversary gift. True love.

Fenway wondered if that's what Sheriff Jeffcoat's plan was: Piper had hopefully asked for her lawyer, and Jeffcoat might be pacing around the room, pontificating, trying to get under Piper's skin. Fortunately, Piper was unrufflable.

Well, maybe not with museum owners who took advantage of artists and investors. But when Piper faced danger, Fenway hoped Piper could tune the sheriff out and just sit there, no matter what the sheriff threw at her.

"We're still interviewing her," Bardot said, "so, no, you can't see her yet."

"But she's free to go?"

Bardot pressed her lips together. "Coroner, I shouldn't even be talking to you about the person of interest in our case. Ms. Patten's a grown woman. She'll get in contact with you when she can."

"There's only a certain amount of time you can hold her without charge."

"You're right," Bardot said. Then she crossed her arms.

Okay, so this wasn't going great. "Deputy Bardot," Fenway said, "You don't know Piper Patten. If you knew her like I do, you'd know she couldn't—wouldn't do this. I'm presenting the investigating team with other options." She dropped her arms to her sides. "If you don't look at any other suspects, the defense—" Then she snapped her mouth shut.

How stupid. Fenway was thinking short term. She was prioritizing getting Piper released today—right now. But she suddenly saw with increasing clarity that she had her priorities wrong. This weekend, getting McVie's moving truck to him, that wasn't the most important thing. The most important thing was getting Piper freed—not today, but making sure she didn't get life in prison for a murder she didn't commit. And that could take time.

The door of the sheriff's office waiting room opened and Sheriff Bartholomew Jeffcoat appeared. Bardot swiveled her head.

"Hey, Izzy," he said, then bobbed his head at Fenway. "Coroner."

"Are you letting Piper go?" Fenway asked.

The sheriff drew himself up to his full height. "About five minutes ago," he said, "we arrested Piper Patten for the murder of Vaughn Trask."

CHAPTER TEN

FENWAY STOOD OUTSIDE THE SHERIFF'S OFFICE, PACING BACK AND forth, her mind going a million miles an hour. How could she get Piper out of this?

Part of her thought she should just let O.K. Ubosi deal with it—he was one of the best criminal defense lawyers in the world, after all. But he didn't know Piper like Fenway did—and besides, Fenway was at ground zero for the arrest. And Piper Patten wasn't a celebrity—she just had the bankroll of a rich—if retired—oil tycoon.

And besides, Ubosi wasn't taking her calls.

Fenway kicked a rock, sending it bouncing over the concrete into the beige stones in the strip between the sidewalk and the parking lot.

She had to think.

Dez—and McVie, and Piper, and pretty much everyone—had been bugging her to stop taking responsibility for every little thing and start relying on other people. Her team. But she was in another state, an hour east of Las Vegas, with her only team member having just been arrested for murder. Her other team members were at the other end of a phone call, true, but it wasn't the same as being able to rely on them. Plus, McVie had his own stuff going on.

She felt her forehead bead with sweat. Easily a hundred degrees in the shade now.

It wasn't doing her any good to wander around the sheriff's office. She trudged the block-and-a-half back to the truck, the sweat on her forehead threatening to drip into her eyes. Fenway unlocked the truck, climbing into the driver's seat, feeling the hot vinyl stick to her skin. The truck was hard to drive; she hated how she had to be mindful of overhangs and underpasses. But she started up the truck, and, feeling the blast of cool air, was thankful that the air conditioning worked well.

If she were investigating this murder, she'd have a list of suspects, and she'd be lining up interviews. Fenway scratched her head. She couldn't use her badge to force anyone to talk with her, but that didn't mean she couldn't ask. And if people didn't realize she didn't have jurisdiction, that wasn't her fault, right?

She pressed her lips together. That was dubious, for sure. But if she was doing it under the guise of the defense...

She pulled her phone out of her purse and tapped her contact list.

The other end rang.

"Fenway—what's happening?"

"Hi, Dad."

"Is Piper okay?"

"They just arrested her for murder."

She could hear Nathaniel Ferris's jaw tighten. "Ubosi gave me his word that this wouldn't—"

"Ubosi is scheduled in court this afternoon, and he's not returning my calls. But I've got some information on additional suspects. I thought he'd probably want to know. Get enough of an alternate theory of the case so that they'd have to release Piper."

"Did you say he's not returning your calls?" Ferris said, and it was more of a statement than a question. "Do you have his cell?"

"No, I called his main office line."

"Let me give his private number to you. I had to bump up the retainer to get it, but now I'm glad I did. I'll call him and let him know *you'll* be calling him, and that I expect him to work with you."

Fenway paused. "I really appreciate this, Dad."

"If not for her, I'd be in jail for killing that asshole professor," Ferris said. "I'm throwing money at the problem and making a couple of phone calls. It's literally the least I can do. I don't know anything about suspects or motivations or anything like that. You've got the talent, Fenway."

"It's difficult when I'm out of my jurisdiction."

A wry chuckle from Nathaniel Ferris. "And somehow I don't think you really believe that."

Fenway was quiet.

"I'll text the number over to you now," Ferris said. "Love you, kiddo. Go kick ass."

Despite herself, Fenway felt a lump in her throat. "Thanks, Dad."

They said their goodbyes, and a moment later, Fenway's phone made a swishing noise. The private cellphone number of O.K. Ubosi. And another text from her father:

Wait ten minutes before you call

Might as well head back to the hotel, then.

She drove back to the Cartwheel Hotel & Casino, trying to figure out what she'd say to the rich celebrity lawyer. She braked a little too hard when she got off I-15 at the Cartwheel exit and she heard some items shift in the back of the truck. Certainly didn't drive like her Accord.

She entered the hotel parking lot and purposely parked about fifty feet away from her old parking spot. A little further to walk, but she wouldn't have to step around the bloodstain.

Fenway got out of the cabin of the truck, closed and locked the driver's door, then saw motion on the other side of the parking lot. Shading her eyes, she turned her head toward the movement.

The red Jetta.

A tall, thin Asian woman with short denim shorts and a tank top with a martini glass design on the front. She was walking toward the Jetta.

That must be Nadine Ryeo.

She looked to be in her early twenties, probably the same age as Orlando Lockberry. Despite the heat, Fenway rushed across the lot, feeling the waves of heat rise from the asphalt.

"No, no, no," Fenway muttered, watching the woman unlock the red Jetta—

And she grabbed a tote bag from the back seat, closed the door, tapped a button on her key fob. The headlights flashed and the horn chirped, and the woman turned back toward the hotel.

Fenway was less than fifty feet away and closing fast. She put her hand in her purse and rummaged around for her coroner identification. "Nadine!"

The woman stopped, turned, and peered at Fenway.

Fenway hurried over to the woman, pulling her badge out. "Sorry—you don't know me, but I'm looking into the death of Vaughn Trask."

Nadine shook her head and started walking away. "I don't know anything about that."

Fenway sped up, sweat dripping down her temple, and caught up to Nadine. "Maybe not, but you knew him, didn't you?"

"I don't see what that has to do with anything."

"You're staying in a hotel room he paid for."

Nadine glared at Fenway out of the corner of her eye, but didn't slow down. "I might be, but I don't have any idea what happened to him."

"Can we just talk for a minute? I'm trying to get a better idea of where he was."

"Like I said, I didn't see him last night."

Fenway glanced at the martini glass design on Nadine's tank top. "Maybe I can buy you a drink while we chat?"

Nadine chuckled. "Yeah, okay, but only if it's top-shelf."

"The top-shelfiest," Fenway said. "I'm dying for a cold drink, myself."

———

A sixty-two dollar martini. That's what it cost. Fenway blinked, but signed it over to her room.

"You're staying here?" Nadine narrowed her eyes at Fenway, leaning back in her chair in the hotel bar. The electronic beeping of the video poker and video slots games from the bar sounded all around. Fenway felt a headache coming on and was glad she'd ordered an ice water in addition to her gin and tonic.

"That's right."

"Since when does the county coroner need to stay in a hotel?"

"I'm not local."

Nadine pushed her tote bag under the table another few inches. "So why are you investigating Vaughn's death?"

Aha. *Vaughn's death.* She didn't call him *Mr. Trask* or anything formal. Not a giveaway, exactly, but it implied their relationship was more than professional.

"We're all interested in seeing justice done, right?" Fenway said.

Nadine turned her head toward the bar. The bartender had a ladder and was grabbing the Excelsior & Monarch vodka—in its telltale aquamarine glass bottle—from the top shelf. The *real* top shelf. Fenway counted herself lucky that it was under a hundred dollars.

"Okay," Fenway said, turning her seat so she was facing Nadine. "So we know you're staying in a hotel room paid for by Vaughn Trask."

"If you say so."

Fenway raised her eyebrows. "You just told me you were. When we were standing in the parking lot."

"I said *I might be.* I don't know who paid for it."

Fenway narrowed her eyes. Technically, Nadine probably didn't see the payment information, so could truthfully say she didn't know. "And you live in Las Vegas."

"Paradise," Nadine replied. Ah—a suburb close to the strip. She couldn't have sounded more bored.

"Why did you come out here? It's kind of the middle of nowhere."

"Vaughn wanted to see me. I had the weekend off."

"The two of you are romantically involved?"

Nadine turned her head to look at Fenway, then raised and lowered her head, taking Fenway's whole appearance in, like a beauty pageant judge would do. "I suppose one could characterize it like that."

Did Fenway want to dig more into that response? Probably not if she wanted more answers. "When did you arrive?"

"I'm not sure of the exact time. Before dinner. I'm sure the front desk could tell you."

"Before dinner is good enough. And you checked in?"

"That's correct."

"Had Mr. Trask been to the room previously?"

"No."

"And you said he never showed up?"

"That's right."

"Did he attempt to contact you?"

"He and I were supposed to meet after dinner." Nadine turned her tongue over in her mouth, probably decided what—or how much—to say.

The bartender arrived with their drinks. "Gin and tonic," he said, setting the tall, icy glass in front of Fenway. "And our Excelsior & Monarch vodka martini, up." He set the martini in front of Nadine, his eyes raking over her.

"Thanks," Fenway said. Nadine said nothing.

Fenway watched the bartender go back to the bar. She wondered what she could say to get Nadine to open up—but no, she was too guarded. Even with her relatively casual tank top, Nadine was easily the most elegant, sophisticated woman in the hotel bar—probably the whole hotel. And it was obvious she and Vaughn were meeting for a hookup.

Oh, that's right: Fenway didn't need to think like a prosecutor. She didn't need to necessarily get Nadine to admit to anything. Just enough where she could get the appearance of a motive. "You knew Vaughn had a wife, though, didn't you?"

"Fiancée," Nadine said automatically, then shrugged.

"They got married," Fenway said. She peered carefully at Nadine's face, but could discern no reaction. "So tell me, was she the jealous type?"

"I wouldn't know."

"You never met her?"

Another shrug.

"You're from Palmdale—is that right?"

Nadine scoffed. "No. I'm from Ruby Dunes. When I went to college, my mom followed me—well, as close as she could afford, anyway."

"Where was college?"

"Santa Clarita Polytech."

"Ah. Not a long drive from Palmdale."

"Closer than here, anyway."

Fenway smiled at the statement, leaning forward slightly. "So you went to high school here in Ruby Dunes?"

"Right."

"Did you know Orlando Lockberry?"

Nadine cocked her head and studied Fenway's face. What was it about Lockberry that got Nadine so on edge? "Yes."

"In high school?"

"Yes."

"How well did you know him?"

"If you saw pictures from senior prom, you would know."

"Oh. You dated?"

"Briefly. It was high school. A long time ago."

"How did it end?"

"I went to college in California. He stayed here. My mom didn't like him, anyway."

"Your mom—Sookie, right?"

Nadine cracked a smile. "That's what her white friends call her. To family, she's Kyung-Sook."

"Sorry."

Yet another shrug.

"Did Orlando take the breakup well?"

Nadine shook her head. "He wanted to keep dating. But I lived five hours away. And I wanted to experience the college life."

"Did he make things difficult for you?"

"What do you mean?"

"Stalking you on social media? Or in person?"

She took a sip of her martini, then set it down with precision. "Nothing I couldn't handle."

"He dating anyone now?"

"I haven't seen him in years."

Now it was Fenway's turn to stop and stare at Nadine. "He was working the front desk yesterday. I think chances are pretty good that he checked you in."

Nadine blinked. "Oh—was that him? I wasn't really paying attention."

Fenway sat back in her chair and watched a bead of condensation form on the outside of her martini glass, then break the surface tension and slide down the side. Was that something, perhaps? A young man obsessed with his high school sweetheart who figured out that she was sleeping with the guy who'd cheated him out of five hundred dollars? Stranger things had happened—people had been killed for less.

"Did you see Orlando at all that night?"

Nadine reached forward, balanced the drink delicately in one hand, and took a slow drink.

"Did you hear what I—"

"I obviously didn't," Nadine said. "I just told you I didn't even recognize him at the front desk. Honestly, I didn't know he was still in town. As I mentioned, I haven't seen him for years."

Uh oh. Fenway was losing Nadine. "When was the last time you saw Vaughn Trask?"

"Last week."

"You two have a regular, uh, meeting time?"

"It depends. Sometimes he comes down to Paradise to see me. Other times, I drive up here."

"How often?"

"Two or three times a month."

"Where do you go when you visit him? Any of the local restaurants? The casino bar?"

Nadine gave Fenway a weary but knowing smile. "We stay in."

Fenway wasn't sure how much she could trust Nadine's answers, but the woman seemed proud of her relationship with Vaughn. "You don't seem bothered by his death."

"He and I had fun," she said simply.

Fenway waited for Nadine to expand on the topic, but she sat silently, then took another sip of her martini.

A noise behind Fenway.

"Nadine!" a shrill voice called.

Fenway turned. An Asian woman appeared, perhaps in her mid-forties, perhaps five foot five, in an elegant blue wrap dress and low heels, looking more suited for a fancy dinner at an expensive restaurant than a midday visit to a bar in the middle of the Nevada desert.

Her face was awash with anger.

In Fenway's peripheral vision, Nadine stood up, her hands balled into fists.

The two women began shouting at each other.

CHAPTER ELEVEN

WERE THEY SCREAMING AT EACH OTHER IN VIETNAMESE? Fenway wasn't sure, but thought the inflections sounded right. She pulled her phone out and quickly tapped the audio button and hit *Record.* She couldn't understand anything they were saying, but she'd bet that whatever it was, it had to do with the reason Nadine was at this particular hotel on this particular day. And that might be important to the murder investigation.

Better safe than sorry, anyway.

Fenway sat in silence while the two women kept arguing. With the resemblance, the older woman had to be Kyung-Sook, Nadine's mother. After a moment, the bartender rushed over.

"Ladies, ladies," he said, "I have to ask you to keep your voices down."

"I will not keep my voice down," the older woman said, pointing at Nadine. "She's the one who—"

"If you don't lower your voice, I'll have to ask you to leave." The bartender motioned his chin toward the casino entrance, where a large, burly man stood in a black polo shirt that strained around his barrel chest and meaty biceps. The burly man looked over with interest but didn't move. "And if you don't leave, I can have additional security personnel here in ten seconds."

Nadine pointed at her mother. "I'm a guest of this hotel. She's bothering me."

Fenway glanced between mother and daughter, then pulled her badge out, giving just a brief flash of it to the older woman. "Okay," she said, "let's go outside."

The older woman shot daggers with her eyes at Nadine, but she stuck her nose in the air and said one last exclamation in Vietnamese.

"I don't live at home anymore, Mother," Nadine said. "You can't make those threats to me."

"We'll see," the elder Ryeo said, turning on her heel and hurrying out through the casino's double doors. Nadine crossed her arms and didn't follow.

Fenway grabbed her purse and her phone—still recording—and ran after the older woman.

"Wait," she called, but the woman didn't slow down.

Once outside, however, the woman stopped in her tracks, her shoulders slumped.

"Mrs. Ryeo," Fenway said, rushing to her side.

Ryeo clicked her tongue. "What do you want?"

"I'm investigating—"

"Nadine doesn't know what she's doing. She's still a young woman."

Fenway paused. "What is it exactly you think—"

"It's all that man's fault, anyway."

"What man?"

"The one who owns that black slab," Ryeo said, pointing derisively at the museum in the distance. "He thinks he knows everything. He thinks he can flash his money around and get Nadine to do what he wants. Someone needs to teach that man a lesson."

"Are you talking about Vaughn Trask?"

"Oh, oh, *now* the police know who he is," Ryeo said, pulling the strap of her purse up on her shoulder. "Not when I complain about him stealing money, but *now,* when it's my daughter in trouble."

Fenway's mind raced in two different directions. Why would Nadine be in trouble? Maybe she and Trask had committed fraud together. That might be a reason for someone to kill him. But she'd said something else.

"Teach Vaughn Trask a lesson?" Fenway asked. "What do you mean?"

"You know what I mean, but I won't say," Ryeo said. "Sometimes a man like that, he only understands right from wrong when he gets hurt."

"Did you threaten him, Mrs. Ryeo?"

She exhaled. "People call me Sookie. Like the woman from that vampire show."

"Sorry. Sookie."

"And so what if I did? He needs to leave Nadine alone."

"Can I ask where you were last night?"

An exasperated puff of breath. "Did he say I threatened him? A man like that, afraid of a woman like me?" She shook her head. "After I left the museum at three o'clock, I went to my sister's."

"Where is that?"

"Benny lives here in Ruby Dunes. Two exits up U.S. 93. I try to get her to look after Nadine, but you know how it is with kids."

"What time did you get to your sister's?"

"Maybe three thirty. I told her what happened, but she and I, we were together all night. Went to Pho Luc for dinner."

"Where's that?"

"Ah, you know, just south of the base. Not as good as other places, but we didn't want to drive all the way to Las Vegas, and I didn't want to cook. And my sister, she doesn't cook the noodles properly. Her cooking is terrible ever since she married that Tây lông."

"Just you and your sister?"

"Yes."

"What time did you get back?"

"Ah, early. Seven thirty, maybe eight."

"And then what?"

"We talked. Stephen is on a business trip, so we stayed up late." She gave Fenway a tight smile. "She has a son at university who is also an ungrateful child."

"And who is Stephen?"

"Her husband."

Ah. The Tây lông, whatever that meant. Probably wasn't a compliment. "Anyone else see you?"

Ryeo shifted her purse to her other shoulder. "What's this about?"

"You said you threatened Trask."

"I told him to stay away from my daughter."

"Or what?"

"Or I would—" Ryeo screwed up her mouth. "Or I would hurt him badly. In areas where, as a man, he would feel it."

"You made this threat at the museum?"

Ryeo frowned. "Any mother would do the same. Any mother who cared whether her daughter was disgracing herself and her family. Maybe some mothers don't care."

"You know he went to see your daughter last night."

Ryeo laughed, a harsh, brittle sound. "He wouldn't dare."

"He did. Bought her a hotel room at the Cartwheel Casino."

Ryeo gave Fenway an ugly frown. "That place has been nothing but trouble."

"Were you in the parking lot of the Cartwheel Hotel last night?"

Pressing her lips together, Ryeo shook her head.

"You didn't go see if Trask was really staying away from your daughter? You didn't stop at the museum?" Fenway wished she had the power of the local sheriff's department behind her—she would definitely take Ryeo in for questioning.

"I will not set foot in that museum." Then Ryeo closed her eyes. "Please do not continue. I do not want to hear what he did to my daughter."

"He didn't do anything, Sookie," Fenway said. "Someone stabbed him before he could go into the hotel."

Ryeo's eyes widened. "You're joking."

"I'm not."

Ryeo's expression of shock dropped as a broad smile spread over her face. "Good."

"Good?"

"Yes." Her eyes danced. "Someone give him what was coming to him. Is he dead?"

"Yes."

Ryeo let out a whoop and spun around like a child playing in the rain. "He's really dead? You are serious?"

Fenway nodded, not quite believing Ryeo's reaction.

When Ryeo stopped spinning, she looked at Fenway, eyes shining; perhaps they were happy tears. "You have made this mother's day."

And she turned, striding across the parking lot, a bounce in her step. Fenway could only stare after her.

———

Fenway went back into the casino's lobby bar, but Nadine and her tote bag were gone—and so was Fenway's untouched gin and tonic.

Probably for the best. She needed to busy herself with more suspects. Because as much as Sookie Ryeo hated Vaughn Trask and obviously wished him harm, she'd been surprised—delighted, yes, but surprised—at the news of his death. Her reaction seemed genuine.

Fenway's phone buzzed. Sarah Summerhill.

She tapped *Answer.* "Hey, Sarah. Any info?"

"I've got lots," Sarah replied. "Starting with Nadine Ryeo. I know she was at the Cartwheel Hotel & Casino—"

"Still is," Fenway said. "I just talked with her."

"You did? How did you manage that?"

"She was getting something out of her car just as I came back from the sheriff's office."

"Ah. How's Piper?"

"They arrested her for Trask's murder."

"Oh, no." Sarah paused. "Think they'll hurry up and arraign her this afternoon?"

"McVie seemed to think they'd wait till Monday."

"How can they do that?"

"I don't like it either, but McVie said if he were in the sheriff's shoes—"

"Oh, right. Piper's got no ties to the county. Nowhere to stay, either. A flight risk if there ever was one."

"I've been trying to contact the expensive celebrity lawyer my dad got for Piper, but he was in court this morning. I don't think Ubosi has been able to even look at the case yet." Then Fenway closed her eyes. Oh, right—her father had sent Ubosi's personal cell number. She needed to call him, and it had been much over ten minutes. Fenway would call as soon as she was off the phone with Sarah.

"You've got the weekend to do what you need to do."

"Not great timing, with me needing to get the truck to McVie's."

Sarah paused.

"What is it, Sarah?"

"You know you don't have to take this on yourself, Fenway. Ubosi is the best in the business. Piper might have to stay in jail for the weekend, but she won't stay much longer. He'll have her out by Monday. And if it goes to trial, he'll win."

Fenway sat at the same table where she and Nadine had been earlier. "I can't just sit here."

"But you *could* drive to Colorado. You're not doing Piper any good by sitting around Ruby Dunes, interviewing people with nothing to back it up."

"I can't just leave."

"And what will you do if someone you're interviewing confesses? Make a citizen's arrest? You don't have handcuffs or a gun. I'm assuming you don't, anyway."

Fenway was quiet for a moment. "I talked to McVie. He might come here after he gets off work today."

"If you leave now—"

"Then I could be at McVie's new apartment by eleven o'clock or midnight. But Piper and I were supposed to drive in shifts. I'm not sure I can drive ten hours by myself today."

"So stop at a hotel in Utah or near the Colorado border. You don't have to do it all in one go."

Fenway tightened her jaw. "I thought you said you had more information for me."

Sarah hesitated. "Okay, yes. You were telling me about Vaughn's new wife—Aurora Horn."

"Right. She was fighting with her mom about Vaughn. She said some things she regretted."

"Trask and Horn eloped two weeks ago. Mom wasn't invited. June thirteenth. The Love Express Chapel in Downtown Las Vegas. No mention of it on either of their Photoxio feeds or any other social media, though. The officiant was a reverend, not an Elvis impersonator, if you were wondering."

"I'm sure that's relevant to the murder."

"The one you're not supposed to be investigating?" Sarah's voice had a touch of saccharine sweetness.

"Uh—yeah."

"I'll tell you what *is* relevant to the investigation," Sarah said. "Vaughn Trask hadn't gotten around to making out a will yet. I'm still digging into his financial statements, but he's got savings accounts, stock portfolios, real estate holdings. He even bought cryptocurrency before it became popular. He's worth at least two hundred million dollars—and that's just what I've found so far."

A sharp intake of breath from Fenway. "I was thinking one of those starving artists killed Vaughn for five hundred bucks and getting screwed out of getting their art on the museum wall. Two hundred million—that changes things."

"And without a will, all that money goes to the wife."

"I should tell the sheriff." Fenway paused. "Where does Aurora Horn live?"

The clicking of a keyboard for a moment, then Sarah spoke. "Address is an apartment in Walker City, but I assume she stays at Trask's house."

"And where's that?"

"In a gated community about halfway between Ruby Dunes and the air force base. Golden Sands. They just put in a golf course. You know the type. Big houses with ten rooms no one ever uses."

"How did you uncover all this?"

"You don't think Golden Sands has a slick website and an online brochure?" Sarah cackled. "The model of mini-mansion he bought is called the *Camberley*. Not really my style. I would have gone with the *Royale*."

"A mini-mansion she'll get to keep."

"Along with two hundred million."

Fenway leaned back in the chair. The bartender was trying his best not to make eye contact. He'd probably gotten rid of her gin and tonic and didn't want to get yelled at. Not that Fenway was the type to yell at servers. For all she knew, Nadine could have finished her sixty-two dollar martini and headed upstairs to her room with Fenway's ten-dollar gin and tonic.

While Aurora Horn had two hundred million reasons to kill her husband, it seemed they had kept their marriage quiet, without so much as a mention on social media. Maybe another relative decided to get millions of dollars by killing him *before* he could get married, not realizing the ceremony had already happened. That was always a possibility.

"Trask have any other relatives?"

"A sister in Philadelphia. As far as I know, that's where she was yesterday, too."

"Parents?"

"Yes. Rural Montana. From a cursory web search, his father is quite involved with the Star Prophet church."

"Ah. That church is pretty insular, right? If Aurora is an outsider, that could explain why Trask and Horn kept their marriage quiet."

Of course, Aurora Horn didn't just have a monetary motive. Trask was sleeping with Nadine Ryeo regularly. Didn't seem like it even slowed him down to get married.

"Might as well send me the address of both Vaughn's house in Golden Sands and Aurora's apartment," Fenway said. "Where does she work?"

More keyboard tapping. "She works as an accountant in the financial services department of a car dealership near Walker City."

"Long commute from here. Gotta wonder how long she was thinking of keeping that job now. Married to a rich guy."

Sarah scoffed. "Listen to you. Right out of the 1950s."

"Seriously? Accounting for a car dealership?"

"Maybe she enjoys the work. Some people like accounting almost as much as you like your job."

Fenway raised an eyebrow. "I suppose. But come on—two hundred million dollars? And she keeps a job where she drives an hour and a half each way?"

"Perhaps she stays during the week in the apartment in Walker City."

"Maybe, but it seems weird."

"You can ask her about her career trajectory when you talk to her. I'm sending you the addresses right now. And the phone number for the car dealership, too."

———

Fenway maneuvered the moving truck onto the on-ramp for Interstate 15, back toward Las Vegas. She pushed the accelerator to the floor. The engine roared, complaining that the day was far too hot to do anything but stay parked in the shade. "Come on," Fenway muttered. "I've got to have you step up now." In the back of her head, her brain admonished her: McVie was paying for the moving truck by the mile, and a forty-mile round trip on top of being at least a day late would make a noticeable dent in his wallet when he was trying to make this move as economically as possible.

But he'd understand. Piper needed another prime suspect to emerge.

After cajoling the truck to ride smoothly at just above sixty miles an hour—and getting passed by a car that looked like her father's Porsche, but bright orange, going at least ninety—Fenway took her right hand off the wheel and tapped her phone.

The voice on the other end sounded rushed. "Suarez Imports."

"Is Aurora Horn in the office today?"

A scoff. "She's working from home. Her in-office days are Tuesday and Wednesday."

"Gotcha," Fenway said.

"I can put you through to her phone."

"No need. Thanks for your time."

Fenway, keeping one eye on the road, opened the text conversation from Sarah, and tapped on the address for the house in Golden Sands. The map application popped up. "Getting directions to 3225 Treasure Dunes Lane."

The next exit wasn't for a few miles, and the landscape was beige and tan and rocky and desolate. A little scrub brush. Mountains on the horizon, jutting into the sky. Fenway knew people who loved the desert, but she didn't count herself among them; maybe she'd been spoiled by the ocean or by living in Seattle, with its rain and constant verdant panoramas.

The road dipped and rose, but the rocky desolation didn't change. She rehearsed what she would say to Aurora Horn, fumbled her words, started again.

The phone announced the exit; she'd been on the interstate just over fifteen minutes. After a few turns, she steered the truck onto Golden Sands Parkway. A wrought-iron gate appeared in front of her.

Oh, of course. Gated community. She'd been so concerned with what she'd say to Aurora Horn, she hadn't thought of how she'd get through the gate.

A guard station on the left. Oh—it was one of those communities that had a person manning the gate. Fancy. And that would make it a little easier; she reached down and grabbed her badge out of her purse. Whatever she could do to get on the other side of the gate, she was sure her county ID would be a part of it.

Fenway pulled close to the guard station—

Oh no. The top of the moving truck wouldn't clear the overhand roof of the guard station—she was too close to the building. She braked hard, her grip tight on the steering wheel.

Fenway looked out of the truck's window; motion in the building. The man inside was waving his hands over his head.

"Back up, back up!" Barely audible through the closed window. Fenway checked her mirrors; no one behind her. She put the truck into reverse and backed up twenty feet.

Then the gate opened.

Ah. She was in a U-Move-It truck. The guard must have thought she was moving in. Fenway gripped the badge more tightly in her hand., then turned the steering wheel hard to the right, giving the guard house and its overhang a wide berth.

After two more turns, the last one onto Treasure Dunes Lane, she drove a quarter mile through a winding street dotted with mini-mansions with elaborate rock gardens on each side.

"Arrived," her app chirped.

Fenway started to pull the moving truck next to the curb, but at the last moment she thought better of it. She parked three houses down. No use having Aurora think Fenway had driven up in a moving truck.

She opened the door, and a blast of June desert wind blew her hair back. Fenway looked down at her clothes; they didn't exactly scream "law enforcement professional," but they'd have to do. She adjusted her sunglasses, jumped out of the truck, and closed the door.

The rock gardens glittered in the sunlight as Fenway walked down the sidewalk. Walking past three houses, with the layout of this ostentatious neighborhood, took longer than she thought. She finally arrived at the circular driveway in front of Vaughn Trask's house. No cars were in the driveway, but a four-car garage attached to the other side of the house—yet another driveway.

A mahogany front door with two small symmetrical glass panes at Fenway's eye height. She'd only seen a door this large on one other house: her father's.

Fenway reached out with her left hand and rang the doorbell. Deep, rich, bell tones; not a Westminster chime, but a beautiful, glittering melody. She gripped her badge tightly in her right.

So little movement, it was almost eerie. No breeze today, just the sun baking the earth. Not even a hum of insects, but a deep, quiet growl: probably the large air conditioners of these mini-mansions, keeping the four or five thousand square feet in each house cool. In the distance, the soft rumble of the interstate.

After a moment, she rang the doorbell again.

She checked the clock on her phone. 1:56 PM. If Aurora had gone out for lunch, she'd surely be back by now. Of course, she might be on a conference call—or maybe the auto dealership was one of those Big Brother-type places that made their employees stay on camera and automatically clocked them out if the computer detected no movement for two minutes or something equally draconian.

She stretched her hand out one more time.

The door swung open, and a white woman in a blazer, cream blouse, and faded burgundy-and-gold Arizona State University athletic shorts stood at the door. Her brown hair in a chin-length bob framed her narrow face, and her large brown eyes peered up at Fenway.

So this was Vaughn Trask's wife.

CHAPTER TWELVE

Fenway held up her badge.

"I expected you to be the package I ordered," the woman said. "Guess it hasn't arrived yet."

Fenway dropped her hand. "Aurora Horn?"

She nodded. "I thought I answered all your questions at the station."

Another person who thought Fenway was with the local sheriff. "Just a few follow-up questions."

"It'll have to be quick," Aurora said. "I've got a conference call in twenty minutes."

Right. Working from home. Business apparel on camera, summer comfort off camera.

"They're making you work today?"

Aurora pressed her lips together and swallowed hard. "Financial reports due for last quarter. Besides, working keeps my mind occupied."

"I'm so sorry for your loss," Fenway said. "I hope we don't go over too much old ground. The interview notes weren't entered into the system."

"Come on in before you let all the cold air out." She stepped aside and Fenway walked into the entryway.

High ceilings, and everything in a southwestern motif: lots of earthtones, angular lines, a corporate vision of wall tapestries and muted oranges and browns. Hardwood floors, not laminate. Fenway took a few steps forward and glanced into the kitchen: expensive appliances, marble countertops. A chef's dream kitchen, and it looked like no one had ever cooked a meal in it.

"Beautiful house," Fenway said, glancing into the living room. The orange and gray couch looked expensive and uncomfortable, but she walked toward it anyway: something about it seemed familiar. "I know you've still got the apartment in Walker City, but I figured you'd have moved in after the wedding."

Aurora followed Fenway into the living room and sat on an armchair that matched the upholstery of the sofa. "Look—we eloped for a reason. We were trying to find the right time to, uh, tell his family."

"Is that why you aren't telling your work about your marriage? Not even for bereavement leave?"

"Something like that."

Fenway sat on the sofa. "Vaughn's family is from a conservative religion, right? Don't want their son marrying an outsider?"

Aurora scoffed. "Oh, please. It's not because of that. It's because their son is rich and can do no wrong. They think I'm after his money."

"Do *your* parents know?" Fenway felt better that she already knew the answer to this question.

But Aurora hesitated. "Uh, yeah, I told her this morning. And— parent, singular. It's just my mom."

"Why wait to tell her?"

"Because she has a big mouth." Aurora scrunched up her face. "Look, maybe I shouldn't talk without a lawyer."

"Why would you need a lawyer?"

"I don't know." She tilted her head. "I already told you I have an alibi."

Fenway took out her phone, tapped on her Notes app, then scrolled through her grocery list. "I apologize, but I don't seem to have that in my notes. Can you..."

"I told the other deputy I was having dinner with a friend of mine. A co-worker. I got on the road at six o'clock. Our reservations were for seven thirty."

"You have a receipt?"

"My friend paid."

"But your server will remember you and your friend, right?"

"I guess so."

"What time did you get back home?"

"I got gas on the way back. Just a couple of exits from here. Credit card receipt said nine forty-five."

"Long dinner."

"A little over two hours. We had a lot to catch up on."

"Name of your friend?"

Aurora folded her arms. "Like I told the deputy, I'll keep her name out of it. With those receipts, you should have no problem confirming my alibi."

"Still gives you enough time to come back to Ruby Dunes before midnight."

Aurora cocked her head. "Midnight? Why midnight?"

Ah. Fenway's visual of Vaughn's rigor mortis told her he'd been dead for at least eight hours. But perhaps the M.E. hadn't made any kind of official determination or hadn't communicated the time of death to the next of kin. But that was a few hours ago; the investigation was young.

"Call it a hunch," Fenway said. "So tell me, why did you think his family would accept you in a month or two? What would change between now and then?"

"I don't think it matters now," Aurora said.

"Oh," Fenway said. "You said it was about money, not religion. You signed a pre-nup."

Aurora flinched.

"And the two of you were probably waiting for the paperwork before telling his family. They're the type who would want concrete proof, not promises that the agreement was in process."

Aurora's eyes flickered, then she cast her eyes to the floor. Fenway was right. She wanted to push more, but further prodding would probably get more resistance. And she wanted to keep Aurora talking.

Fenway thought for a moment, then decided to pursue a line of questioning eating at her—one that might surprise Aurora. "What were you really fighting about?"

Aurora blinked. "We weren't—what do you mean? When?"

"The last time you spoke to him," Fenway said, "it was at the museum, right? Just before you left to go have dinner with your friend?"

Aurora's face crumpled, then she dropped her head down. A sniffle, but then she looked up.

"He'd cheated on you before, Aurora. Was he doing it again?"

Her lower lip trembled.

"He was, wasn't he? I interviewed a woman in her early twenties, a blackjack dealer from Vegas. Does she sound familiar?"

Aurora gritted her teeth and stared at the wall behind Fenway.

"When did you find out about the cheating?"

"I—" Aurora's voice broke, and she crossed her arms. Whether she didn't want to break down, or whether she didn't want to give Fenway more to work with, it was clear Aurora wouldn't be speaking much more.

Ordinarily, Fenway would have kept pressing her, but she wanted to avoid Aurora calling the sheriff's office to complain. Then, for sure, Sheriff Jeffcoat would have words for Fenway. Maybe it would even get her on the suspect list. And it sure wouldn't help Piper's case. No, the next time Fenway talked to Jeff-coat, she wanted it to be on her own terms.

And Aurora had already given Fenway a lot of information. She had an alibi until nine forty-five—well, really, more like ten or ten fifteen by the time she could have made it back to the Cartwheel parking lot. She'd already told Fenway about her husband's infidelity. Aurora knew who the other woman was.

And there was the matter of a pre-nuptial agreement. Fenway guessed—especially if they'd rushed through it in their hurry to elope—that the terms were not in Aurora's favor. That might give Aurora a motive to kill her husband, especially if the pre-nup prevented Aurora from leaving the marriage with money. But Fenway was sure Aurora wouldn't provide any more information about what might be in that pre-nuptial agreement.

Perhaps more importantly, Aurora had exited the museum at around six o'clock—just after Fenway and Piper had. When Piper had dropped her purse and Fenway had retrieved her lip balm from rolling under a white SUV.

Ah—perhaps Aurora would answer another line of questioning —one that wasn't so emotionally charged.

"What kind of car were you driving last night?" Fenway asked.

Aurora furrowed her brow. "An Acura MDX."

"That's an SUV, isn't it?"

"Yes."

"What color? Black? Dark blue, maybe?"

Aurora scoffed. "In Vegas? You better believe it's white. Hard enough to keep cool here. I'm not getting a dark color. Besides, with the wind and sand? I'd never keep a black car clean."

"It's here? Parked in the garage?"

Aurora scowled, but she nodded. No, Fenway could tell that Aurora wouldn't let her see it without a warrant—and getting one would be out of the question.

Fenway got to her feet. She wasn't sure if the white SUV in the NNoV8 parking lot the evening before had been an Acura, but if

Piper's knife had gone under Aurora's SUV, it wasn't a stretch to think it could end up in Aurora's purse. "Thank you for your time, Ms. Horn. And, again, I'm sorry for your loss."

She walked to the front door and opened it herself, then felt Aurora's eyes on her as she walked across the circular driveway to the sidewalk. The front door closed firmly behind her.

Fenway wondered if Sarah could get her hands on that prenuptial agreement, if it even existed. If the terms were unfavorable to Aurora, the document might be enough to get the sheriff to consider Aurora as a viable suspect.

She walked down to the moving truck. A silver Lexus was parked behind it. Ugh. Fenway hoped the car didn't belong to one of these overzealous HOA types. She'd be moving the truck soon, anyway.

As she got closer to the Lexus, the driver's door opened, and a thin, tall, dark-skinned Black man in an expensive-looking tailored gray suit got out of the driver's side. She blinked. She'd seen him on TV before: Okpara Ubosi. His dark, piercing eyes were distracting, the focal point of his thin, gaunt, clean-shaven face. Short hair, a clean-cut low fade. He was good-looking, but not nearly as handsome in person as he was on camera.

"Fenway Stevenson?" he said. His accent wasn't quite British, but spoke of finishing school and a posh upbringing. That's right—he'd grown up in West Africa, according to the background information from the televised trial. Nigeria, wasn't it? He'd perhaps been upper class. From the looks of the Lexus, he still was.

"That's me. You're Mr. Ubosi, right? I think I saw you in the news on the Erik Zoltar case. Congrats on the acquittal."

Ubosi nodded and smiled, a disarming, friendly smile. "You're a bit of a celebrity yourself."

"Only in Estancia," Fenway said.

Ubosi shook his head. "Your little adventure in Los Angeles didn't escape my notice."

Fenway cleared her throat. "A return phone call would have been fine, Mr. Ubosi."

"Please call me O.K.," he said. "And I'm not here because I wanted to meet you, Ms. Stevenson."

Fenway raised her eyebrows. "No?"

He motioned to the house. "Your father paid me to represent Ms. Piper Patten in the murder of Vaughn Trask. I've just met with Miss Patten, and now I believe you're here for the same reason I am: this is the murder victim's residence."

"Don't you have investigators for this sort of thing?"

Ubosi smiled again. "Not when your father is paying me full whack."

"Full what?" Fenway said.

"Top dollar, as you Americans would say."

"Right." Fenway crossed her arms. "So how much do you know about Trask's wife?"

Ubosi nodded. "Married two weeks ago at the Love Express Chapel in downtown Vegas, Ms. Stevenson."

Fenway was impressed: Sarah's intel had been solid. "If I can call you O.K., you can call me Fenway."

"Am I to assume your presence means that you've already questioned the Widow Trask?"

Fenway nodded. "Sorry if I threw off your game, but, you know, I called you several times this morning."

"I wish you wouldn't undermine the defense's case, Fenway. I hate it when the people paying me for representation are disappointed in the outcome."

"Piper's my friend. I'm good at investigating." Fenway shrugged. "And as far as I can tell, we're on the same side. No reason you can't use my talents to your advantage."

Ubosi rubbed his chin. "I remember I was researching a case a few years ago for an automobile repair shop. I had to interview several employees, and I noticed the sign above the counter. It said,

'Auto repair: fifty dollars per hour. Sixty if you watch. One hundred if you help.'"

Fenway chuckled. "I'm not like the other girls. If I tell you everything I found out, I'll be saving you hours of time."

Ubosi narrowed his piercing eyes, studying Fenway, then sighed, walked around to the passenger side of the Lexus, opened the door, and motioned Fenway to get in. "Can I buy you a coffee? There's a terrible roasting company on the other side of the interstate. Overpriced, snooty, and poor quality. My treat. Especially if you will be saving me so much time."

Fenway walked to the moving truck. "I'll follow you. I get the heebie-jeebies in neighborhoods like this."

———

The moving truck couldn't navigate the coffee shop's small parking lot, so Fenway parked on a side street half a block away.

The coffee shop was decked out in an over-the-top nautical theme, with interior style choices of oars and pirate flags and life preservers. *Coffee Castaway.* Cute. Fenway picked up a smell of the over-roasted coffee beans masking a slightly sour odor. Ubosi wasn't kidding: the coffee would be terrible.

Fenway usually ordered a latte, but with the heat, she wanted something cold. She almost ordered an iced coffee. Then seeing the old coffee stains on the counter that no one had properly wiped up, Fenway reached down and plucked a soda out of the refrigerated drink section next to the counter. Ubosi selected a sparkling water and held out his credit card. Platinum, naturally.

Fenway took her soda over to a table in the corner with two straight-backed metal chairs. Didn't want to get too comfortable if she'd be giving Ubosi information: she'd have to stay alert, make sure that every detail was accurate so he'd be able to get Piper out. She thought back to a cop show she used to watch up in Seattle:

how many times had the prosecutor said, "Why didn't you tell me that?" And the detective responded, "I didn't think it was relevant!" And the prosecutor said, "Well, the killer's going free. Think it's relevant now?"

So Ubosi would get fully unfiltered Fenway, whether he liked it or not.

Coffee Castaway was mostly deserted: a lone laptop user worked at a high-top table on the other side of the café, next to a palm tree painted amateurishly on the wall.

Ubosi finished paying and walked purposefully over to the table, taking a seat. "So, Fenway, it seems you've gotten a head start on my team."

"What do you want to know first?"

"What do the police have on Miss Patten?"

Fenway opened the can of soda with a click and a pop. "Circumstantial evidence," she said, then took a sip. "Yesterday evening, Piper lost a knife her father gave her. An inscription on it."

"Do you have any idea how that happened?"

"She dropped her purse in the parking lot of the NNoV8 museum when we were leaving. A lot of stuff spilled out. I think it happened then."

"But you didn't see the knife fall out of her purse."

"I saw it in her purse before that, but not after—not that I looked for it."

"When did you notice it was missing?"

Fenway thought for a moment. "Piper noticed it was missing. Well—uh, let me tell you exactly what happened. We got back to the hotel room about eight thirty—"

"From the museum?"

Fenway shook her head. "No—hold on. Let me start at the beginning."

So Fenway told Ubosi, in excruciating detail, about everything: the walk to the museum, the two people who followed them through the last few exhibits—Stanley Schup and his wife. Then how Fenway had exited the exhibits to find Piper in a heated conversation with Vaughn Trask.

"And a woman recorded it on her phone," Fenway added. "I didn't get her name, but maybe she or the people she was with purchased a ticket by credit card. Might track them down that way."

"Our investigators *have* done this before," Ubosi said drily.

Fenway soldiered on with her story. Pulling Piper out the gift shop exit, then talking her down and going to the Mexican restaurant, ordering the margaritas—

"How many did you have?"

Fenway grimaced. "Three apiece. And they weren't small."

"Was Piper intoxicated?"

Fenway took another sip of the soda. "Neither of us got behind the wheel. Even so, I don't know if three margaritas in a two-hour period would be over the limit, necessarily. We weren't stumbling home or giggling uncontrollably."

Ubosi nodded.

Then back to the hotel. Fenway getting out of the shower to find that Piper was gone, and then, when she came back, helping her look for the knife in the parking lot.

"Did you walk next to the moving truck?" Ubosi asked.

Fenway pursed her lips. "We went *by* the moving truck. But it was dark. If there'd been a body lying on the ground between the concrete barrier and the truck, I'm not sure either of us would have noticed. I don't think I shined the flashlight there." She thought a moment, taking another drink of her soda. "But remember, Piper had already gone looking for the knife. She might have looked next to the truck."

Ubosi frowned. "That's what I'm afraid of."

Fenway furrowed her brow—then it hit her. "Oh, I see. You think the prosecution will say that instead of looking for the knife

—which Piper, they'll claim, had never lost—she scoped out loca-tions where she could kill Vaughn Trask."

"Something like that, anyway."

"Here's the problem with that line of reasoning," Fenway said. "Piper had never met Vaughn Trask before. She'd have no way of knowing that he was meeting his mistress at the Cartwheel Hotel that late."

Ubosi's head snapped up. "What? His mistress?"

Fenway nodded. "Yes. A woman named Nadine Ryeo who works as a blackjack dealer in Vegas. I interviewed her. And her mother showed up too. Not a big fan of Mr. Trask." She related her discus-sion with both Nadine and Sookie.

"Two additional suspects, one of whom expressed delight at the man's death. Interesting. Has the sheriff interviewed either of them?"

"I don't know, but I don't think so. Not the way either of them acted." Fenway tapped her chin. "Sookie was a little too gleeful when I told her Trask was dead. If she had killed him, I think her reaction would have been different. She would have at least *acted* remorseful to hear about his death. But I don't know her."

"Who else knows about the mistress?"

"I assume Trask's business partners, who all have secrets of their own at the Cartwheel. And, as I just learned, his wife knows, too. I was trying to get her to tell me about the details of their pre-nuptial agreement, but she was—or at least she acted—too upset to continue talking about it."

"Aurora Horn is in the house? Right now?"

"That's correct."

"Depending on the contents of the pre-nuptial agreement," Ubosi said, "Horn would have motive."

Fenway nodded. "She's got an alibi until about ten o'clock. And I don't know when the time of death was." She leaned forward. "But even though a bunch of people knew about Trask coming to see Nadine, Piper wasn't one of them. As far as she was concerned, he'd have no reason to come to the hotel or be on that sidewalk in the parking lot."

"Sidewalk in the—"

"The murder scene," Fenway said. "Blood spatter there would be consistent with the location of the stabbing, and then just enough evidence of drag marks to make me think the killer moved the body between the moving truck and the concrete barrier."

Ubosi leaned back, chin in hand. "It's a good point. Of course, the prosecution might say Piper left the hotel to go confront Trask, and ran into him as he was walking to the hotel."

"Less likely, though. And that particular location on the sidewalk?" Fenway took out her phone and scrolled to the pictures she'd taken earlier, then turned the phone so Ubosi could see.

"Ah. Fairly well hidden between those vehicles."

"Exactly." She scrolled to the previous picture. "And this is the blood spatter which makes me think it was right there."

Fenway sent Ubosi the photos of the murder scene, then he asked her questions for another hour. Fenway answered as completely and honestly as she could, all the way through discussing her interview with Aurora Horn. Finally, Ubosi drained the last of his sparkling water, set the bottle down carefully on the table, then leaned forward, resting on his elbows, and steepled his hands.

"I appreciate you speaking with me," he said slowly. "It's helpful."

"You're welcome."

"I would usually request that someone in your position doesn't investigate further," Ubosi continued. "Often, it's because amateur investigators do more harm than good."

"I sense a *but* coming."

"You've been on the prosecution's side of the law," Ubosi said carefully. "So I know you understand what will get the defense into trouble, and what can effectively poke holes in the prosecution's case. So as much as every fiber of my being is screaming against it, I won't tell you to stand down." He flicked his eyes to Fenway's face. "Not that you would listen to me, anyway."

"I might," Fenway said. "I want to do what's best for Piper."

"If you choose to continue, then contact me whenever you find something." He reached into the inside pocket of his suit jacket and pulled out a business card, then took a pen from his shirt pocket and scribbled on the back of the business card. "My personal cell-phone. If you give this to anyone else—especially the media or to anyone associated with district attorney offices in Nevada—I can and will make your life difficult. Even in California." He cocked his head.

"I understand," Fenway said. She didn't tell him her father had already given it to her.

"As far as the information you've uncovered so far, I can use much of this to discuss with the D.A., and I could use much of it at trial, assuming it goes there. If I follow up on your leads and uncover more, we might have enough for reasonable doubt. Particularly if the police aren't following up on other leads."

"But the circumstantial evidence doesn't look good," Fenway said.

"No. And we have no evidence of any kind, circumstantial or otherwise, that directly points to anyone else."

"But the mistress—"

Ubosi held up a finger. "The knife. The murder weapon. The prosecution knows it belongs to Ms. Patten." A second finger joined the first. "The argument in the museum lobby. If you're right about a woman recording it on her phone, the prosecution will find it." He wiggled his two fingers together, then his ring finger joined them. "And Ms. Patten has no alibi. You can provide coverage of some of the time in question, but you've admitted she wasn't in your sight the whole time—and she was in a building adjacent to the murder scene, which won't look good to a jury."

"And you're saying it'll be an uphill battle to get her out of jail?" Fenway asked.

"Assuming she doesn't accept a plea bargain—and assuming another suspect doesn't emerge—I expect this to go to trial." Ubosi got to his feet. "I've won with less. But I've also lost with more."

———

The side street where Fenway had parked the moving truck was a dead end, and navigating a three-point turn—which rapidly became a nine-point turn—in the narrow street with only the side mirrors to guide her was a harrowing experience. Fenway's back stuck to the seat through her shirt from the nervous sweat, not just from the heat. She almost bashed the truck into a pole, but at least there were no overhanging branches ready and willing to rip the roof of the truck off.

She finally got back on the interstate, heading back to the hotel, and contemplated her next move. Ubosi had seemed reticent to take Fenway's help at first. But after she revealed the information Ubosi didn't have—Trask's mistress and the pair of two-million-dollar life insurance policies—Ubosi had almost given his tacit approval for her to keep investigating.

The air conditioning had trouble keeping up with the oppressive heat of the late afternoon, and Fenway briefly worried if the heat would damage any of McVie's stuff in the back of the truck—or if the nine-point turn she just navigated had broken anything.

She took the Ruby Dunes exit, and the clock on the dashboard read 5:48. She'd spent most of the day looking for other suspects, and she'd spent a surprisingly long time in the coffee house with O.K. Ubosi.

Despite the information she'd uncovered, Fenway felt like she was spinning her wheels: Piper was still at the police station, or in a holding cell, or maybe she'd been processed by now. But no arraignment until Monday, probably. Poor Piper—what a terrible way to spend the weekend.

She turned into the oversize vehicles lot at the Cartwheel Hotel & Casino. It was close enough to dinner. Maybe another meal at the Mexican place. They didn't have lengua tacos like Dos Milagros, but the enchiladas looked good.

Next to the concrete barrier was a small Kia Rio.

And standing next to the Kia Rio was Craig McVie.

CHAPTER THIRTEEN

FENWAY'S HEART FLUTTERED WHEN SHE SAW MCVIE—AND immediately she was horrified she was so sweaty and gross. Of course, McVie was standing in the direct sun, in a black fitted shirt, tight on his biceps and across his chest, and khaki pants. He looked like a corporate shill at a tech convention. There was even a small logo on his polo shirt.

Then it hit her. This was his work uniform—or as close to a uniform as he had. That logo read *Payback Systems*.

He had been at work earlier in the day; this had been his first week on the job. And here it was—not even six o'clock yet, and he was here, in this parking lot, only about five hours since she had last talked to him. An hour flight from Denver to Las Vegas, and another hour to drive from the airport to Ruby Dunes. Maybe a little longer in that tiny subcompact. McVie would have barely been able to squeeze into it.

Oh no. He'd really gone to some great lengths to get here.

Fenway slowed the truck to a stop, put the truck in Park, then engaged the parking brake. She surreptitiously smelled her left armpit—not great, but she was expecting far worse. She took a deep breath. Would he be upset? Would he blame her for staying in town when her father's lawyer was willing to fight for Piper? She exhaled, opened the door, and climbed out of the truck cab. McVie had already walked to the truck.

"Hey, Craig—"

And he enveloped her in a hug.

"Oh."

"I'm glad you're okay," McVie said into her ear, and gently kissed her just below the temple. He squeezed her a little harder, picking her up so that her sneakers left the ground by an inch or two.

"But Piper—" Fenway began, and then the stress in her shoulders loosened and she relaxed into McVie's embrace. He smelled like hard work and travel, but underneath the hundreds of miles of airplane and rental car, there was his unmistakable scent. Fenway buried her face in his neck and felt like crying—relief, fear, sadness, anxiety. If she could just stop time and be here, be present in this moment for more than the few seconds they had.

McVie set Fenway down. "Sorry," he said.

"It's okay," Fenway said, smoothing down her T-shirt. "I needed that, too."

They stood, Fenway holding McVie's hand, his other arm wrapped around her back. "I left messages with a couple of my friends who work for Vegas P.D., but no one has contacts in Ruby Dunes. Is there anything I can do to help Piper? Maybe I can go talk to the sheriff?"

"I don't know," Fenway said. "Her lawyer is on it. That's where I was—meeting her lawyer at a coffee shop. I told him everything I found."

McVie raised an eyebrow. "You're investigating the murder?"

"As if you expected anything different." Fenway elbowed McVie playfully in the ribs. "Lots of circumstantial evidence against Piper. The murder weapon is her knife. There's a recording of her shouting at the victim in his museum from yesterday evening. And she doesn't have a good alibi."

"Aren't *you* her alibi?"

"She left the hotel room while I was in the shower, and after I fell asleep, I can't swear she didn't leave, either. I mean—she left in the morning when I was still asleep, and I didn't notice."

"But you know she didn't kill him."

"Only because I know her. You were right on the phone earlier —if I were the sheriff, there's no way I wouldn't have arrested her, given the evidence at hand." She dropped his hand. "But—I didn't ask you to come help me."

"Don't be silly, Fenway. Of course I'm going to help you and Piper."

"I thought you couldn't leave before five."

"When we got off the phone, I looked at last-minute flights to Vegas. The only available seat was on a flight leaving in an hour and a half—all the evening flights were booked." He, too, dropped his arms to his sides. "Then I talked to my boss. I didn't think he'd say yes, but I told him I started a week early as a favor to the company, and he finally said it was okay to take part of the afternoon off."

Fenway nodded. So what next? Did McVie rent that Kia Rio, or did he take a FlashRide? Was he hoping Fenway would leave Piper in Vegas and drive the truck the rest of the way? She tried to wrap her head around the logistics, then gave up. "So—what do you want to do now? Take the truck and get on the road?"

McVie cocked his head. "Um...well, I guess I could—"

"Just thought you might not want to drive ten hours straight through tomorrow."

His face fell. "Oh. Right, well, yeah. That makes sense. I guess I could hit a cheap motel in a few hours. I just thought maybe I could do something to help Piper. And spend a little time with you."

Fenway quickly reached for his hand. "I'm sorry. Jumping to conclusions. Just—I didn't expect you to come. At least, not this early. I thought maybe you'd wait to see what happened with

Piper." She ran her thumb over the back of his hand. "And the evidence is all circumstantial, but it's strong. I've got to dig a little more."

McVie gently squeezed Fenway's hand. "Since you're working on this murder investigation in an unofficial capacity, we could work together, at least for the rest of the day. I could be just as unofficial as you."

Fenway raised her eyes to meet McVie's. "Just like old times."

McVie smiled. "If it's okay with you, I'll stay tonight. I'm supposed to have brunch with Megan tomorrow, but I think I can move it to Sunday."

Fenway stepped forward and put her arms around McVie again, and he hugged her back. "I *am* really glad you're here."

A vibration on Fenway's left hip. "Is that a cellphone in your pocket?"

"I'm just happy to see you," McVie said, keeping his left arm around Fenway while pulling the phone out. He raised his eyebrows, then turned the screen toward Fenway. Sarah Summerhill. He tapped the screen.

"Hi, Sarah. What can I do for you?"

A pause.

"I just arrived in Ruby Dunes about fifteen minutes ago. And yes, she's right here." He took the phone away from his ear and tapped the speakerphone icon.

"Hey, Sarah," Fenway said.

"I've called you a few times. You didn't answer."

"Oh. I guess I left my phone in the truck."

"Wanted to let you know—the apartment that Aurora Horn is renting in Walker City?"

"Right."

"I went onto the SinCityRentals website. An apartment in her building is available for rent. I called the building manager and confirmed that it's the same apartment she rented."

"That's not too crazy. We thought she was moving in with Trask

—they are officially married, even if they haven't told their families."

"The building manager asked if I wanted to make an appointment to see the place tonight. I said I was calling for my boss, and that you could be there by seven-thirty."

Fenway furrowed her brow. "Why would I need to visit Aurora Horn's apartment?"

"You think she should be a suspect, don't you? And if she's staying in Trask's house—well, if they're married, maybe it's her house now—maybe she's left something in her apartment that could throw more suspicion on to her."

"Oh—she hasn't moved out yet?"

"Nope. The manager said he okayed it with her. If you find something, Piper could at least get released on bail."

"It's kind of a long shot."

"Do you have shorter shots?"

"I was hoping to talk to Trask's business partners. The museum is open for another half hour."

"Then I'll call back and see if the building manager can stay until eight."

McVie's eyes twinkled. "We can go together. Say we're looking at our first place."

Fenway frowned. "I don't know. It's a long time to be on the road."

McVie shrugged. "If I'm taking the moving truck on Saturday, I have to add you as a driver on this Kia anyway. And I couldn't do it at the car rental at the airport without you being there. Isn't Walker City only about ten minutes from the airport?"

"Yeah."

"Well, then," McVie said, "since we have to add you to the rental, we might as well stop in Walker City on our way."

Fenway pressed her lips together, then nodded. "Okay. But the museum comes first."

———

Fenway held the door open to NNoV8, and McVie looked at her out of the corner of his eye.

"I was here with Piper yesterday," Fenway said. "They might recognize me. And maybe not talk to me."

"You're the one with the badge."

"Don't you have a private investigator's license?"

McVie folded his arms. "You know a badge gets more people to talk."

"But if they recognize me from yesterday—"

"Fine. I won't argue with the door wide open." McVie walked in, then pulled his wallet out, his private investigator license in his hand. He walked up to the ticket agent; fortunately, the woman, in an aquamarine silk blouse, cat's-eye glasses, with her hair pulled into a severe bun, hadn't been there the day before.

"Are you ready to innovate?" she asked.

"Excuse me?" McVie asked.

Fenway elbowed McVie gently. "She wants to know how many tickets we want."

The woman gave McVie a small smile. "That's right."

Fenway eyed her suspiciously. Only thirty minutes before closing time, and yet they were willing to take two full-price tickets. She glanced around the museum; there was no sign that one of the co-founders had just been murdered.

"I'm—" McVie began, but Fenway elbowed him gently in the ribs. He looked at her, then she pulled out her badge and flashed it at the ticket taker. "Were you here yesterday?"

The woman pursed her lips. "No—look, I told the deputy earlier—"

"My apologies," Fenway said. "We need to talk to the co-owners, anyway. Mr. Schup and Mr. Shellwater. Are they here today?"

"*Doctor* Schup," the woman said. "And of course they are. You people told them they had to stay in town."

"Not everyone heeds our advice in our investigations when a crime has been committed," Fenway said. "Let's speak to Mr. Shellwater first."

"Of course. Let me get him for you." She rose from her chair behind the counter and turned toward a hallway behind her.

"Is there somewhere we can speak privately with Mr. Shellwater?" McVie said.

The woman looked at McVie over the top of her glasses. "This is a museum, not a conference facility."

"Surely you have a meeting room or a private office. Even a utility closet would work."

The woman nodded, still not addressing the issue, and disappeared down the corridor.

Fenway glanced at McVie. "Now what?"

"Now we wait."

They took a step back from the ticket counter. McVie swiveled his head to the left, taking in the doors painted black.

"I went on the website before coming here," he said. "Seems like a lot of tech-speak about blockchain and NFTs."

"Yep."

"Also seems like something Piper would have been excited about," he said.

"She was. I believe her complaints were about the execution. Seemed like a rip-off to her. Not really art."

A smile touched McVie's lips. "That sounds like her."

"And she was also ticked off that the museum was messy. Broken-down cardboard boxes. Packing foam. I even tripped over a black curtain that was on the floor in the middle of the spotlight room exhibit. It'll be a miracle if they don't lose a million-dollar slip-and-fall lawsuit."

"I can contact my friend at OSHA. See if he knows anyone in the Las Vegas unit."

"Sure," Fenway replied. "Couldn't hurt. Might make Piper feel better—though she might lose her investment."

"Her—her investment? She *invested* in this place?"

"With the bonus check you gave her."

McVie shook his head. "And here I thought she was smarter than me." He walked toward the counter, leaned forward, then craned his neck.

"See the woman coming back?" Fenway whispered.

McVie shook his head, then motioned Fenway to follow him.

"What are you—"

He put his finger to his lips, stepped around the counter, and walked quietly down the corridor.

Fenway's jaw dropped open. McVie was usually such a Boy Scout—now he was creeping uninvited down a hallway?

The museum building wasn't very large, and the corridor was narrow. A metal door on the left with a placard next to the door: *Electrical.* Fenway wondered if they ran the programming for the NFTs and the electronics in a server room onsite or in the cloud.

They walked past the door and stopped just before the corridor opened into a bank of offices. Voices further on: the ticket-taker in addition to a lower-register voice Fenway recognized as Brock Shell-water. On the right, another door, this to a smoked glass-encased office. The surreal natural light of the desert shone through the smoked glass; there must be a window in the office. And the plac-ard: *Vaughn Trask.*

McVie turned back toward Fenway and motioned with his head. He reached out and turned the door handle. A soft click and the door swung open.

They went inside and closed the door behind them.

Vaughn Trask's office. A desk in front of the large window. A monitor sat on the desktop with its back facing the door. An execu-tive leather chair behind the desk, and three chairs around a small round table, with an orange-and-red rug underneath it, the same motifs as in Trask's home. Against the near wall, a low bookcase, full of hardback books—business books, from a quick glance.

And it was hot. At least ten degrees warmer than the rest of the air-conditioned office. And she could still hear the voices of the other office workers down the hall; the office wasn't built to be soundproof.

She stepped forward to the desk and opened the center drawer. A keyfob—an Alfa Romeo logo on it. That must be the sports car she'd seen in the museum lot that hadn't moved.

A noisy computer fan. Fenway walked behind the desk—and there was the culprit, in both heat and noise: a Qasper PC tower. Top of the line, with its telltale metallic green finish. Fenway had seen the ads on online videos, and she had to admit the metallic green looked cool—it sure made the computer stand out. Piper said the metallic green just added cost to the machine, providing no tangible benefit; odd that she had such a soft spot for artistic sensibilities until it came to the tools she had to use.

The Qasper PC looked nearly brand new. Humming and whirring. Fenway raised her head: a monitor and keyboard on top of the desk—and a spot where a laptop would have been located. But the top-shelf PC had cables coming from the back in a tangle that looked like they might connect to the monitor and keyboard. Fenway reached out for the mouse to see if she could wake up the monitor, then hesitated. Fingerprints. But if the sheriff's office had already taken the laptop, they would have already assessed the office. Would have been the first thing she'd done if she were leading the investigation.

Fenway took out her phone and texted Sarah.

> Can you find out if the Correos County sheriff has taken Trask's laptop from his office at the NN0V8 museum?

Fenway hit the arrow and a low-pitched electronic ping signified the sending of the text. McVie glanced up.

"Sorry," Fenway whispered, and turned the volume down on her phone all the way.

A buzz in her hand; Fenway looked down. Sarah had given Fenway's message a thumbs-up.

McVie had turned away, examining the artwork on the walls, but there were no filing cabinets. Fenway waved to catch McVie's eye, then pointed under the desk. McVie walked around the desk and saw the noisy computer, then looked at Fenway, a question in his eye.

"The laptop is gone," Fenway whispered. "Maybe the cops took it."

"So what's the PC doing here?"

"It's really active." Fenway scratched her temple. "Since this museum is all about NFTs, maybe it's mining crypto?"

McVie's brow furrowed. "How does that work?"

Fenway opened her mouth, then closed it again. She thought for a moment, then whispered, "I'm not really sure. Piper would know, I bet."

McVie nodded, then walked around the desk again.

Another buzz in her hand. Sarah—already responding.

> Sheriff's office visited the NN0V8 museum at 9:34 AM. Removed 7 boxes of evidence. Not sure how big the boxes were or what was inside. CSI arrived 10:08, left 14:33.

Fenway rubbed her forehead. Maybe the laptop had already been gone, or maybe this noisy PC was Trask's main machine. But, with CSI being there over four hours, at least Fenway could be sure the museum's offices had already been fingerprinted.

She reached out and moved the mouse. Then clicked. Nothing.

Fenway got on her hands and knees. She took a deep breath and crawled to the tangle of cables. There, underneath the web, was a KVM switch; in one position, the keyboard, video, and mouse would control one PC; in the second position, it would control another PC. An old-school way to make a desk look like there's one computer, when there are really two.

The switch was about six inches wide and four inches deep, held a foot-and-a-half off the floor by the tension of the cords running from the front and back.

Fenway rolled onto her back, moving her head behind the switch. Monitor, ethernet, a USB remote plug she assumed was for the mouse and keyboard. And a thin cable plugged into a port labeled *Wired Remote*. Fenway followed the cable, and it ran mostly parallel to the monitor cord.

She pulled herself into a sitting position, then rose to her feet. Scooting herself around to the back of the desk, she ran her hands from the video cable coming out of the monitor until she found the thin cable next to it.

The thin cable ended at a circular black plastic case sitting on the monitor stand, about two inches in diameter and half an inch high. For a moment, it looked like part of the monitor stand itself. Fenway ran her fingers over the top of the case, and it gave slightly. She pushed—and there was a quiet click.

The monitor came to life.

Fenway rushed to the other side of the desk.

A spreadsheet. Or—no. It was a database, and it was updating live.

With dozens of names in the left-hand column. Fenway grabbed the mouse and scrolled—no, not dozens of names. Hundreds. Thousands.

She leaned forward. The first column was all names. Then another two columns full of a mishmash of characters—ten or twelve each. She scrolled up; maybe there were column identifiers at the top of this sheet. But no such luck. She scrolled a click to the right, the names going off-screen, but two more columns coming into view.

In the Column D, a percentage: 100%. And in Column E, another percentage: 51.0%. And Column F: *Complete*.

That was odd.

She scrolled down. Row 1571: Column D read 97%—now 98%. Column E, 49.3%. Column F: *In process.*

The percentages of Column D fluctuated. Further down, the percentages of Column E uniformly lowered: 48.3%. A hundred rows farther down: 46.7%. Fenway kept scrolling. Around Row 3100, the percentages of Column E dipped into the teens. More scrolling: Fenway got to Row 5000, and both percentages were at zero. As the rows went down, Column F changed from *In Process* to *Not Started.* And Columns B and C changed from the gobbledygook character strings to *To Be Assigned.*

She scrolled up to an entry where Column D was at 99.8% and Column E was at 24.3% She watched as Column D notched up to 100%—then Columns B and C flashed. Were those different character strings? And Column E popped up to 25.1%.

Questions swam in her head. What did those columns represent? Why did Columns B and C just change? If only she had labels for the columns. How many rows were there, anyway? And the names in Column A: who were they? And what did it all mean?

Fenway scrolled down, and scrolled and scrolled and scrolled, until finally a wash of white hit her vision. She scrolled back up: the last entry was in Row 9178.

And unlike the preceding rows, Columns B and C had no character strings, nor did they say *To Be Assigned.* Instead: *Not applicable.*

Columns D and E were both 0%.

And yet Column F read *Complete.*

That was even stranger. 0%, nothing assigned in the second and third columns, and yet it read *Complete* rather than *Not started.* Fenway scrolled to the left. What was the name associated with this final entry?

She blinked.

Orlando Lockberry.

CHAPTER FOURTEEN

Fenway grabbed her phone and took pictures of the screen, then scrolled up and took another picture. She got a snapshot of the first few rows, all at 100% and 51.0%, then a few of the rows where a change in percentages from one to the next was visible.

McVie stopped looking around the rest of the office and moved to stand behind Fenway. He furrowed his brow.

"I don't know what it means either," Fenway murmured, "but the computer is crunching this. It means something."

"Why didn't the cops take the PC?" McVie whispered back.

"Maybe they only thought the laptop was relevant. Maybe the other owners convinced them that the PC needed to be on for the business. I don't know. But look." She scrolled to the bottom and pointed at *Orlando Lockberry*.

"Am I supposed to know that name?"

"The desk clerk at Cartwheel Hotel & Casino. He's one of the artists whose NFTs are featured in the exhibitions here. He's the only one with physical artwork on display." Fenway peered at the screen. "In fact, one of the early press releases for this museum said there were more than six thousand artists taking part. I wonder if this is the list of artists."

"So, what's the other stuff?"

"I don't know. The columns don't have headers or labels." She pointed at the PC. "But that computer is the most powerful thing on the market right now, and it's working like crazy. And these percentages are going up, a little at a time. When this column"—she indicated Column D with her index finger—"hits 100%, it starts over, and it looks like Columns B and C switch to another set of characters. It looks like the whole thing stops when Column E hits 51%. That's when Column F switches to *Complete*." Fenway rubbed her forehead. "I'll send these to Dez and Sarah, but I bet Piper could figure this out fast."

"Why don't you see if that hotshot lawyer your dad hired can have another meeting with his client?" McVie asked. "You might not be able to speak to Piper, but they'd let him talk to her."

"And I can give Ubosi these screenshots to show Piper and see if she knows what they mean."

"If he's as good of a lawyer as his reputation suggests, maybe he can even bring you with him."

Fenway nodded.

Voices outside the door.

Fenway jumped, then leaped forward and hit the button on the KVM switch again. The monitor went black. McVie calmly stepped around the desk and pulled out a chair at the round table and sat, coolly folding his hands in front of him. Fenway followed suit, although she felt her pulse race and a bead of sweat skate down between her shoulder blades.

The door opened, and the woman who'd been at the front counter stuck her head in, then frowned.

"What are you doing in here? You're supposed to be waiting in front."

"That's not what the guy in the teal polo shirt told us," McVie said, a confused note in his voice.

"What guy?"

"He came in just as you went in the back. He asked what we were doing, and I said we were there about Mr. Trask. Then he asked why we weren't waiting in his office. So here we are."

"Wait—a museum visitor said that, and you just assumed you could come back here?"

"A visitor?" Fenway frowned. "He looked like an employee to me." The lie came easily to her lips.

The woman's frown turned into a scowl. "You can't be in here. Besides, Mr. Shellwater is too busy. He can meet with you tomorrow morning."

"Oh," Fenway said. "I would have thought that his insurance company would want us to sign off so he can get his claim approved—"

"Margaret, it's okay," said a voice from outside the door. "Go back to the ticket desk."

"But they're—"

"It's okay," the voice repeated.

Margaret's head popped back out of view, and the door opened wider.

Brock Shellwater appeared, still with slicked-back light brown hair and bushy eyebrows, as well as the ill-fitting suit jacket he'd been wearing earlier in the sheriff's office break room. "Now, listen, you were in this room for half the day already."

"Not me," Fenway said. "CSI." Though she didn't know who from law enforcement had visited.

"Whoever it was, they were with the cops. And we're just trying to run our business here."

"I'm familiar enough with life insurance payouts," Fenway said, "to know you and your business partner won't collect on the multi-million-dollar policy you had on Mr. Trask unless you're cleared of wrongdoing in his murder. And insurance companies love to have excuses not to pay."

Shellwater smacked his hand against the doorframe and swore

under his breath. "I *told* Stan we should have come clean about the life insurance policies."

"Yes, because now it looks like you have something to hide."

"What happened to Vaughn was a tragedy," Shellwater said through gritted teeth. "But believe me, he was worth more to us alive, if you're going to accuse us of a financial motive."

"How so?" Fenway raised her eyebrows. "The museum doesn't look like it's making a profit. Certainly nothing close to giving you and Dr. Schup two million dollars apiece."

"There's a lot more that goes into the valuation of a private museum than the number of visitors," Shellwater said.

If the constantly updated database on Trask's computer was any indication, there was a lot more that went on than the police knew about. Fenway thought about mentioning the odd spreadsheet—and the superpowered PC under the desk—then thought better of it. She wasn't in a position to confiscate the PC; that was something the sheriff's office should do. And if she let Brock Shellwater know she suspected something strange with the PC, she was willing to bet the PC would magically disappear.

"Walk us through this valuation process," McVie said.

Shellwater folded his arms. "We've got dozens of investment experts who have assured me that what they recommend makes sense. I've got the capital to make the outlays, and I expect this to be quite lucrative for me."

Fenway raised her eyebrows. "Hard to do when you're currently bleeding money."

"We'll have investments paying off soon enough." Shellwater held the door open. "Without Vaughn, it'll be harder to make those investments come to fruition."

What investments was Shellwater talking about? Fenway assumed Shellwater was confident that if the police looked into his investments, the financial information would corroborate his story. But Fenway knew numbers could be manipulated.

If only Piper were here to look into Shellwater's investments.

Sarah could do some of the digging, but for sniffing out finance information that was misleading or falsified, Piper was second to none.

"Now," Shellwater said, "I've been more than accommodating up till now. You and the police have more questions, talk to my lawyer."

———

Outside the museum, walking back to McVie's rented Kia in the oppressive heat, Fenway pulled O.K. Ubosi's contact in her phone and called him.

"Good evening, Fenway."

"Hello, O.K.," Fenway responded. "I'm sending you over some information I got off the PC in Trask's office at the museum."

"The office—" Ubosi frowned. "How did you get in there?"

"We asked," Fenway said.

"We?"

"I have—" Fenway almost said *my boyfriend*, but then decided to be more professional. "I have a private investigator who flew in this afternoon."

A sigh. "Spectacular. You know I have my own investigators working to free Ms. Patten."

"I'll send you the screenshots I took," Fenway continued, ignoring Ubosi. "Piper might know what they are. Some sort of database that was updating live. Maybe you can meet with her this evening and ask."

"I'm on my way back to Las Vegas," he said.

"And that's where we're going, too," Fenway said. "Well, the airport, anyway. Can you see if you can meet with Piper around—I don't know, maybe nine o'clock? Nine-thirty?"

"On a Friday evening?"

"I know it's inconvenient," Fenway said, "but I also know you have a reputation for going the extra mile for your clients."

Another sigh. "I'll contact the sheriff's department to see if I can arrange it," he said. "But on a Friday evening, I wouldn't expect much."

"Fourth amendment," Fenway said. "Right to consult with one's attorney."

"Within a reasonable time frame," Ubosi said.

"There's nothing unreasonable about a Friday evening when Piper's in a holding cell in the sheriff's office."

"Sometimes I don't think rich clients are worth it." Ubosi sighed.

Fenway was silent for a moment as she could almost hear the gears turning in Ubosi's head.

Finally he spoke. "Fine. I'll call the sheriff's office and insist on a meeting with my client this evening. But I need to grab some dinner first. I'll try to be there at nine thirty."

"Thank you, O.K."

———

Thankfully, no one stood in line at the rental counter, and Fenway had her driver's license in her hand when she and McVie stepped forward to the agent's workstation. Ten minutes later—and an extra ten-dollar-a-day charge—the agent added Fenway as an authorized driver. Walking back to the parking garage, Fenway glanced at her watch. "We've got about forty-five minutes to make it over to Walker City to Aurora Horn's apartment."

"Plenty of time." McVie grinned, but Fenway saw the tightness in his shoulders, the creases in his forehead.

"Is everything okay?" Fenway asked.

"This is stressful, that's all." They got to the rental car and McVie tapped on the fob to open the doors. "I wasn't expecting to work this week, I wasn't expecting to stay in a hotel, and I wasn't expecting to fly to Vegas to get my rental truck."

Fenway nodded as they got in. She wanted to be sympathetic,

but this was no picnic for her, either. The seventeen-hour drive would have been painful enough without the complication of Piper's arrest for murder. "What's the building manager's name?"

McVie started the ignition. "Javier Romero. Seemed helpful on the phone."

"Of course he does. He wants to rent the place out right away. And with Aurora being all the way back in Ruby Dunes, it's easier to get her permission to get in and out of the apartment." Fenway's stomach rumbled. "Almost eight o'clock. Should we stop and eat something?"

"Let's make sure we're not late. I don't trust Vegas traffic."

Sure enough, the freeway was bumper-to-bumper, even this late in the evening. The sun had dipped behind the mountains, and the twilight half-darkness shrouded the road. McVie tried to find a radio station, but every time he changed the channel, a commercial was playing. Finally, he switched it off.

They passed a few minutes in silence, inching along the freeway. The engine noise wasn't enough to replace conversation, and a sense of awkwardness crept up Fenway's back. Finally, she cleared her throat. "Were you able to talk to Megan this week?"

McVie grunted. "Only briefly. She was always running out the door."

"Oh. Does that mean she made friends?"

"I don't know. She wouldn't tell me much." He sighed. "I expect it at this age, but it doesn't make it any easier."

Fenway nodded, and the brake lights ahead dimmed as the traffic started moving. "And how's Amy?"

"Taking her mid-life career change well, I guess."

"That's right—she sold the real estate company." After her new husband passed away—although he'd left Amy enough money that Fenway was surprised she chose to work again, particularly after selling her business.

"Now she's the chief operations officer for a loan services organization. Change of pace. She says it's good for her."

Oh—they'd talked. Fenway grimaced. Of course they'd talked. They still co-parented Megan, for one thing. But Fenway didn't want to talk about McVie's ex-wife. "Besides the strict time clock thing, is the job okay?"

"Still getting my feet wet. Seems like Payback Systems has a lot of unnecessary red tape. Of course, coming from a two-person P.I. firm, I suppose everything would seem overly bureaucratic."

"Yeah." Fenway shifted in her seat. "How much longer?"

"I should be there at least a year. We'll see what happens with Megan after she graduates. Maybe she'll want to come back to California."

That wasn't what Fenway meant by *how much longer*, but she figured out how to respond. "Or maybe she'll decide to go to college two thousand miles away. Gotta let her go sometime." The words were out of Fenway's mouth before she could stop herself— and she heard how judgmental they sounded. "I mean, uh, just that she'll be an adult, and if she wants to go far away…"

"Yeah," McVie said noncommittally.

The traffic cleared over the next mile, and soon they'd accelerated until they were going the speed limit.

They'd only been apart for a week, but Fenway and McVie weren't clicking yet—and they were both distracted by their own concerns. McVie was helping Fenway despite his work and moving problems, but they were both stressed. Not an ideal way to start their long-distance relationship.

Fenway opened her mouth to talk, but nothing came out. A mile went by, then two, then Fenway's phone buzzed. It was Dez.

"Hey, Dez." Fenway tried not to let the relief show in her voice. "Everything all right?"

"Heh," Dez said. "I'm hiding out in your office with the door closed."

"Hiding?"

"From Sheriff Donnelly," Dez said. "She and the ADA had a shouting match this morning."

"Why?"

"Pondicherry doesn't think the evidence against George Pope is strong enough in the Mathis Jericho murder."

Fenway rubbed her chin. "Yeah, well, I don't either. But I know how much Donnelly wants that case to be wrapped up." And Fenway knew she didn't believe Pope had committed the second murder. She closed her eyes and saw the text from Donnelly in her head.

Congratulations on solving the two murders

"And now Donnelly's stomping around because you're not here," Dez continued. "She wants you on this case right now. Wants it to be your number one priority."

"I don't report to her," Fenway said reflexively.

"Yeah, well, try telling *her* that."

"Okay—thanks for the warning."

They said their goodbyes just as McVie's phone announced an upcoming exit at Walker City Boulevard.

"Good, we're almost here." It was a banal thing for Fenway to say, but she had to break the awkward silence.

"We'll have to hurry to get back to the county jail by 9:30 to meet Ubosi."

"This'll be quick." Fenway gazed out the window at the businesses on Walker City Boulevard: souvenirs, pawn shops, check cashing, smoke and vape. No wonder Aurora wanted to stay at her husband's house.

Five minutes and three turns later, McVie and Fenway found themselves in a residential area with fourplexes and apartment buildings. The GPS on McVie's phone dinged. *"The destination is on your right."*

McVie parallel parked between a decade-old Jeep covered in dust and a black Infiniti with chrome wheels, then turned off the ignition. "How do you want to play this?"

Fenway shrugged. "Your idea earlier? That works for me. We're moving in together. Looking for our own place."

"Gotcha." He got out of the car and Fenway followed suit.

The apartment complex was a two-story building, all right angles with cheap-looking windows and gray paint. A gutter hung at a slight angle along the flat roofline.

"Seen better days," Fenway said.

"I can ask the building manager about those gutters," McVie said.

"We're not *really* moving in together, Craig. I don't care about the gutters."

McVie looked at Fenway out of the corner of his eye. "I know, Fenway. But we can't very well go snooping in Aurora Horn's apartment while the building manager is hovering over us. That means I'll have to get him out of there. And you know this investigation way more than I do. You have a better chance of finding what you need if you're in the apartment by yourself."

"Oh. Right. Good point."

They walked across the gravel garden area to the business office. The concrete walkway was cracked, the sun low in the sky but beating on the front of the apartment building. McVie reached around Fenway and opened the door. A burst of cool air escaped, and Fenway walked through the doorway.

The office was obviously a repurposed apartment. Low-pile carpet, in jewel-toned burgundy-and-beige, ran through the living room. Where a sofa and coffee table would ordinarily be sat a scratched maple wooden desk that looked to be at least thirty years old. A wiry man with olive skin, perhaps twenty-five years old with a thin mustache, rose from behind the desk. His wide brown tie wavered as he stood and smoothed down his short-sleeved goldenrod dress shirt.

"Mr. McVie?" he asked, his voice deep and strong.

"That's me," McVie said. "We were interested in looking at the apartment."

The skinny man reached out his hand. "Javier Romero, building manager. We spoke on the phone. Let's head up there."

McVie shook the man's hand. Fenway noticed the building manager didn't even acknowledge her. She was annoyed, but it was probably better that he didn't pay her mind—she could slip unnoticed around the apartment.

Romero led them back outside into the sun, then turned the corner and went up a flight of cement stairs. A green door that clashed with the gray of the building stood at the top of the step, and Romero had his key out as he approached.

The front door was open a few seconds later and McVie and Fenway entered the apartment, a mirror image of the business office. Fenway looked down; the carpet here was tan. A blue sofa was against the interior wall, a black rectangular coffee table in front of it. Fenway glanced around: the apartment was sterile in its cleanliness.

Fenway walked into the kitchen. The countertop tile was beige, the grout clean but starting to wear. The appliances were spotless but aged, and the eggshell paint on the cabinets had faded. A silver trash can, its cover closed, sat at the wall to the right of the sink.

"I think you'll find we're conveniently located," Romero said. "The Strip is only ten minutes away—"

"I'm a little worried about the gutter that's hanging down," McVie said.

Fenway glanced on the counter. A pile of mail.

"The gutter?" Romero said.

Keep him talking, Fenway thought. Romero and McVie went into another room, McVie expressing concern.

She stepped forward and leafed through the pile—six or seven pieces.

A credit card offer. Another credit card offer. An ad for window blinds. One for air conditioning service. A water bill.

The front door opened, and McVie and Romero stepped out of the apartment.

She walked around the apartment. A double bed was against the wall in the bedroom, perfectly made, like no one had slept in the bed for at least a few days. Fenway opened the closet: a few items hung inside, but the styles were out of date. Aurora had probably moved most of her life out of this apartment already. Fenway quickly opened drawers, but most were empty; a few had linens or clothes in them. No file cabinets or computers; nothing that documentation could be in. She walked out of the bedroom, back into the kitchen.

Oh—she had missed a manila envelope next to the microwave. It was torn open, nine by twelve inches. Fenway picked it up. Empty.

The return address: Bowen, Toti, and Nelson, Attorneys at Law. A stamp: *Open Immediately.* The postmark was a week ago. It was addressed to Aurora Horn.

Fenway put back the envelope. Hmm. She pulled her phone out and searched for Bowen, Toti, and Nelson, then clicked on the first result.

The Premier Family Law Firm in Southern Nevada.

She tapped on *Practice Areas.* Family law. Wills and trusts. And there it was: Pre-nuptial Agreements. She tapped, and a new page loaded. She saw the word "pre-nuptial" and Fenway pressed her lips together.

Where might the contents of the envelope be? Maybe Aurora had taken it with her to Vaughn's house.

She picked up the envelope again and examined the top. A rip that went halfway along the edge, then went down about an inch to the right of the clasp. That suggested Aurora had opened the manila envelope quickly. Perhaps in anger. Maybe Aurora had been expecting the package—and didn't think she'd like what the envelope contained.

Considering the legal practice areas of Bowen, Toti, and Nelson, Fenway would bet that the contents were Aurora's official copy of the pre-nuptial agreement. And the fact that the package had gone to Aurora's apartment instead of the house she shared with Vaughn Trask? Maybe that had made her angrier.

So—if the envelope *did* hold the pre-nuptial agreement, and if Aurora didn't like what it said, then what would she have done with it?

Fenway walked over to the trash can and stepped on the foot button. The top of the can popped up.

A sheaf of papers on top—maybe ten or twelve sheets in total. The sheaf had been ripped in half.

The title on the first torn page: *Pre-Nuptial Agreement, State of Nevada.*

CHAPTER FIFTEEN

Fenway reached into the trash and pulled out the sheaf of papers, taking care to pull both halves of the ripped papers out. Something sticky was on the back page of the bottom section. Fenway looked around the kitchen. The paper towel roll was next to the sink, and she brought the sheaf over and set the paper face down on the counter.

She kept an ear open for the front door opening again. Fenway didn't have an evidence bag, but she opened a kitchen drawer for a zippered plastic bag. A small box of gallon baggies sat in the third drawer from the bottom next to the refrigerator. She put both halves of the stack of papers inside, zipped the top closed. She unzipped her purse—obviously too big to fit.

The front door opened.

"I assure you it can pass inspection," Romero said.

Shit, shit, shit. Fenway hurriedly folded the plastic gallon-size baggie and pushed it into her purse.

"We'll think about it," McVie said. "Hey, honey?"

"I'm here," Fenway said, shoving the baggie down into her purse —but the corner stuck out awkwardly.

"Just checking out the kitchen." A note of warning in her voice; hopefully McVie could delay Romero a moment longer—

"That gutter looks like it could go in the next high wind."

"It's something we can fix quickly," Romero added, still from the living room.

There. Not too elegant, but at least the baggie wasn't sticking out.

Much.

Fenway put her purse over her shoulder and her forearm over the top of the baggie. Ugh—her spy skills left a lot to be desired.

"What do you think otherwise?" Romero said.

"It's got potential," Fenway said, walking from the kitchen to the living room.

Romero stood in front of the coffee table; McVie had his hands on his hips.

"Some cute things," Fenway said, letting a slight note of disgust creep into her voice. "I don't know—the layout's okay. Kitchen is functional. Enough room for a one-bedroom, but I was hoping for something with a little more character."

McVie held his hand out. "We'll be in touch, Mr. Romero."

Romero shook McVie's hand, disappointment showing on his face, then McVie turned, grabbed Fenway's hand. "Ready to go?"

She pushed the purse with her elbow behind her back, the plastic baggie sticking farther out of the top. "Sure, sweetie." Ugh. As odd as *honey* sounded to her ears, *sweetie* tasted equally weird on her tongue.

They hurried down the concrete steps and went back out to the car, not waiting for Romero to lock the door behind them. "I should drive," Fenway said.

"Why?"

"I found the pre-nup in the garbage."

"You snooped through Aurora's trash?"

Fenway walked around the driver's side, opening the door and letting out a blast of hot, stale air. "I know it's not admissible in court against Aurora Horn, but it can help establish reasonable doubt if Piper goes to trial."

"And what do you want me to do while you're driving?"

"Oh, *honey*, you can read through the pre-nup." She sat, the steering wheel burning to the touch.

McVie got in, chuckling. "Yeah. We're not really a *honey* and *sweetie* couple, are we?"

"I don't know what you're talking about, pookie-bear." Fenway grinned and patted the baggie with the pre-nup. "See what made Aurora Horn so mad she ripped the document in half. It might be the same thing that made her angry enough to kill Vaughn Trask."

"Why me?"

"Because—" Fenway paused and turned on the ignition. "Because you know the legalities of this kind of stuff in a way that I don't."

"Because I've been divorced."

"Um, yeah. You've gone through legal documents like this. I haven't."

"Gotcha," McVie mumbled. He must have known Fenway's request made sense, though he obviously he didn't like being reminded of Amy and his failed marriage.

The drive back to Ruby Dunes took nearly an hour. The sun, which had dipped behind the western mountains, grew weaker and weaker, and McVie had to squint to make out some of the text on the page. Finally, as they crested a hill on Interstate 15, McVie let out a deep sigh.

"What?" Fenway turned the headlights on.

"The pre-nup. Not exactly structured fairly."

"I take it Aurora got screwed?"

"It protects her if Vaughn Trask cheats—"

"Which he was doing."

"—but a few paragraphs later, it says if Aurora cheats, no matter whether Vaughn cheats or not, he pretty much gets everything."

Fenway drummed her fingers on the steering wheel. "You're right; that doesn't seem fair."

"I don't know Nevada law, but I think this is unenforceable."

"Aurora might not have known that."

McVie nodded slowly. "I guess we need to let someone know." He slipped the torn pages back into the gallon baggie.

"Like the sheriff." Fenway clicked the turn signal to take the Tenth Avenue exit. "And I think we can still make it on time to the county jail. O.K. Ubosi is supposed to be there in fifteen minutes." She turned right at the bottom of the offramp, and a few moments later, Ubosi's silver Lexus came into view, parked next to the curb.

Ubosi got out of his Lexus, waiting as McVie and Fenway pulled up behind his car. Fenway reached into the back seat, grabbed her purse, and put the baggie into it.

McVie got out of the car, and Ubosi watched him carefully.

Fenway got out, closing the door behind her, and motioned to Ubosi with her chin. "Craig McVie, this is O.K. Ubosi."

The two men shook hands. "This your private eye?" Ubosi asked.

"More or less," Fenway said. "He uncovered a couple of things."

"I guess you two have been busy."

"As a matter of fact, we have," Fenway said, pulling the baggie out of her purse.

Ubosi raised his eyebrows.

"The pre-nuptial agreement between Vaughn Trask and Aurora Horn."

Ubosi examined the baggie. "Obviously ripped in half. I assume it's signed. This is the official version."

"Correct. Notarized on the last page."

Ubosi opened the baggie, took out the first torn page, and skimmed it. "Where did you get this?"

Fenway shook her head. "Anonymous tip."

Ubosi nodded. "I see. Anything I should know about what it says?"

"If Trask is unfaithful to the marriage," McVie said, "Aurora gets sixty percent of the joint assets after the marriage and twenty percent of Trask's assets before the marriage. That last percentage goes up the longer they're married."

"That seems more than reasonable."

"But," McVie continued, "if Aurora is unfaithful—even if Trask is also unfaithful—Aurora only gets ten percent of the assets that Trask brought to the marriage *after* the date of the wedding, and none of his assets before."

Ubosi rubbed his chin. "That doesn't seem fair, but only if Aurora was planning on being unfaithful."

"Or if she'd already been unfaithful," Fenway pointed out. "And we know Trask was sleeping with Nadine Ryeo."

"And she didn't catch this before she signed it?"

McVie shrugged. "It's buried in the middle of another paragraph that discusses definition of assets—some of the driest legalese I've ever read. Easy to see how Aurora could have missed this when she signed it. Especially if the adultery clause were added in late in the process." He clenched his jaw. "Amy tried that with me. It's a good thing I read stuff."

Ah, yes, McVie the Boy Scout.

Ubosi rubbed his chin. "I don't suppose either of you have a bombshell to drop about Aurora's fidelity to the marriage."

"Not yet," Fenway said.

"We need to connect all the pieces to weave a believable tale to the jury," Ubosi said. "So, in order for us to use this torn document, we need the rest of the story."

"To demonstrate that Aurora Horn had a motive to kill Vaughn Trask. And needed to do it before Trask pushed for the pre-nup to be signed."

"The theory of the crime needs to be complete before a jury would consider reasonable doubt."

"Yeah, I get it," Fenway said. "Means, motive, and opportunity.

But I know Aurora's SUV was in the NNoV8 parking lot, and I'd bet Aurora's SUV was the vehicle Piper dropped her knife under."

"You'd testify to that?"

Fenway was quiet for a moment. "No. I'm pretty sure, but not a hundred percent."

"Then I can't put you on the stand." Ubosi looked at Fenway out of the corner of his eye. "Unless you really *did* see Piper Patten's knife go under Aurora's SUV."

Fenway shook her head. "No, and I don't want to do anything on the stand that'll call my credibility into question." She cocked her head. "But I *could* testify that Piper dropped her purse, knocking a lot of stuff out of it, right next to Aurora's SUV. Let the jury draw their own conclusions."

Ubosi pressed his lips together and shook his head. "That doesn't lead the jury to draw that same conclusion. You think that because you want your friend to be innocent. But that won't rise to reasonable doubt in a jury's mind. Worse, they might conclude you're grasping at straws."

Fenway sighed.

McVie tapped his watch. "It's 9:27. You need to get inside if you're going to talk to Piper."

Ubosi turned back to Fenway. "I'd like you to come in too."

"Good—I was kind of hoping you'd ask."

"I'm not doing it as a favor. You're observant, and you know Piper better than I do. She might talk to you in ways that she won't to me."

Fenway cocked her head at McVie. "You okay going back to the hotel?"

"Sure."

Fenway took a step forward toward McVie and put her arms around his back and pulled him to her. He bent down slightly and kissed her lightly on the lips.

They broke their embrace and McVie walked back to the car.

Ubosi chuckled. "I wondered where you had found a P.I. on such short notice."

"He's Piper's boss, too. I didn't have to promise him anything untoward." Fenway smirked at Ubosi as McVie drove away. "That's just a bonus."

"You Californians," Ubosi said, then put a serious face on. "You've done this before, right?"

"Done what?"

"Spoken to suspects being held before an arraignment."

"Mostly from the prosecution's side."

"So you know the police can't listen to conversations between a lawyer and his client."

"I know they're not supposed to. I know *I* haven't."

"With a couple of exceptions," Ubosi said, "the jails and prisons haven't listened to my conversations with clients. I've only caught them once, and the judge threw out the case. But I bring it up because everything up to where my client is brought in can be recorded—*and* used in court. And if I leave the room for any reason, then they can record and use that, too."

"So they're monitoring our comings and goings."

"Which means we need to keep our voices down. If what we say bleeds through the walls, they can't use it in court, but it might give them clues where to get evidence against Ms. Patten."

"That'd be hard to do, since she's innocent."

Ubosi cocked an eyebrow.

Fenway exhaled. "Yeah, yeah, I heard that as it was coming out of my mouth. Might be the most naïve thing I've said in the last year."

"As long as you keep all this in mind."

"I will." She ran her tongue over her teeth. "I took photos of that database, O.K. I'd like to show the rows and columns to Piper. See if she can make sense of it."

"If she's as good with cybersecurity as you say she is—and from what I've researched on her, she definitely is—then I think that's a great idea."

Fenway took her phone out of her purse and opened her photos app. She scrolled back and found the first photo she took, and zoomed in. A little blurry, but she could read everything onscreen.

She scrolled through the rest; the other photos were clearer.

"What questions do you want to ask her?"

"I want to know what we're dealing with. My team didn't know what the database was—not at first sight anyway—but they suspected a management console for some sort of remote access tool, and that sent their red flags up."

Fenway checked the time on her phone. 9:29. "Whatever you want to do, it's time for us to do it."

They walked up the sidewalk to the walkway that led to the front door, Ubosi in his tailored suit, Fenway in her shorts and T-shirt. She felt embarrassingly underdressed but didn't want to mention it to Ubosi; he'd know she had no other clothing options besides two other pairs of shorts and T-shirts. Besides, going to see Piper in jail wasn't like showing up in court.

They walked through the front doors of the jail, and a long counter ran down the side of the wall, a blue-uniformed deputy sitting behind the lone workstation about ten feet away. The woman's black hair touched her shoulders—and then she looked up, the monitor no longer obscuring her face.

"Nice to see you again, Deputy Bardot."

"Ah, Coroner Stevenson," Izzy Bardot said.

Ubosi raised his eyebrows.

"Deputy Bardot was kind enough to give me a ride to the sheriff's office this morning," Fenway said. "This is Okpara Ubosi. Piper's lawyer."

"Pleased to meet you." Ubosi nodded curtly.

"Long day, deputy?" Fenway asked.

"Mortenson called in sick," Bardot said. "I don't mind the overtime. Visiting hours are over, though."

"We're here to see my client," Ubosi said. "I cleared it with Sheriff Jeffcoat a few hours ago."

"And Coroner Stevenson?"

"I'm relying on her information to get a complete picture of the situation."

A smile touched the corner of Bardot's mouth. "Spoken like a true attorney." She rose. "Follow me."

Unlike the county jail in Estancia, there were no metal detectors. Bardot led them through an off-white door behind the workstation, and the dingy gray walls of the back offices greeted them. A large room, about twenty feet square, held five desks and a holding cell where Fenway expected to see Piper, but instead, a mustachioed white man with a deeply tanned face and a crew cut looked solemnly out at them.

Another door; this one was a much smaller room with another holding cell. Piper, now wearing an ill-fitting orange shirt and trousers, stood up from the bench on the side of the cell. "Fenway?"

"Piper!" Fenway said, not able to keep the relief and excitement out of her voice. She hurried to the bars of the cell. "You doing all right?"

"Fine," Piper said—then turned her head to face Fenway. Was that a black shadow under her eye, hidden by her long red hair over one side of her face?

"Deputy Bardot!" Ubosi's voice was sharp and deep. "What happened to my client?"

Bardot took a step back from the bars. "We had a drunk and disorderly brought in here. I guess she took one look at Ms. Patten and thought she was the one who slept with her—"

"I don't need to know the details. Have you taken steps to ensure my client's safety?"

Bardot nodded soberly. "We've separated them."

Fenway leaned forward, her forehead nearly touching the bars. "Piper, are you hurt?"

"Mostly my pride," Piper said, her voice with a hint of tremor. "The deputy took care of it fast. Mistaken identity, I guess."

Ubosi turned to Bardot. "We'll need a room to conduct our meeting. Somewhere you can't hear us."

"Got a conference room in the back," Bardot said. "Little small, but there are only three of you."

"I appreciate it," Fenway said, but Ubosi shot her a look.

Don't get too friendly with the enemy, his eyes fairly shouted.

"You should see the other chick," Piper cracked.

Bardot grunted. "After she punched Piper in the face, the assailant lost her balance, fell, and cracked her head on the bench. Lost consciousness for a minute. Had to go to the E.R. in Duncan Wells."

"Don't listen to her," Piper muttered. "I used my Jedi mind tricks."

Not the time for jokes, but Fenway suppressed a smile anyway.

Bardot stepped forward, key in hand, and unlocked the cell. "Follow me, everyone."

She walked past the holding cell, Piper following, then Fenway and Ubosi bringing up the rear. They went through an archway, then into a short corridor, where another industrially depressing gray door stood at the end. Bardot opened it, and the door creaked open. "All yours," Bardot said. "There's a panic button in there if Ms. Patten does any of her evil telekinesis on you, too."

CHAPTER SIXTEEN

Fenway turned on the light, and the room was suddenly ablaze with harsh fluorescent light, the buzzing bulbs possibly a couple of decades old. The metal table in the center of the small room was just big enough for four people, two on each side. Aluminum folding chairs.

"No expense is too great for this place," Fenway deadpanned.

Ubosi motioned to the far side of the table, and Piper sat. "I've seen worse," he said.

"And this room smells like Pine-Sol, not like feces," said Piper. "So that's an improvement over my previous digs."

Ubosi cleared his throat and set his bag on the table. "Ms. Stevenson, do you want to ask Ms. Patten..."

Fenway already had her phone out and was leaning over the table. "Have you seen anything like this before?"

"What am I looking at?" But Piper's eyes lit up. She knew.

"I took pictures of the PC screen from Vaughn Trask's office at the NNoV8 museum. I believe it shows a database."

Piper stared at the screen for a moment. "I take it the numbers were changing while you were taking pictures?"

"Right."

Piper glanced at Ubosi and pointed at Fenway's phone. "Can I hold it for a minute?"

"Certainly."

Piper took the phone from Fenway, peered at the screen, then enlarged the photo of the database. She zoomed back out, swiped to the next photo, zoomed in, squinted. She took almost two minutes scrolling, zooming, squinting.

"You know what this is?" Fenway prodded.

"From the first second I saw it," Piper replied, "but I didn't believe it."

"What is it?"

Piper pointed to the percentages. "These numbers weren't just changing—they were increasing, right?"

"Right."

"And these names." Piper pointed at the list of names on the left. "Do you know who these people are?"

"I assume they're artists who've agreed to have their art converted to NFTs," Fenway said.

"But you haven't confirmed it?"

Fenway glanced at Ubosi.

"We're working on it," said Ubosi.

Piper rolled her eyes. "Can I open up a browser on your phone, Fenway?"

"Uh, sure."

Piper bent over the phone, both her thumbs flying over the screen keyboard. Fenway sucked in a breath. This was like food and water to Piper. She'd been away from her laptop and all screens for almost a full day.

"Okay," Piper said. "The NNoV8 website has some content hidden—it's commented out—and I've already seen about a dozen of the names in the database that are in the invisible content. That pretty much confirms what I think this is."

"Which is what?"

"I've heard about unscrupulous NFT buyers doing this to artists on a one-to-one basis. But not something at this scale." Piper turned the screen around so Fenway and Ubosi could see it, although there was no understanding the whirls and squiggles onscreen. "A buyer offers to purchase a painting or a piece of digital art by an artist, but offers to buy the NFT, not the actual piece of art."

"I'm following you so far," said Ubosi.

"So the buyer asks the artist to use a particular piece of software to convert the art to an NFT. Then they offer to turn on the tracking for the NFT in the software, so the artist can determine where the artwork is displayed and when the sale will close. The software also gives payment information to the artist's bank account."

Ubosi was silent.

"It *looks* like a legitimate piece of software, because it does everything the buyer says it'll do: converts the NFT and tracks it. Nice interface—at least the ones I've seen."

"But it's not?" asked Fenway.

Piper shook her head. "No. You see these percentages?"

"Do those track the progress of the NFT conversion?"

"Nope," Piper said. "The NFT has already been converted. These track the progress of cryptocurrency mining."

Ubosi's face fell. "You mean—the software takes over the artist's computer and uses it to mine crypto?"

"That's exactly what I mean," Piper said.

"Okay, I've heard a lot about cryptocurrency," Fenway said, "but I wouldn't be able to explain it."

"Basically," Piper said, "cryptocurrency depends on an extensive network of decentralized computers to verify and record transactions. Like a bank ledger, but not at a bank. A bank would be centralized. This is *decentralized*. So the trusted verification processes take place on hundreds of thousands of computers around the world."

Fenway bit her lip. "That doesn't sound secure."

"That's why the verification calculations are so complex, and they take a *lot* of power. So that kind of energy usage is monetized. The blockchain owner rewards the verifiers with cryptocurrency."

"But not with this," Ubosi said. "The malware takes over the computer to do those complex calculations, but the malware owner is the one who's rewarded with the cryptocurrency."

Fenway looked skeptical.

"Energy costs eat up most of the cryptocurrency profits," Piper said. "It was great ten years ago, when you could mine virtual coins and make good money. Now, after all the energy required to do the calculations, miners barely break even."

"That's ridiculous," Fenway said. "How much energy are we talking about?"

"Powerful computers running complex calculations for hours every day?" Piper scratched her head. "Thirty or forty dollars a month in energy costs per machine, I would think. But if the machine is powerful enough, maybe a couple hundred."

"But don't you need specialized computers for crypto mining?" Ubosi said.

"Artists may not have a lot of money, but if they're digital artists, they're spending what little money they have on powerful computers that can work as fast as their creative brains. Not super-computers, but compared to taking over a typical home computer for crypto mining, the processors are way faster. Besides, the issues are usually speed and energy consumption, and since the software is hijacking the computer, both those issues are moot."

"So Vaughn Trask was taking over hundreds of artists' computers to mine cryptocurrency under the guise of tracking the artists' NFTs?"

"Not hundreds of artists—*thousands*," Piper replied. "If you're paying for the electricity bill of two thousand PCs, that'll eat up the profit of your crypto mining *fast*. But if you split that cost among the artists—well, maybe they'll see an extra hundred bucks a month in electricity bills, and their computers will burn up faster, but Vaughn Trask isn't paying for it."

"So their business model isn't dependent on bringing people through the door of the museum. It's literally taking artists' computers and hijacking them to create tens of thousands of dollars in cryptocurrency."

Piper squinted at the screen again. "Not tens of thousands. Millions."

Fenway sat back in her seat. "This is fraud."

"I agree," Ubosi murmured. "The U.S. Attorney will see it the same way."

"If Stanley Schup and Brock Shellwater knew about this, they could both go to jail for a long time," Fenway said.

"Even if they claim they had no knowledge of this malware," Ubosi said, "the software was using NNoV8 company property, on NNoV8 property, both during and after NNoV8 business hours."

Piper cocked her head. "Doesn't that open them up to legal liability?"

"If someone finds out about it? At this scale?" Ubosi frowned. "It would put them out of business. It might bankrupt every investor involved."

"Does this database access a common piece of malware?" Fenway asked. "This isn't the first time I've heard of hijacking someone else's computer to mine crypto. First time I've ever been this close to it, though."

Piper shrugged. "I don't know of any malware with this kind of functionality, but a good programmer could piggyback an NFT tracker program onto a crypto-mining program—I don't expect this malware to be any different."

"Is there a way for us to track who uses this program?" Fenway asked.

"Why?" Ubosi asked. "It's already on NNoV8's computer."

"But we don't know who's getting paid..." Fenway trailed off. "I guess the bar for reasonable doubt is a lot lower than the bar for the prosecution."

"We can piece together a story that the other owners at NNoV8 knew about the malware—or should have known," Ubosi said. "That way, we guide the jury to connect the dots without *proving* they're connected."

"But I thought you said—"

"If it's not a conclusion people would normally draw, yes, we'd need more," Ubosi said. "But this? Trask was using his work computer. If Trask were using his personal computer in his house, we'd need to connect the dots with proof. But for a work computer? No—the jurors will make the connection for us."

"But what about who actually *killed* Trask?" Piper said. "You're suggesting we just say the malware opened the owners up to millions of dollars of legal liability, so *they* killed Trask? Where's the proof?"

Ubosi folded his hands in front of him on the table. "Reasonable doubt, Ms. Patten. I don't need a smoking gun. I just need to make the jury believe there's a smoking gun that isn't in *your* hand."

Piper sat back, a worried look on her face, but said nothing else.

"Will you be all right tonight?" Fenway asked.

"Not like I have a choice," Piper answered.

Fenway turned to Ubosi. "We need to give these photos to the sheriff, right? Make sure they head to NNoV8 tonight to retrieve that PC from the office."

Ubosi ran a hand over his short hair. "What I don't understand is how the cops missed it the first time. They took the laptop. They should have taken the other computer, too."

"We can see what Deputy Bardot has to say."

"Or Sheriff Jeffcoat."

Fenway turned back to Piper. "You need anything?"

Piper folded her hands in her lap. "Just get me out of here as soon as you can. I don't need another fistfight."

They rose and Fenway hesitated—she wasn't really a hugger—

but stepped forward and gave Piper an embrace. She wanted to say something, but everything on the tip of her tongue seemed hollow.

Ubosi rapped on the door, then opened it. "Deputy, we're ready."

Bardot walked up. Piper walked out of the room first, and they trudged down the short corridor in silence, then back to the holding cell, where Piper entered and Bardot locked her in.

"Thank you for letting us see my client," Ubosi said.

"I was here anyway," replied Bardot.

"You heading home soon?"

"Deputy Wegman just got here. Looks like my time-and-a-half gravy train is over."

"I have another question," Ubosi said. "I've gotten a tip that there's a PC in use at the NNoV8 museum. Specifically, in Vaughn Trask's office. It's running a piece of malware that is hijacking the computers of all the artists who take part in the NFT-based exhibits."

Bardot furrowed her eyebrows. "What?"

"It's taking over their computers to mine cryptocurrency," Fenway said. "Probably costing the artists thousands of dollars."

"Where did you hear this?"

"Anonymous tip," Ubosi said. "But my investigators are working on it."

Fenway suppressed a grin. Sure were a lot of anonymous tips lately.

Bardot ran a hand over her face. "I wasn't on the team that went into Trask's office." She scratched her head. "But I think Deputy Wegman was. Come with me."

They walked out to the reception area, and a young man in a light blue uniform shirt, matching Bardot's, sat behind the workstation.

"Chaz?" Bardot asked.

The deputy raised his head.

"Were you at the museum earlier?"

"Yeah."

"And you went into the murder victim's office."

"Yeah."

"I've heard a tip that there was a PC in that office that we failed to take with us."

Chaz shook his head. "Laptop on the desk. I took pictures of it before I bagged it up and gave it to the county CSI team. I'm pretty sure they entered it into evidence."

"Not the laptop," Fenway said. "A tower PC—high-powered. Under the desk."

Chaz frowned. "I don't know anything about that. The sheriff told me to go get the computer from the decedent's office. That's what I did."

"Did you *not* check to see if there was a second computer in there?" Bardot asked the deputy.

"It's a powerful machine," Fenway added. "It'd make—" She paused, restarted. "Computers like that make a lot of noise. Should have been pretty obvious."

Chaz pressed his lips together. "CSI asked me to take a computer. Laptop was sitting right on the desk and I took it."

"You didn't think—"

Chaz rose from his chair. "As Sheriff Jeffcoat is fond of saying, he doesn't pay me to think."

Bardot closed her eyes, pinched the bridge of her nose, and bowed her head slightly. "Thanks, Chaz."

Fenway stared at Chaz, then turned her head to Bardot, then finally glanced at Ubosi. The lawyer's face was impassive, almost blank.

Bardot turned away from the workstation and strode out the front door.

Fenway looked at Ubosi, who gave a slight shrug, then followed Bardot out. Fenway hesitated, then went after them both.

"Deputy Bardot," Ubosi called—not sternly or loudly, but firmly. Bardot had a cellphone next to her ear.

"Can't talk now," Bardot said. "You can't come with me, either."

Ubosi stopped on the sidewalk, watching Bardot disappear around the corner—possibly toward the parking lot with the sheriff's cruisers. She was talking on the phone, but Fenway couldn't hear what she was saying.

"What do you think?" Fenway asked.

"I think the sheriff will go straight to NNoV8 to get that PC," Ubosi said.

"Which they should have done to begin with." Fenway crossed her arms, despite the heat of the early night, and stared at the sidewalk.

"But," Ubosi said, "if you hadn't taken pictures of what that program did, we might not know the extent of the fraud Vaughn Trask was part of."

Fenway raised her head; a police cruiser emerged from behind the building and turned left, accelerating quickly.

Ubosi jutted his chin toward the cruiser. "That's the direction of the museum, correct?"

"Right." Fenway dropped her hands to her side. "Think we should follow them? Maybe we can help them figure out what's on that computer."

Ubosi shook his head. "They might need to bring in the computer forensics team from Vegas, but they won't let us help." He cracked a smile. "You've been on the prosecution's side for too long."

Fenway watched the cruiser turn onto the freeway, then she turned to Ubosi. "What do we do now?"

"I don't think there's anything else *to* do. When they find that NFT tracker, or malware, or whatever it is on Vaughn Trask's PC, they'll see that hundreds of artists had much more reason to kill him than your friend Piper."

Fenway blinked. "Artists? I thought the other owners would have much greater motive if Trask were to put the museum in a position to commit fraud."

"We can discuss both possibilities."

"So you think they'll let her go?"

Ubosi shrugged. "None of the other artists and neither of the owners were in possession of the murder weapon. The district attorney may decline to bring this to trial, as I believe this provides us a solid basis for reasonable doubt. Unless the police uncover other evidence against your friend, I believe the D.A. wouldn't risk what's almost certain to be a not guilty verdict, or at the very least, a hung jury."

"I guess that's good news." Fenway took a few steps on the sidewalk, away from the county jail. "Still, if they decide to take it to trial, Piper could be locked up for the foreseeable future."

Ubosi screwed up his mouth in thought. "I plan to bring this evidence up at the arraignment on Monday. I don't know if Piper can be ROR'd, but I would imagine bail would be reasonable."

Something Fenway's father could afford, anyway. Fenway nodded.

Ubosi gestured toward his car. "Now, I believe your investigator-slash-paramour has returned to the Cartwheel. Shall I drop you off on my way back to Las Vegas?"

———

Fenway opened the door to the hotel room. McVie had figured out which of the queen beds was Fenway's, and he was fast asleep in the side next to the center nightstand. She knelt next to her suitcase between the two tiny armchairs under the window and pulled out pajamas that she hoped were from the same set. Phone in hand, she crept to the bathroom, closed the door, turned the lights on—good, the pajamas matched. And the bathroom was a little misty. A damp towel hung on a hook on the back of the door. McVie had taken a shower; after running around in the heat all day, Fenway should take one too. She sneaked out of the bathroom, grabbed a hair wrap from her suitcase—McVie was still fast asleep—and stepped back into the bathroom.

After she was clean and cool—she'd kept the water on the cold side— she dried off while scrolling on her phone's browser, looking for any information that could help Piper.

Stan Schup and Brock Shellwater both had a series of business articles on LinkProfs that thousands of people subscribed to—but most of the articles were recycled platitudes about the cutting edge of technology, with only vague references to blockchain. Not a single reference to NFTs.

She put her pajamas on while searching Nadine Ryeo's social media accounts, but found nothing. She checked Sookie Ryeo's account too, but there were no new posts.

Fenway got a low battery warning on her phone—and realized with a start that it was past eleven. They had spoken to Piper for longer than she thought. With a sigh, Fenway clicked the side button to put her phone to sleep. She hoped it would be as easy for her to get some rest.

Turning the light off, she opened the bathroom door as quietly as possible. She stepped around Piper's bed, unused tonight, with her black suitcase at the side of the bed next to the interior wall. She dropped her sweaty clothes from the day on top of her suitcase, then decided to put them inside. The zipper caught for a moment, then gave way and she unzipped it all the way.

Fenway wondered if Piper would have any additional adventures in the holding cell. Piper had probably gotten lucky that her intoxicated assailant had fallen after a single punch. She might not be so lucky next time.

And she wondered how long it would take for the computer forensics team to find the malware program on Trask's PC, reaching out and infecting thousands of artists' computers.

At least she had that strand of hope to cling to.

She got into bed carefully. Fenway glanced over at McVie, sleeping peacefully on his side. She wondered if she could wake him. They wouldn't be together for at least another few weeks. So he'd probably welcome a little physicality. Maybe start with a kiss or two on the back of his neck. Maybe draping her hand around him, her open palm on his bare chest.

Oh, her phone. She needed to plug in her phone. The charger plug was attached to the power outlet on the nightstand, and she reached over McVie to grab her phone and connect it.

As soon as she touched the phone, it buzzed in her hand. Ubosi.

> Dep Bardot reached out to me
>
> No PC in Vaughn Trask's office
>
> Cords, switch, & monitors all in place
>
> But no one admits to moving it

Fenway closed her eyes and took a deep breath, then texted back.

> Thanks for letting me know

She plugged her phone in, turned the notifications to silent, and lay back on her pillow, listening to McVie's gentle breathing. Turning on her side, she lifted her arm to put it over McVie, then held it in the air for a moment before dropping it to her side and rolling onto her back.

Fenway stared up at the ceiling for a long time.

PART 3

SATURDAY

CHAPTER SEVENTEEN

A low voice. "I didn't tell her I'd be anywhere today. I thought I'd be unpacking the truck."

Fenway opened her eyes. McVie, shirtless, his back to her, on the other side of Piper's bed. He had his cellphone pressed to his ear.

"I get that you'll have a hard time cancelling your spa day, but I'm literally ten hours away. There's no way I can—"

Silence.

Fenway gently rolled onto her right side and reached for her phone. Ugh. A few minutes before six. She'd finally gotten to sleep after an hour. It had helped to have McVie in bed with her; his breathing was the white noise she needed to concentrate on so her brain wouldn't continue to race at a million miles an hour.

Then McVie lowered his voice into a whisper. "She is *not* trying to take me away from spending time with my daughter."

Fenway's ears perked up. That surely was a reference to her. Was Amy accusing Fenway of taking McVie away from his daughter? Was she really crazy enough to suggest that Fenway could arrange

Piper's arrest so McVie would have to spend the night with her away from Colorado?

"This is already stressful enough without you making wild accusations."

A pause.

"Yeah, well, at least she was single when I started dating her. And you and I, if you'll remember, were separated."

Another pause.

"We certainly were. Maybe not per the legal definition, but you'd already kicked—"

McVie took a deep breath.

"You know what, Amy? This is water under the bridge. You've moved on, I've moved on. You've gotten what you wanted."

Fenway debated if she should get up. She needed to pee, for one thing. And McVie should really take this conversation outside. Maybe he should put on a shirt first. Although the view from here wasn't bad at all.

"Yeah, yeah, I know, you didn't want me to come, but you still need your me time, right? If I hadn't moved to Colorado, who would you have asked to take Megan to her game?"

Fenway pushed herself into a sitting position, and McVie glanced over at her and grimaced. "Sorry," he mouthed.

Fenway pointed at the bathroom door.

McVie nodded and took two steps to his right, away from the bathroom.

Thunk.

McVie let out a yelp, followed by a few curse words.

Fenway flinched.

"No, not you," McVie barked. "I hit my toe on a suitcase on the floor. Dammit, that hurt."

Fenway got up—and yes, now her need for the bathroom was much more urgent. She hurried around the foot of the bed and into the bathroom.

"Doesn't change the fact that I'm a ten-hour drive away," McVie said as Fenway closed the door and turned on the modesty fan.

Fenway hadn't brought her phone in, so she stared at the wall. A sterile painting of the desert, mountains in the distance. Rocks. Sand. A cactus. Beiges and browns and harsh yellows. It depressed her; some people thought the desert was beautiful and loved living in it. Not Fenway; she'd take the rain and fog and greenery of the Pacific Northwest every time. Even Estancia, with its ocean views, cypress trees, and lush springtimes were aligned with her desires. But the desert? She couldn't wait to leave.

She finished up, flushed and washed her hands, then opened the door of the bathroom. McVie stood in a T-shirt that was a size or two too large for him, and he was sitting on the edge of Piper's bed, pulling on a pair of jeans.

"Sorry," he said, "but I've got to go. I guess Amy told Megan I'd be at a softball game today. I won't make it, but if I leave now, I might get back in time to take her out to dinner tonight."

Fenway bit her lip. Maybe Fenway should have powered through it last night and awakened McVie. She had thought maybe they could spend part of the morning connecting—maybe over break-fast, or maybe in bed.

But her thoughts all focused on getting Piper out of jail. She was too distracted, just like she'd been too distracted—and exhausted—the night before.

"I know this is a crappy situation." McVie tried to sound apologetic, but he was angry and frustrated. "I really appreciate you offering to drive my truck all this way."

"It's not a problem," Fenway said automatically.

McVie looked at her out of the corner of his eye. "It absolutely *is* a problem. If I hadn't asked you to do this, you'd be at home in Estancia, probably going out dancing with Rachel or having Piper try to convince you to go to a neuroscience lecture at Nidever University. Instead, she's in jail, you're stuck in a hotel room in the middle of the desert, and I'm fighting with my ex."

Fenway let a small smile touch her lips. "I didn't have any of that on my bingo card for this year, that's for sure."

"I don't know how I can make this up to you," McVie said.

"You don't need to worry about it. Let's just get through this weekend. They'll arraign Piper in two days, and then my dad will pay her bail and get the two of us on a plane back to Estancia."

"I'm supposed to be a private investigator, and I can't even keep my own employee out of jail when she's accused of something she didn't do."

"And I'm a coroner and I can't even look at the victim's body."

McVie reached out a hand, and Fenway grabbed it. "I appreciate you, Fenway. I hate that this is hard, and I hate that I can't pull myself mentally out of this."

Fenway shrugged. "I know it's hard. New job, new apartment, new state. I went through this a year ago, you know."

He nodded, caressing her fingers gently with his thumb, then pulled her into his lap.

She squeaked. "I haven't brushed my teeth."

He smiled—it was forced, though Fenway could tell he was trying his best to make it genuine. "Then go brush your teeth. I at least need a goodbye kiss from my girlfriend before I get on the road."

———

Twenty minutes later, Fenway bent down and unzipped her suitcase—

And the zipper pull came off in her hand. She stared at it for a moment.

"Did your suitcase just break?"

Fenway shook her head. McVie knelt down and wiggled the other zipper pull until the suitcase was open.

"Take your stuff out," McVie said. "I'll be right back." He stood and hurried out of the hotel room.

Fenway pulled on a new T-shirt and shorts, then emptied everything out. She'd have to do laundry if she was going to stay much longer.

McVie was back with a small gray-and-pink rolling suitcase, about the size of Fenway's. "Will this do?"

"Um, yeah. This was empty?"

"It is now. Towels and sheets. The advantages of having everything I own out in the parking lot," McVie said, grinning, then grabbing Fenway's broken case. "I'll see if I can fix this."

"Thank you, Craig."

"It's the least I can do."

Fenway walked McVie out to the U-Move-It truck. "Call me when you get home," she said. "Just so I know you're safe." She grimaced because she sounded like her mom when Fenway would go out at night as a university student.

McVie nodded. "Of course. And we'll figure this out. You're important to me. I'm going to make this work."

Fenway nodded. She wanted to say something about Amy's overreaching, about setting proper expectations with Megan, but kept her mouth shut. Not her place. McVie opened the door of the truck and Fenway leaned forward and kissed him. Not a peck on the cheek; on the mouth, wrapping her arms around his back, with a little of the lingering passion left over from the hotel room.

"As much as I'd like round two, I'm already running behind," McVie protested.

"I know," Fenway said, dropping her arms.

McVie climbed into the cab, turned the engine on. "I'll miss you."

Fenway nodded, McVie closed the door, and a few moments later she watched as the U-Move-It truck's brake lights dimmed as McVie pulled out of the parking lot onto the road toward the freeway.

Fenway sighed. She'd have to fly out to see him. Maybe in two or three weeks. Assuming she could get this mess sorted out with Piper.

She turned in the parking lot—even this early in the morning, the day was heating up—and trudged back to her hotel room.

When she had closed the door behind her, she sighed. The room was stuffy despite the air conditioning, and it just reminded Fenway that she wouldn't be seeing McVie for a while. She looked at the thermostat; McVie had set it at seventy. Not environmentally friendly, but the trip out to the parking lot in the morning sun had warmed her up.

She plopped herself on the bed for a moment, her mind going back to getting Piper out of jail. If the PC had been removed, probably by one of the NNoV8 owners, she had to make sure that reasonable doubt came from elsewhere.

Was there anywhere to look for Trask's tower PC? It could be anywhere; if she'd been trying to get rid of it, she might have driven out into the desert and dumped it in a cave or a hole in the ground. No one would have been able to locate it.

But there were other suspects, too. Aurora Horn: there was still the matter of the torn-in-half pre-nup. Nadine Ryeo had the opportunity, too, although Fenway didn't know whether she had a motive. And Sookie—if she wanted to keep Vaughn Trask away from her daughter, leaving him stabbed in the middle of the hotel parking lot was certainly an effective way to go.

Should she take a shower? She'd just taken one the night before, and with the promise of another hot day, she wouldn't stay cool and clean for long. No, she'd forgo a morning shower. She had work to do.

Fenway picked up her phone on the nightstand. She tapped the screen, the Photoxio app came up, and Sookie Ryeo's feed refreshed.

Fenway blinked.

A photo of two mimosas, a tag from Albie K's.

Best brunch in Ruby Dunes — #sistersforever

Sookie's sister. The one who Sookie had supposedly been with the night Trask was murdered. What had Sookie said? Fenway shut her eyes tight. Seven thirty or eight. That's what Sookie had said.

Fenway glanced at the timestamp. *A minute ago from Ruby Dunes, NV.* They were both at Albie K's right now.

She could check out Sookie's story; Fenway needed to eat anyway, and weekend brunch at Albie K's might be better than the hotel diner. At least she'd feel like she was *doing* something. And Fenway could gauge Sookie's reaction. Sookie had been positively jubilant when she'd heard Trask was dead, so Fenway doubted she had much of a poker face.

And she wouldn't even have to drive. She grabbed her purse and was out the door.

Just in the few minutes she'd been in the room, the sun had started to bake the asphalt of the parking lot, the heat rising in waves as she walked to Albie K's.

Fifteen or twenty cars sat in the diner's parking lot. Even though few people lived in the area, perhaps it did a decent business with the hotel and casino clientele.

Fenway walked in through the front door. She saw Sookie Ryeo sitting at a booth with another woman who slightly resembled her, dressed more casually and with short, straight hair just past the bottom of her ears. A two-person table next to the booth was open.

"Just one?" the woman behind the host stand said.

Fenway pointed to the table next to Sookie. "Can I have that table near the window?"

The woman nodded, grabbed a menu, and led Fenway to the table. The woman put the menu down in front of the chair opposite the window, but Fenway took the chair on the other side of the table, facing Sookie.

Fenway sat, staring at the menu, not looking at Sookie, but knew she was in Sookie's line of sight. If Fenway held her head just right, she could see Sookie out of the corner of her eye, but wouldn't appear as if she were looking at her.

She ordered a Bloody Mary for her beverage; seeing Sookie had reminded her that the waitstaff had taken her gin and tonic away before she'd had a chance to drink it when she was interviewing Nadine. As soon as the server turned her back, Fenway regretted her order. She needed to be sharp for the day ahead, and the Bloody Mary would make her sleepy and damage her ability to focus.

But if Sookie were to see the Bloody Mary on the table in front of Fenway, she *might* lower her inhibitions about talking. Looked like Sookie and her sister were drinking mimosas, so, hey, when in Rome. Or when in Vegas.

Fenway pulled out her phone, wanting to look busy. Might as well try to figure out Sookie's sister's name. Photoxio—did Sookie tag her sister? Not in the last photo. Fenway scrolled back a couple of weeks. Oh, there it was: *Benny Jones*. Ah—Sookie had called her brother-in-law a Tây lông. Maybe that had something to do with the *Jones* part of the name. The woman across from Sookie looked exactly like the woman tagged as Benny Jones on Photoxio.

Sookie gave Fenway two or three glances while sipping on her mimosa and talking with Benny. The two women spoke Vietnamese, and Fenway couldn't understand what they were saying. The server appeared with Fenway's Bloody Mary, and Fenway looked up from her phone. She gave the server an order of a breakfast burrito—she really missed Dos Milagros—and then, as soon as the server turned, Fenway caught Sookie's eye.

She smiled widely, and Sookie smiled back—forced and uncomfortable—and Fenway stood and walked over to their table. In addition to the mimosas, the sisters had two half-eaten plates of Portuguese sausage and eggs between them.

"Mrs. Ryeo," Fenway said. "So good to see you again."

"Uh, yes. Forgive me, I don't remember who you are."

"Coroner Fenway Stevenson," Fenway said. "We spoke yesterday. Just wanted to tell you how helpful it was to know you were with your sister on Thursday night."

Benny flinched.

"Uh..." Sookie's eyes darted to Benny. "Of course. I was happy to help." She startled, then changed her face to one of sadness and sympathy—though Fenway suspected it was more a performance for her sister than Fenway.

"Anyway," Fenway said, "just thought I'd say hello." She turned to Benny. "Sorry to interrupt your brunch."

Fenway went back to her table, taking out her phone again. After a couple of minutes, Benny excused herself from the table, then made eye contact—long, lingering eye contact—with Fenway as she passed her table.

Fenway didn't react, and reached out to grab her Bloody Mary. She pulled a pickle off the skewer and bit into it thoughtfully. How long did she have to wait? Maybe another ten, fifteen seconds.

She took another bite of the pickle, then wiped her hands on the cloth napkin on her lap, and rose from her chair. Fenway could feel Sookie's eyes on her as she walked to the restroom.

Benny was standing at the sink when Fenway pushed open the door to the restroom.

"Hello again," Fenway said.

"My sister did not visit me Thursday night. She did not come to my house until yesterday morning." Benny crinkled her nose. "She stank. Like cigarettes. Like she hadn't showered." She pushed the door open and took a step out of the restroom.

"Wait—"

Benny shook her head. "I must go."

The door closed behind Benny and Fenway stared after her for a moment, then absently washed her hands in the sink.

Stayed out all night and smelled like a casino. Possibly the Cartwheel, which was a hundred feet from the murder scene.

Anyone could have happened upon Piper's knife in the parking lot. Maybe Sookie was just biding her time. Lying in wait in the parking lot. Then gambling the rest of the night away. Why not? She was already gambling with her life to get away with murder.

Fenway started to push the door to the bathroom open, then hesitated. It would look too odd if she immediately came back to her breakfast, so she counted to a hundred before returning to her table.

Sookie and Benny were gone.

Fenway sighed and sat heavily in the chair, then got up and sat in the other chair, the one opposite the window. If Sookie and Benny had gone, she might as well stare at something besides the inside of the restaurant.

Her breakfast arrived a few minutes later, and she wolfed it down. Sookie no longer had an alibi—something she should tell Ubosi—but Aurora Horn's torn-up pre-nuptial agreement was still weighing on Fenway's mind.

She paid as quickly as she could, then crossed the parking lot to the hotel. She had to get the rental car's key and drive back to the house that Vaughn Trask had—

Fenway stopped in her tracks.

McVie's moving truck. Sitting in the parking lot, in the same spot she'd left it the night before.

CHAPTER EIGHTEEN

Fenway scratched her head. Had it been there when she came out? She didn't think so. But if she'd simply overlooked it, where was McVie?

She pulled her phone out. Ah—a message from her investigator-slash-paramour, as Ubosi had phrased it.

> Apparently the sheriff doesn't want the moving van leaving the county. Got pulled over and strongly encouraged to return to Ruby Dunes.

Less than an ideal situation for McVie. He had until Monday morning to drive the truck home and unload, and ten hours of driving ahead of him—and it was already Saturday morning. Ugh.

She dragged her sneakers on the dusty asphalt as she passed the moving truck, then climbed the stairs to her room. On the landing, McVie sat cross-legged, like a little kid, with his back against the wall next to the door. He'd bowed his head over his phone, and he was furiously typing with two thumbs.

"Morning, Craig."

He looked up at her and smiled, although the smile was a little forced. "Long time no see."

"I'm sorry."

"I'm trying to work it out with Payback Systems now. They want me back there today—I guess there's some background checks another team gave up just before quitting time last night—but I'm, you know, a ten-hour drive away."

"Plus your dinner with Megan."

McVie dropped his head. "I moved out to Colorado so things *wouldn't* be so stressful for Megan. So she could have both her parents there for her. And here I am—"

"In an untenable situation," Fenway said gently. "She'll understand."

McVie scoffed. "She's seventeen, Fenway. Even if she understands, she'll act like she doesn't."

"Lays the guilt on thick, does she?"

"With an assist from Amy."

"Okay, well—can I get you back to the airport so you can fly back to Denver?"

McVie sighed. "I can't really afford an eight-hundred-dollar last minute ticket."

"No more miles?"

McVie shook his head.

"I can pay for it," Fenway said.

"No," McVie said. "I can't let you do that."

"You can't lose this job," Fenway said. "Not when you just got it."

"I'll be fine. They're being unreasonable just to see how far they can push me. But I've seen this before—the boss tries to push new employees around. Hell, I got the business end of that when I got promoted to sergeant back in Estancia."

"Yeah," Fenway said, "but the police have a powerful union. You don't have a union, right?"

"Well, no—"

"So maybe you should get on that plane."

McVie pushed himself to his feet. "I'll take the moving truck over to the sheriff's office. If they want to search it, they can search it."

"That would be a bad idea. All the stuff you have in there? They'll have to take all of it out. They might not be careful with it."

"Law enforcement respects law enforcement."

Fenway shook her head. "You're not law enforcement anymore."

"Yeah, but not by choice. I wasn't re-elected."

Fenway could barely suppress a grin. "You ran for mayor, not sheriff, remember?"

"Well, yeah, but public service is public service."

Fenway raised her eyebrows. "It's your stuff, Craig, and it's your choice. They find anything in there they can use against Piper, though, and you won't get your moving truck back."

McVie walked to the railing above the stairs and leaned his elbows on it. "I don't know what to do. I need to leave."

"Call Ubosi."

McVie shut his eyes tight, then opened them. "I don't think so. Conflict of interest. He can't protect me *and* Piper."

"Ubosi knows the cops will look for something to use against Piper. If you and the truck are gone—especially since they didn't cart the truck into evidence on day one—that'll make Ubosi's life a lot easier. And you better call him now. The sheriff might be working on a warrant for the truck as we stand here yammering."

McVie pointed at the door. "Can you let me in?"

"Oh. Sure." Fenway held the keycard in front of the doorknob and a click sounded. She turned the knob and pushed the door open.

"Thanks." McVie stepped in. "You coming?"

Fenway followed McVie in and grabbed the car key off the nightstand. "Thanks again for lending me the suitcase."

"It's really no big deal."

Fenway twirled the car key ring around her finger and nodded.

She'd never had a boyfriend who helped her out without asking before. Was he this thoughtful because Fenway had rejected his proposal? Was this just his Boy Scout nature? She felt a headache coming on; maybe she was dehydrated from the heat, or maybe she was overthinking her relationship. Fenway cleared her throat. "I'm going to ask Aurora Horn about that pre-nup. Want to join me?"

McVie gave a slight shake of his head. "No, I think I'll call Ubosi. See what he says about when I can leave in the truck."

———

Fenway pulled in front of the guard house at Golden Sands twenty minutes later. It was still early, just past eight o'clock; Aurora might still be in bed, but Fenway needed to speak to her.

The guard stopped her, but Fenway flashed her badge. His eyes darted between the badge and Fenway's face—and her shorts and T-shirt—but he stepped back and opened the gate.

This time, Fenway parked in front of Aurora's house; no need to hide a moving van today. She opened the door. The morning was already hot, and Fenway suspected the needle would move north of one hundred degrees Fahrenheit by lunch.

She strode to the front door and rang the doorbell.

Nothing; no dogs barking, no sound inside the house.

After a moment, she rang the bell again, then took a step back and raised her voice. "Aurora Horn? This is Coroner Stevenson again. It's urgent that I speak with you."

That was *just* loud enough that Aurora would know that if Fenway had to repeat her words, the neighbors might hear her. Both a request and a warning. Fenway waited another ten seconds, then rustling sounds from inside. She held her badge up to the doorbell camera.

The door opened a moment later, and Aurora Horn, her hair flat on one side of her head and sticking up at a few crazy angles on the other, appear in the doorway. "It's eight on a Saturday morning," she croaked. "This couldn't wait?"

"My apologies for the wake-up call," Fenway said. Even from the front step, Fenway could smell the stale alcohol emanating from Aurora. She'd probably drank herself to sleep the night before. Aurora's eyes were bloodshot, red-rimmed, slightly vacant. Perhaps she'd been crying as well as drinking. "But no," Fenway continued, "this couldn't wait."

Aurora rubbed her left eye with the heel of her hand. "Okay, so what is it?"

"Your pre-nuptial agreement."

Aurora dropped her hand to her side; her vacant look disappeared. "I suppose Mr. Bowen was *kind* enough to provide a copy to the police." She hesitated for a moment, then stepped out onto the front step with Fenway, closing the door behind her. Obviously, Fenway wouldn't get an invitation inside. Aurora opened her mouth, then decided against it. Ah, Fenway hadn't asked a question, and Aurora was smart enough to not provide an answer to a question that wasn't asked. Maybe coached by a divorce lawyer.

"I got information that you didn't care for the terms that were in the final pre-nup that you signed."

Aurora ran her tongue over her teeth, thinking. Then: "I was under pressure to get the pre-nup signed before the wedding. My lawyers had negotiated terms, then I found out Vaughn's lawyer slipped some language in after we'd sent the final edits over. I received an agreement that I apparently signed, but my lawyer and I hadn't approved." She gritted her teeth.

Probably an honest answer.

"Can you tell me who receives the bulk of Mr. Trask's estate now?"

Aurora shifted her weight uncomfortably. "Not—no."

"You hesitated. Why?"

Aurora ran a hand over her face. "I don't think Vaughn left a will, but I'm not sure. I'm letting the lawyers figure that one out."

"If Mr. Trask didn't leave a will, everything goes to you."

"I don't really know the law in these cases," Aurora said. "I'm sure *something* goes to his parents."

Fenway studied Aurora's face for a moment. It seemed like she believed what she was saying, but she could be a good actor.

"And did you go to see Mr. Trask on Thursday to discuss the unwanted additions in the pre-nup with him?"

Aurora pressed her lips together.

"You've already admitted to going there. And fighting with him. You fought about the pre-nup, didn't you?"

"Okay," Aurora said. "Fine. I went to see him."

"And what did he have to say about the pre-nup?"

"He blamed the lawyers. Said one of them just got ahead of himself." She tightened her jaw. "And that I was overreacting." She sniffed, then clamped her mouth shut.

"You drove a white Acura MDX to the museum that day?" Fenway asked.

Aurora's eyes lost the confrontational spark. She nodded glumly.

"I saw the agreement," Fenway said. "There's an adultery clause, where you get more than half his assets if he cheats. But if *you* cheat, you get next to nothing. Even if *he* cheats. Is that the section you objected to?"

"I thought—" Aurora stopped herself, then continued, her voice calm. "I didn't study it. It was the principle of the thing."

Fenway cocked her head. "Are you sure, Ms. Horn?"

Aurora licked her lips. "What do you want me to say?"

"I just want the truth," Fenway said.

Aurora was silent.

"The police could get warrants to find out who you were cheating with," Fenway continued. "Did you leave a paper trail? A hotel bill, a dinner at a restaurant?" Fenway cocked her head. "Maybe your affair partner is single, and he paid for it. Wouldn't think to hide a paper trail, would he? If he doesn't have a wife or girlfriend to worry about, he wouldn't care if a fancy dinner or a hotel room shows up on his credit card statement."

Aurora's shoulders relaxed—oh, Fenway was on the wrong track. She studied Aurora's face. Where did she go wrong? Maybe the guy was married or had a girlfriend. Maybe the guy was poor, and Aurora had to pay for everything? Fenway blinked—Aurora's affair partner wasn't necessarily male, either.

She'd made the mistake of asking questions she didn't know the answers to. Fenway had gotten used to Sarah and Dez—and before they left the employ of the county, Mark and Piper—to research everything before she started questioning suspects.

O.K. Ubosi would tell the sheriff's office about the pre-nup, though, and they would probably do at least a little due diligence on it. If the sheriff didn't follow up, Ubosi's investigative team surely would, and they had a lot more resources at their disposal than Fenway at the moment.

Aurora crossed her arms. Yeah, she wasn't in the mood for saying anything else. Catching her off-guard early on a Saturday had only gotten Fenway so far.

"Thanks for your time, Ms. Horn," Fenway said. "Have a good rest of your weekend."

Then Fenway was off the porch, walking back to her car.

And really, what was she thinking, not being more prepared? If Aurora Horn *was* the killer, now Fenway had tipped her off that Aurora's pre-nuptial agreement was casting a light on her as a suspect. She swore under her breath. Fenway felt the gnawing of uncertainty that she hadn't had since her first few months as county coroner.

Wait—she was judging her own actions by the wrong standards? Fenway wasn't trying to catch a killer. She wasn't even trying to prove Piper's innocence. She was trying to find reasonable doubt— and to convince the county's D.A. that they shouldn't hold Piper for this murder.

Fenway got in the rented Kia Rio and started the engine,

turning the air conditioning from medium to high. Impatience was getting the better of her; she wanted Piper out of jail immediately, and she wanted McVie to get his belongings into his new apartment.

After putting the car into gear, Fenway made a U-turn in the street, then drove to the exit of Golden Sands. She rubbed her forehead as she passed the guard station.

If the sheriff was making a big deal about keeping the truck in the county, then he better have something to back it up. Fenway suspected he was just throwing his weight around. Maybe he thought Fenway was behind the wheel and *she* was the one leaving the county. No idea what her legal rights were in Nevada regarding this, though. Maybe Ubosi would know.

She pulled off to the side of the road, about halfway between Golden Sands and the freeway, and dialed Ubosi's number.

"Good morning, Ms. Stevenson. You're up bright and early."

"Did you get a call from Craig McVie?"

He paused. "I got a call from an unknown number. 805 area code."

"That's him."

"I let it go to voicemail."

"The sheriff stopped Craig on the way out of town. He was driving the moving truck, and they said he needed to turn around and stay in the county."

Ubosi paused. "I don't believe they can do that."

"Honestly, I think they saw the moving truck and thought it was me."

"Why would they want you to stay in the county? You've been nothing but a pain in their neck. I would think they'd be delighted you weren't creeping around underfoot."

"Unless they really think there's something in the truck that'll convict Piper."

Ubosi paused. "I suppose that could be the case, but it just seems so odd."

"I have the idea to stop by the sheriff's office and tell them they either need a warrant or they need to let Craig go."

"No, I wouldn't. That's—"

Fenway waited for Ubosi to finish, but he'd stopped. "O.K.?"

"Sorry. I'm going over it in my mind. I don't think a judge—not the ones in Correos county, anyway—would sign a warrant for the truck. For one thing, they'd need to look for something specific. So if they *do* manage to get a warrant, they'll have to fill out what they're looking for. That'll give us a better idea of where they're going with their case."

"So—you think I should do it?"

"I'm Ms. Patten's lawyer, not yours, Fenway. I can't give you legal advice. But if you're asking if it'll help Piper's case, then yes, I'd prefer you do it." A slight pause. "Let me know how it goes."

"And did you tell the sheriff's office about Aurora Horn's torn pre-nup?"

"The sheriff won't be in until noon today," Ubosi said. "I've made an appointment. Doesn't seem like they're very keen to get evidence that contradicts their theory that Ms. Patten was the killer."

"How about your investigators?" Fenway asked. "Have they figured out where the missing PC is?"

"It's barely been twelve hours," Ubosi said. "And it's the weekend. I'm getting my best people on it, but you need to give me a little time to put the pieces in place."

Fenway grunted. "One of my greatest strengths is my impatience."

"And another is that you don't care who you piss off."

"That's me. I'm an open book." Fenway put the car back in gear. "I'll contact you after I find out whether they're getting a warrant."

———

Twenty minutes later, Fenway strode into the sheriff's office. The moving truck wasn't in the parking lot—McVie had listened to her, after all. The deputy behind the reception desk was someone Fenway hadn't seen before. Short brown hair, freckles covering his cheeks. The desert sun didn't agree with him.

"I'd like to speak to whoever stopped my moving truck from leaving the county," Fenway said.

The deputy looked up, confusion clouding his face. "I'm not involved with that case," he said. "Do you know who the officer in charge is?"

"I know Sheriff Jeffcoat was the first law enforcement officer on the scene—"

"Is this the Trask murder?"

"That's right."

"The sheriff is off this morning, but Deputy Bardot is in."

Fenway nodded. "Great. I can talk to her."

"Have a seat." There was an edge to his voice that told Fenway she was riding the line between being firm and being an entitled asshole.

"Thank you," Fenway said, as kindly as she could manage, and took a seat on an uncomfortable beige plastic chair.

After a moment, Deputy Bardot stepped into the waiting room, and Fenway stood. "Good morning, deputy."

"Fenway," Bardot said. Oh—now they were on a first-name basis. "I think I know—"

"You can't keep the moving truck here indef—"

Bardot held one hand in front of her, palm out. "Hang on, hang on, let me explain—"

"Do you have a warrant?"

Bardot motioned to the front door. "Let's talk. I'll buy you a coffee. Something better than the swill they have here."

"I don't want a cup of coffee. I want my—" Fenway paused. What exactly should she call McVie? Ah, hell, it didn't matter. "My boyfriend's truck to be released. He's moving this weekend, he's got to be back at his new job on Monday—"

"Let's go." Bardot pushed past Fenway on her way out the front. Holding the door open, she thrust her chin at Fenway. "You coming? I'm not letting the hot air in for longer than I can help it."

Fenway opened her mouth, then closed it, hearing her words echo in her head. She sounded just like the entitled rich women she'd interviewed. She switched her purse to her opposite shoulder and walked outside. As soon as she stepped across the threshold, the hot air hit her in the face—along with a mixture of exhaust from the freeway. Ugh. The temperature must be in the mid-nineties already. Maybe she could blame her foul mood on the heat.

"Decent place two blocks away," Bardot said. She wore a short-sleeve uniform shirt and long, olive green trousers. She must be *really* warm, although perhaps she'd lived here long enough to get used to it.

Fenway followed Bardot across the parking lot to the street. No sidewalks here; they stayed on the side of the road next to a chain-link fence.

"I guess I shouldn't have hauled you back here," Bardot said.

"That's right. You don't have a warrant. You can't compel the truck to stay."

"I wasn't trying to compel the *truck* to stay. Even if we wanted to search it, it's been two days since the murder. The truck has been out of our control, parked in an unsecured lot. If we find evidence in the truck, Ubosi will get it disallowed before the ink is dry on the evidence form."

"Then why couldn't my boyfriend leave?"

Bardot paused, then stopped in the street. She looked behind her; no movement from the sheriff's office. "I don't think Piper Patten is guilty," she murmured, so low Fenway almost couldn't hear. "But I think Sheriff Jeffcoat wants a quick win."

Fenway raised her eyebrows. "Did he hear about the pre-nup?"

Bardot shook her head. "All he cares about are the headlines for the arrest. If Patten gets off on a technicality or is released in a few months, he'll already have made political hay out of this."

Fenway narrowed her eyes. "So why are *you* helping me?"

"I'm not." Bardot touched the side of her nose. "Not as far as you know. But you're the only person who's looking at anyone who *isn't* Piper Patten."

"Pretty stupid to limit your options," Fenway said. "The D.A. might not even take the case without assurance that he can win a case against Piper."

"We'll see," Bardot said. "I know we're only an hour from Vegas, but this is our first homicide in the county in four years. And the county sheriff is an elected position. If people remember Jeffcoat put away the killer—even if it's just for a month or two—his reelection chances go up a lot. In fact, he might not even get a challenger."

"No promotion in his future?"

"He'd make more in Vegas, sure, but he'd have to do some actual police work there."

"All right," Fenway said, "so let's assume I believe that you're looking at other suspects out of a sense of duty—"

"Justice."

"A sense of justice," Fenway said. "Why keep the truck in the county?"

"Because," Bardot said, shaking her head. "I thought *you* were driving it. If I want justice to be done, I can't do it myself. I'd like you to stay. At least another day or two."

"Okpara Ubosi has a whole team of investigators."

Bardot chuckled. "Can you imagine? Me keeping my job after I provide aid and comfort to a defense lawyer? Jeffcoat would eat me alive."

"If I stay, can you foot the hotel bill?"

Bardot scratched her nose. "I'd like to, but no."

Fenway was silent for a moment. "But you can let McVie drive home?"

"Sure. Give him my apologies. I'll call the highway patrol and cancel the APB."

Fenway gritted her teeth. Bardot put an APB on the moving truck because she wanted to keep *Fenway* in the county. And Fenway hadn't even been in the truck. Bardot should get written up at least. But Fenway suspected they were a tight-knit bunch. Bardot would probably not even get a slap on the wrist.

Fenway pulled her phone out and tapped the telephone app, then tapped the screen again.

"Hey, Fenway."

"Hi, Craig. I'm at the sheriff's office, just clearing a few things up. You can head out now."

"Not before I make a couple of phone calls," Bardot said in a stage whisper.

"How long will that take?"

Bardot screwed up her mouth. "Maybe twenty minutes."

"You can be on the road at nine thirty," Fenway said into the phone. "I know that's three hours later than you wanted to leave, but it's better than nothing."

"Great," McVie said. "It'll give me time to finish up my breakfast."

"You ate without me?"

McVie laughed. "Don't give me a guilt trip, Fenway. I saw the receipt from Albie K's on the nightstand. I hope Albie K's was better than the hotel diner."

Fenway grinned. "I guarantee it was."

"Almost makes me miss Dos Milagros." McVie paused. "I'd like to see you before I leave, but I'm so late as it is. I'm going to hit the road."

"You can give your key to the front desk. I need to extend another night."

"Okay. I miss you already."

She hung up and looked plaintively at Bardot. "All right, let's go. That iced coffee isn't going to order itself."

CHAPTER NINETEEN

Bardot bought Fenway an iced latte—an extra-large, since Bardot wasn't picking up the hotel bill. She gave the barista *Joanne* for her name, and Bardot raised her eyebrows.

Fenway stepped out of line in front of the espresso machine. "No one believes me when I say *Fenway*. Or they mis-hear it and write something totally different."

"Who's Joanne?"

"My mom." A pang of the past, of watching her mother work two, three jobs to provide for them, thinking of the painting of the cypress trees still hanging over Fenway's bed back in Estancia. "I swear, I'm not a mafia informant or anything."

A smile touched the corner of Bardot's mouth. "Keep me in the loop if anything else comes up as you're investigating."

"You're not sticking around to watch me drink my latte?"

"I've gotta get back to work."

Fenway folded her receipt and put it in her purse. "You know, I could really use some background information."

Bardot folded her arms. "On what?"

"Nothing you couldn't disguise as due diligence. The financial situation of the NNoV8 museum, for one thing."

Bardot laughed, a deep, throaty laugh. "No way. I won't chase other suspects down for you."

"You'd need to do it anyway. Even if Sheriff Jeffcoat doesn't want you chasing other suspects, you know the D.A. will want this information. He won't want O.K. Ubosi surprising him in court."

Bardot was silent.

"It's your call, Izzy. If you want to be proactive for the D.A., I just ask that you let me know anything I can do to... to, uh, serve the cause of justice."

Bardot shook her head. "That was a terrible save." She sighed. "But fine. I'll see what I can do."

"Thank you."

Bardot nodded stiffly, dropped her arms to her side, and walked out of the coffee shop. Fenway took a seat at the side, one of the two-person tables next to the small, wheeled tray with cream, sugar, and other mix-ins.

She took out her phone and called Sarah Summerhill.

A sleepy voice answered. "Fenway?"

Oh no. Fenway had lost track of the days. "Sorry, Sarah—it's Saturday. I wasn't thinking."

"Did you get Piper released?"

"No."

"Well, then." Sarah immediately sounded more alert. "What can I do to help?"

"I've got a couple of suspects who are looking more and more suspicious."

"Joanne?" the barista called.

Fenway got up to get her iced latte and relayed to Sarah what she'd found: the NFT tracker that Piper thought was malware, the NNoV8 founders with their potential legal liability, their life insurance policies; Aurora Horn, with her torn pre-nuptial agreement; Sookie Ryeo, with her alibi that her sister wouldn't cover.

Sarah sighed.

"What is it?" Fenway asked.

"You don't have jurisdiction to look into any of this," Sarah said.

"Piper's lawyer is all right with me investigating."

"That's not what I mean," Sarah said. "You know how cops get in trouble when they run background checks on the people they're dating?"

Fenway closed her eyes. "Of course. Misuse of the NCIC system is a crime in California."

"In every state. Even Nevada."

"And if I ran background on the suspects when it's not even my case," Fenway continued, "you're saying it'd be just like that. Enough for me to face criminal charges?"

"Correct. You'd get in a lot of trouble."

Fenway shook her head. "Why didn't that occur to me?"

"Because your desire to get Piper out of jail blinded you."

"I guess." Fenway rubbed her chin. "And maybe because you ran the plates of Nadine's Volkswagen Jetta."

"Not using the NCIC system. Loophole for the win!"

Fenway chuckled. "So what can we do that's, you know, legal?"

"Public information. Stuff I can get from the web, from corporate reports, that kind of thing. Non-NCIC searches." Sarah paused. "There might be another way, though."

Fenway's ears perked up. "I'm listening."

"You said there were hundreds of artists in this database on Trask's work PC, right?"

"Thousands."

"From all over the country?"

"Maybe even all over the world. I haven't dug into it."

"If you can find one of those artists who lives in Dominguez County..."

Fenway's eyes went wide, and she smacked her knee. "Then NNoV8 will have committed fraud against a Dominguez County resident. And that might give us a reason to dig into NNoV8's financials."

"It's a thought. It might not work to get evidence used in court—there are still jurisdictional issues. But it gives you a justified reason to run a background check or an NCIC search on anything related to NNoV8."

"Sarah, have I told you you're a genius?"

"Not nearly often enough."

"Hang on."

Fenway put the phone on speaker, then pulled up the photos she'd taken of the PC monitor in Trask's office at NNoV8. Ugh. At her phone's resolution, she'd have to zoom in all the way to read the names, and then going back and forth between the photo and a browser to find where the artist was located? It would take hours. No, probably more like days.

"Sarah, I think I'll have to send these photos of the monitor to you. I didn't get the entire database, but I've got maybe seven pictures where names are visible. Maybe thirty names on each. That'll get you two hundred of the six thousand or so."

"I'll see what I can do."

"I'm sorry, Sarah. This is a lot of manual work to read those names from the photo and then do a web search."

Sarah chuckled. "OCR, Fenway. I can convert those photos to a spreadsheet in a few minutes." She lowered her voice conspiratorially. "You can even get an app for your phone."

Fenway shook her head as if clearing cobwebs out. Of course—optical character recognition was a thirty-year-old technology. Did she have blinders on when it came to this case? The murders she usually investigated had a set of rules she needed to follow; she found it almost impossible to think from the other direction, to try to intentionally create reasonable doubt instead of making sure a case against a suspect was as airtight as possible. And that cognitive switch was obviously throwing her off her game.

She took another drink of her iced coffee and turned the plastic cup in a circle, the name *Joanne* written in Sharpie on the side.

Then a thought struck her. Her mother's old art group. "Hey—have you heard of the Dominguez Art Collective?"

Sarah paused. "Sounds familiar. Maybe I've seen fliers up in Java Jim's."

"My mom was a member for a while, and they were always trying to get her to restart her membership, even after she moved to Seattle." Fenway tapped her chin. "Maybe start with names you can find on their membership list. Or make a call to their head office. They might cooperate if they think some of their members have been victims of fraud."

"It's Saturday. They're probably closed."

"Galleries. Farmer's markets. Art walks. It's late June in Estancia —this is the time the Art Collective throws together a bunch of events."

Sarah sighed. "This no longer sounds like something I can do from my laptop in the comfort of the bed in my apartment."

"I'll make it up to you." Fenway paused. Sarah sounded like going outside would be cold and terrible, not a hundred-degree summer day. Then it struck her: Estancia was still a coastal town. The coastal fog wouldn't burn off until noon, and until then, it would be in the fifties—maybe the low sixties. Right now, that sounded heavenly.

"This is a nice-dinner kind of favor, not a Java Jim's latte favor," Sarah said.

"You won't even do this for Piper?" Fenway selected the seven photos, tapped her screen a few times, and emailed all the pictures to Sarah.

Sarah grunted. "Oh, the guilt trip. I see how it is. Tell you what, I'll take care of this out of the goodness of my heart, and you buy me a pheasant dinner at Maxime's out of the goodness of *your* heart."

"I can do that." Fenway paused. "One more thing, Sarah. I took a picture of the very last line of the database. There's an artist listed: Orlando Lockberry. That line is different from the others."

"You've sent me the photos already?"

"Just now. Can you look at the database and figure out any reason he'd be treated differently than any of the other artists?"

"Sure." Sarah sighed. "Raúl canceled our brunch plans anyway."

"Just close your eyes and think of Maxime's," Fenway said. "If the sheriff drops the charges, I'll even spring for a bottle of wine."

"A *quality* wine. Not the rotgut stuff you usually drink."

"Deal."

———

Fenway stayed at the coffee shop for another hour. It was just past ten when she pried herself out of her chair and walked in the shimmering heat back to the sheriff's office, where she'd parked the rental Kia. She opened the door of the sedan and a blast of heat escaped. Jeez—did that singe her eyebrows?

She leaned forward, balanced on one foot while depressing the brake, and started the engine. The air conditioning was already on, but she turned the thermostat down to sixty degrees and cranked it up to high. Although the cloth seats wouldn't burn the back of her legs, she stood up to let the car cool down before she got in.

"Hey!"

The voice behind her made her jump, and she turned to see Izzy Bardot.

"Deputy Bardot—Izzy."

"Just to let you know, I've contacted a bunch of the computer repair shops in the area."

Fenway blinked. "Oh—the missing PC from the NNoV8 office? You've been busy while I was finishing my latte."

"I don't have the serial number of the PC yet, but I went through Vaughn Trask's credit card transactions. He bought a computer directly from a company called Qasper, with a Q."

"Yeah, that sounds right. The high-end PCs that are all in that cool metallic green finish."

"Oh, right. I've seen those ads. Anyway, he bought a Qasper computer tower, top-of-the-line everything. Processor that would put my laptop to shame. Techie terms that I didn't understand. I paid less for my first car than he paid for this computer."

"So it didn't come from NNoV8's purchasing department."

"I don't know if he expensed it or not; we're still going through his laptop. But I want you to know I'm taking this seriously." She paused. "And I expect to be informed of what you find."

"It's in my best interest to get my friend out of jail as soon as possible," Fenway said. "Why wouldn't I give you evidence?"

"You wouldn't if it makes your friend look bad," Bardot said. "And you wouldn't..." Then she trailed off.

"What?"

"We've had a couple of run-ins with Okpara Ubosi before," Bardot said. "He likes to make the cops look stupid. Threatens lawsuits. Unlawful detainment, civil rights violations, that kind of thing."

Fenway shrugged. "I can't really help that."

"Yeah, well, it wouldn't be the first time that Sheriff Jeffcoat would be on the wrong side of a lawsuit because of Ubosi."

Fenway cocked her head.

"Jeffcoat has learned a lot in the last five years," Bardot said quickly. "He's not usually the kind to jump to conclusions anymore."

"That's exactly what he's doing, though."

"It's just—this has the potential to be, um, uncomfortable."

Fenway was quiet.

"As a fellow law enforcement officer, I figured you'd be sympathetic to our situation."

"Ah." Fenway nodded. "Well, look, I don't want to cause any trouble for you or your department. I mean, you've got the wrong suspect in custody. I know I'm making your life—Sheriff Jeffcoat's life—difficult, but better we get this out in the open now than for Ubosi to spring something on you at trial."

Bardot nodded. "I can see where you're coming from, but I told you, Jeffcoat wants the quick win. I just don't want the sheriff's office to be the target of a multimillion-dollar lawsuit, then decide they have to cut a couple of deputy positions."

Fenway pressed her lips together.

"As I said, I hope you'll be sympathetic to my situation."

Fenway held out her hand. "I'll let you know anything I find."

Bardot shook her hand. "And I'll take your evidence seriously."

As Bardot walked away, Fenway knew she wasn't getting a fair deal—*I'll bring you everything I find, and you promise to consider maybe looking into it*—but Izzy Bardot was a better teammate than an enemy. Fenway would still be looking over her shoulder, but this was another glimmer of hope that perhaps Fenway could leave Las Vegas with Piper Patten in her passenger seat.

And speaking of things that weren't fair...

Fenway called Dez. One ring. Two rings. Three.

"Mmf. Fenway?"

"Were you still asleep?"

Annoyance. "It's Saturday, Fenway. We have no active cases until Pondicherry officially reopens the Mathis Jericho case on Monday morning. I am taking advantage of these two days off."

"Sorry."

"I'm awake now. What do you want?"

"I wanted to know if there were any updates with Donnelly. Specifically about the Jericho case. But it sounds like there won't be any movement until Monday."

Dez exhaled. "I managed to successfully avoid Gretchen on Friday. If anything changes, you'll be my first call."

"Okay. Sorry to bother you." Fenway hesitated. "Sorry, Michi!" she shouted.

"Oh, for heaven's sake, Fenway, I'm not on speakerphone. And

Michi's out getting bagels." Then her tone softened. "Sorry—I didn't even ask how Piper's holding up."

"I've got a few leads," Fenway said, although she had no idea how viable any of them were.

A pause. "That's not what I asked."

Fenway closed her eyes. The sooner she could get Piper out, the better she'd be doing. "I saw her last night. Seemed in good spirits." She almost mentioned Piper's black eye, but then decided not to.

"All right. Let me know if I can help."

"That depends. Are you going back to sleep?"

"Only until the bagels get here."

———

Fenway turned everything over in her head as she pulled out of the sheriff's office parking lot. There was a plan to get access to NNoV8's financial records, but nothing yet that would get information on Sookie Ryeo (or her daughter, for that matter). Nothing on the pre-nuptial agreement between Aurora Horn and the decedent —although maybe Ubosi's investigators would find something. The NNoV8 angle was good, though, but Fenway was unconvinced that either of the other co-founders were responsible for Trask's murder.

No doubt they were shady, protecting their interests at all costs, probably riding gray areas of legality to bilk money out of artists, purposely turning a blind eye to what Vaughn Trask was doing.

Well, hang on. Fenway was jumping to conclusions, probably because of her mistrust of rich people. Probably because of her terrible relationship with her father over the last twenty years. Fenway sighed. She needed to get back into therapy.

But the conversations she'd overheard between Dr. Stanley Schup and Brock Shellwater—those weren't exactly the topics innocent people discussed with each other.

"Focus, Fenway," she muttered to herself, exiting the freeway toward the Cartwheel Hotel & Casino. She had to force herself not to catch the bad guy, instead concentrating on reasonable doubt. Anything that could show the sheriff's office that Piper shouldn't be the prime suspect. She didn't need to lead them to arrest the killer. She just had to convince them to release Piper.

Fenway pulled into the parking lot of the hotel and casino. No U-Move-It van. McVie was gone again. She looked up and down the parking lot. The Cartwheel wasn't a giant casino resort like the ones in Vegas, so this was just a lot, not a covered parking garage. No trees. The rental car didn't even have a windshield shade. Yes, the fog that covered Estancia on summer mornings would be more than welcome now.

She parked close to her hotel room, turned off the engine of the comfortable air-conditioned car—and the air immediately heated as soon as the airflow stopped. She started the engine again, cracking the windows, then shut off the car again. That might save ten or fifteen degrees.

Fenway got out, the heat of the asphalt in the parking lot soaking through the soles of her sneakers. The metal handrail on the stairs was hot to the touch, but most of the concrete steps of the staircase up to the second floor were thankfully in the shade. A bead of sweat ran down her temple before she got to the landing. She trudged in the outdoor hallway to the room she and Piper shared.

She pulled her keycard out of her purse and held it above the doorknob, the click of the door unlocking. Turning the knob, Fenway pushed the door open.

The rush of air-conditioned cold air on Fenway's skin made her shiver, but she sighed in relief. After a year in the relatively cool coastal climate of Estancia—and twenty years in Seattle—she'd never thought of air conditioning as so necessary.

The housekeeping staff had been there and gone. A slight scent of lemon cleaner in the air. The bed she and McVie had slept in was made.

A note in the middle of the bed, on the bedspread.

Fenway blinked. Oh, she had to remember to get another night; even if she and Piper could leave today—not a very realistic possibility, admittedly—she'd still need a home base. Better to spend another hundred bucks on this room than any of the other options available to her.

She reached out and picked up the note.

The printed letters were sloppy, almost like a toddler's, all capital letters.

LEAVE IT ALONE OR YOU'RE NEXT

CHAPTER TWENTY

Fenway dropped the note onto the bedspread and stepped away from it as if it were a bomb. Her mind spun a million miles an hour. She had to do something. She was in danger, and they— whoever *they* were—knew where she was. Knew where she was staying.

She should call the police.

She should call Okpara Ubosi. He'd be able to use this. A death threat against the one person who was trying to get Piper out of jail? That would certainly be reasonable doubt.

Fenway wanted to call McVie. She wanted McVie *there*, to hold her and tell her everything would be all right.

She wanted to call her mother.

A lump formed in her throat. For the first time in her new career as coroner, she thought her mother could shine a light on this. She knew how artists thought. Joanne Stevenson had known about scams; she'd tell Fenway what to look for, who to talk to, the language she should use when talking to artists. She'd know.

And even though her relationship with her father had improved in the last few months, the twenty years of mistrust and pain weren't gone overnight. Or even over sixty or seventy nights.

She closed her eyes.

Okay, first things first. This had to be something she told Izzy Bardot about. As much as she wanted McVie to comfort her, he couldn't do anything. He had his own stuff to worry about: his new job, getting home in time to have dinner with Megan, not to mention unloading all his stuff into his new apartment.

Fenway took the phone out of her purse and called the sheriff's office.

"Correos County Sheriff's Office. This is Chaz."

"Deputy Izzy Bardot, please."

"One moment."

A click. No hold music, no message saying how glad the county was to serve the residents. Almost refreshing.

A full minute ticked by before Chaz came back on. "I'm sorry, Deputy Bardot is on another call. Is there something I can help you with?"

Fenway paused for a moment. She didn't trust anyone in the sheriff's office except Bardot, and even that trust was conditional. But this was too important to the case *not* to report. And time was probably of the essence; the more time that elapsed between now and whenever Fenway made the report, the less seriously the sheriff's office, even Bardot, was likely to take it. No matter what promises the deputy had made.

"I need—" Fenway began, but her voice cracked. She cleared her throat. "I'm calling to report a death threat."

Chaz's voice grew serious. "A death threat? Against whom?"

"Me," Fenway said, her voice squeaking. Ugh, she hated that.

"Hold on," Chaz said.

Again with the absence of any hold music.

"Sheriff Bartholomew Jeffcoat."

The last person she wanted to talk to. Still, there was protocol.

There were expectations if this could have a hope of being used to get Piper out of jail.

"I understand you've received a death threat?" Jeffcoat continued.

"Yes," Fenway said. "Hello again, Sheriff."

A pause. "I'm sorry, I don't recognize your voice. Who is this?"

"Fenway Stevenson. The coroner from California." She plowed ahead before waiting for a response. "I went to—" No. She couldn't say she'd interviewed Aurora Horn or talked to Izzy Bardot. "I had breakfast, then went to a coffee shop. When I got back to my hotel room, there was a death threat written on a piece of paper. Someone put the death threat on the bedspread, right in the center of my bed."

Jeffcoat paused. Even in the silence, Fenway could feel the sheriff's skepticism soaking through the phone line. "I see."

Fenway debated with herself: should she say anything about his skepticism, or should she just focus on the facts?

She shut her eyes. She didn't know Jeffcoat well enough to know how he'd react to either of the options Fenway could take. She flipped a coin in her mind. Heads.

"I know how this looks, Sheriff."

"How is that, Ms. Stevenson? How exactly does it look?"

Fenway grimaced. Perhaps that wasn't the right direction to go. Still, she was committed. "It looks convenient. An anonymous note left on my bed that says *leave it alone or you're next*? It implies that someone besides Piper is behind the murder of Trask, and that the real killer is threatening me. And that's awfully convenient for me. For Piper."

"And you know I'm compelled to make a police report."

"I'm not that familiar with Nevada state law."

"And now your expensive hotshot lawyer can poke holes in the case. Now you've got something to tell the jury that could introduce doubt in their minds. I'm not stupid, Ms. Stevenson."

"I never said you were."

"I can move to get this excluded."

"Look, Sheriff," Fenway said, "My life has been threatened. I'll have to find another place to stay tonight."

"Also convenient."

"Decidedly inconvenient for me," Fenway said. "But I can see it from your perspective." What was it that Bardot had said? *I hope you'll be sympathetic to my situation.* "I'm a law enforcement officer myself."

"Not in Nevada you aren't."

"I mean for my job. For my career." As short as it had been till now, anyway. "And I know if I were in your shoes, I'd be looking for ways to prove my story is false."

"Doesn't mean Ms. Patten's lawyer won't use this to their advantage, though." He harrumphed. "Are you still staying at the Cartwheel?"

"Yes."

"I'll be over to examine the room shortly."

"No, I—" Eek. A visceral reaction. Fenway didn't want Sheriff Jeffcoat going through her things. Then a tinge of panic. Through Piper's things, too. And Jeffcoat was the sheriff. He could plant something that would make Piper look guilty. She knew it happened, and she heard Bardot's voice in her head: Jeffcoat wanted this case closed quickly. He was up for election in the fall, and this case might very well make or break his re-election chances. Fenway closed her eyes and a wave of nausea threatened to overtake her. She tamped it down but tasted bile anyway. This wasn't good. She should have insisted on waiting until Bardot was off her call. Stupid, stupid, stupid.

"That's great," Fenway lied. "I'm glad you're taking this seriously."

"Did you touch the note with the death threat?"

"Yes. I picked it up to read it."

"So your fingerprints are on it?"

"That's correct," Fenway said. The skepticism in his voice deepened. Yes, it was very convenient that Fenway's fingerprints were on the paper. Fenway could have written the note herself, placed it on the bed, et voilà: instant reasonable doubt.

"We'll be able to get better information when we get there," Jeffcoat said. Yeah, and there'd be more opportunity to plant evidence in their hotel room. A terrible thought sprang unbidden into Fenway's head: maybe the evidence would point toward *Fenway*, not Piper. Maybe the sheriff would let Piper go only to arrest Fenway with planted evidence. After all, Fenway was the pesky one; she'd had access to Piper's knife, she'd had ample opportunity. The only thing Fenway didn't have was motive, and if the sheriff could plant evidence of that, there was no telling what fresh hell would await Fenway.

"Stay in your room until we arrive," Jeffcoat said, and Fenway ended the call before saying goodbye. This wasn't good.

She closed her eyes for a moment. Ubosi—he was the next logical call. She dialed his personal number.

"Good day, Fenway," he answered.

"I just got a death threat," she said. "Came back to my room after breakfast and meeting Deputy Bardot for coffee. It was on the bed when I came back in."

"Don't touch it," Ubosi barked.

"Too late," Fenway said. "I thought it was a note telling me I'd need to extend my stay. So I grabbed the paper, and it says *leave it alone or you're next.*"

A pause. "That's exactly what it says? Word for word?"

"Yes."

A long exhale from Ubosi. "I don't have to tell you this is excellent news for Piper."

"Yes. I get that. Reasonable doubt all day and twice on Sunday. But the sheriff is skeptical."

An audible gasp from Ubosi. "You called the sheriff?"

"Come on, O.K., I *had* to. If there's no police report on this, it didn't happen."

Silence.

"Even if," Fenway continued, "the sheriff thinks I wrote the note myself, we have to file a police report. If they *don't* make one, then you're a good enough lawyer to suggest that the police hyper-focused on Piper. And if they *do* make a police report, they'll be forced to follow up on it."

"I know," Ubosi said.

"But," Fenway said, "they're coming here."

"Where's here?"

"My hotel room at the Cartwheel. I shared it with Piper on Thursday night—the night of the murder. And I'm afraid they're going to plant evidence against Piper." Fenway paused. "Or maybe even me."

Ubosi chuckled. "I think you've been watching too many cop shows."

"Or maybe I've caught one too many corrupt cops," Fenway retorted. Well, it had only been a couple, but that had been a couple too many.

Ubosi said nothing.

"How quickly can you make it here?" Fenway said. "I think we need to have you here when they search the room."

Ubosi grunted. "I'm an hour away, and I'm in my pajamas. You think you can stall them?"

"I suppose I can insist on a warrant."

"They've got probable cause. You're the one reporting a death threat. The note's on your bed. It's not unreasonable to assume the perpetrator left something else there." He sighed. "I'm not sure I could argue that they need a warrant. A death threat requires immediate action."

Fenway swore under her breath. "You don't have someone in your employ who lives closer to Ruby Dunes? Someone who could get here in less than twenty minutes.?"

"Let me see what I can do."

They said their goodbyes, and Fenway hung up.

How did this happen? It was obviously *after* the housekeeping staff had made the bed.

Again, first things first: she needed to change rooms. She checked the clock on her phone: 10:23. The sheriff probably wouldn't be there until half-past, maybe even longer. And since Fenway was a law enforcement officer, Sheriff Jeffcoat might decide he needed a warrant after all. That would take a while. On a Saturday, it might take an hour or two to find a judge willing to sign a warrant. And it might take another hour for Jeffcoat and his team to even create a warrant.

Fenway rubbed her temples, her fingers in a circular motion. She could be a pain in Jeffcoat's ass, for sure. She could insist on a warrant. That would probably give Ubosi enough time to get out of his PJs and into real clothes and get his butt to Ruby Dunes. He wouldn't like it, but her father was paying him for this. No expense too great to save Piper, who had saved him from jail. Or, for that matter, save his daughter, with whom he had just gone from estranged to tenuously civil.

And the sheriff had told her to stay in her hotel room. But she wasn't going to.

She texted Ubosi.

> I'm going to stall. I'll insist on a warrant.
> Get here as fast as you can.

She didn't want to give the sheriff the opportunity to plant anything in either of their bags, so Fenway hurriedly threw her toiletries and cables into McVie's gray-and-pink suitcase, grabbed it along with Piper's cherry-red duffel, then opened the door to her room—and almost immediately bumped into a tall brass-plated luggage cart, suitcases and bags piled high.

"Sorry about that," an employee dressed in the bell uniform said. "Want me to take these to the front desk for you?"

"Oh," Fenway said. "Sure."

The employee took the cases from her and put them on top, then rolled the cart down toward the elevator.

"Shall I follow you?"

"Sure."

————

Fenway followed the bell desk employee into the lobby of the Cartwheel Hotel & Casino and turned to the front desk. The employee pushed the tall brass cart parked next to the bell desk, about twenty feet away, then walked through a doorway into the back—probably luggage storage.

Orlando Lockberry was behind the front desk, in a white polo shirt with the Cartwheel logo. Much more professional than the rumpled blue shirt he'd had on the night before.

"I need to extend my stay for another night," Fenway said.

"Sure," Orlando said.

"But it needs to be a different room."

Orlando furrowed his brow. "Another room?"

"I—" Fenway paused. She almost started crying, but took a deep breath, tamping her emotions down. "I got a death threat. On my bed. They know where I'm staying."

Orlando blinked. "They—they what?"

"I got a death threat. On my bed." Fenway narrowed her eyes at Orlando. "Somebody got into my room and threatened my life."

"Oh—oh no," Orlando stammered. "I'm so sorry."

"Well, it's not your fault, but the hotel needs tighter security."

"When did it happen?"

"After housekeeping was in the room."

"Oh." Orlando grimaced. "I'm afraid housekeeping is one area where we're not as secure as we could be."

"What do you mean?"

"It's just that if someone comes to the door when the room is being cleaned, housekeeping doesn't always check to see if they *should* be in the room."

Fenway cocked her head. "That's—"

"Unacceptable, I know," stammered Orlando. "But there's not a lot I can do about it. Housekeeping isn't paid to be private security. Honestly"—and here, Orlando lowered his voice—"it costs a lot less to reimburse guests for the loss of property when that *does* happen, rather than hire extra security staff during the housekeeping rounds." He frowned. "And besides, it makes the housekeeping staff resentful. Like they're being watched constantly."

"The cops are going to be here soon to go over my room," Fenway said. "And they'll probably want to talk to the housekeeping staff."

"I think that would be Naddie," Orlando said.

"Naddie?"

"Nadezhda," Orlando replied. "Refugee from Ukraine. Hardest worker at this entire hotel. Has a six-year-old. Cutest kid." He shook his head. "Her husband was killed in the first Russian attacks. She and her kid fled across the Polish border with nothing but the clothes on their backs."

Fenway hesitated. She wanted to talk to Nadezhda, but didn't want to come across as a harsh police authority figure. Still, preparing Nadezhda for the American police interrogation that would no doubt come with the territory on this? It was probably a good idea. "Is Nadezhda still working?"

Orlando nodded. "Yeah, she finishes up around eleven. Lunch break, then another sweep of the rooms at two."

"Where can I find her?"

"Uh... she's working the third floor of the casino rooms right now." He leaned forward. "But don't go too hard on her. After what she and her kid have gone through? She doesn't get paid enough to check room keys while she's trying to clean up these shitty hotel rooms."

"I just want to know who went into my room."

"Yeah, well, she's got a healthy mistrust of authority. As you can well imagine."

Fenway nodded. "Can you put me in a different room tonight?"

"I think so." Orlando turned to his computer and clicked on the keyboard, moved the mouse, then frowned. "Where are you now?"

"443."

"Do you want something in the plaza rooms?"

"The plaza rooms?"

"The area where you are now. So you don't have to walk through the casino."

Fenway grimaced. "I bet I was in danger because someone saw the room I went into. As much as I hate the casino, I think I'll be safer if no one can sit in the parking lot and see what room I enter."

"Yeah, good idea." Orlando leaned forward again. "They're usually twenty bucks more, but I'll put you in one for the same price."

Fenway nodded. Orlando thought he was doing her a favor, but because the hotel had been derelict in their security, it was the very least he could do. Most companies would comp a night—or even the entire stay. But Fenway didn't have the strength to argue. "Thank you, Orlando."

"My pleasure." He tapped again. "Check out is at eleven o'clock, so if you could move—"

Fenway shook her head. "I can't move until after the police search the room."

Orlando frowned. "I see. Understandable. I guess management will have to suck it up." He smiled, though the humor didn't reach his eyes. "Come back and see me when the sheriff is done, and I'll see if we have a room available. I think we can put you on the third floor in the tower. Guests should be checking out shortly."

"Thanks. I appreciate it. And I *did* get my luggage out of the room. Is it possible to store it here?"

Orlando flashed a charming smile. "Of course." He turned his head toward the bell desk. "Ah. Mateo seems to have vanished." He walked around the front desk to the bell desk, grabbed two luggage tags, and grabbed the pink-and-gray suitcase and the cherry-red duffel from the pile of suitcases on the cart. He pulled the tags around the handles, then pulled the numbered stubs off both tags and handed them to Fenway.

"Thank you, Orlando." Fenway put the stubs in her wallet.

"My pleasure." He cocked his head. "Maybe you'd let me buy you a drink tonight."

Fenway's heart sank. She'd hoped Orlando was a decent guy, but he was still trying to get in her pants. And this after McVie—all six-foot-four, big-biceps McVie—had left the state.

And yet, without Orlando bending the rules for her, she'd be in a worse spot. Maybe she'd meet him for a drink later; buy him a beer to thank him. And maybe he'd try to insist on paying, but she'd keep things professional.

Would certainly be better than to have him back out of whatever he was doing now. As distasteful as it might be to meet him for a drink. Especially if he had any hope that Fenway might be open to cheating on McVie for a one-night stand.

But she'd—she'd done worse before. She'd made other compromises. And here she was. She'd gotten through it.

So she smiled. "I appreciate all you're doing," she said, then took the key and turned back to go to her plaza room. She had been intentionally vague. And vague was good.

Orlando leaned forward. "And I probably shouldn't be telling you this," he said, "but the woman who Trask was supposed to see on Thursday night?"

Nadine Ryeo. She nodded.

"She's extended her stay through the weekend." Orlando arched an eyebrow. "Did I hear right that you had it out with her in the hotel bar?"

"I asked her a few questions," Fenway said. "She didn't like answering them, but I wouldn't say we had it out." Nadine's *mother*, on the other hand...

"Yeah, well, Nadine's still here," Orlando said. "Maybe *she's* the one who snuck into your room. It's not like she's the pinnacle of moral superiority."

CHAPTER TWENTY-ONE

FENWAY HURRIED BACK TO HER ROOM WITH A FEW MINUTES TO spare before the sheriff was supposed to arrive. But it was too late —she found the front door wide open, the sheriff inside, the death threat note on the side table, a tech leaning over the table with a fingerprint kit.

"Hey, hey, hey," Fenway said, "you weren't supposed to be here for another ten minutes."

"And you were supposed to stay in your room," Jeffcoat said.

"I didn't consent to a search."

"Imminent threat to life," Jeffcoat said. "That trumps any privacy—"

"You need a warrant."

"Not in a hotel room we don't," Jeffcoat said. "And I'd think you'd take your personal safety more seriously than this."

"You'll forgive me if I want to protect my rights," Fenway said. Jeffcoat was wrong about the search warrant, too—the Supreme Court even said so—but they were already in the room.

The sheriff shrugged. "You don't have to cooperate with us, but it'll go easier if you do. We'll also take a quick look around the room. Let me know if anything else is out of place."

Fenway bit her lip. Surely, the sheriff would notice that there were no suitcases or bags in the room. He wouldn't like that—but at least it eliminated any opportunity to rifle through Piper's stuff.

Then another thought struck. What if whoever had left the death threat had also planted evidence in the hotel room? Whoever had killed Trask had almost certainly gotten blood on their clothing, too. What if the killer planted the bloody clothes in the hotel room, too, and Fenway hadn't seen them when she was packing in a rush?

She walked around the hotel room. Except for the bed being made, the note, and their bags gone, everything was pretty much where she left it. "I see nothing out of place."

"Thank you, Ms. Stevenson," the sheriff said. "I'm afraid I'll have to ask you to step outside until we're finished." He harrumphed. "I'd suggest you get another room if you're staying for another day."

Fenway sighed. "Already on it."

There was nothing else Fenway could do. She stepped out of the room, pulled her phone out, and pulled up Ubosi's messages. No response from him yet, but she sent him another message.

> Never mind, the cops are already here
> searching my room

A pause, then three dots appeared.

UBOSI
> They already got a warrant?

FENWAY
> No they said the death threat posed
> imminent danger so they had probable
> cause to search

Fenway grinned. She'd only known Ubosi for a day, but he had definitely figured out what made her tick.

There was a member of the housekeeping staff she needed to talk to.

She walked down the concrete stairs and saw Izzy Bardot walking across the parking lot, toward the stairs. Bardot caught her eye and motioned with her head.

Fenway sighed. Bardot wore a frown.

Fenway stopped at the bottom of the stairs. "Hi, Izzy."

"Fenway," Izzy said, then gently took Fenway's elbow and pulled her down the first-floor hall.

Fenway opened her mouth, but Bardot obviously wanted to talk.

"I thought," Bardot said, "that you were going to keep *me* informed of everything."

"I got a death threat," Fenway said. "And I *did* call you. You weren't available to talk."

"Why didn't you say you'd wait until I was off the phone?"

"Because," Fenway said, "if I hadn't reported it immediately, I'd be accused of planting it. Waiting until I could talk to a friendly cop, and not the sheriff, who I knew would make my life hell—I didn't think that was a good option."

Bardot raised her eyebrows. "He's not making your life hell right now?"

"Yes," Fenway hissed, "I can see the error of my ways."

Bardot let go of Fenway's elbow and paced in a circle. "I just don't know what we should do," she said. That was good—Bardot was using the term *we*.

"I'm about to talk with the housekeeping staff member assigned to clean my room," Fenway said.

Bardot nodded. "That's a good idea. You think they saw whoever left you the note?"

"It's possible. Someone who works for the hotel had to let them in. Or I guess these door locks aren't top-of-the-line. Maybe someone who knew how to break in did it."

Bardot stopped pacing and crossed her arms. "I've seen that look on the sheriff's face before," she mumbled. "He's gotten the idea that your friend did it, and he's like a dog with a chew toy he doesn't want to give up. But now he thinks he'll have to."

"You're not worried—" Fenway began, then shut her mouth. No. She wouldn't accuse the sheriff of planting evidence.

"I'm not worried about what?"

Fenway shook her head.

"No, really, what?"

"Never mind."

Bardot blinked. "Ah. You think the sheriff is so tied to his idea that your friend did it, he'll make sure to get evidence to convict her?"

"Or whoever left the note planted evidence, and Sheriff Jeffcoat will find it."

Bardot pressed her lips together, then dropped her arms to her side. "I'm not gonna lie, the sheriff and I don't get along great. But he would never plant evidence."

"But if he *found* planted evidence?"

"Well, now, that's another story." Bardot started pacing again. "But what is it you think will get planted? Our theory of the crime is that Piper got so angry with what Trask had said in the museum, that she felt ripped off or whatever, and that when she saw him in the parking lot, she just snapped. What could Jeffcoat possibly plant?"

Fenway felt a little relief. At least this wouldn't be prosecuted as a premeditated crime. Lesser charges. Then Fenway snapped herself out of it: if Piper was convicted, she was still looking at twenty years in prison.

"I've been gone for too long," said Bardot. She pulled a small notebook out of her pocket and scribbled on it, then tore out the page. "My personal cellphone. Call me next time you feel you need to report something to the sheriff's office that can't wait."

———

Fenway walked across the sweltering parking lot to the casino. Pulling the door open, she entered a sea of air conditioning and stale cigarette smoke. Trying not to cough—or think about having to treat her hair for the smell later—she strode across the casino floor. Then did a double take.

Sookie Ryeo. Sitting at a slot machine.

Of course. This is where she'd probably been the night Vaughn Trask had been killed. Should Fenway talk to her? Tell Sookie that she'd lied to Fenway before?

She pulled the phone out of her purse and looked at the time. 10:51. Only nine minutes until Nadezhda was off her shift.

Ugh. No. She had to talk to Nadezhda first. If Fenway could get to the housekeeper right at the end of her morning shift, maybe Fenway could talk to her for a few minutes on her break between eleven and two. Maybe Fenway could get her lunch at the Mexican place. Her stomach growled, and Fenway shook her head. She'd had breakfast not four hours before. Lunch should be able to wait a little longer. Still, if Fenway offered, maybe Nadezhda would be more likely to talk.

She stole another glance at Sookie. She seemed glued to the slot machine. If Fenway were a betting woman, she'd put a fifty-dollar-chip down that Sookie Ryeo would be in this same spot after Fenway spoke to Nadezhda. Even if there was lunch at the Mexican restaurant first.

Orlando said Nadezhda was working on the third floor of the casino rooms. Of course, that was twenty minutes ago, maybe longer. But it was a place to start. Fenway crossed the casino, going toward the sign that read *Casino Room Elevators*, and after a labyrinthine walk between roulette tables, the Pai Gow area, and past the faux-marble archway for high rollers, she saw the elevator bank on her left.

An elevator was waiting on the ground floor, its doors open, and she stepped in and pushed the button for the third floor. The doors closed with a squeak, and Fenway felt the shift under her feet as the elevator started pulling her up toward the sky.

The doors opened, and Fenway stepped out. Three hallways after she exited the elevator bank: one to the left, one to the right, one straight ahead. She peered down all of them. A housekeeping cart was about ten rooms down on the right corridor, and Fenway hurried to get to it.

She arrived at the cart, slightly out of breath, and the door was open. She rapped her knuckles on the open door.

A woman appeared in a Cartwheel hotel uniform—Nadezhda.

"Is this your room?" Nadezhda said. "Five minutes, I am done. You come back?"

Fenway shook her head. "I just need to talk when you're finished."

Nadezhda's brow furrowed. "Talk?"

"You cleaned my room the last two days. On the plaza side. I just have a question for you."

Nadezhda's eyes narrowed. "Is something wrong? I do not take anything."

"I know, I know," Fenway said. "I'm not angry. Nothing is missing. I just want to talk."

Nadezhda hesitated. "I take this cart back. I have break at eleven o'clock."

"I could buy you lunch," Fenway ventured.

Nadezhda shook her head. "I go home. My son."

"Bring him along. I'll buy him lunch, too."

She hesitated, then shook her head. "No, not a good idea."

Fenway paused, then took out her badge.

Nadezhda recoiled.

"You're not in any trouble," Fenway said quickly. "I just need to ask you a few questions. Ten minutes, if you don't want lunch."

"I have done nothing. I work hard for—"

"No trouble," Fenway repeated. "I just need to know what you saw."

Fenway could see the gears spin in Nadezhda's head. Finally, she spoke. "When?"

"I will meet you in the hotel lobby when you are done with your shift. Ten minutes. Then you can get home to your son and be back in plenty of time for your afternoon shift."

She gave Fenway a curt nod, then went back into the room.

Fenway put her badge away, then turned and walked back toward the elevators. She shuffled her feet on the low-pile, red-and-gold carpet and swore softly under her breath. She'd completely botched that interaction. Orlando had even warned Fenway about Nadezhda's reticence to talk to the police—and yet, at the first sign of hesitation, Fenway had pulled out her badge. "Be better, Fenway," she admonished herself, riding the elevator back down to the casino level.

Maybe Nadezhda wouldn't even show up.

Fenway crossed the carpeted floor of the casino, in and out of the video poker machines and gaming tables. She had enough time to talk to Sookie. Probably.

She followed the signs to the registration desk and looked to her right to where Sookie had camped at the slot machine a few minutes before.

No. Empty.

Good thing Fenway wasn't the betting type. She'd be down a fifty-dollar chip.

She walked around the slot machines; maybe Sookie was at another one. There! She saw a short woman with straight black hair. But no, that wasn't her. Fenway sighed and turned back toward the main carpeted walkway.

And a woman ran right into her, knocking her purse off her shoulder.

"Oh—sorry," Fenway said. Then she saw: it was Sookie.

"Mrs. Ryeo," Fenway said.

"You're following me," Sookie said.

Fenway bent down to get her purse. Fortunately, nothing had fallen out of it but her phone, which had bounced a surprising distance across the carpeted floor.

"I'm not following you. I'm here interviewing one of the employees." Fenway grabbed the phone and pulled her purse back up on her shoulder.

"First, you follow me at brunch. Next, you're here at the casino."

Fenway raised herself to her full height; she towered over Sookie. "If you hadn't noticed, Ruby Dunes doesn't have a lot of options for breakfast. And I'm staying at this hotel. What's *your* excuse for being here so often?"

Sookie scoffed, though her eyes flashed uncertainty. "It's a free country. I don't have to answer that."

Fenway wanted to tell Sookie that she knew the Ryeo sisters hadn't been together the night of the murder, but didn't want to out Benny. She got the feeling Benny was afraid of Sookie. Then she had an idea. "In fact, I'm talking to a few different employees here. They say you were on the casino floor. In the evening. I'm looking into getting a warrant for the footage. Will I see you were here at the time of the murder? If you disappeared from the floor, the video will show that too. Maybe I can see when you went out to the parking lot—"

"I don't have to listen to this."

"Sure, I guess you'd rather talk to the sheriff. Or if you want to go back to Palmdale, we could get the FBI involved, since you're crossing state lines." It was all a bluff, but again, Fenway just needed reasonable doubt.

Sookie laughed. "Look at me. I'm a tiny woman. Overpowering a man like that? No one will believe it. No one will believe *you*."

The older woman turned on her heel and walked away.

All the way to a roulette table, where she sat down.

Fenway considered following her and asking her more questions, but she knew Sookie had been here at the casino, not one hundred feet from where Vaughn Trask had been killed. That should be enough to get Deputy Bardot to get moving, asking for casino footage at the very least. If Sookie had left the casino at any point during the possible time of the murder, that would be enough for reasonable doubt. Sookie had a better motive than Piper, an established opportunity, and could easily have found the knife in the parking lot. Ubosi would eat that for breakfast, as he'd said.

Fenway walked through the casino back to the lobby. Orlando was no longer behind the front desk; instead, Teddi stood there. Fenway smiled at her.

"You're still at the hotel?" Teddi asked.

"Yeah. I'm moving rooms, though." Fenway cocked her head. "Orlando didn't tell you?"

"Tell me what?"

"I—" Fenway glanced around, then stepped closer to Teddi and lowered her voice. "I got a death threat."

"A death threat?" Teddi leaned in. "If we still had that blue-and-gold Colver .38 in the safe, I'd lend it to you."

"I don't think I'd need it. The sheriff is in my room right now."

"That's it?" Teddi said. "Sheriff Ready-for-His-Closeup is on the case?"

"He is," Fenway said. "Teddi, who has access to the keycards that would open my room?"

Teddi paused. "The system tracks all the keycards we make. "

"There are master keycards, though. And housekeeping can get in."

Teddi shook her head. "That's all under wraps. We have good security here."

"Except for the cameras, right?"

"Well..." Teddi leaned forward. "Okay, so hotel security has master keys. Obviously, the front desk people can make keys. But I swear to you, I didn't go anywhere near your room. And Orlando was sitting at the front desk all morning."

"He takes breaks, though, right?"

Teddi shook her head. "He does, but he'd never do something like that."

Fenway nodded. Teddi might have rose-colored glasses on when it came to Orlando; Fenway recalled how Teddi had swooned over his art. "But let's say," Fenway said, "someone convinced someone else to give them a key, just for ten minutes. Or tricked them into giving it away."

Teddi put a hand to her chest. "Are you suggesting that I—"

"Not you, Teddi. I mean, maybe it was an unintentional thing. Maybe housekeeping got tricked into letting someone in."

A sigh from Teddi. "That happens more often than hotels want to admit. People leave valuables in their rooms all the time, and maybe somebody sneaks by housekeeping."

Fenway nodded. "Anyway, I'm moving from the plaza rooms to the casino tower."

Teddi cracked a smile. "Ha. 'Tower.' Three floors. That always gives me a laugh."

"Have to get past security to get to those rooms, right?"

Teddi nodded enthusiastically. "Don't get me wrong, it's a lot more secure. Moving to the casino tower is a good idea."

"Were you working with Orlando at the front desk this morning?"

"Nope, didn't start until eleven, just a few minutes ago."

"Did you see anything this morning when you came in? Somebody going into my room on the plaza side?"

"Oh, honey, I wouldn't notice anything. I'm not a morning person. That's why starting at eleven works for me. I have a full pot of coffee in the morning, but I still drive here like I'm a zombie."

Fenway nodded. "I gotcha. I'm dead in the morning before coffee, myself." She cleared her throat. "Just waiting for Nadezhda to come meet me. Then I'll see if I can find Orlando to ask him."

Teddi cocked her head. "Naddie? What do you want with her?"

"She's the one who cleaned my room this morning. Thought she might have seen something. But I might have scared her off."

Teddi scoffed. "She doesn't scare that easy."

Fenway smiled, then stepped back. Teddi was still smiling at her. Oh, this was going to be awkward if Nadezhda didn't show up soon.

Fortunately, a hotel guest walked up to Teddi with a question, and Fenway was saved—and then Nadezhda, dressed in jeans and a light blue blouse with short sleeves, came through the door behind the counter. Her forehead was creased. Fenway caught her eye and gave her the friendliest smile she could.

Nadezhda walked around the side of the counter and Fenway met her next to the concierge desk.

"Thank you for meeting me," Fenway said.

"I do not have much time."

"I will be quick," Fenway said. "You cleaned my room this morning, correct?"

"I do not know which room—"

"Sorry, sorry. Room 443. In the Plaza Rooms side."

"Ah, yes, 443 would be my room."

"Did anyone come to the door while you were cleaning?"

Nadezhda's eyebrows knitted. "Uh—no. No one came to the door."

"Did you leave the door open when you cleaned?"

Nadezhda shook her head. "Not the Plaza Rooms. Those are open to the outside. Anyone can come in. Especially since the cameras broke." She pursed her lips. "Are you missing something?"

"No, no. Someone put a note in my room."

"Oh. I do not know. Where was the note?"

"On my bed."

Nadezhda jutted her chin out. "I tell you, no note on the bed when I left Room 443. Or any room today. I make the bed, I clean the bathroom, I vacuum, I take the towels and leave clean, I make sure everything is the way it was when I come in. No notes today."

Fenway studied Nadezhda's face. If she'd been in an interrogation, she would have asked more probing questions. She probably would have done some research on Nadezhda, too. But she didn't have that luxury. "Thank you," Fenway said simply. "I'll let you get home."

Nadezhda nodded and walked past Fenway out the front door of the hotel.

She might be lying, but Fenway didn't think so. Someone else had let the person in who put the note on Fenway's bed. There were dozens of hotel and casino employees. Sookie, Nadine—they probably just needed to ask another member of the housekeeping staff to let them in, or bribed Teddi or Orlando or one of the other front desk employees. In fact, if a bribe was in the equation, the two remaining owners of the NNoV8 museum would have plenty of money to do that.

Fenway waited a few moments, then exited the hotel lobby as well. If she was going to change her room to the casino tower, she'd need to do it as soon as the sheriff left.

Then she thought for a moment. If someone in the hotel had

given the intruder access, was it really safe staying at the Cartwheel another night?

Fenway shook her head. The Cartwheel was the only hotel in a twenty-mile radius. And if someone had bribed a hotel worker to provide access to Fenway's room, they could just as easily do that in the next hotel down the road. The hotels in Las Vegas were probably more secure, but she didn't want to drive an hour and a half to get down there—then back here when she needed to continue finding something that could convince the sheriff to let Piper go.

She'd keep her stuff and Piper's stuff in the trunk of the rental car, and she'd sleep with the safety lock on and maybe even a piece of furniture against the door. Fenway was freaked out enough where she'd be doing that no matter where she slept tonight—even if she went all the way to Vegas.

She walked up the concrete stairs to her room. The red-headed deputy was leaving, a squarish case in his hand, as Fenway walked up.

"How much longer?" Fenway asked.

"We're all done."

"Great," Fenway said. "You find anything?"

"That's a question for Sheriff Jeffcoat."

"And where is he?"

"Already gone." He paused. "We took the note, by the way. Analysis."

"I see," Fenway said. "Where's Deputy Bardot?"

"She's gone too."

"So you're out? I can come back in now?"

"As far as I'm concerned."

Fenway nodded, and the deputy moved past her.

She entered the room and closed the door behind her. Silence.

Fenway was suddenly aware of her heart racing and took a deep breath. She'd been running around all morning, talking to people who didn't want to talk with her, trying to balance everything with McVie, with Ubosi, with the sheriff's department—and a wave of exhaustion hit her. She looked at the bed. Half her brain wanted to take a nap; the other half was screaming at her to be vigilant.

Fenway sighed, then walked around the room to make sure she hadn't left anything. She'd officially change rooms. And then she needed lunch—and more caffeine.

CHAPTER TWENTY-TWO

When Fenway went back to the front desk, Teddi was flustered and caught flat-footed; she'd checked the availability of a room in the Tower, but none of the available rooms had two beds. Fenway wasn't sure that would be an issue with Piper being an overnight guest of the Correos County Jail, but if Piper got out after the last flight back to Estancia left, it might be a problem. Then it was just that Teddi wouldn't have a room available for Fenway for another hour or two.

"I'm so sorry," Teddi said. "There are a couple of rooms that asked for late checkouts. You'll be able to check in later this afternoon."

"Not a problem," Fenway said, smiling in a way she hoped looked genuine.

It was almost one o'clock. And she was hungry. Now, the most important question she'd have to answer all day: the Mexican place, or Albie K's? No question: Mexican, even if the place was a poor comparison to Dos Milagros.

But as she began the walk down the street to the Mexican place, she changed her mind. It was too hot for anything but lizards to be out in this heat. She made a ninety-degree turn in the hundred-degree heat and went for the cool confines of Albie K's.

As she opened the door, a seat at the empty bar called out to her. A cold beer, maybe a turkey with guacamole. Just the salve for this scorching hot day.

As she sat at the bar, exhaling like someone triple her age, her phone buzzed. She reached into her purse and pulled it out. Sarah.

"Hey, Sarah."

"Got a hit on a name in that database," Sarah said. "Iris Abernathy. Newer artist, mostly mixed media. Got a couple of her sculptures at a small gallery in Windkettle. Her website says she graduated from Central Coast College of the Arts last year."

"She's from Estancia?"

"P.Q.," Sarah said.

That was good enough; Paso Querido was still in Dominguez County, so within Fenway's jurisdiction. "Have you contacted her yet?"

"Ah, that's outside my job description," Sarah said. "And just so you're aware, I'm hourly, and now that this is officially a fraud investigation for a victim in Dominguez County, I'm putting in for overtime."

"Of course," Fenway said. "Send me her number. I'll call her right away." Her stomach, quiet since thinking about Mexican food when she needed to interview Nadezhda, suddenly roared to life. "Or maybe after I grab something to eat."

"Incoming," Sarah said.

Fenway heard the ding of a text arriving. She sighed. The beer would have to wait until after she talked to Iris Abernathy.

She said goodbye to Sarah, motioned to the bartender and ordered a club soda and a sandwich, then stared at her phone. Should she call her now?

Fenway shifted on the stool. No time like the present. She dug in her purse and got out her earbuds, put them in, and heard the chunky electronica sound notifying her of the connection with the phone. She tapped Sarah's text message, then tapped the phone number for Iris Abernathy.

Would Abernathy pick it up? Maybe not—an unknown local number was sure to be a sales call, right? Sure enough, it went to voicemail. Fenway spoke clearly, succinctly. "Iris, this is Coroner Fenway Stevenson from Dominguez County. I'm investigating a fraud case involving the NNoV8 museum, and I believe you have been a victim. Would you contact me as soon as possible?" She left her number. Did that sound too much like a scammy call? Oh, well—if not, she'd call back and tell Iris to call the coroner's office. Sarah could put her through—well, not on the weekend, but she'd cross that bridge later.

She ended the call and put the phone on the counter. Maybe she *would* order that beer. She caught the bartender's eye and ordered a beer—no wait, a gin and tonic. They'd cleared the one she ordered at the hotel bar before she could even take her first sip.

And her phone buzzed on the counter. Iris Abernathy.

"This is Fenway Stevenson."

A slight pause. "I got your message. You—you say you're looking into a fraud case?"

"That's correct. You've done business with the NNoV8 museum in Ruby Dunes, Nevada."

"Well, I—uh, yes. I put my art in a, uh, what did they call it? A technology installation."

"Did you convert your artwork into NFTs?"

"I hadn't done it before, but I had some artist friends who did. I don't have a blockchain account, but the man from the museum said I didn't need one."

"Did he give you a software program to do it? One that didn't need a blockchain account from you?"

Another pause. "Dammit," Iris muttered under her breath. "Dammit, Iris, you are such an idiot."

"No, no," Fenway said gently. "This museum looks like it's on the up-and-up." Ugh, one of her father's favorite sayings. "Backed by financiers with impeccable reputations. New technology. There's no way you could have known this. They weren't throwing up any red flags."

"A blockchain account is expensive," Iris said. "Extravana wanted over five hundred bucks for the Proof of Work."

"And NNoV8 required the Proof of Work method?" Fenway was skating on the edge of her technology knowledge, but she hoped her tone was confident enough to pull it off.

"I guess." She groaned. "I just want to paint. Can't I just paint? Why do I have to know all this shit about blockchain and finances and authentication? I've got too much in my head already with color theory and perspective and—"

"Are you near your computer?"

"Uh, it's in the other room."

"Can you go in there? See if it's on?"

"I don't think so. I put it to sleep when I'm not using it."

"See if it's running. Maybe it's warm."

"Hold on." A rustling, a fumbling of keys. The sound of chair legs dragging across the floor, then footfalls, first on a hard-surface floor, then softer ones on carpet. "Okay, I'm in my home office. What the hell—it's roasting in here."

"So the computer is on and probably actively running a resource-intensive application," Fenway said. "We suspect that when you allowed their software to make NFTs of your work, a piece of malware attached to the program began running on your machine."

"It's supposed to be tracking how many people are viewing my art."

"Except we don't think that's what it's doing."

Iris gasped. "Oh no—am I getting my identity stolen? Credit cards? Is my—"

"We believe they're mining cryptocurrency."

Silence.

"Your computer is running all the time, running a program that creates cryptocurrency, and it'll put your electricity costs way up."

"That—that was the tracking software, they said."

"I don't think so," Fenway said gently.

"Let me get this straight," Iris said. "They went through this whole thing to run a computer program for cryptocurrency?"

"Have you seen your electricity bill over the last few months?"

"I figured it was the start of summer. I got a window air conditioner, and I just thought I bought one that sucked up a lot of electricity."

Fenway debated with herself for a moment, then decided to ask. "It would really help our investigation if we could look at your computer and analyze the software."

"Uh—I want this piece of shit NFT tracker off my machine *now*. And I'm going to tell that bastard at NNoV8 that he's in breach of contract."

Depending on what was in the terms of service for the NFT tracking software were—the document most people agreed to without reading—NNoV8 might not be in breach of contract. If this got out to the media, certainly NNoV8 would get raked over the coals, but legally speaking, it was unlikely that anything would happen.

"Was this bastard's name *Vaughn Trask*?" Fenway asked.

"Yes, that's it. Vaughn Trask. Seemed like he understood artists. Made me feel good about agreeing to the installation. I thought I was future-proofing my career."

"One more thing, Iris. Where were you…" Then Fenway's brain put the brakes on her words. Don't antagonize her. Iris Abernathy lived four hundred miles away. She just said she'd talk to Trask about breaching the contract. She probably didn't even know he was dead—and if she did, she was going through great pains to establish the idea that she *didn't* know. Asking her where she was the night of the murder would accomplish nothing—and it might put her on guard enough where she wouldn't bring the computer in to have Patrick Appleby, Dominguez County's resident IT guru, look at it.

"I'm going to make a few calls," Fenway said. "Once I arrange things, you'll be able to get your machine over to the sheriff's office, and our IT guy will copy your hard drive so we can analyze this software, and then he'd eradicate every piece of the software off your machine."

Silence for a moment, then Iris said, "Okay" in a small voice.

They said their goodbyes just as the bartender put Fenway's sandwich down in front of her.

She looked at her phone. Patrick Appleby didn't work on Saturday—not without a direct order from his manager. Not that he was contrary, but he was rigid in his approach to everything. So she'd have to call Jordan Daniels, his manager, first. That would be a faster conversation. She picked up her phone and called his cell. But no answer. Well, noon on a Saturday in late June. Family gatherings, kids' baseball or soccer games.

Fenway called Sarah.

Sarah picked up on the first ring. "You get in touch with Iris?"

"Yes. And I think she'll bring her computer in, but I want to tread carefully with Patrick. Can you talk to Jordan Daniels and Patrick and see if they'd be willing to come in today to analyze the malware on Iris's PC?"

Sarah chuckled. "You know, I may not know as much as Patrick or Piper, but I could do some work on this myself. If it's over my head, I'll call Jordan and ask him to arrange it."

"I sense a large overtime check coming your way."

"I know this is important."

"Yeah—I don't want Piper spending any longer in county lockup than she has to."

"I'll call Iris right now."

They said goodbye, and Fenway picked up her sandwich and took a big bite.

As good as the brunch had been, lunch was disappointing. Both the turkey and guacamole were bland. The toasted sourdough wasn't sour, the guacamole wasn't spicy, and the layers of lettuce, tomato, and guac were more slippery than anything. Fenway finished half the sandwich and looked skeptically at the remainder.

The front door to Albie K's opened and Orlando appeared. He hesitated when he saw Fenway. He'd changed his clothes; a button down slim-fit gray linen shirt. Dark blue jeans. He looked like he wanted to look good without trying too hard.

"Orlando?" Fenway said.

He smiled his radiant, easy smile and sauntered over to the bar.

"Another lunch interview?"

"Uh," Orlando said, "I dunno."

"Oh, come on, I won't say anything," Fenway said. "You meeting someone, or do you want a beer or something?"

"I'm—I'm just here for a few minutes." His eyes darted between Fenway and the bartender.

Ah. He was meeting someone for an afternoon date. And from the looks of it, he planned to meet with a romantic partner, and yet was still attempting to keep Fenway—and maybe Piper—in the *maybe she's into me* column. She'd been single, almost alarmingly so, before she and McVie became serious. So she understood.

Orlando took his phone out of his pocket, tapped the screen. A look of relief, or maybe disappointment, crossed his face.

"She running late?" Fenway asked.

Orlando flinched. "Oh. Uh, yeah. Only a few minutes."

"All right, don't let me ruin your whole vibe thing." Fenway noticed her gin and tonic for the first time; the bartender must have put it down when she was on the phone with Iris. He was stealthy, that one, and from the knowing look he gave Orlando, he was used to running wingman-style interference for him.

Fenway took a sip of the gin and tonic. Ick. The well gin they used was terrible—but what did she expect? Maybe the one at the hotel lobby bar would have been better. She set it down.

Then it came to her. She hadn't asked Orlando Lockberry about the database. About how he was the only name in it with a 0%, but a *Complete.* Other names had 100% and *Complete*, still others had a 0% and *Not Started.* Was it a glitch in the database, or was it something else?

But she didn't want to just come out and say it—put him on the defensive. How could she ease him into it?

She could always try gratitude.

"Hey," Fenway said, "Just wanted to let you know I appreciate you changing my room. Often, something like that happens, and it's like pulling teeth to get the hotel to do anything."

Orlando reddened and waved his hand. "Don't worry about it. I'd hate for you not to feel safe."

Fenway grinned. "Yeah. Well, it caught Teddi a little off-guard, but I should have my new room in a couple of hours. Trying to get my friend out of jail is tough enough without having to worry about where I'm going to sleep tonight."

"Sure thing."

"You were at the front desk the whole time?"

"This morning?" Orlando's brow furrowed, then relaxed. "Oh, you want to know if I saw anything suspicious? Like someone asking what room you were in?"

"Or anyone giving their master keycard to someone else?"

"That's a fireable offense," Orlando said. "And no, no one asked what room you were in." He tapped his chin. "Someone did yesterday, though."

Fenway straightened up. "Who?"

"White guy, about six four. Looked like a cop, if I'm honest. Wore a black polo shirt with some kind of corporate logo on it."

"Payback Systems?"

Orlando snapped his fingers. "That's it. I didn't give him a keycard. I didn't tell him what room you were in, either, or even if you were staying here."

"My—my significant other," Fenway said. She couldn't remember if she'd told Orlando she had a boyfriend or fiancé. This covered all the bases. "So probably not him. He left this morning, anyway."

"Well, you can't be too safe."

"And I appreciate it." Fenway grabbed her drink, then feigned surprise and set it back down. "Before I forget, I found out something. As one of the artists at NNoV8, you probably need to know."

"What is it?"

"I found out NNoV8 was distributing a piece of malware to all the artists. It was attached to a program that converts art into NFTs, but then it takes over your computer and starts mining cryptocurrency."

Orlando blinked and then furrowed his brow. "What?"

"Yeah. Crazy what scams they come up with now. I saw the malware in action, too." Oh—should she not say this? Well, whatever, she wanted to know why his name was different from all the others. "When I saw the dashboard for the malware, all the artists had a percentage next to their name. If it was a hundred percent, it was marked *complete*; if it was lower than a hundred percent, it was marked as *in process*, and if it was zero percent it said *not started*." Fenway turned slightly in her stool to gauge Orlando's reaction, but his face was stone. "But your name was different."

Orlando cocked his head, the same impassive look on his face. "How so?"

"You were at zero, but your row was marked *complete*."

"I guess I don't understand."

"Zero percenters were all *not started*, but yours was *complete*. You have any idea why that is?"

Orlando shrugged. "I don't know what to tell you. Maybe I never got infected with this malware thing."

"Did you load the museum's NFT tracker onto your computer?"

"I mean, I did, but maybe it was an old version? Or maybe my antimalware got it? I don't really know."

"Yeah, well, I just thought you should know. I've told a few other artists, and they're freaking out."

"I suppose I've seen up close and personal how low and frankly immoral Vaughn Trask can be. Nothing he did would surprise me."

Outside, the crunching of tires on the gravel lot next to Albie K's. Fenway looked out the front window.

A white Acura MDX.

The scene replayed in Fenway's head: Piper dropping her purse. Right next to a white SUV. And Fenway couldn't swear to it, but it had probably been an Acura MDX.

Aurora Horn.

CHAPTER TWENTY-THREE

Fenway rushed outside, waving her arms, just as Orlando was getting into Aurora Horn's Acura MDX.

"Wait—wait, hold on," Fenway called. Orlando turned, the passenger door open.

Aurora Horn, who had changed from that morning's pajamas into a glittery tank top and a black pencil skirt, sat in the driver's seat. Color rose to her cheeks.

Fenway had leapt to the conclusion that Aurora was cheating on Vaughn with Orlando—but the blush all but confirmed it. "I'm sorry to bother you again," Fenway said, feigning being out of breath so she could think. How did she want to play this?

"We're in a hurry," Aurora said.

"It'll just take a second," Fenway said. "I meant to ask you the other day—"

Orlando shot a glance at Aurora, who ignored it.

"—about your MDX. I thought I had seen it in the parking lot of the museum on Thursday afternoon, but I wasn't sure."

"I already told you I was in the museum lot," Aurora said.

Then a lie sprang to her lips. "I confirmed an MDX came back *after* originally leaving."

"How do you know?" Orlando asked. "The museum doesn't have cameras in the parking lot."

"An ATM camera," Fenway said, though she had no idea if there was an ATM around. "Saw an MDX driving toward the museum."

"How can you be sure it was Aurora's MDX? Could have been any white Acura SUV that stopped at the museum."

Fenway arched an eyebrow at Orlando—conveying *Oh, had she driven this way to see you at the hotel?*

"I mean," Orlando stammered, "there are restaurants here, or the hiking trail up on the left. Maybe it wasn't even her car."

But Fenway kept her mouth shut and studied Aurora's face. The dusky red blush had reached the tips of her ears.

"No one we talked to at the restaurant remembers you, either," Fenway said. Wild guess. But Aurora's body language and demeanor were telling Fenway that Aurora was hiding a secret.

"Okay, fine," Aurora said. "I was here. At the museum. And you're right. I got that pre-nuptial agreement, and the first thing I thought was that Vaughn had trapped me. He knew..." She paused, looked down, took a deep breath, and continued. "I thought he'd found out about me and Orlando."

Orlando took a small step back, bumping into the SUV with the back of his legs, and turned toward Aurora. "I—I thought we said—"

"We *did* say no one else would find out." Aurora looked back up at Fenway, her face resigned. "But, you know, Orlando, when confronted with the truth, sometimes you've got to admit things you don't want to admit."

"So you came back to the museum?"

"I was too upset to argue properly," Aurora said. "And I didn't want to make a scene. I didn't want any of the museum employees to think I was—"

Orlando interrupted. "Aurora had nothing to do with this."

Fenway nodded. Maybe Orlando was a player who'd tried to hit on both Piper and Fenway, but that didn't necessarily preclude gallantry. Besides, since Aurora was married to Vaughn, it's not like Orlando and Aurora were exclusive—though who knows what arrangements they'd made?

"And if he found out about you and Orlando," Fenway said, "if you signed that agreement, he could divorce you and you'd get practically nothing." She glanced at Orlando; no surprise registered on his face. "Tell me, when did you find out *he'd* been cheating?"

Aurora shook her head. "He's probably been cheating on me since we started going out. I've caught him three times. Twice before we were engaged, and then again the week after we were married—with that blackjack dealer."

"Nadine Ryeo?" Fenway asked.

"I don't know her name. I just know Vaughn gets her a hotel room sometimes, usually when I'm spending the night at my apartment or when I'm out of town."

Fenway tilted her head in Orlando's direction. Aurora pursed her lips. Fenway saw the story laid out in front of her: Orlando using the information he had working the hotel's front desk to inform a beautiful woman that her husband was cheating on her, offering her a shoulder to cry on, then one thing led to another.

"I know how it looks," Aurora said, "but I wasn't anywhere around here. Look at that camera footage. I bet it shows that I left well before Vaughn was—" She hesitated, then swallowed hard. "Before he was killed."

"If you left beforehand," Fenway said, "maybe you saw something."

Aurora scrunched up her face. "I didn't see anyone except Vaughn. He said he'd just met with the NNoV8 people."

"I'd asked him about getting paid for my art," Orlando said. "Or getting the other investors to give me back my rights to my paintings."

"I was the one who suggested Orlando bring up the idea of

displaying *Desolation*," Aurora said. "You know, 'here's what the art looked like before it became an NFT.' Use Orlando's work as the sample piece. That way, Orlando would get promotion of his work, and it could tell the NNoV8 story a little better."

Orlando nodded. "Visitors would actually know they're experiencing real art, instead of just watching NFTs interact with each other through some soulless algorithm."

"And Vaughn agreed," Aurora interjected. "*Desolation* has been part of the installation for a couple of months now." She shook her head. "I get that they want to switch Orlando's painting out for another artist, but it's such a shame."

Fenway nodded, wanting to steer the conversation back to Thursday night. She wanted to tell Aurora Horn of everything she suspected, to see how she'd react: that Piper had dropped her knife under the MDX, that Aurora had picked up the knife when she'd come back out to her car. Maybe she drove around for a while, trying to calm down, or maybe assessing her options. In the end, later that night, she'd likely driven back to the hotel, knowing that Vaughn was on his way to spend the night with Nadine again. Maybe she'd just wanted to scare him, or maybe she'd wanted to get out of the marriage with her dignity intact. But maybe things went sideways, and she ended up stabbing him.

Or maybe Aurora had intended to kill Vaughn anyway, and figured since it wasn't her knife, she could get away with it.

Fenway would have to call O.K. Ubosi. This might be enough for reasonable doubt, but before she told the sheriff's office about Aurora's MDX and her increasingly convincing motives, she wanted the attorney's opinion.

"We're running late," Aurora said. "Am I under arrest, or am I free to go?"

"You're free to go," Fenway said. "Though I'm sure the sheriff's office will want to speak with you in the next couple of days."

For a second, Fenway regretted saying that—being told that the sheriff wanted an interview might scare Aurora off. Then she realized that if Aurora disappeared, that would be even better for Piper —Aurora would look guilty for sure.

Orlando climbed into the MDX and shut the door, then wouldn't look at Fenway as Aurora reversed out of the parking space and drove off. They drove out of the parking lot and turned left on the road toward the freeway.

A ping on her phone. It was a text from Sarah.

> Iris is on her way with the computer

> I'll let you know what I find

All right, then. Back to the bland turkey-and-guacamole sandwich.

———

She took two bites of the remaining half-sandwich, looked forlornly at the rest, and took the top piece of bread off. Reaching toward the wire condiment rack on the bar, Fenway grabbed the El Toro Bravo hot sauce and shook a generous amount onto the turkey. She replaced the bread and took a bite. Still bland; now with a vinegary hot sauce. She didn't want a hot sauce sandwich.

Chewing the big bite, Fenway reached toward the condiment rack again and spun it. Nope, nothing in there could save this sandwich. She made a mental note to stick to brunch and BLTs if she came here again.

Hopefully, it was a mental note she'd never have to use.

She swallowed, then took a second sip of the gin and tonic. It hadn't improved. Fenway centered herself on the stool and stretched her arms above her head. Time to call Ubosi and let him know about Aurora Horn's affair.

Fenway grabbed her purse, and the phone buzzed. Oh, maybe that was Ubosi.

She pulled her phone out. It was a text from an unknown number. And it was just one word.

Bitch

Fenway cocked her head. Was this from the same person who'd left the threatening note in her room? She scratched her head, picking up the watery yet astringent gin and tonic. Hmpf. She sniffed it. It even smelled cheap.

Of course, the text would be from a number she didn't know. Was it from Aurora? From Sookie? From Nadine? From one of the NNoV8 owners?

Hmm. An 805 area code. The area code for Dominguez County, down to Santa Barbara; it wasn't the Las Vegas area code. She rubbed her chin. What area code was Palmdale, where Nadine Ryeo was from and where Sookie Ryeo still lived? She wished she knew her area codes better. But even if Palmdale was a different area code than 805, it was still possible for a cellphone to have any area code the requestor wanted. If it were a burner phone, all bets were off, too: people could buy a burner phone in Las Vegas and find out during activation that it had a Detroit area code.

She decided to call the number to see who it was, then her finger paused over the *Call* button.

An 805 area code. Maybe it was from a case in Fenway's past. She'd certainly made her share of enemies solving the murders she had.

Then it dawned on her: her last case. The murder of Mathis Jericho. The case where George Pope was sitting in prison for a murder he admitted to, but also one he didn't. She remembered the now-sheriff, Gretchen Donnelly, being cagey in her last discussions. And she'd been so busy moving McVie—and trying to get Piper out of jail—that she'd barely talked to Dez about it in the last two days.

Could this be the cellphone of one of the drug dealers who'd been tangled up with Mathis Jericho? Or one of Jericho's friends?

Maybe even someone who'd depended on Jericho, like the owner of the storage facility where Mathis Jericho worked. If it was one of their cellphones, maybe she should leave it alone.

Or maybe it was Gretchen Donnelly herself. Fenway didn't have Gretchen's cellphone number in her phone. And it wouldn't matter if it were a burner, anyway.

She couldn't envision a scenario in which it *was* Gretchen who sent the text, but she tapped the Favorites button on her screen and then called McVie.

"You miss me already?" McVie said. The loud hum of the rental truck engine in the background almost drowned out his voice.

"Making decent time?"

"I'm on I-70 now," McVie said. "Still about seven hours left, and I won't make it for dinner with Megan tonight, but we're going to have brunch tomorrow."

"Good," Fenway said. "I know you were worried about seeing her."

"Yeah. My boss is blowing up my phone, too, but I told him I was on the road, on my way back. Can't ask me to move three states away, insist I arrive early, and then insist I work on my off time when I'm supposed to be moving stuff. Figured I'd draw a line in the sand now, or I'd spend the next year having him walk all over me."

"Yeah."

A pause. "You didn't call me just to hear the sound of my voice."

"I got a weird text."

"From who?"

"I don't have the number in my phone. 805 area code, though. I was thinking it might be someone who's connected to the last case. And then I was thinking it might be Sheriff Donnelly."

"What does the text say?"

"Um—it just says 'bitch.'"

Another pause. "That's it? That's the whole message?"

"Yes."

"Doesn't sound like Gretchen. But you said it was from an unknown number?"

"Not a number that's blocked—I just don't know it. And I don't have Gretchen's cell in my phone. I thought maybe I could read the number to you and you could tell me if it belonged to Sheriff Donnelly."

"I'm not sure I know her cellphone number off the top of my head."

"Maybe someone else at the county."

McVie laughed. "Once I plug the number into my cell, I have officially erased it from my memory. There's no chance I'll recognize it."

"Maybe if you see the number, it'll ring a bell?"

"Aww," McVie said in a softer voice. "You *did* just call me because you missed me. You wanted the excuse."

Fenway felt the color rise to her face. "Do you want to hear the number or not?"

"You really think Gretchen would stoop to this level of juvenile animosity?"

Fenway ran the last few interactions with Gretchen through her head. That last text: *Congratulations on solving the two murders.*

No, probably not. Gretchen would have made it more cryptic, less confrontational.

"Humor me," Fenway said.

"Sure." McVie sounded like he was repressing a laugh.

Fenway read out the number.

Silence.

"Did I lose you?" Fenway asked.

"Read the number one more time," McVie said.

Fenway did.

More silence.

"Am I right?" Fenway asked incredulously. "Was it Gretchen?" Then she had a thought. "Hang on—did Amy send me this text? Did I do something to your ex-wife where she felt—"

"It's not Amy," McVie said gruffly.

"Then who—" Then it dawned on Fenway. It wasn't Amy; it was Megan. McVie's daughter must be blaming her for McVie missing the softball game and dinner. Because Fenway's the one who needed help. Because McVie dropped almost everything and came to Las Vegas.

Not because Fenway wanted help. It was because the moving truck had to get to Colorado. Though Fenway supposed it might look like she was playing a game to get to see McVie away from his family. "It's okay, Craig."

"It's *not* okay," McVie said. "Look, I love Megan. I'd do almost anything for her—I'm moving a thousand miles away so I can live in the same town as her. But come on. This is ridiculous." A rustling; McVie might have been tapping on the screen. "When did you say this text was sent?"

"Ten minutes ago, maybe."

"Look at your texts—let me know the exact time."

Fenway did. "Twelve minutes ago."

McVie grunted loudly. "And I hung up with Megan exactly fourteen minutes ago."

"I can see how she'd think I was—"

"No," McVie said firmly. "I get you're not her favorite person. She didn't like Rick much either, and she let Amy know it, too. But there's a difference between dislike and disrespect. And this is—" McVie paused, took a deep breath. "Erase the message. I'll talk to her."

"You don't have to—"

"I'm not talking to Megan on *your* account, Fenway." McVie paused, the road noise coming back fully. "Well, I kind of am. But that's not the point. It's not rude because you're my girlfriend. It's rude because it's—it's, well, it's just rude."

"Okay."

"I'll call you later. Let you know I made it home safe."

"Thanks, Craig." Fenway hesitated. Should she tell McVie about the threatening note? Could he do anything about it besides worry? Would he turn the truck around and try to rescue her? And he was focused on Megan and her inappropriate texting. No—it could wait. "Love you."

"I love you, too. I'm sorry the last few weeks have been so messy."

"It happens."

They ended the call and Fenway picked up the gin and tonic again—and caught another whiff of it. Ugh. It wasn't even worth it.

———

"It's not ready yet?" Fenway asked.

Teddi shook her head from behind the front desk. "I'm sorry, Ms. Stevenson. I thought it would be ready earlier, but now the computer's saying the room won't be ready for check-in until four."

Fenway took the phone out of her purse. 2:47. She wanted nothing more than to decompress for a few minutes in the cool air conditioning of her hotel room. She still had to call Ubosi and tell him about Aurora Horn.

But the text from Megan had thrown her for a loop. It was funny: had she gotten a mysterious text calling her names even a year-and-a-half ago, when she was still working at the walk-in clinic in Seattle, she'd have been obsessed about who sent the text for days, and it would have gotten under her skin. But now, she'd thought it might be a dangerous drug dealer, or someone threatening her to leave this case alone, and she was unfazed.

But McVie's daughter? That was another story.

And the note threatening her to leave this case...

"Teddi," Fenway said thoughtfully, "I know there are a few people from next door who use this hotel to meet up with affair partners."

Teddi shrugged.

"Any hotel employees ever do that?"

Teddi laughed. "Anything the general manager does is on his own time. I don't get involved with that."

Fenway leaned forward, resting her elbows on the counter. She suspected Teddi was goading her into spreading a little intra-office gossip, but she didn't have time for that. "You ever see Vaughn Trask's wife in here?"

Teddi furrowed her brow. "Wife?"

"They got married a couple of weeks ago."

"Oh. Well, not that I can recall. Her big obnoxious SUV, yes. But her? I might not have checked her in, of course, but I probably would have seen her name at some point. Not if she were here for just one or two nights, but if she were a regular, like Vaughn Trask and Stanley Schup? Yeah, I'd know."

"Okay, thanks." Fenway stood. "Four o'clock?"

"Might be a little earlier."

"What am I going to do with myself for forty-five minutes?"

Teddi pulled out three pieces of glossy paper the size of index cards. "Hotel bar coupons?"

"Maybe in a bit." Fenway took one, and Teddi pushed all three over to her. "Thanks."

Fenway put the coupons in her purse, said goodbye to Teddi, and went out the front door of the hotel.

Oof. When would she get used to the blast of hot air whenever she exited buildings in this heat?

She'd been cooped up inside for too long. She needed to stretch her legs. Maybe a lap around the hotel and casino. Even in this heat, it was better than being in the stale air. Besides, one lap in the heat wasn't going to kill her.

She walked toward the plaza rooms. "Plaza rooms" was a dumb name, but then the museum was dumb too. The turkey sandwich was dumb. Vaughn and Aurora both cheating on their marriage before they even told their families was dumb.

She turned down a walkway between two of the taller buildings, feeling the relief of the shade. Fenway was glad for the respite; it was cooler in the shade, but still warm.

The walkway emptied out on the back side of the plaza rooms into a loading area and a flat gravel lot.

Oof—a sour smell hit Fenway. She looked to her right, an eight-foot concrete wall. Fenway walked toward the wall. Was this the dumpster area Teddi had talked about earlier? Fenway smiled to think of Vaughn Trask and Nadine Ryeo wanting an exciting getaway and getting that sour smell wafting into their den of iniquity. She stepped around the wall. Yep, just as Teddi had said, the dumpsters were overflowing. Black plastic garbage bags were stuffed in the top, and a few lined the ground next to the dumpster.

"What a mess," Fenway mumbled to herself. The dumpster was about six feet high, just an inch taller than Fenway. If she stood on her tiptoes, she could see inside. Styrofoam, flattened cardboard boxes, mostly plain and brown, a broken two-by-four. The occasional box that people hadn't even bothered to break down. A half-squashed box with *Americana Linens* in a designer font and photos of a calm bedroom. Another white box labeled *Highball Glasses 24 Count*. And a sparkly green plastic cube peeking out of the corner of the dumpster.

Fenway tilted her head. The sparkly green was oddly familiar.

She blinked. The same green as the color of Qasper PCs.

Now what would a Qasper PC be doing in the dumpster of a Cartwheel Hotel?

Fenway shook her head. Qasper made high-end computers for consumers. Not for corporate workstations. Even if Cartwheel needed powerful server machines to run its video poker and other applications, they wouldn't use Qasper.

"Maybe it's not a PC," Fenway muttered.

She took a few steps closer to the dumpster. The sour smells got stronger—definitely some milk products had been out in the heat for a couple of days. Fenway didn't have gloves, but she stood on her tiptoes and looked at the plastic sparkly green case.

The Qasper logo, melded to the case, just below the lip of the dumpster.

She walked halfway around the dumpster, looking in, and saw a ream of paper, untouched, sitting on top of a pile of black plastic trash bags. Fenway tore the ream open and pulled out two sheets of paper. The paper was thin and Fenway's sweaty hands stuck to it. Gross, but in this situation, it was good. She stuck a piece of paper onto her palms, covering her fingers. Can't leave any prints on the PC, right? Otherwise, the sheriff's office might accuse her of planting it there.

She hurried back to the corner of the dumpster where the Qasper PC was, reached her hands in, careful to keep the paper between her fingers and the computer. With a hand on either side of the box, she pulled up.

Nope. Wouldn't move. But Fenway would bet anything that this was the PC that had disappeared from Vaughn Trask's NNoV8 office.

CHAPTER TWENTY-FOUR

"You just *walked* by the dumpster?" Deputy Izzy Bardot said, studying Fenway's face. They stood in the shade on the side of the plaza rooms, the gravel crunching under their feet. Two other Correos County deputies were behind the concrete wall, supposedly pulling the Qasper PC box out of the dumpster. Fenway had been standing out in the heat for more than an hour, waiting for them to show up after calling Bardot. She called Ubosi as she waited, leaving him a message.

"Remember when we talked about the Qasper PC?" Fenway asked. "That cool metallic green color?"

"Uh, sure."

"I saw that metallic green color sticking out of the corner of the dumpster. I thought it might be the missing PC from Trask's office." Fenway put her hands on her hips. "And just like we discussed, I let you know before anyone else."

"You haven't even told that fancy lawyer of yours?"

Fenway smiled. "He was my first call after you."

Bardot nodded. "And you're a coroner. You sure you're not a detective?"

"I know Piper didn't do it, Dep—uh, Izzy."

A smile touched the corner of Bardot's mouth. "I looked you up. You've had a pretty good run solving murders back home."

"More murders than I care to solve," Fenway said. "I thought I was moving to this idyllic beach town, and instead I'm in the middle of a dozen murders."

"Still fewer than Vegas gets in an average month," Bardot said.

"And I know I told you about the pre-nuptial agreement between Trask and Aurora Horn," Fenway said, "but I also saw Aurora come pick up Orlando Lockberry today at Albie K's. Aurora admitted to me that the two of them have been having an affair."

Bardot tilted her head. "Lockberry, huh? Isn't he one of the artists at NNoV8?"

Fenway nodded. "Yeah, but he was the only one I saw in that database who *wasn't* affected by the malware. He told me he didn't know anything about it, though. Said maybe his PC's security programs caught it."

Bardot pursed her lips. "He worked the front desk, right? At Cartwheel?"

"Still does."

"And didn't you tell me that Trask would use the Cartwheel to meet up with that blackjack dealer? The one with the mother who you suspect might have killed Trask?"

"Sookie Ryeo," Fenway responded. "She's the mother. Yeah, I think she's a suspect. She was at the casino the night Trask was killed." She grinned. "In fact, that's why I was at the dumpster in the first place. The other front desk clerk told me she put Vaughn Trask in the room right above the stinky dumpster for one of his dalliances."

"I expect he didn't like that much."

"No," Fenway said. "In fact, that was the way Orlando showed his art to Trask in the first place: Trask came to the front desk complaining about the smell, Orlando comped a suite for him, and then started asking Trask to put his art on display at the museum."

Bardot rubbed her chin. "And you think Trask put his art in the museum to make sure Orlando didn't blab about his cheating?"

"Of course I do."

"And maybe that's why Trask didn't use Orlando's computer for that cryptomining hack."

Fenway nodded. "That makes sense. No use poking the bear." Fenway blinked. "But with the wording of the pre-nup? Aurora thought Vaughn had figured out she was cheating. Maybe even who she was cheating with."

Bardot nodded. "You said Aurora's car was in the lot."

"That's right. And I think Piper's knife was under her SUV."

"So," Bardot said, "she now has access to the knife, according to you. She has a hell of a motive: the pre-nup means that Aurora Horn stands to lose millions. Plus, the cushy lifestyle she was getting used to."

"The apartment complex in Walker City *is* pretty gross."

"And the lack of cameras in both the NNoV8 parking lot and the Cartwheel lot? It makes sense that she'd do it there."

Fenway thought for a moment. "The front desk workers know all about the camera situation. I wonder if Orlando said something to Aurora."

Bardot rubbed her forehead. "It's not enough to arrest Aurora. Not yet. But it's enough to convince the D.A. that there's no way a jury will convict Piper Patten of the murder. This has 'reasonable doubt' stamped on its forehead and shouting from the rafters."

Fenway's heart leapt. This was the best news she'd heard since Piper was arrested, but she tried to keep her face impassive. Wouldn't do to look delighted. "That's great. When can I come get Piper?"

"I'll have to work all this out with the sheriff." Bardot sighed. "And it means a couple of hours of paperwork. But if all goes smoothly, Miss Patten could be a free woman in time for you to have a celebratory dinner."

And get the hell out of Ruby Dunes. Fenway nodded.

"Maybe you could stick around and help us get more evidence against Aurora Horn," Bardot said.

"I thought coroners weren't considered law enforcement officers in Nevada."

Bardot smirked. "We could deputize you."

Fenway stifled a giggle. "I appreciate the offer, Izzy, but I think I've had enough of the desert for one week. I've got to get back to work on Monday, and I've got plane tickets to sort out." Right—she and Piper both had plane tickets from Denver to Estancia Sunday afternoon—that was in less than twenty-four hours. Hopefully she could rebook, but even if she lost the money for those tickets and had to pay a couple of thousand dollars to fly home from Vegas, it would be worth it. She had the money, now that she had a year of coroner salary under her belt and still lived in her father's apartment complex. Hell, her dad would probably pay for the new plane tickets.

"Let's not get too far ahead of ourselves," Bardot said. "I'll let you know what Sheriff Jeffcoat does."

"At least he's got another prime suspect to go after."

"True. At least there's that. It'll take some of the sting out."

Fenway snapped her fingers. "Oh—I almost forgot. Back in Dominguez County, we found an artist who we believe was the victim of this NNoV8 scheme. Her PC should be at our offices now, and we're looking at it, seeing if it's infected with the malware."

Bardot dropped her arms to her side. "This might be a federal fraud case. If Sheriff Jeffcoat can wash his hands of this entire thing and push it off to the FBI, even better. Then it won't look like he arrested the wrong person and it'll just go out of our jurisdiction forever."

"It must be exhausting to work with a sheriff who cares so much about how everything looks to the public."

Bardot shrugged. "Believe it or not, Jeffcoat is better than most of the bosses I've had. At least he mostly stays out of my way."

Fenway thought back again to the Dominguez County sheriff, Gretchen Donnelly, and her cryptic statements after George Pope was arrested for the murders of both Seth Cahill *and* Mathis Jericho. Yes, Sheriff Donnelly mostly stayed out of Fenway's business, but the Jericho murder felt like Fenway would get her toes stepped on.

She really needed to be back at work on Monday.

————

The deputies finished up about thirty minutes later, and it was four thirty by the time Fenway went back to the hotel. Just standing out in the area behind the plaza rooms, even in the shade, made Fenway sweat more than running five miles back home.

But she entered the hotel lobby and couldn't help smiling from ear to ear. It was late enough by now that she should be able to check into her new room on the casino side. But maybe she'd relax a little, perhaps get a decent gin and tonic, and get all the bad feelings out of her system. Who knows? Maybe in half an hour, Izzy Bardot would call and say Piper was being released, and then Fenway could call the airlines, change her departure from Denver to Las Vegas, and be home before midnight.

She ordered a gin and tonic from the bar. "Royal Juniper," she said. Yes, it was about three times as much as the well gin, but this was worth the celebration. And she'd bet it would be a million times better than the terrible gin and tonic at Albie K's. She'd only been able to choke down two sips of that terrible drink.

She sat at the bar and texted Ubosi, letting him know she'd found the PC suspected to be the one from the NNoV8 office, and that Aurora Horn's affair made her the prime suspect now, and that Bardot would try to get Piper released that day.

Ubosi texted back.

> If you ever decide you prefer the vibrant nightlife of Vegas to the sleepy little hamlet where you currently live, just let me know

> I've always got an investigator position open for you

> Guaranteed it's more than you're making now

Fenway smiled at the text screen. It was nice to have options, even if she had to deal with the Mathis Jericho situation when she got home.

The bartender brought her the expensive gin and tonic, nodded solemnly, then stepped away. Fenway reached over, brought the gin and tonic to her nose and sniffed. Then closed her eyes.

Yes. That was divine. She opened her eyes and took a sip.

Heaven.

She could sit for thirty minutes or an hour, waiting for a text from Bardot that would tell her whether the sheriff's office was releasing Piper—and when. She hadn't been able to take a breath for two days. Even longer than that, really; when McVie had first decided to move to Colorado, Fenway had been juggling her case-load and helping him move. It was too much, though at the time she hadn't thought so. Her shoulders were tight; she had to relax. She closed her eyes, brought the gin and tonic to her nose again, and took a deep breath through her nose.

Ah, that's the stuff.

Her next aromatherapy session should be a big gin-and-tonic scented candle. They made those, right?

She opened her eyes again and looked at her phone. One missed call. She tapped the screen and called Sarah Summerhill back.

"So it's definitely malware," Sarah said as soon as she answered. "I copied Iris's hard drive, found a PC shell no one was using, and air-gapped it."

"Air-gapped?"

"Not connected to any other computer. Or the internet. Don't want our stuff getting infected."

"Sure."

"I'm not good enough to figure out where it's going or who this belongs to. I'll need Patrick for that."

"You've done a lot to help already," Fenway said. "And I think they're letting Piper go."

"Really? Even with the murder weapon clearly belonging to her?"

"Vaughn Trask's wife had opportunity, had the means to get Piper's knife, at least assuming the cops believe me, and had a way better motive than Piper."

"So this whole PC thing has been in vain?"

"Not necessarily. We found the PC that Trask was using—or at least, I think it's the same PC. Someone dumped it in the trash behind the hotel next to the museum."

"Obviously someone without much computer experience—you don't just throw the whole machine away."

"Let's see if the hard drive is still in the machine," Fenway said.

"Even so," said Sarah, "you're no closer to finding out who the real killer is—"

"That doesn't matter. So many others with the means, motive, and opportunity, my contact at the sheriff's office thinks it'll be too tough to convince a jury beyond a reasonable doubt. Especially with Okpara Ubosi as the lawyer."

"Even though Piper admits she owns the murder weapon?"

"I guess." A nagging doubt crept into Fenway's mind. The knife. It was the most damning thing against Piper, and all the evidence that Fenway had uncovered with Aurora Horn, Sookie Ryeo, and the malware on the PC might not be enough for the sheriff to agree to release Piper. Fenway ran her hand through her hair. Would it be enough if she were the coroner on this case? Would she be in ADA Pondicherry's office, asking him to keep the woman who owned the murder weapon in jail through the weekend?

Fenway cleared her throat. "I suppose we'll see. Things are different here. I hope they release her."

"Me too."

"Can you send me any information that you found out about Iris's PC?"

"Not before Patrick looks at it. And I've been trying to reach Jordan with no luck. I think someone said he was going hiking this weekend. He might be out of cell range."

Fenway pressed her lips together. Not ideal, but this could probably wait till Monday. She crossed her fingers. Maybe Piper would still get out.

Just then, her phone buzzed in her hand. Fenway took the phone away from her face. It was Ubosi.

"Hey, it's the lawyer. I gotta take this."

"Okay. I'll keep you updated."

Fenway clicked over to the other call. "Hello, O.K."

"Hello, Fenway," he said. Something in his tone made Fenway's heart sink.

"Good news, I hope." But she knew it wasn't.

"I'm afraid not," Ubosi said, clicking his tongue. "Sheriff Jeffcoat called me personally. He apologized, but they're still keeping Piper Patten locked up this weekend. The arraignment is on Monday morning."

CHAPTER TWENTY-FIVE

Fenway and Ubosi continued talking for a few minutes. Ubosi detailed what Fenway should expect at the arraignment. He'd be driving up to Ruby Dunes that evening and discussing things with Piper. He was pushing for a *not guilty* plea—which Fenway had, until this point, taken for granted. Ubosi said he'd been requesting Piper to be released due to lack of evidence.

"I may call on you to take the stand," Ubosi said.

"But I can't say definitively that the knife fell out of Piper's purse," Fenway said.

"You can testify to the time Piper said it was missing."

"I can. But isn't that after the time Vaughn Trask was killed?"

"M.E.'s report hasn't come back yet. Probably won't get it until later on Monday."

Without exculpatory evidence, Piper would be held after the arraignment, Fenway was sure of it. "And we can't introduce all the other theories of the crime at an arraignment."

"Correct."

The judge couldn't even consider other evidence, even if it were offered—Fenway knew that from her research when her father had been arraigned. "So we're stuck here."

"I would expect it will take until mid-next week, at the earliest, before this gets resolved."

Fenway felt a pang of guilt. She'd been running like crazy to catch the killer—no, she reminded herself, to get enough evidence that the D.A. would conclude the case wasn't worth taking to trial. And she'd been so busy with that, she hadn't even visited Piper in jail beyond the single meeting she'd had with Ubosi. "Hey, O.K., when are visiting hours over?"

"At the jail? They end at five."

Shit. That was only five minutes, and there's no way she'd get there in time.

"I can bring you with me tonight," Ubosi said. "You haven't seen Piper today?"

A hundred excuses jumped onto Fenway's tongue, but she mumbled, "No."

"You've been busy trying to get her out." Ubosi tutted. "And you almost did it. You've gotten a lot further than my investigators."

"Has your team uncovered anything useful?"

"Vaughn Trask's arrest record. Twice for fraud, charges dropped both times."

"Any of his previous fraud victims potential suspects?"

"No," Ubosi said, the disappointment showing in his voice. "One's dead, one's out of the country. But we have no shortage of other suspects. I'm having them interview the people who stayed at the hotel on Thursday night. Maybe someone recorded something."

"Like Trask fighting with someone else?"

"I'm hoping," Ubosi said patiently, "that someone recorded the parking lot of the NNoV8 museum after Piper dropped the knife and the killer picked it up."

"Seems like a needle in a haystack."

"It's a long shot," Ubosi admitted. "But long shots never come through if you don't put in the work to find them."

Fenway was quiet.

"The good news," Ubosi said quickly, "is that everything you've uncovered has almost certainly assured reasonable doubt in the jury's mind." He coughed lightly. "If this goes to trial, that is."

"But Piper will be stuck here until then."

Ubosi hesitated. "Possibly."

Fenway rested her chin in her palm. "She'll lose everything. McVie will lose his P.I. business without Piper to run it. Piper will lose her apartment, any chance she has for a career."

Ubosi was silent.

"How do we convince the D.A. to drop the charges?"

"I'll talk to the D.A.," Ubosi said. "The fear of reasonable doubt is high enough now that I should be able to get the charges dropped. But, Fenway, this is a high-visibility murder. There might be a huge amount of pressure on the D.A. to keep Piper in custody. Trask, Schup, Shellwater—these guys are all a big deal in the investor community. Not many funds devoted to artistic endeavors that aren't all about A.I. This fund fails, they'll be the laughingstock of the financial world."

"Oh, please," Fenway said. "People have short memories. Especially when you have money."

"True."

"And besides," Fenway said, "don't you think that adds more motive for Schup and Shellwater to get rid of Trask? Especially if he was doing shady stuff with the NFTs and with cryptomining?"

"This can all be argued at trial."

Piper doesn't have the time to wait until trial, Fenway thought.

No, Fenway would have to find the killer herself. And she'd have to do it without the help of the sheriff's office or Piper's expensive lawyer.

———

Fenway finished the last of her gin and tonic ten minutes after hanging up with Ubosi. She pushed the empty glass toward the back of the bar, and the bartender appeared.

"Another?"

Fenway shook her head. "I wish. I have to get to work."

"On a Saturday afternoon?"

"I have a terrible boss." Fenway grinned at the bartender. She glanced at her phone; it was past five thirty. She probably needed to get some dinner at some point, but she wasn't hungry. And she had at least two hours before Ubosi would be at the Correos County Jail to visit Piper again.

And she was hamstrung, not able to get any financial information on NNoV8. Once Patrick figured out where the malware had come from, maybe the county could subpoena NNoV8's records in a fraud investigation. But Izzy Bardot had a good point: once the fraud case crossed state lines, it would likely be a federal case, and the FBI would take it off her plate. Besides, she was the coroner, and her purview was murder, not fraud. Given her situation with Sheriff Gretchen Donnelly, she didn't want to hand this case over to the sheriff's office, even though she would be forced to.

Might as well regroup. She wasn't going anywhere.

She put the drink on her room tab—still 443, even though she'd officially moved out—and stood. She remembered too late that she had free drink tickets, then sharp needles shot down to her foot. Her right leg had fallen asleep from sitting on the stool for so long.

Fenway needed a plan. And how was she going to get past the fact that the murder weapon belonged to Piper?

Aurora was the lowest-hanging fruit. But she already knew Fenway was onto her, and there was no way she would admit to finding the knife under her SUV.

Maybe Fenway could prove the knife would have fallen out? An experiment duplicating the purse falling off Piper's shoulder? Load up the purse with the exact same stuff, and then film everything falling out?

Fenway shook her head. There's no way that would work.

The pins and needles left Fenway's leg. She could walk again. She walked around the bar toward the front desk.

If pressing Aurora wouldn't work, what about Schup and Shellwater? Surely one of them had thrown away the Qasper PC—or had ordered one of their underlings to do so. Maybe Fenway could find one of those underlings. Destroying evidence; surely that would hold some weight over the proceedings in Piper's favor. And the timing might be good; it was almost six thirty. The museum would close soon, and the big-shot owners were probably out at a thousand-dollar dinner in Vegas or at a high-rollers' table. Or in hotel rooms with their affair partners. Perfect time to get the employees talking.

Then, halfway across the lobby, the fatigue hit her. The gin and tonic hadn't helped, but she suddenly felt the fatigue in her muscles, in her bones. She wanted to curl up and go to sleep. And she wanted McVie there, for him to hold her in his arms and—

Bitch.

The word from Megan's text slapped her across the face.

"She's just a kid," Fenway muttered, continuing her way to the front desk. She called her mother that during high school. Just twice. And Joanne Stevenson hadn't even flinched. Pretended she hadn't heard it. And both times, Fenway would be racked with guilt lying in bed the night after, too proud to apologize.

Maybe Megan was going through the same thing. Or maybe Megan was angry with her mother. Or maybe with McVie. But it was safer to be angry with Fenway—and when your father has a girlfriend who's closer to your age than to his own age, resentment can build. And build. Fenway still didn't have the best relationship with Charlotte Ferris, even though it was a lot better than before.

And there was Orlando Lockberry, behind the desk, typing on his workstation, his brow furrowed in concentration.

"Hi, Orlando."

"Oh." His head snapped up. "Hello, Miss Stevenson."

"I tried to get into my new room earlier today, but Teddi said it wouldn't be ready until four."

"She left me a note about it," Orlando said. "And yes, your room is ready now." He winked. "I've upgraded you to a suite, like I promised. No extra charge."

"That's so sweet. Thank you."

"Hey, after what you've been through? Least I could do." He typed again, his head toward the monitor. "Just let me get you situated, and I'll program the room key." He was silent for a moment.

"I thought Piper would be released today," Fenway said.

Orlando's brow crinkled. "Really?"

Oh, Fenway shouldn't talk about this anymore—not when it was Aurora Horn who was the prime suspect. She still had to deflect. "Yeah, I thought all the evidence we found would convince the D.A. that the jury would for sure find enough reasonable doubt. I guess it's not enough to release her."

There, that was suitably vague. Now to change the subject.

"I appreciate the room upgrade," Fenway said. "I only expected to be staying the one night, so when all this happened, I'm just grateful that I don't have to worry about a place to stay."

"And you're on an executive floor," Orlando said. "Extra security."

"That's great," Fenway said. "Oh—and I almost forgot my bags."

Orlando grinned. "I can get those for you in just a moment." He turned back to the monitor.

Fenway pulled her wallet out, undid the clasp, and saw the two stubs tucked into the fold.

Wait.

Fenway blinked.

"Orlando," Fenway said slowly, "how did you know those bags were mine?"

Orlando looked up. "Sorry?"

"When you were helping me earlier, you took my suitcase and Piper's duffel bag off the luggage cart."

Orlando blinked. "I think Mateo helped you."

"No," Fenway said, "it was you."

"Well, they're two unique cases," Orlando said. "I must have seen them when you checked in."

But she'd just switched suitcases with McVie that morning after the zipper had broken—there was no way Orlando would have known.

Unless he had been in the room after McVie had left—and before Fenway took the suitcases out.

Had Orlando let Aurora into the room to put the note on the bed? Did he think the two of them had enough of a future that he was willing to cover up evidence that she'd murdered her husband?

Then a scenario flashed in her head: Orlando and Aurora talking in the parking lot of the NNoV8 museum on Thursday evening, maybe on Orlando's dinner break. They talk, trying not to make it appear like they're romantically involved. Aurora telling Orlando about the pre-nup. Aurora gets in her Acura MDX and drives away. Orlando is going back to the second half of his shift. He's in a white polo with the Cartwheel logo. He watches his lover drive out of the parking lot.

And there, on the ground, where her car had been only seconds before, a folding knife. *You'll always make us proud.* Orlando picks up the knife.

He'd told Trask that he'd hide Trask's affair from Aurora, and he'd traded it with Vaughn Trask to get his art on the wall in the NFT project. He'd traded his supposed silence to avoid getting the malware on his machine, when all the other artists had.

But when he'd found out about the pre-nuptial agreement from Aurora, he knew all that could come to an end. His secret wouldn't need to be hidden anymore—Vaughn Trask would no longer lose millions if Aurora found out he was cheating.

Fenway heard Aurora's voice in her head. *I get that they want to switch Orlando's painting out for another artist.*

Vaughn Trask had planned to put another artist's painting on display. He didn't think Orlando held anything over his head anymore.

So Vaughn and Orlando had a confrontation in the parking lot. And Orlando brought Piper's knife. Maybe he'd intended to put it in the lost-and-found, but out of laziness, or maybe self-preservation, he hadn't.

And the confrontation had gone sideways.

He stabbed Trask right where it would do the most damage—the left chest, just above the sternum. Not the heart, protected by the rib case, but just above, where it would sever large veins and cause immediate loss of consciousness and a quick death.

Because Orlando had known from his anatomy class. Even if the Michelangelo story was apocryphal, Orlando probably knew. He'd gotten an A in upper-division anatomy.

That first night he checked them in, he'd worn a rumpled blue dress shirt that didn't fit him right. Not the white polo shirt he'd had on every other time she'd seen him. Orlando might have stabbed Trask in the perfect place to kill him quickly, but there would have been a lot of blood. And it would have ruined a white polo shirt.

She looked up at Orlando. He was staring at her, searching her face. The death threat was from *him*.

And Orlando had murdered Vaughn Trask.

Did it show in her eyes?

He held the room keys in his hand, and, still maintaining eye contact with Fenway, put the card key on the counter between them.

"You must have seen me with those bags this morning, I guess." She smiled and tried to keep her voice casual, light.

Orlando smiled back at Fenway, but the grin had a sickly look, his eyes menacing. Fenway fought the urge to recoil. But Orlando's hands were under the counter. She couldn't see them.

Fenway opened her mouth, then hesitated. He knew he was caught. How did she want to play this?

"Don't do anything rash, Orlando," Fenway said. "There's security all over this casino. You murdered Vaughn Trask."

Orlando slowly pulled a gun out from under the desk and pointed it at Fenway.

It was a Colver .38. Blue handle, gold stars. The same one Teddi said had been turned into the lost-and-found.

Now Fenway knew how it had disappeared from the safe.

"Don't follow me," Orlando said.

Then, holding the gun close to his stomach, still pointed at Fenway, he walked out from behind the counter, then glanced toward the front entrance. He turned his head slightly to see where he was going.

"On second thought," Orlando said, "you're coming with me."

CHAPTER TWENTY-SIX

"You don't need to do this," Fenway said.

"Oh, so you'll just let me walk out of here?" A sardonic note in Orlando's voice as he took a few steps closer to Fenway. "Because I think if I leave, you'll be on the phone with the cops in ten seconds. I'll be lucky to make it to the interstate." He motioned with the gun. "Now move."

Fenway hesitated. She knew the odds of her survival were low if she were taken to a second location—and Orlando hadn't had time to make a plan. He'd thought the threatening note would scare Fenway into silence, get her out of town, probably. Taking Fenway hostage was an ad lib out of desperation. And Fenway knew he'd already killed once.

She walked toward the entrance, trying to catch the eye of the burly man in the black polo shirt next to the front doors, but to no avail.

Orlando followed two steps behind, just far enough for Fenway to be unable to reach him. "Act normal," Orlando growled. "Not like you have a gun pointed at you."

"I'll have to take acting classes before getting taken hostage next time," Fenway said. Another furtive glance at the burly man, who stood with his arms folded, his head turned toward the slot machines.

They walked out the glass doors onto the polished concrete walkway in front of the casino, the hot desert air scorching her face. Other people were walking in, talking to their friends or significant others. They didn't see the gun that Orlando pointed at her. Didn't see the panic on her face. She tried to catch their eyes, any of them, without making it obvious. A woman in a pink wrap dress, her hair in a ponytail, glanced at Fenway's face. Fenway tried to send a message of help telepathically. But the woman didn't stop. Didn't even break stride.

"Where are you parked?" Orlando said.

"Me?"

"I'm not taking *my* car," he said.

"My car is parked on the other side of the lot," Fenway said, the lie coming easily. The Kia McVie had rented was less than thirty feet away, but Orlando didn't know that. Fenway squinted. A silver Ford sedan, parked in the open area next to the concrete divider between the oversize lot, halfway between the casino and the NNoV8 museum, about a hundred yards from Albie K's. Fenway wasn't sure what she'd do once she got to the silver Ford—it would become obvious the car wasn't hers. Was she a good enough liar that she could pretend that she'd forgotten what car McVie had rented?

She flexed her fingers, then clenched and unclenched her fists. *Oh no, this isn't my car. It looks like the car I own back home, but it's not the rental.* She gritted her teeth. It even sounded dumb in her head.

And even if Orlando believed her, then what? Would Orlando panic and run to his own car? Maybe he'd take Fenway's cellphone, thinking it would take Fenway a few minutes to run back into the casino and call the police.

Or maybe he'd shoot Fenway in the parking lot, since they'd be far away from everyone else.

Still better odds than him taking her to a second location.

"Was it self-defense?" Fenway asked.

"What?"

"You stabbing Trask. Did he surprise you in the parking lot, tell you he'd kill you if you told everyone his plan to make millions in crypto?"

Orlando scoffed.

"Or maybe he was sick of the blackmail and he wanted to kill you—"

"More walking, less talking," Orlando said.

"Nobody's come to pick up his car," Fenway said.

"What?"

"His red Alfa Romeo." Fenway pointed across the parking lot, over past Albie K's, all the way to the NNoV8 museum. "It's just sitting there. No one's even driven it back to his house."

"Yeah, well, Aurora doesn't want it."

"Seems like a waste. You get together with her after you work all this out, you'd probably be driving it."

"How about we get to your car?" Orlando asked gruffly, but there was a note of envy in his voice. Yes, he wanted what Vaughn Trask had.

"You're probably wondering how I figured out Trask was stealing cryptocurrency."

"I don't really care how—" Orlando began.

"We tricked our way into Trask's private office at the museum." The gears in Fenway's mind spun. "Found his computer under his desk. Oh—and he'd left his car key in the top drawer of his desk. And his office wasn't even locked."

And Fenway didn't say that no one would be looking for Trask's Alfa Romeo convertible—but she'd planted the seed.

They were almost at the silver Ford sedan, parked in the casino lot about five feet away from the concrete barrier. McVie's moving van had been on the other side of this barrier, in the oversize lot, not twenty-four hours before.

Fenway started shaking. "Oh no, oh no, oh no…"

"What is it?" His tone was terse, hurried.

"I—I left my car keys on the table at the bar."

"You mean—" Orlando pulled the gun up, keeping his elbow at his side. "You don't have the keys to your car?"

"I don't—" Fenway put a waver in her voice. "I can go back and get them. We can go back and get them."

Orlando grunted, kicking at the asphalt. He turned his head and looked back at the casino, swore, then spat on the ground, then turned his head.

"You did this on purpose," he said.

"No, I—"

Orlando raised his gun—and Fenway ran.

She ducked behind the Ford sedan.

No pistol report.

He cursed loudly, and Fenway darted out from behind the car to jump the concrete barrier. Again, no shot, and she bent double, running as fast as she could toward the museum.

"Hey!" he shouted, but now she was at least thirty yards away.

The museum parking lot loomed ahead, seeming almost impossibly far away, and she started running diagonally, zig-zagging—maybe she'd be harder to shoot.

Still no shot.

She was running out of breath; she hadn't sprinted so much in a long time. Fenway got to the edge of the NNoV8 lot, ducked behind a gray SUV, and stopped to catch her breath. One of the few vehicles in the lot—it was Saturday evening, almost closing time. She heard Orlando's footsteps on the asphalt, maybe twenty yards away, and bolted toward the front door of the museum.

Thirty yards. Then ten. And she ran right next to the red Alfa Romeo. If Orlando even thought of the possibility of escaping in Vaughn Trask's convertible, he'd pause before shooting.

Orlando still twenty yards behind her, heading into the museum too.

She didn't have much choice. She couldn't go around the perimeter of the museum without exposing herself—Orlando would have a clear shot of her in just a few seconds.

Maybe, even though there'd only be a few people in the museum, that would give Orlando just enough pause to not pursue her. Maybe go back to the Cartwheel and drive off in his own car, heading to Mexico. Or maybe he'd try to go to Trask's office at the museum and steal the keyfob from his top drawer.

She grabbed the entrance door and ran inside. No pistol shot; no glass shattering.

"Hey—you can't come in," Roberto said, standing behind the registration desk. "We're closing—"

"Help!" Fenway yelled. "He's got a gun! Call the police!" And she ran past Roberto, yanked open the door marked "01," and ran inside.

Darkness.

Only the sound of Fenway's frantic breathing. Get ahold of yourself. Orlando would be on his way in any second.

What was the first exhibit?

Fenway took a tentative step forward, then a light on the far side of the room illuminated.

Right. This was the funhouse mirror lightbulb thing. Where Piper had gotten angry with the execution of the exhibits.

Ugh—if Fenway didn't want to get executed *in* the exhibits, she had to move. She ran across the narrow hallway. The lightbulbs delayed in their illumination, growing closer as she ran, then turning on behind her as she passed the midway point of the room. Soon she was on the other side and dipped through a curtain.

All right, the first exhibit had passed. But Fenway realized her mistake: Orlando had been in this museum before. Probably many times. Fenway had only gone through the exhibits once, and didn't know any of the hidden doors or ways in.

And this was the oddly shaped room with Orlando's painting on the wall. *Desolation.* Fenway glanced as she ran by. Still loved the colors. A real shame—she might have bought one of his pieces in another circumstance.

Loud voices muffled outside. Orlando had come in. Roberto's voice, terrified. Orlando yelling. Was that "get down"? Possibly. Fenway entered the next exhibit through another black velvet curtain and stared across the dark room. Which one was this?

She stepped forward, and a blaze of light bathed her from above. Oh, that's right, the spotlight room. And on a glass panel on the far wall, a black and white swirl of files taking the shape of Fenway.

She should have stayed outside. She'd have been exposed out there, but she was trapped in here.

Hang on.

She stepped back until the velvet curtain touched her back. The light went off. She felt the wall to her right and took a step. Still darkness.

A door slammed behind her. Orlando was in the first room. He'd cross it in a matter of seconds, then be running past *Desolation* into this room. She kept her back to the wall. There was no way she'd make it to the exit before Orlando came into this room. And if Fenway made a break for it, she'd certainly light up the entire room and be—

Oof. Fenway fell backward.

She landed flat on her back. She'd tripped over something—oh, the black curtain, still lying on the floor, right where Piper had kicked it over during their visit on Thursday night. The staff really *couldn't* pick up after themselves.

And that gave her an idea. She grabbed the curtain with both hands; it was heavy, but she lifted her arms above her head and got the bottom of the fabric about an inch off the ground. Holding the curtain in that awkward position, she slid back closer to the entrance, then stepped on the back of her right sneaker with her left foot. The shoe came halfway off, and she moved her right foot, the sneaker dangling from her toes, so it wasn't behind the curtain.

Footsteps, slow, coming closer.

The door to the spotlight room opened. Orlando, his white polo shirt barely visible in the darkness, was in the doorway.

Fenway kicked her shoe off, and it flew across the room.

Ten spotlights across the ceiling flashed on, then off, one after the other, following the shoe—blinding in the brightness, brighter and brighter.

Bang. Bang.

The sound of two of the spotlights exploding when the bullets hit. Fenway gritted her teeth.

He'd actually pulled the trigger.

Orlando stepped forward, his eyes searching the darkness, looking away from where Fenway had her back to the near wall. He took another step, right next to Fenway.

Fenway jumped onto Orlando, holding the black curtain in front of her, and their bodies collided, the fabric of the curtain over his face.

Then she pushed with all her might.

Orlando's legs tangled in the curtain, and Fenway fell with him, the Colver .38 falling with a thud on the floor, and Fenway landed with all her weight on top of him.

He grunted as the wind went out of him, and Fenway scooted herself up so that her knee was on his right hip and her forearm was across his collarbones, just below his neck. The black curtain completely covered him: his face, his nose, his arms.

"Orlando Lockberry," Fenway said, panting with exertion, "you're under arrest for the murder of Vaughn Trask."

Sarah's voice in her head: *you're out of your jurisdiction.*

That was fine by her. She could hold Orlando like this for the next couple of minutes before the sheriff arrived.

They'd have to arrive soon, right?

Then four bulbs went on at each corner of the room. Emergency lighting, maybe?

And ten seconds later, the door opened again.

An abrupt laugh. "You sure you don't want me to deputize you, Fenway?"

Ah. Izzy Bardot.

"No deputization necessary, Bardot," Fenway said. "I just made a citizen's arrest of Mr. Lockberry."

"That him under the blackout curtain?"

"Careful," Fenway said. "He had a gun. It's on the floor somewhere."

"And you're sure he's the killer?" A sound of metal skittering on concrete; Bardot had kicked the Colver out of reach.

"He's the one who left the death threat note in my room," Fenway said. "I'm betting he found the knife when Aurora drove her SUV out of the museum parking lot on Thursday night. And he was blackmailing Vaughn Trask—until Trask figured out that Orlando and Aurora were sleeping together."

"Is this true, Mr. Lockberry?" Bardot said, pulling her handcuffs out of her utility belt and digging for his right hand under the curtain.

"I want a lawyer," Orlando said, his voice muffled.

"I figured as much," Bardot said. "Unfortunately, I've heard the best criminal attorney in Nevada has a conflict of interest."

PART 4

SUNDAY

CHAPTER TWENTY-SEVEN

Six a.m. came early. Fenway blinked at the late June sun peeking through the curtains. Fenway had been at the sheriff's office for what seemed like forever.

After Bardot had brought Orlando into custody yesterday, Fenway had pulled up in her rental car. A minute later, O.K. Ubosi drove his silver Lexus into the parking place next to the Kia. Fenway and Ubosi had been in the waiting room when Sheriff Jeffcoat arrived.

Giving her statement had taken a few hours. Jeffcoat hadn't even been able to meet her eyes as he signed the paperwork for Piper's release. During the process, Fenway had glanced over at Ubosi; she'd never seen anyone look so smug, even though Fenway was the one who'd done all the work.

And been shot at.

Fenway blinked and yawned, then got up and opened the door into the suite's second bedroom. Piper was still sleeping soundly—the first time since Thursday night she'd been in a proper bed. Fenway pulled on her sweat shorts and her shoes. She went down in the elevator and walked through the stale air of the smoky casino until she left through the front door.

The desert was surprisingly cool at six in the morning, and she put in her ear buds. The scenery wasn't as pretty as the butterfly waystation near her apartment, but Fenway could now see how the desert had its own beauty.

Unfortunately, the gravel lot behind the hotel offered none of that beauty.

She started her running playlist on her phone, and just a few minutes later she was past the NNoV8 museum, headed toward the hiking trail she'd heard about. With any luck, she'd be able to get five miles in and be back in plenty of time to shower and get ready for brunch with Piper and Izzy Bardot.

She saw a green sign ahead—was that the hiking trail?

Her earbuds dropped the music volume, and the phone rang. She tapped her earbud. "Hello?"

"Fenway?"

She didn't recognize the voice. "Sorry, who's this?"

"Assistant District Attorney Vel Pondicherry."

Ah, the ADA from Estancia. "How can I help you?"

"On Friday, I dropped the charges against George Pope for the Mathis Jericho murder."

"I figured as much."

"Can we meet for coffee?"

Fenway chuckled. "Probably not. I'm in Las Vegas. Well, a little town an hour northeast. It's a long story. With any luck, I'm coming home this afternoon."

"Then can you come to my office first thing tomorrow morning?"

"Absolutely."

They said their goodbyes, and the music started playing again. Fenway ran on. Yes, it was a sign for the hiking trail. She turned and started on the trail. Maybe it would just be cactus and scrub brush, but anything was better than the burning asphalt of the road next to the casino.

———

At ten thirty, the dining room at Albie K's was packed. Only a twenty-minute wait for a table, though. Could have been worse for Sunday brunch.

Fenway and Piper sat on two metal straight-backed chairs as more people came in, sighing loudly at the increasing wait times. Fenway kept looking out of the corner of her eye at Piper, whose black eye was only a day-and-a-half old, and looked bad despite a heavy application of makeup.

A buzz on Fenway's phone. It was Izzy Bardot.

> Almost there

Fenway turned to look through the front window as a beat-up Mitsubishi Eclipse pulled into the lot, Bardot visible through the windshield, then drove past. She'd have to park on the other side of the lot.

Two minutes later, Bardot rushed in, out of breath.

"Oh, good," she said. "You're not seated yet."

"I never thought I'd say this," Piper said. "But I'm glad to see you again."

Bardot grinned. "In happier circumstances this time. I'm sorry for what you went through."

"After a hot shower, I'm feeling like myself again." Piper elbowed Fenway. "And now when I play *Never Have I Ever*, if someone says, 'I've never been arrested for murder,' I'll have to drink."

"You're welcome," Bardot deadpanned. She sat down in the empty seat next to Fenway. "Did you get your flights straightened out, or are you two stuck here another night?"

"Booked on the 3:15 back to Estancia," Fenway said. "No offense to Ruby Dunes, but I think I've had about all I can take of NFTs and the Cartwheel casino."

"If you need help with that Qasper PC with all the malware on it," Piper said, "let me know. McVie Investigations provides consulting services for law enforcement agencies, and you'll find our prices to be very reasonable." She reached in her purse and handed a business card to Bardot.

Fenway looked out of the corner of her eye at Piper. Not only was she a great techie, she was turning into an assertive salesperson.

"If our techs can't do it," Bardot said, "then we'll call you."

"Call me anyway," Piper said. "I've got some ideas where you can start. Free of charge."

Bardot nodded, putting the card in her purse.

Fenway sighed. "Doesn't feel like it's only been two days."

"Believe me," Piper said, "it felt more like two years in there."

The woman behind the host station grabbed three menus. "Joanne, party of three?"

Fenway stood. "That's us."

The woman stared at Piper's black eye for a moment before leading them to the same table where Sookie and Benny had sat the morning before.

"Welcome to Albie K's," the server said. She was brunette, her hair pulled into a tight ponytail atop her head. "Can I start you off with—"

"Bloody Mary," Piper said. "The Albie K Special. Beer back."

The server blinked, staring at Piper's black eye.

"You should see the other chick," Piper said.

"True," Bardot said. "She's in the hospital."

The server flinched, then nodded. "Anything else?"

"Coffee," Fenway and Bardot said at the same time.

They sat in silence while they looked at the menu, and when the server brought the Bloody Mary—complete with a piece of bacon, a kebab stick with alternating blocks of white and yellow cheese, and a mound of pickled vegetables—the three of them ordered.

When the server left, Bardot fixed Fenway with her gaze. "So how did you figure out it was Orlando and not Aurora?"

"This sounds stupid, but he knew what our suitcases looked like," Fenway said. "Everything clicked into place when I realized the rules changed for him when Aurora got that pre-nup. And I remember Teddi—that's the other desk clerk—showed me one of Orlando's pictures—it was a nude of a woman in an orange-and-gray blanket. The blanket had the same design as the sofa in the house when I went to interview Aurora. I think there's a matching blanket, and Orlando was, shall we say, inspired after one of their sessions."

"Do you think that painting is how Trask figured out Aurora was cheating with Orlando?"

"The way Teddi showed off Orlando's artwork on her phone to anyone who'd look? She showed me the orange-and-gray blanket nude to me before I even knew her name. I figure she showed it to Vaughn—or showed it to Dr. Schup or Shellwater. However it happened, I bet it got back to Trask."

"So he threatens to take everything away from Aurora Horn, and Orlando snaps?"

"Trask threatened to take the art off the wall in the exhibit, too," Fenway said. "But it might have been enough to threaten Aurora. Whether Orlando had genuine feelings for her or just thought of her as his meal ticket."

Bardot nodded. "Orlando isn't talking."

"I'm not surprised. Aurora Horn's footing the bill for the lawyer, I take it."

"Time will tell," Bardot said simply, then turned to Piper. "And I'm glad you're out of that jail cell."

"Not as glad as I am," Piper said, then took a drink of her Bloody Mary, trying to hide her face. Not just her black eye, but her entire expression—her face clouded with worry.

Fenway pressed her lips together. She was free, true, but Piper would have to carry McVie Investigations for the next year. She was smart enough and capable enough to do it: background checks, financial transaction research for smaller police departments on the West Coast, maybe even the occasional jilted lover wanting dirt on their soon-to-be-ex. Not always work that played to Piper's strengths, but she'd get through it.

Though Fenway hoped this would be Piper's only Bloody Mary.

Fenway's phone buzzed in her purse, and Fenway grabbed it. McVie.

"I have to take this," Fenway said, sliding out of the booth, and Piper raised her eyebrows knowingly. Yeah, yeah, all right, Piper caught her.

She answered the phone when she was halfway out the door. The sky was still clear, but there was a breeze today, a good ten degrees cooler than the day before. "Hey," she said, hating how breathless she sounded. "Ready to move into your new place?"

Silence.

"Craig? Hello."

"I don't—" McVie said, then cleared his throat. "Everything's all messed up, Fenway. I—I didn't know who else to call."

Fenway's eyes widened. "What's wrong?"

"On a Sunday morning, if you can believe it," McVie mumbled. "They call me and tell me I was a no-call no-show yesterday. On a Saturday, after I'd worked a full week, when I was in the middle of moving my stuff here."

"Oh, Craig, that's terrible." Fenway brought a hand to her forehead. "I know how much it sucks to start a new job from behind the eight ball, but—"

"No, no, it's not like I got a mark against me. They let me go."

"They—they let you go?"

"Still on my first ninety days. I'm a probationary employee. They can let me go for any reason."

Fenway sucked in a breath. "Oh no."

"But that's not the worst part."

"You getting fired isn't the worst part?"

"They contacted the property management company—"

Fenway shut her eyes and winced.

"And pulled their confirmation of employment. So I was supposed to take ownership of the apartment today, and when I showed up in the moving truck at eight this morning—"

"The building manager was there and told you that you couldn't move in." Fenway gritted her teeth.

"All this happened before I met Megan and Amy for breakfast. Sort of a 'sorry for missing dinner last night.' And I wasn't myself. I had to tell my ex that I didn't have a job or a place to live."

Ouch. "I'm so sorry, Craig. That must have been rough."

"And Megan pipes up and says, 'You can just move in with us.'"

Fenway blinked. What the hell? Her heart pounded.

"Was this a surprise to Amy, too?"

McVie's nostrils flared. "I would have thought, after she married Rick, that she'd moved on. But apparently, she thought me moving to Colorado was an invitation to get back together. She kept saying, 'I know I made mistakes, but I'm a different person now.' A fresh start, she said. New state, new house."

Fenway's pulse raced.

"I'm *not* moving in with them," McVie said firmly. "Amy and I were married for a long time, and the last half of our marriage was terrible. We tried to make it work, and it didn't. And I'm with you now. And even if I were single, I'd never go back to Amy."

Fenway breathed a sigh of relief—but had nothing to say. She didn't want to make anything worse.

But how *dare* Megan. And how dare Amy.

"So I told both of them no. I told Megan I loved her, that she was important to me, but I wasn't considering getting back together with Amy."

"How did she take it?"

"I don't know—Amy jumped in. She said I'd live to regret not getting back together with her, and she kept—well, she said some pretty hurtful things." McVie laughed; it was a nervous, insecure laugh, one that Fenway had never heard out of McVie's mouth before. "But, you know, I got suspicious."

"Of Amy?"

"No, of Megan."

Fenway was quiet.

"Did I lose you?"

"No," Fenway said, "I'm still here."

"So I grabbed Megan's phone from off the table. I'd talked with her about how disrespectful it was to text you like she did yesterday, but, you know, Amy just brushed it off. Not much I can do when I'm not the custodial parent." He scoffed. "Well, Megan didn't like me taking her phone, but it was unlocked. And I'm her father. So I scrolled through her texts. And then I scrolled though her calls."

Fenway sucked in a breath.

"She'd called my work on Friday when I'd left early. It was in her call log. And not a quick call, getting my voice mail and hanging up. It was a seventeen-minute call."

Oh no.

"I finally got it out of her. But we were arguing—pretty loudly, I guess. We had to leave the restaurant. Then we were yelling at each other in the parking lot. She'd called my boss."

"She *called* your boss? I thought teenagers wouldn't talk on the phone for any reason at all."

"Well, apparently, she figured out my boss would take an accusation of me cheating on Amy if she actually talked to him instead of texting."

Fenway's jaw dropped. "She did *what?*"

"Yep. She told him I'd cheated on her mom with you. Asked if he wanted to employ someone who did—" Craig's voice broke.

"A violation of some morality clause?"

"Which they didn't need to cite, since I'm probationary. But yeah, they said they had a morality clause, and told me it was a violation."

"What—what did Megan think would happen?"

"She—" He coughed. "She thought my boss would give me an ultimatum. My job or you." A slight growl in his throat.

"But that's not how it works," Fenway said under her breath.

"Then when I lost my job *and* my apartment, Megan thought she'd just speed up her plan to get the two of us back together."

Fenway bit her lip.

"I don't know, maybe Amy put her up to it. Rick left Amy so much money, she thought I wouldn't need a job if we got back together, I guess."

Fenway wanted to know so much information. What would he do now? Try to find a new job, a new place to live? It would be expensive to stay in a hotel and get a storage unit while doing all that, but it wasn't out of the realm of possibility. And obviously, his relationship with Megan was more damaged than he thought—and dealing with Amy would be a challenge. Divorce was rough— Fenway was living proof of that—but it was probably rougher to be with two people who hated each other. And Amy made it clear that she hated McVie. Or maybe she hated being rejected more.

"You haven't said anything yet, Fenway."

"I'm so sorry you're going through this," Fenway said. The amount of restraint she had to exhibit here was monumental. The future was up in the air. She wanted to scream at Megan for screwing up McVie's plans. She wanted to scream at Amy for hurting McVie. She wanted these problems to all go away. "I—I'm glad you can talk to me about it."

"Yeah," McVie said. "Anyway, that's the update. Plus, I'm paying for therapy."

"For Megan?"

"And for myself. She's obviously furious with me. And a big part of me doesn't blame her."

Fenway pursed her lips. She'd been furious with her father, too.

"She just wants her family back together," Fenway said quietly, as she remembered starting school up in Seattle, the first year after her mother had taken her away from Estancia and her father. How much Fenway had wished things could go back to the way they were. "I can understand that."

"Yeah. My parents never divorced, but I think I can understand that too." A pause, then McVie spoke gingerly. "You told me no when I proposed."

Fenway was quiet.

"Do you—I don't know—does part of you want the excuse not to deal with me and my bullshit anymore?"

"What do you mean?"

"Sometimes—sometimes people find it too hard to break up. So when something like this happens, like when an ex wants to get back together, it's easier to just let it—"

"No," Fenway said, as firmly as she could. "I told you, I want to be with you. I just don't want to feel trapped into speeding up our relationship when you're a thousand miles away."

"Okay," McVie murmured. "But I'd understand. This is a lot. I hate drama, and this is a boatload of drama."

"No. I—I love you, Craig."

McVie exhaled; Fenway could feel the relief through the phone connection. "I do too."

"Yeah."

Silence for a moment.

"Are we—are we good?" McVie asked.

"We're good."

"Okay—I've got work to do. I have to extend the truck for another—uh, I don't know. Day. Week. I have to figure out where I'm going."

"Maybe your work as a P.I. can qualify you for another place. Storage unit for a week, maybe find a place you can move in fast. You can look for another job. With your résumé, you could get something within a month." She scratched her neck, just below her ear. "I could lend you some money if you need to spend a week or two in a hotel while you find a place."

"Or maybe I should just come back home," McVie said quietly.

Fenway was silent.

Was that what she wanted? Selfishly, yes, but would McVie be a shell of himself, knowing that he wasn't close enough to Megan to repair their relationship?

"I don't have the money to be here without a job for more than another week," McVie continued. "I spent a lot of money this week on the hotel. I got my paycheck for the week of work—I can deposit it tomorrow morning—but it doesn't pay for much. Not enough to cover even a week of expenses." He sighed. "And I don't know what I'm qualified for here if it's not a security firm like Payback Systems. Maybe I can commute to Denver, but that's at least an hour each way."

Commuting to Denver? Fenway hadn't checked the map in a week, but that was about sixty or seventy miles from Amy's house into Denver. That would mean less time with Megan—the whole reason he'd moved to Colorado.

"But if you moved back to Estancia," Fenway said, "you'd be able to pick up your P.I. business right where you left off. And Piper wouldn't feel like she needed to keep the business afloat all by herself."

"That's true."

"But, you know, you moved to Colorado to be with Megan."

McVie was quiet. "I did."

"If I'd tried to get my parents back together and it backfired like this," Fenway said, "I'd be devastated if my father left."

McVie sighed. "Megan told me that she doesn't want me around if I'm not with Amy. And I refuse to be with Amy."

"She doesn't mean that."

"But she's put me in such a bad position. Maybe it *is* time for me to let Megan go. She'll keep making her own decisions, even if I think they suck. Learn the consequences of her actions. I can't be there to save her all the time. And it gives her such a terrible message if I let her walk all over me."

Fenway screwed up her mouth. *Don't be selfish. Don't be selfish.*

McVie chuckled mirthlessly. "Hell, moving back to Estancia would be the easiest thing logistically. Cheapest, too. I can keep running McVie Investigations. And I can keep the moving truck loaded up. Call U-Move-It and extend the truck for another two or three days, then drive it back to Estancia."

"Yeah, you could do that."

"It'll probably cost me another few hundred bucks," McVie mused. "But that's cheaper than getting a hotel for a week here and renting another storage unit." He paused, thinking. "Plus, I have that storage facility in Estancia for another three weeks, and I could extend it if I needed to. That'd give me time to get an apartment there."

"You could stay with me," Fenway said.

Then her eyes went wide with horror. Had those words just come out of her mouth?

"You know," Fenway continued, trying to keep the panic out of her voice. "Until you find your own place."

McVie was quiet.

Fenway covered her eyes with her free hand. Why had she suggested that? She wasn't ready for him to move in. A night or two, maybe. But an open-ended offer? No. No, no, no.

"I won't lie," McVie said. "That would be a huge relief."

"Great," Fenway said. "That's absolutely great."

CAST OF CHARACTERS

Fenway Stevenson: *A former nurse practitioner with a master's degree in forensics, she moved to Estancia a little over a year ago. Fenway has a rocky (but improving) relationship with her father. Appointed to fill out the coroner's term, she ran for election—and won. Her official four-year term started January 1.*

Her family

Nathaniel Ferris: *The richest, most powerful man in the county, the oil magnate founded and owns Ferris Energy. After his wife took away the then eight-year-old Fenway to Seattle two decades ago, he threw himself into his work, but had hardly seen or talked to Fenway in the twenty years before she came back to town.*

Charlotte Ferris: *The former beauty pageant winner married Nathaniel a decade ago when she was 25 and he* *was 50—the weekend of Fenway's high school graduation.*

Co-workers and law enforcement personnel, past and present

Piper Patten: *Formerly in the county's IT department, this willowy redhead is a whiz at forensic accounting and data gathering. She helped Nathaniel Ferris prove his innocence in a murder case, and now works for McVie.*

Sergeant Desirée "Dez" Roubideaux: *A detective in the coroner's office, Dez has worked for the county for over twenty years. She's a dedicated, determined investigator despite her wisecracks.*

Craig McVie: *The former sheriff of Dominguez County, he lost the mayoral race in November. Recently divorced from Amy, he's now a private investigator. He and Fenway officially started dating after the election.*

Miguel "Migs" Castañeda: *The legal specialist in Fenway's office, he passed the bar exam a few months ago. Everyone expects him to leave the office to become a lawyer.*

Sarah Summerfield: *The coroner's assistant.*

Deputy Brian Callahan: *Another sheriff's deputy, he has also applied for the detective position in the coroner's office—and he's dating Rachel.*

Vel Pondicherry: *The assistant district attorney for Dominguez County.*

Bartholomew Jeffcoat: *The county sheriff in Ruby Dunes.*

Izzy Bardot: *A Ruby Dunes sheriff's deputy.*

Chaz Wegman: *A rookie Ruby Dunes deputy.*

Suspects, witnesses, and persons of interest

> ***Vaughn Trask:*** *A co-owner and co-founder of a bleeding-edge technology museum.*
>
> ***Dr. Stanley Schup****: Another co-founder of the technology museum, he coordinated and funded much of the equity investment.*
>
> ***Brock Shellwater****: Another co-founder who is in charge of the finances.*
>
> ***Orlando Lockberry and Teddi Blankenship****: The hotel clerks at the Cartwheel Hotel & Casino, where Fenway and Piper are staying.*
>
> ***Nadezhda Shoharov****: A member of the housekeeping staff at the Cartwheel.*
>
> ***Aurora Horn****: Trask's jealous wife.*
>
> ***Nadine Ryeo****: Trask's affair partner, who is a blackjack dealer in Las Vegas.*
>
> ***Sookie Ryeo****: Nadine's mother, who lives in the high desert in California.*
>
> ***Benny Jones****: Sookie's sister, who lives in Ruby Dunes.*
>
> ***Javier Romero****: An apartment building manager in Walker City.*
>
> ***Iris Abernathy****: An artist and an NNoV8 client from Paso Querido in Dominguez County.*
>
> ***Okpara "O.K." Ubosi****: one of the most famous criminal lawyers in Las Vegas.*

MORE BY PAUL AUSTIN ARDOIN

The Fenway Stevenson Mysteries
Book One: The Reluctant Coroner
Book Two: The Incumbent Coroner
Book Three: The Candidate Coroner
Book Four: The Upstaged Coroner
Book Five: The Courtroom Coroner
Novella: The Christmas Coroner
Book Six: The Watchful Coroner
Book Seven: The Accused Coroner
Novella: The Clandestine Coroner
Book Eight: The Offside Coroner
Book Nine: The Warehouse Coroner
Book Ten: The Digital Coroner

The Woodhead & Becker Mysteries
Book One: The Winterstone Murder
Book Two: The Bridegroom Murder
Book Three: The Trailer Park Murder
Book Four: The Executive Murder

The Time Loop Detective
Book One: A Time for Murder

Dez Roubideaux
Bad Weather

Collections
Books 1–3 of The Fenway Stevenson Mysteries
Books 4-6 of The Fenway Stevenson Mysteries
Fenway Stevenson: Rookie Year

Non-fiction
From Zero to Four Figures:
Making $1,000 a Month Self-Publishing Fiction

Sign up for *The Coroner's Report,*
Paul Austin Ardoin's fortnightly newsletter:
http://www.paulaustinardoin.com

I hope you enjoyed reading this book as much as I enjoyed writing it. If you did, I'd sincerely appreciate a review on your favorite book retailer's website, Goodreads, and BookBub. Reviews are crucial for any author, and even just a line or two can make a huge difference.

ACKNOWLEDGMENTS

My mom, Carolyn Ardoin, passed away when I was writing the first draft of this book. She was the last proofreader I had on every mystery book I've written—and no matter how many professional editors I had, she always caught a few typos, punctuation errors, or misstatements. If any errors are in this book, it's because my mom didn't proofread it. I'm grateful to her support of my writing career, for her doctors for caring for her so well in the last eight years of her life, and for the extra time we had together after her diagnosis.

Many thanks to my cover designer Ziad Ezzat of Feral Creative and Jamie Sanfelippo, who keeps my newsletter, social media, and other marketing activities sailing smoothly.

Special thanks to the Wordforge Novelists group in Sacramento, whose comments and guidance are, as always, invaluable. Shout-out to the Just Write Milwaukee and Shut Up and Write Milwaukee groups, who have given me a great writing community in my adopted city.

Thanks to my early readers, including Dana Luco, Beverly Ange, Dr. Christina Bellinger, Nicole Prewitt, Gavin Ralph, Genesis Hansen, Dr. Monique Koll, and D.F. Hart.

To my wife and kids: I'm deeply grateful for your continued encouragement and support.

ABOUT THE AUTHOR

Paul Austin Ardoin is the USA TODAY bestselling author of *The Fenway Stevenson Mysteries*, *The Woodhead & Becker Mysteries*, and is a contributing writer to *Indie Author Magazine*. His work has appeared in the anthologies *Bottomfish*, *Sweet Fancy Moses*, *The Paths we Tread*, *12 Shots*, and *Turning the Tide*.

Born and raised in Northern California, Paul holds a B.A. in creative writing from the University of California, Santa Barbara and an M.B.A. in marketing from the University of Phoenix. He lives in the Milwaukee area, where he enjoys Milwaukee's surprisingly excellent symphony orchestra and unsurprisingly excellent fried cheese curds.

www.ingramcontent.com/pod-product-compliance
Lightning Source LLC
Chambersburg PA
CBHW021241190726
48289CB00005B/1438